How to
Break
My Heart

How to Break My Heart

A Novel

KAT T. MASEN

ATRIA PAPERBACK

New York   Amsterdam/Antwerp   London
Toronto   Sydney/Melbourne   New Delhi

ATRIA
PAPERBACK

An Imprint of Simon & Schuster, LLC
1230 Avenue of the Americas
New York, NY 10020

For more than 100 years, Simon & Schuster has championed authors and the stories they create. By respecting the copyright of an author's intellectual property, you enable Simon & Schuster and the author to continue publishing exceptional books for years to come. We thank you for supporting the author's copyright by purchasing an authorized edition of this book.

This book is a work of fiction. Any references to historical events, real people, or real places are used fictitiously. Other names, characters, places, and events are products of the author's imagination, and any resemblance to actual events or places or persons, living or dead, is entirely coincidental.

First Atria Paperback edition September 2025

ATRIA PAPERBACK and colophon are trademarks of Simon & Schuster, LLC

Simon & Schuster strongly believes in freedom of expression and stands against censorship in all its forms. For more information, visit BooksBelong.com.

For information about special discounts for bulk purchases, please contact Simon & Schuster Special Sales at 1-866-506-1949 or business@simonandschuster.com.

The Simon & Schuster Speakers Bureau can bring authors to your live event. For more information or to book an event, contact the Simon & Schuster Speakers Bureau at 1-866-248-3049 or visit our website at www.simonspeakers.com.

Interior design by Kyoko Watanabe

Manufactured in the United States of America

1 3 5 7 9 10 8 6 4 2

Library of Congress Control Number: 2025939166

ISBN 978-1-6682-0195-4
ISBN 978-1-6682-0196-1 (ebook)

This book is dedicated to my one true love that will never break my heart—incredibly delicious, so tasty, and makes me moan more times than I can count. . . . The almighty donut!

Playlist

"About You" by The 1975

"This Is What You Came For" by Calvin Harris & Rihanna

"Vampire" by Olivia Rodrigo

"Somebody to You" by The Vamps

"Photograph" by Ed Sheeran

"Cardigan" by Taylor Swift

"Atlantis" by Seafret

"Save Your Tears" by The Weeknd & Ariana Grande

"Never Be the Same" by Camila Cabello

"4ever" by The Veronicas

"Wings" by Birdy

"I Love You, I'm Sorry" by Gracie Abrams

"Birds of a Feather" by Billie Eilish

Eva

*D*id *you hear that?"*

Maddy tightens her grip on my arm, halting her steps as an owl hoots among the tall, overgrown trees. The haunting yet gentle sound echoes around us in the dark woods, while her hold on my arm is so tight she's nearly cutting off my circulation. You'd think she was about to be eaten alive by the harmless creature.

A small huff escapes my lips. "This was your idea, remember?"

I had better things to do tonight than sneak into a secret high school graduation party thrown by her older brother, Aston, and his jerky friends.

"I know," Maddy whispers, eyes wide as she scans our surroundings. She starts to move again, taking small, cautious steps. Glancing down at her sparkly teal cowboy boots, I wonder what she was thinking when she chose that footwear and shake my head. Maddy will use any occasion to dress up. "I refuse to miss out on the most *epic* party of the year just because we weren't invited."

I pause mid-step, shifting my gaze onto her while crossing my arms. "Madelina Eleanor Beaumont," I say, raising my voice. "You said we *were* invited, but your parents said no. Did you seriously just lie to me all because of some guy?"

Maddy forces a small smile. "I may have embellished the

truth a little. Don't hate me, okay? Once we're there, you'll forget all about it, and we will have the best time. Besides, he isn't just *some guy* . . . Camden Winters is the *guy of all guys*."

It takes a lot of effort not to roll my eyes. She can be in love with Camden all she wants, but the guy has serious red flags. Of course, being my best friend, she chooses to ignore my warning. The moment Maddy turned sixteen last spring, she suddenly got a case of boyitis.

"Maddy! You're going to get in so much trouble with your father. What if he grounds you over summer break? We can kiss all our plans goodbye. Have you forgotten our week in Europe with your aunt? I need to eat cheese in some ridiculously expensive castle in France."

"Will you just relax?"

"Says the person ready to shit their pants over an owl," I mumble.

I should have known Maddy was telling half-truths. Unlike my parents, who have no idea what the word *discipline* means, Maddy's parents are strict. Her father is the mayor, and God forbid Maddy or her older brother do anything to ruin his reputation. The mere fact I'm best friends with her is a problem. At least, it seems that way to me. Mr. Beaumont is always cold around me, as if I'm unworthy of his time or energy. My very presence is an inconvenience to him. But as my mom always reminds me, you can't please everyone.

It explains why this party is being held at the abandoned house by Peppermint Lake—no one will find us here. Rumor has it the place is haunted . . . but maybe now isn't the best time to remind Maddy of that fact, since she just held on to me tighter when something rustled behind the trees.

"We're almost there, according to my map," Maddy informs me, glancing down at her phone. The rustling behind the trees grows a little louder, and she casts a nervous glance over her shoulder. Suddenly, she lets out a terrified scream, breaking away from me, and begins slapping at her face. Her phone flies out of her hand, smacking into my chest.

I catch it, my eyes widening. "What the heck? What's happening right now?" I yell over her incessant shrieking.

"It's attacking me. Get. It. Off!"

With a quick swipe, I switch on the phone's flashlight. A tiny mosquito is buzzing around her face, and I can't help but burst out laughing. Reaching forward, I grab her flailing arms to calm her. "Maddy, get a grip. It's a mosquito."

She stops panicking, and a look of *what the hell* crosses her face. Maddy reaches out to take her phone. "I knew that. I was just messing around."

"Uh-huh, sure. Let's keep moving," I reply.

The first time my dad took my older brother, Elliot, and me fishing was to this exact spot. While the lake was beautiful, fishing was not. Still, there is something about this part of the lake that is mesmerizing. The water is crystal clear blue and shines in the moonlight, reflecting gentle ripples and sparkles that take my breath away.

That day, we sat on the rusty old pier, with our rods in hand, as Dad told me and Elliot this town would be good for us. It's destined to leave a mark on our soul, and our future will always come back to this humble place. He said it with wisdom in his eyes, but honestly, all I saw was this beautiful lake in front of me.

Elliot complained the town was boring, but of course he was older and ready for adventure.

I smile briefly at the memory, then suddenly get distracted by music.

The sound of the Calvin Harris and Rihanna song "This Is What You Came For" becomes louder as we finally step into a clearing. I reach for Maddy's hand and pull her through the bushes.

Tonight is a full moon—which my mother says symbolizes a time of release and completion, whatever that means—and it's so bright I can see the state of the dilapidated home from where we're standing. The roof appears intact, as does the large porch surrounding the house, but even from this distance, the broken glass, which was once stained-glass windows, exposes the flaws of this once-beautiful property.

Most of the kids, at least thirty, are gathered around the bonfire or dancing beside the large speaker, celebrating freedom. Suddenly, the idea of retreating back through the woods seems tempting. Senior girls can be cruel, even though I've avoided most of them at school, being in eleventh grade myself. There's this tension between the two grades, and frankly, I'm so glad they're graduating. Seniors always think they rule the school.

"Oh my God, can you see him? He's so beautiful," Maddy gushes.

I glance over to where Camden is standing. He's wearing his letterman jacket, arm around a girl, and drinking what I assume is beer since there's a keg only a few feet away. Sure, he's good-looking, but the guy is a 100 percent bona fide jerk. I have no idea why Maddy obsesses over him, especially since he's her brother's best friend. He does this thing with a toothpick in his mouth, chewing it like he's a badass, which annoys me, but Maddy finds it "*sooo* hot!" Her words, not mine.

My eyes wander toward where Aston is sitting. Unlike the other boys, he appears subdued. The girls around him try to touch him, but he's uninterested.

I hold my breath, watching him intently, trying to ignore the butterflies creeping in. Yeah, okay, Aston is hot. But not once has he shown any interest or spoken more than two words to me.

When I sleep over at their house, he stays in his room and ignores me. About two months ago, I ran into him in the bathroom when he'd just gotten out of the shower. He yelled at me, and given that I was still in shock from seeing him half naked, things got awkward from there.

A six-pack, a towel barely covering his lower body, and water cascading down his chest . . . I was speechless.

Before that, he was just Maddy's older brother.

I bite the corner of my lip, observing him quietly until Maddy tugs on my arm.

"C'mon," she pleads as we walk down the slight embankment toward the bonfire.

Aston immediately spots us, shaking his head in disapproval. As he stands, the girls clinging to him nearly tumble off. He towers over all of them, his stance intimidating.

Maddy rushes over with her arms crossed, ready for battle. "I know what you're going to say . . ." she begins. "But Daddy won't find out."

"He better not, or it will somehow be my fault. It always is," Aston warns her.

Maddy grins, then makes her way to the keg. One of the other guys hands her a red cup, but Aston quickly swipes it away from her.

"I'll let you hang. *But* . . . there's no chance in hell you're going home drunk. Deal?"

"Fine." She sighs heavily before turning to face me. "Eva, let's go get something to eat."

I avoid everyone's stares and have this sudden urge to chill by the snacks since no one else is there. It's not like I don't know most of the kids here from school, but seeing them here is a whole other scenario.

"Okay, we need a game plan," Maddy gushes through a mouthful of chips, and a few crumbs fall out the side. "How do I get Camden alone?"

"Alone for what?"

Maddy laughs. "Eva, what do boys and girls do alone? You can't be *that* naive."

Are we really *having this conversation?* I'm not exactly a prude, but losing our virginity should be memorable, not at some senior party with a douchebag and his annoying toothpick.

"I don't think you've thought this through . . ." I say gently.

When did she become so careless? "This is a big deal, and Camden is . . . well, he'll just take what he needs, and that's pretty much it. Please don't tell me you think he's going to give up going to college and stay with you."

Maddy bows her head, and her brows furrow. "No. I'm not stupid."

"Okay, glad we cleared that up," I mumble. "Look, kiss him, fool around if you must, but don't make a big decision based on the fact that you think he's hot."

My reality check drives a wedge between us—I see it in her face.

Maddy wanders off to talk to some of the girls she knows, leaving me to mingle on my own. Some guy tries to carry on a conversation while stuffing his face full of pretzels, but it's obvious he's had too much to drink—he's been talking for a solid five minutes about the brilliance of the person who invented the shape of the pretzel.

This is why I'm single.

The boys at our school are so . . . *meh.*

Bored and ready to abandon this lame party, I walk toward the other side of the house and away from the noise. It's much quieter near the water, and as I slow my steps to take it all in, I trip on a small broken branch and fall onto the dirty ground.

"Crap!" I whimper as my knee begins to sting.

With great effort, I struggle to pick myself up, but a pair of black jeans appears in front of me. Slowly, I glance upward as Aston crouches to my level. His curly dark hair falls over his eyes, but he quickly slicks it back with his fingers to reveal his beautiful face.

"Already hitting the keg, huh?"

I shake my head, trying to cover my embarrassment. "I'm not Maddy."

"No, you're not my sister." His smirk is annoyingly sexy. "Are you hurt?"

"A little."

Aston extends his arm as I reach out for support. At a slow and agonizing pace, I manage to stand. Not only does my knee sting, but the fall also tore my jeans, so now there's a big rip exposing *a lot* of skin.

"Sit down here." He motions to a large log near the edge of the water. "Let me take a look."

I take a seat while Aston kneels in front of me. My pulse quickens at the smell of his cologne, making the simple act of breathing impossible. His deep green eyes trace my body, causing me to shiver. Then, his eyes gaze upon mine while a smile graces his lips. He has one of those smiles that lights up his entire face. Not that I've seen it often. Around me, he's usually annoyed.

"I think you'll survive. A little broken, but still pretty perfect."

"I never was perfect," I inform him as he takes a seat beside me. "Far from it."

"We all see things differently," he murmurs, then tilts his head slightly as if to better observe me. *"Everleigh."*

I'm not fond of people calling me by my full name, but the way he slowly drags it out leaves me speechless. As we stare out over the lake, I fidget nervously with my hands. Maddy told me her father insisted Aston spend the summer in London to work with a business associate before starting college in the fall. I decide to bring it up since London sounds pretty cool, and sitting here in silence is awkward as fuck.

"So, tomorrow is the big day, huh?"

His shoulders slump as he leans forward to rest his elbows on his knees. "Yeah, the big day."

"You don't seem too excited. I've only read about London, but it looks like a beautiful city."

"Well, when you're following your father's directions, it's hard to get . . . *excited*," he answers.

"I'm sorry."

"What are you sorry about? The fact that I'm his firstborn

son and heir to our family's fortune? Or how he controls every aspect of my life for *his* benefit?"

I turn to face him, filled with this sudden urge to pull him out of whatever negative space he's in. London is amazing, but no one should be allowed to dictate your life. At least my parents always taught me to follow my own dreams.

"So . . . say no?" I blurt out. "What's the worst that can happen?"

Aston sighs dejectedly. "You underestimate my father's control over our family."

"That's because you let him." I raise my voice. "Come on, you have everything going for you. You're smart, a straight-A student without even trying. Coach loves you. Your athletic ability is the best the school has seen. I mean, I'm not one to watch lacrosse, but so I've heard. Not to mention, you're pretty. So tell me, why on earth do you think your father should dictate your life?"

"You think I'm pretty?" Aston cocks his head with a playful smile on his lips. "Unusual choice of words, Miss Woods."

"You know what I mean."

"I don't think I do."

"Handsome, hot, sexy. But that's beside the point. What I'm really trying to say is—"

Warm lips smash against mine, and I gasp. It takes me a second to realize Aston Beaumont's kissing me.

Oh. My. God!

Aston Beaumont is kissing *me*.

His tongue gently pushes through my lips, and my heart beats like a drum inside my chest. A million thoughts are running rampant through my head, but the only thing I can focus on is how he tastes like perfection.

We find ourselves in perfect harmony, slow, sensual kisses igniting my entire body. Then, he explores every inch of my mouth with desperation. Desire travels right between my thighs as his hand slides beneath my sweater and against my stomach.

The tips of his fingers rub against my belly, causing me to gasp as he inches closer to the button of my jeans.

Am I about to lose my virginity?

I have only just lectured Maddy on being responsible, yet here I am, about to have sex with her brother. With a desperate need to ignore any rational thoughts, I reach out to caress his face. My bold move causes him to moan inside my mouth as the pop of my jeans button sounds between us. Savoring the touch of his skin, I try to bring him closer to me, but then he pulls away, out of breath.

"I shouldn't h-have . . ." he stammers, quickly rebuttoning my jeans. "I'm leaving tomorrow, and you're Maddy's best friend."

I shake my head slightly to bring myself back to reality.

But the reality is my best friend's older brother just kissed me, and we were moments away from something more.

I've been avoiding my feelings for the last year. Denial is a vicious game I play with my emotions, because it's easier than getting hurt. The moment I admit to myself that I have a crush on Aston Beaumont will be the moment my life changes forever.

Surely, if he kissed me first, he *must* feel something.

I can't be imagining all this.

And it's not like we're going to get married or anything.

Though we would make cute kids.

"It's okay," I barely manage to say, trying to catch my breath with this sudden burst of confidence. "I want this to happen. I think . . . um, I like you, Aston. I mean, I've had feelings for a while."

A gentle wave crashes against the sand bank, shifting my attention momentarily. This kiss, in this spot of all places, is something I will never forget. I want to savor it all—the way the water glistens under the moonlight and how, if you listen carefully, the frogs become quiet as if they are at peace listening to the thrum of my heartbeat.

"Everleigh . . ."

The warning in Aston's voice and the weight of his gaze make my heart stop abruptly, and suddenly the creatures surrounding us are loud and obnoxious. It's as if they know something is wrong and are warning me of what's about to come.

What the hell did I just do? Did I admit I wanted him to kiss me? Did I admit my feelings to the one boy who is completely off-limits to me?

Maddy would kill me if she found out.

Her stern words about Penelope Anderson ring in my head. After Penelope moved to Cinnamon Springs and insisted on becoming friends with Maddy, it didn't take long before she was showing up at all of Aston's games—and the truth came out. It was ugly, Maddy was furious, and to this day I don't know if Penelope successfully got with Aston. She ended up moving back to the West Coast before senior year, and we never heard from her again.

I'm far from a mean girl, but if someone befriends me just to get with my brother, the gloves are off and claws will be out.

It was all very dramatic, but still, those words stuck in my head and it often plays on repeat just to remind me my crush can go nowhere.

"I have to go."

I place my hands on my stomach to try to control this overwhelmingly bad feeling,

I stand and run back toward the bonfire before he can say anything else. Suddenly, I want to be as far away as possible from Aston.

No one seems to notice my flushed cheeks or my torn jeans. Everyone is happily dancing away, even Maddy, who's busy with some other guy now. And that doesn't seem to bother Camden, who is making out with a girl who had her hands all over Aston earlier.

I sit beside the fire with a soda can in my hand, staring into the flames.

Aston's lips felt like pure bliss. Every part of me ached for his kiss. My body felt like it was possessed, and nothing could stop me.

Until . . . Aston pulled away.

"Here he is." Jake, another senior, chuckles as Aston returns to the bonfire. He avoids my gaze, taking a seat in an empty chair. I steal a careful glance at him. He doesn't look happy.

"Are you ready?" Jake asks Aston.

"It's so barbaric," Tiffany, the girl kissing Camden, complains loudly.

"It's a ritual, and who are we to break tradition?" Jake moves toward Aston with a needle and a small bottle. Aston removes his shirt as I watch in confusion, with a sudden thickness in my throat.

"What are they doing?" I quiz the guy beside me.

"He's getting inked. To symbolize the end of an era."

With the needle in his hand and some ink beside him, Jake begins to carve into Aston's chest. Most of the girls are unable to look, squeamish at the sight of the needle grazing his skin. Aston doesn't flinch, not even when Maddy turns pale and almost passes out.

Instead, he is staring directly at *me*.

My weakness has always been his eyes, the same green eyes that consumed me and drew me into a kiss I'll remember for the rest of my life.

But something about his stare is worrying.

"Ready to leave this town, Beaumont?" Camden teases with an obnoxious laugh. "London has interesting women, not boring girls like this godforsaken place."

Tiffany smacks his arm. "I'm not boring. You're such a jerk."

"Sweetheart, you weren't calling me that ten minutes ago, when I gave you the best orgasm of your life."

What a fucking loser. Thank God Maddy didn't touch him. I glance over at her to make sure she's okay, and, judging by her relaxed smile, I think she's realized she avoided a walking STD.

"I'm done with this place," Aston declares with a look so cold it makes me shiver. "And you're right, I need a *real* woman. There's *no one* left for me here."

My lips begin to tremble, but I force myself to keep it together, refusing to show him just how much I despise him right now.

Aston Beaumont knew how to win my heart . . .

. . . and break it.

All in one night.

A mastermind, some may call him.

But not me.

He's the biggest asshole to ever exist.

I could leave this party right now and allow my tears to get the better of me, or forget Aston Beaumont ever existed.

Out of sight, out of mind.

Tomorrow, he'll be on a flight to London and gone from my life forever.

The perfect cure for my broken heart.

CHAPTER 1

Eva

Present

Valentine's Day has to be the worst day of the year.

My usually peaceful café is filled with couples making googly eyes at each other while they share heart-shaped donuts filled with vanilla cream. Monetizing holidays seemed like a good idea, but the more I stand behind the counter quietly judging people, the more I regret my decision to partake in this ridiculous Hallmark holiday.

I close my eyes briefly, remembering my vision board and all the things I wanted to achieve this year, many of which involve money. Money that customers spend in my café.

It's been a slow season due to unprecedented snowstorms blanketing the town and roads, and the usual tourism trade is down this year compared to last. Many of the businesses in Cinnamon Springs are hustling to make ends meet.

Hence my idea to make a splash today.

A man sitting opposite his lady friend lifts the heart-shaped donut to her mouth, and she giggles before taking a bite. She follows by licking her lips, and I swear on all unholy gods, this is the beginning of an incredibly poorly acted porno movie.

I hear cheesy music playing in my head, and it's far from romantic.

"When did I become so cynical?" I ask mindlessly while Billie stands beside me, carefully restocking the glass display with fresh cinnamon twists. The warm, spicy and sweet smell is by far my favorite. It reminds me of my childhood, when my mom would make donuts for us every Friday after school. "All these people look so . . ." I trail off, unable to find the words.

"In love?" Billie laughs, closing the display to avoid any un-invited visitors. Given that we live in a small town surrounded by woods, pesky little suckers love our sweet treats. "I love this day. There's something in the air—"

"Denial?" I cut her off.

Billie places the tongs back and then rests her hand on my shoulder. "It's time to start dating again. When was the last time you went on a *real* date?"

I scrunch my nose. Dating is *not* on my vision board and therefore isn't something I'm actively pursuing.

The last guy, Henry, was, um . . . nice.

That's just it—*nice*.

He would politely open the door, pull out my chair, and do everything to show he respected women. But, when it came to conversation, he was the single most boring person I have ever had the misfortune of dining with. I almost fell asleep during our second dinner date from all the wine I drank just so I could power through.

"Months, maybe. I've stopped counting," I mumble, finally answering her question.

"So, what you're trying to say is you're not getting laid, hence the attitude today?"

Billie is as laid-back as they come. We met in college when she was assigned to my room at the last minute. Maddy had been so indecisive about joining me at Cornell—she'd always wanted to study in California. It boiled down to this—separation anxiety. So, after many tears from Maddy and lots of reassurance from me that we would still be best friends, we took the leap and went our separate ways, so to speak. Insert me, an empty dorm room, and Billie, who coincidentally grew up just a couple of towns over from Cinnamon Springs.

I warmed up to her quickly. She loved to bake, and so did I, even though I wasn't as good as Billie, so our room was filled with all sorts of mini appliances as we experimented with different recipes. We quickly became the hit of the building, especially with the late-night-munchies crowd—though we did get a few warnings for pushing the limits of the fire code.

Thankfully, nothing ever burned down—though I am pretty sure the fire warden developed a nervous twitch.

With our love of baking and my business degree, it was a no-brainer—we set out to open our own café, Donuts Ever After. We put together a business plan and went to the bank for a loan after graduating from Cornell, but then Billie's mom was diagnosed with a rare heart disease and needed immediate medical treatment. It meant Billie had to move back home to care for her mom physically and financially.

Our dream was put on hold.

But as if the universe knew we needed a lucky break, my parents decided to sell a piece of land they owned in Wyoming and gifted me and my brother a share of the profits. It was enough to start the café and hire Billie as a baker. It suited us both. She didn't need the added pressure of investing in a business, especially with her mother's medical bills piling up, and I needed her because she was a superstar in the kitchen. Without her recipes, we would have served only coffee and iced tea. Sure, I could bake, but no way was I as good as Billie.

The perfect place presented itself—Cinnamon Springs, where I spent most of my teenage years. It never occurred to me to go back, given I'd moved away for college.

My parents have always enjoyed being on the road. Growing up, we moved every few years, somehow making a journey across the country until one day my dad heard about this town that needed a horticulturist to focus on crop cultivation. It was kind of perfect in the end. Dad settled into a job he loved, and Mom worked the farmers markets every week. They would sell organic fruits and vegetables from our property, and quite often, Mom would bake cookies to give to the kids who accompanied their parents.

We moved to Cinnamon Springs when I started middle school. Of course, it didn't take long for my parents to get itchy feet again. After a lot of tears and begging, they agreed to stick it out until I finished high school.

Since then, my parents moved and my brother left for Europe, but something always pulls me back here. I'm not even mad about it. The moment my parents drove down Main Street all those years ago, I knew this place had something special. I still remember gazing out the window and admiring all the cute little storefronts. It looked like a movie set. Cinnamon Cones, home of the best ice cream in town; Betty's Bookshelf, the most popular bookstore within a twenty-mile radius; and the diner on the corner called Happy Days. Later, I learned it was owned by a couple who, no surprise, were obsessed with the TV show *Happy Days*. The husband, Al, even wore a leather jacket and styled his hair like Fonzie. Mom had to explain about the TV show since it aired well before my time—and when I say *well before*, I mean decades.

It all feels like a lifetime ago now.

Bringing myself back to the present, I turn to Billie with a grin. "A girl can please herself," I remind her.

"Sure, but a hot guy can do it better."

I purse my lips, crossing my arms beneath my chest. "And where are the hot guys?"

Billie shrugs. "Not in this town, that's for damn sure."

We both find ourselves in this sudden slump, thanks to me. Billie is a beautiful woman, so it surprises me she's single. Guys always lavish attention on her. It's the ginger-colored hair, which falls effortlessly down her back like she's a modern-day Rapunzel, but instead of being trapped in a tower, she works for a grump in a donut shop.

That grump being *me*.

I'm not usually a pessimist, but this winter feels different. And not necessarily in a good way. The picturesque snow only reminds me of the wet puddles customers drag into the store. The hot chocolate I usually devour tastes too sweet, especially when you add marshmallows. And everyone knows they're the best part.

I don't know what's wrong with me lately. It's almost like all my dreams have been put on hold for no other reason but time. It gets away from me and refuses to stand still so I can just have a moment to breathe.

All this and it's only February. The hype of New Year's resolutions is fading into the distance along with my love of this cold season.

A chair creaks, and my attention shifts back to the couple. The guy leans in, whispers something into the woman's ear before she giggles again and runs her high-heeled shoe up his leg.

"You need to stop them," I warn Billie, cringing involuntarily. "I think she might give him a foot job, and I don't think I'll be able to sleep tonight if she does."

"Why me? You're the owner," Billie complains. "We had a deal. I make the yummy desserts, and you handle customers doing *foot jobs* in the store."

I let out a huff. "I don't recall this agreement. However, I will put an end to this for the sake of not having to bleach our brains."

I take a deep breath and approach the couple's table. They instantly pull away from each other when they realize I'm standing beside them.

A forced smile graces my lips as I ask, "Is there anything else I can get you lovebirds today?"

The woman's cheeks turn crimson. "We, um . . . are fine. The donuts are delicious."

"Yes," the man adds, clearing his throat. "Would we be able

to purchase a box to take with us? We could have them for dessert tonight." He glances at the woman with what I assume is supposed to be a sexy grin, making this all the more cringey. The longer I stand here, the harder it is to control the urge to shudder.

"Of course, I'll get them packaged up and brought right over." As I walk back to the counter, Billie tries to hide her laughter.

I pinch her arm the moment I reach her. "Gross, they're going to have sex and use our donuts in their dirty games," I whisper.

"Okay, stop! I will deal with them because I love you so much," Billie offers with a teasing grin, then nods over my shoulder. "Besides, you have a visitor."

I turn around swiftly to see Maddy, who's at the door with a beaming smile. It's been two months since I last saw her because she was vacationing with her boyfriend in the Bahamas. I've lost count of how many times they have vacationed in the year they've been together. Maddy is truly living her best life while I'm watching potential porn movies acted out in my café.

"Oh my God, you're here!" I run toward her and straight into a tight embrace. She smells just like I remember—strawberries and cream. As we pull away, I take a moment to really look at her. She is sun-kissed, but what catches my eye is the hint of gold in her usually dark brown hair. Last year, during her quarter-life crisis, she impulsively got bangs. Now, they've grown out enough to just tuck behind her ears.

Her gemstone-green eyes sparkle with anticipation, and I realize she's waiting for me to notice something. I glance over her again, but nothing seems unusual. She's dressed in denim jeans with a black top and an oversize ivory knitted cardigan.

Then, she raises her hand and waves *it* at me. The diamond catches the light, nearly blinding me as Maddy thrusts her hand in front of my face, her smile practically bursting with joy.

I squint at the ring, trying to make out the cut. I am no expert on carats, cuts, or top designers, but even I know this ring is massive and worth a lot.

"It's a big ring," I say slowly.

"I know, but do you know what type of ring it is?"

"Tiffany?" I answer with a scrunched face.

"It's an engagement ring!" Maddy shrieks. "I'm getting married!"

My fingers instinctively trace the edge of the ring while Maddy's words begin to sink in. *Did she just use the M-word?*

Oh my, I mouth, yanking her hand toward me to get a better glimpse. "Maddy, are you for real? Or is this some prank because you're bored, and you know I'm heading to the doctor for a checkup and worried they'll find something and then tell me I have one week to live?"

"Now who's being melodramatic?" she teases. "Myles proposed. And the best news is, we're getting married in a month. Here, in Cinnamon Springs!"

I shake my head, trying to slow my thoughts because my overstimulated brain has many, many questions.

"One . . . month?"

"Yes! And before you even think it, I'm not pregnant."

"I wasn't thinking it," I lie.

"Of course you were." Maddy tugs my arm, guiding me to one of the empty tables outside. "Myles's grandfather is unwell. I mean, he's ninety-six, which is a miracle in itself, so who knows how long he has left? It's super important to his family that he's part of the day, so Myles asked if I would be open to planning it quickly. I mean, it's a wedding. How hard can it be?"

I snort, covering my mouth the moment it slips out. "A wedding is a big event and a month isn't a lot of time. For starters, how many people are you inviting? Have you considered what venue can hold all your guests? And so quickly? You'll need a wedding planner."

"There'll be about a hundred people, including Myles's family," Maddy rushes to respond. "My father secured the Grand Honey Lodge. It's the perfect location. Plus, they will do all the catering. As for the wedding planner, I've contacted three, but they said it's too short notice, no matter how much I tried to entice them with a bonus."

"Oh."

"Myles's mother has insisted on planning it, since apparently she is part of some charitable committee and plans events all the time." Maddy's face changes, as if she's trying to convince me she's happy Myles's mother will take over.

"Okay, so that's covered, I guess. What about your dress and your bridesmaids?"

"Well, here's the thing . . ." Maddy smiles, resting her hand on top of mine. "No one in the world means more to me than you. So all I need is for you to say yes to being my maid of honor. The bridesmaids will be Myles's cousins Ramona and Hailey since he's an only child, and he's close to them."

"I . . . I would be honored." My eyes blur as I reach out to hug her.

We were never the type of girls to gush about marriage and babies. Our lives focused on college and then real-world responsibilities. Maddy switched her major from literature to theater, much to her father's disapproval. After one trip to see *Hamilton*, Maddy decided she was destined for the stage. Well, not the stage itself, but behind the scenes.

She's always had a fascination with costumes. Once, for a town fair, she made us dress up as Tweedledum and Tweedledee for a pie-eating contest. She made the costumes herself and insisted we would win the grand prize of two hundred dollars for the effort. In the end, we were runners-up, and I was throwing up cherry pie for a solid four hours after that competition.

The runners-up got free pies from Shirley's Pie House.

We never picked ours up.

After interning for what felt like forever, Maddy got her dream job in Manhattan, despite her father being less than pleased she chose a career in theater. It's there she met Myles—he's a talent scout who invests in up-and-coming theater productions. The funny thing is, they had crossed paths before at family events but had never spoken to each other.

"I'm shocked, but if you love him, this is great."

"I do love him, Eva."

"Then, it's settled." I clap my hands with excitement. "Let's get you married. You tell me what you need, and I will do my best to make it happen. It's not like I have anything else going on in my life right now." I let out a nervous laugh.

Maddy sighs. "You know me better than anyone else."

"Yes, some say we were conjoined twins in a previous life," I tease, then follow with, "But?"

"It's just, work is going to be crazy over the next month with the premiere coming up for that show we've been working on. We actually need to postpone our honeymoon until after opening week. I know it's not the right time to get married, but if it stays small and intimate, it shouldn't be overwhelming, right? I can be present for both. The drive to Manhattan is only two hours. Less, if I put my foot on the gas and pretend I'm Dom Toretto."

I reach out to touch her hand. "You're capable of anything you put your mind to. But if you need more help, I'm always here."

"I just don't want Myles's mother to make it her day."

"So, don't have her plan it. Why don't you leave the boring stuff you don't care about to her, and give me the fun stuff you do care about. I don't care for china patterns but I do care about saying goodbye to your single days with an epic bang."

Maddy's eyes water. "You would really do that for me?"

"Like I said, my life is about as exciting as a bear going into hibernation."

Her mouth quirks as she giggles. "So I'm really not burdening you, and maybe all this wedding planning might send good karma to the universe and deliver you the most perfect man?"

"Okay, now you're reaching." I laugh.

Maddy glances at her watch, scrunching her face. "Ah, crap! Listen . . . I have to meet the minister in ten minutes. It was the only time he could see me. How about we catch up tonight at your place? I could really use some girl time, and we can talk about the wedding in more detail."

"Sure, but you know it's Valentine's Day. Don't you have a fiancé to spoil?"

"We decided to hold off until the wedding," she admits with an unsure smile.

An unflattering laugh leaves my mouth. "*You* . . . not have sex for one month? Oh, this won't end well. I'm not dealing with a bridezilla."

Maddy chuckles. "Hey, what doesn't kill me will make me stronger, right?"

I shake my head with a grin. Maddy is many things, but patient is *not* one of them.

Billie joins us, and Maddy quickly announces her news. The ring is brought out again for display, and Billie gushes over the diamond. Since Maddy needs to go, she rushes through the upcoming plans while Billie listens attentively.

Before leaving to see the minister, Maddy hovers behind the counter and takes a glazed donut, shoving it in a brown paper take-out bag. Billie frowns but offers to make her a to-go coffee as well.

"Thanks, Billie." Maddy sighs dejectedly. "I'll need a strong one, too, if the minister brings up my virtue."

"The virtue you gave away when we traveled to Europe that summer before senior year? I'm sorry . . . what was his name again?"

The summer traveling around Europe was the best time of our lives. We backpacked and met other people our age. It was just one big party and many drunk nights walking the cobblestone streets in uncomfortable heels in whatever country we were in at the time.

Maddy rolls her eyes. "Can we not bring him up, please? I shudder at the thought."

"Okay, okay . . ." I raise my hands with a giggle. "I promise not to ruin your memorable day. See you tonight."

She leans in, kissing me on the cheek before heading toward the door, where she pauses just shy of the couple and dramatically pretends to gag. They have progressed to kissing, and I'm almost certain I catch a glimpse of tongue.

That's it! They need to take this elsewhere.

"Oh, shit," Maddy says, turning back to me, "I just remembered, my brother can help you with all the wedding stuff, too. I still have to tell him, but I'll do that after seeing the minister. Aston won't say no since he knows I'll annoy him until he caves. So don't worry about having to do it all yourself. That's if Myles's mother doesn't drive us all to the nuthouse. Did you know it's bad luck seeing a nun or monk on your way to your wedding ceremony?"

What the . . .

My brain is jumping back and forth between the so-called help I'm to receive and the nun or monk just randomly appearing on a wedding day. Cinnamon Springs doesn't have nuns or monks that I know of. God, this is so beside the point.

Her brother??

"Um, a nun, right . . ." I mumble.

"I know. Myles's mother is a piece of work." Maddy waves with a big smile. "Bye. Love you!"

And in a flash, she's gone, leaving me completely speechless. The moment she dropped the word *brother*, my stomach twisted.

The *last thing* I want to do is spend one minute with Aston Beaumont.

It's been eight years since I saw him. No, that's a lie. Actually, he was passing through town once with his father, and I saw him across the street. It was summer break, and I'd decided to visit for a few days. When I spotted him, I freaked out and ran the other way, and afterward, I felt stupid. So much so, I did tequila shots with some random tourists passing through town and ended up singing "It's Raining Men" during karaoke hour onstage in front of the busy Friday-night crowd. It wasn't my finest moment.

My phone buzzes in my pocket, alerting me to my appointment.

"Great," I mutter under my breath. "What café owner books a doctor's appointment to renew her birth control on Valentine's Day?"

Billie's warm smile is enough to calm my overwhelming thoughts.

"Go to your appointment. We close in an hour anyway, so I'll see you tomorrow."

I nod with a forced smile, but deep inside, my resentment spreads by the second.

How can one guy—a jerk, to be precise—still make me feel this way years later? I've moved on, and I'm sure he's moved on.

It was one stupid kiss.

A billion years ago.

We were kids.

End of story.

CHAPTER 2

Eva

With a deep breath, I remove my green apron and hang it up in the back. The café isn't big by any means, but we have a small office right behind the kitchen. There's a desk with my laptop for when I have to do paperwork and other tasks.

Above the desk is a corkboard with photos pinned to it. My eyes wander to the one of me and Maddy drenched in tomato juice from partaking in La Tomatina in Spain. We laughed so hard that day, I swear we both peed our pants.

Beside that photo is one of Maddy frowning with a bruised wrist from the Gloucester cheese-rolling festival. I smile at the memories. Who would have thought that two girls seated next to each other in freshman biology, both trying not to throw up while dissecting a dead frog, would end up here?

My best friend is getting married.

I press my palm to my chest to suppress the overwhelming feeling of life moving fast. One minute, we're just kids doing stupid kid things, and the next, we're planning weddings.

After grabbing my purse, I wave goodbye to Billie. She's busy talking to the couple who have finally managed to pull their tongues away from each other. Maybe this is the beginning of their love story, and my café plays a part in their forever . . . or a kinky night involving the donuts Billie made this morning.

As I walk out the door, I smirk, leaving that awkward encounter for Billie to handle, and head toward the clinic just a block away. The crisp winter air is exactly what I need to clear my head.

The door to Fairy Lane Treats opens as the owner, Mrs. Dorothy, steps out. I brace myself for the inevitable, certain that she has two main goals in life—to sell candy and to set me up with whatever single man she can get her hands on.

Her pink-stained lips raise into an overbearing smile. "My dear, aren't you looking beautiful on this special holiday."

"Thank you, Mrs. Dorothy, as are you."

"Stop." She flicks her hand with a giggle. "It's my and Mr. Dorothy's fortieth anniversary today."

"Oh wow! Forty years married." I let out a whistle. "That's true love."

"No, my dear." She glances around to make sure no one is listening, then leans in close. "Forty years since we first fornicated."

I freeze. "Fornicated?"

"We weren't married yet," she whispers. "But I don't want you to follow in my footsteps."

"Oh, right. Yes, I wouldn't want to be a bad girl," I lie, then force a smile to stop the word *fornicated* from repeating in my brain.

"Now, there's a young fellow I'd like you to meet . . ."

Mrs. Dorothy rambles on as I nod, pretending to listen but zoning out while glancing around the street to see what is happening.

I chose Cinnamon Springs because of my fond memories, yet everyone moved on.

My parents moved to Utah years ago, finally living their farm life with a gazillion animals. Every time Mom calls, they've added some new member to their ever-growing flock. I heard her throw around the word *grandkids* but hung up before the conversation segued to my love life, or lack thereof.

My brother, Elliot, lives in Cannes. We still keep in touch, but I miss him terribly. It's not the same with everyone so far away. He's busy building his life as a pastry chef at some high-end restaurant with women throwing themselves at him. That's according to Mom, anyway.

Maybe a trip to see him might cure whatever funk I'm in right now, but the last time I attempted to do that, my flight was canceled, and a hurricane stopped me from leaving the States. I took it as a sign and stayed home.

I return my focus to Mrs. Dorothy as she smiles with eyes wide in anticipation.

"So, how about dinner tonight?" she asks, watching me intently. "I'm sure Basil can make it if I ask him."

Surely, a red flag is being set up on a blind date with a guy named after an herb.

"I'm sorry, Mrs. Dorothy, I have plans tonight. Maybe another time?"

She nods politely. "You let me know, dear. I'll have you know my sister, Winnie, is a spinster."

And this is my cue to leave.

I distract Mrs. Dorothy by complimenting her on the new storefront. The big rainbow lollipop spinning in the window is sure to draw a crowd, I tell her as I make my exit.

To avoid being stopped by anyone else, I walk faster with my head down and ignore all eye contact. When I reach the clinic, I breathe a sigh of relief.

The chime on the door dings as I enter. There aren't any other people waiting, which must be a world first. Usually, this place is overcrowded in winter, with all the viruses spreading around.

The receptionist greets me with a friendly smile. "Miss Woods, I was afraid you forgot about your appointment."

"I'm so sorry, Mrs. Weston. It's been busy at the café today. You know, Valentine's Day and all." I release a breath, wondering if I should just back out now. What's the point of staying on birth control if my sex life is nonexistent? It's not like I'm on any dating apps, and quite frankly, the men in this town are . . . blah. Manhattan is only two hours away, but city men are often so arrogant. Like Aston.

My lips purse at the thought of him. *God, I really need to get over this.*

"Take a seat, my dear. Dr. Wilde is with another patient, but he won't be long."

I sit on the plastic chair and reach for an old magazine. As I flick through it aimlessly, I begin praying this routine checkup turns out okay so I can continue taking the pill for future me, who is supposedly going to have *all the sex.*

Then, I tilt my head with confusion and glance at Mrs. Weston. "Dr. Wilde?" I ask from across the room. "Is he new? Where is Dr. Green?"

The door to the office opens, prompting me to turn around. And when I do, the sexiest of grins is all I can focus on. God, his lips look soft and inviting—full and the perfect shade of pink. I just know he would be a great kisser.

I'm unable to speak, but I force myself to lift my gaze to meet his chestnut-brown eyes, desperately trying to swallow my urge to say something foolish like *Hellooo, Dr. Hottie.*

He glances down at the chart. "Miss Woods?"

"Um . . ." I croak, much to Mrs. Weston's amusement. "Yes, that's, um, me."

"Come into my office," he offers politely, standing by the door as he waits for me to enter.

As I walk past him, the scent of his cologne consumes me.

Ding. Ding. Ding.

Turns out my libido is alive and functioning perfectly.

Just breathe.

Be yourself.

Act cool.

He closes the door, taking his seat behind the wooden desk. I wonder what it would be like to have sex right here. Would we push all the papers off the desk like you see in movies? It'd create a mess, though, and who's cleaning that up?

God, I've lost the plot.

"I'd like to introduce myself . . . I'm Dr. Wilde. I'll be Dr. Green's replacement while he's recovering from surgery."

I smile awkwardly, silenced by my dirty inner monologue, which has now thought about how sexy his lips would be buried between my legs.

Once again, he glances at the chart. "So, you're here to stay on birth control, is that correct?"

And as if the universe—*Cupid, perhaps*—decided to give me a break, I smile in return and straighten my posture. "Yes, Dr. Wilde, I plan on being sexually active."

"Let's take a look at your medical records, shall we?"

Dr. Wilde sits across from me, reading a folder filled with notes about my medical history. I sit in the awkward silence, wondering what he's thinking. My overstimulated brain is conjuring up a million different scenarios.

And why is this room so damn hot? It's still winter. Despite the snow stopping earlier in the week, it's lingered on the lampposts and around the town square where the gazebo sits. The trees, while bare, have snow still covering their branches. If you drive farther into the mountains, there's plenty of snow for sledding.

I spot the thermostat on the wall. It's not even that hot, but beneath my ivory wool coat, sweat begins to form, and I'm pretty sure my cheeks are flushed.

The problem is not the room. It's the hot young doctor sitting in front of you.

I'm drawn to the way he concentrates while reading, brows narrowing to focus. His hair is a lighter shade of brown, almost a dark blond, which is parted to the side. My eyes then gravitate toward his sharp jawline, which is freshly shaven. The more I observe him and his desire for my medical history, the more panic begins to creep in.

I'm far from being a hypochondriac, but then I remember the time Dr. Green had to do an emergency tampon removal in my senior year of high school. I called on Maddy, as my best friend, to help me first, but she started freaking out. Her freak-out made me freak out even more, which I believe to this day lodged the tampon even farther up my vaginal canal. Mom also tried, but by then, there was no choice but to seek intervention.

Even though Dr. Green assured me it's quite common, I was completely mortified. It was a month after I'd lost my virginity to Henry Painter, this guy from my English class, so I assumed it was the perfect time to start using tampons. Boy, was I wrong.

We'd dated for four months before we did the deed, but after the tampon incident, I realized I wasn't ready for a relationship—and all the stuff that came with it—and called it quits.

"According to Dr. Green's notes, you're in good health."

My shoulders loosen as I release the tension I'd been building up. "That's always good to hear."

He chuckles while reaching for the blood pressure machine beside him. "Let me check your blood pressure first."

As he wraps the Velcro strap around my arm, I glance at the desk again. There's no photo frame with wedding pictures or kids. Nothing in this space would indicate he is married, including his bare ring finger. My lips curve upward slowly, but then the loud sound of the Velcro ripping brings me back to reality.

"So, tell me a bit about yourself," he says, gazing at me with eyes that distract me from why I'm here at this consult. "What do you do for a living?"

"I own the donut café on Ginger Grove. It's called Donuts Ever After."

His grin distracts me, along with his perfectly white, straight teeth. "Ah yes. I've heard good things about the place. A friend of mine suggested the gingerbread donut. *To die for*, according to her."

Does he mean girlfriend?

I smile in return, thinking of ways to extract this information. "Oh, really? So, I guess you're new to town."

"Yes and no." He leans back in his chair, relaxing his posture and fixing his lab coat. "Dr. Green is a family friend, so we've been visiting him for as long as I can remember. I moved here from Chicago a few weeks ago."

"And, um . . ." I twist my hands but put on a smile so as not to appear like I'm stalking his personal life, even though I clearly am. "By yourself?"

He nods, followed by that sexy grin. *That grin will get me into a whole lot of trouble.* Thinking of him in a nonprofessional way is surely violating some sort of doctor-patient regulation. *I wonder if he would leave the coat on.* It's like a role-play dream except he is an actual doctor, which makes it ten times hotter.

"Yes, unfortunately. I recently broke up with someone."

I pout my lips. "I'm sorry. Breakups are never easy."

He places his hand on the desk with a thud. "Enough about me. We are here for you. So, you want to continue birth control?"

"Yes, I like to be responsible in case, you know, I meet someone." I gulp, then shake my head. "Better to be prepared than not. The last guy I slept with was . . ." I try to do the math in my head but then become hyperaware Dr. Wilde is staring at me with a smirk. "Okay, too much information. I'm sorry."

"Miss Woods—"

"Please call me Eva. Everyone else does."

"Eva," he says smoothly. "What we discuss in this office is confidential. I like my patients to know they can talk to me about anything."

"So, what you're trying to say is you give medical *and* relationship advice?" I question with a laugh. "My best friend, Maddy, would be here in a heartbeat if she found out."

"Look, you're doing the right thing by being responsible. There's nothing wrong with consenting adults enjoying their, let's say, *freedom.* I'll just write this script for you as I'm sure you have better places to be."

Great, he's pushing me out the door.

I sigh loudly, unaware I had done so until he raises his chestnut-brown eyes to meet mine. Something inside of me stirs, and I can't remember the last time a man made me feel this way.

Why does he have to check all the boxes but be off-limits?

His hand extends. "Here is your script, Eva."

"Thank you, Dr. Wilde." I quickly stand, then reach out to shake his hand. The moment I do, I regret my decision. His hand is warm, inviting, and *large.* It is a simple touch, but enough to make me realize I am lonely. "I guess I'll see you around."

With my purse in hand, I turn to go. As I reach the door, Dr. Wilde calls my name. When I turn around, he's sitting at the edge of his desk with his arms crossed.

I notice how muscular he looks with the coat tightening around his biceps and swallow the lump caught inside my throat.

"Outside the office, you can call me Marco . . ." His lips upturn and there's a gleam in his eyes. "Everyone else does."

I nod, then tilt my head, smiling.

Maybe, just maybe, things are not as off-limits as they seem.

CHAPTER 3

Aston

This guy must have the smallest dick.

My fingers tap against the wood-grain table with an impatient beat. It's just after four in the afternoon, and this meeting has gone on for *far* too damn long. A meeting that could have been an email—but Chalmers insisted we talk about numbers inside the boardroom of our downtown office with every executive team member in attendance.

A waste of goddamn time and resources.

Chalmers is old-school and is always the last to get on board with the latest technology. He even wears those corduroy sport coats with elbow patches. They should be buried along with his stale cigar and coffee breath.

The only reason he's on the board of directors is because of my father.

The absolute bane of my existence.

"Listen, Chalmers," I begin while trying to curb my irritation. "We need to project the future, not fixate on past performance. Times are changing, and our focus needs to be on development and market demand. We are in the digital era, and commercial investment is heavily tied in with e-commerce growth."

Beside me, Will, another board member, snickers. He understands exactly why Chalmers should be in a retirement village in

Boca, not trying to impart his so-called wisdom onto us *young folk,* as he so annoyingly likes to refer to us.

The room is cold, and the air conditioner is blasting too high for my comfort. I spend most of my time inside this building, more than in my penthouse, it seems. *So why the fuck can't the maintenance guys get this shit right?* We pay them more than enough money.

Unsurprisingly, Chalmers ignores my direction and goes on some tangent about the budget. Closing my eyes briefly to calm the fuck down, I open them to the sound of my phone vibrating in my pocket. I pull it out of my suit jacket, scanning my eyes over the text.

Little Brat
Do you know what day it is?

My sister, Madelina, is the biggest pain in my ass. We were born a year apart, so for all of my life, she's been my bratty little sister who annoys me. When I was growing up, my parents hired nannies to take care of us because their social life took precedence. Madelina craved attention, and when our parents were too busy to notice, she focused on making my life hell. She would whine all the time, copy my every move, and despite the many times I warned her to stay out of my room, Madelina would end up sleeping at the foot of my bed when she was scared of thunderstorms.

Now, we're adults, but nothing has changed.

At all.

Me
Thursday?

The three dots appear and bounce for what seems like forever. My eyes lift away from the screen as Chalmers rambles about the stock market crash of 2008.

Jesus fucking Christ—this man needs to be stopped.

My phone vibrates again, forcing me to shift my attention to the illuminated screen.

> **Little Brat**
> It's Valentine's Day!

> **Me**
> And?

The screen flashes with a call, but I hit decline and then quickly type a message.

> **Me**
> I'm in a meeting

> **Little Brat**
> Anyone hot in the room?

> **Me**
> Go away. I'll call you later.

I place my phone back in my pocket and focus on the topic at hand. Just as I'm about to tell Chalmers to cut the bullshit, the door opens, and everyone turns their heads.

Lo and behold—it's the king himself.

My father.

All the men at the table straighten their shoulders. Will and I are the only ones who seem unperturbed by his presence. It's his same old routine. He'll stroll into the boardroom all high-and-mighty to scare the team into doing things *his* way. Then, he'll leave to play golf with his billionaire so-called friends while we are left to clean up the mess.

Then there is my mother, who's somewhere in Europe at some wellness clinic she checked herself into. My parents have the most dysfunctional marriage, which probably explains why I don't do the whole relationship thing. There's never been any woman I would want to spend all my time with. No matter how much they get me off in bed.

"I see we are having another unproductive meeting," my father immediately reprimands everyone in attendance. I gather he read my frustrated expression the moment he set foot in the room. "Chalmers, you setting these young ones straight?"

"I'm trying, Beaumont. They're too caught up in the digital future," Chalmers mutters.

I clench my hand into a fist, trying to control my fury over my father's innate lack of consideration for the hardworking people in this room. *Chalmers excluded.*

Nepotism has nothing to do with the fact that I worked, and continue to work, my ass off. I've dedicated every waking moment to this company to prove I could take over the role of CEO despite others thinking they were better than me. I started at the bottom, learning everything I could to prepare myself.

Since I was promoted last year, our profits have exceeded our projected forecasts, and the value of our investments has skyrocketed. I pride myself on my ability to get things done, despite my father warning me failure is not an option.

"Is there a reason you have graced us with a visit?" I challenge my father with a raised brow. "I'm sure there is a golf club calling your name."

My father's counterfeit smile comes as no surprise. "My, my . . . the apple doesn't fall too far from the tree, now, does it, son?"

He knows exactly how to get to me. How to manipulate me into thinking I'm just like him. Honestly, I couldn't think of a fate worse than turning into my father. I'm here because he placed an ultimatum on me a long time ago. An ultimatum that included taking over the family empire. It was either me or Madelina. I knew exactly what went on behind the scenes of his empire. It's nothing but a damn boys' club—plain and simple. There's no way in hell I would subject my sister to that kind of environment.

Late-night board meetings with aged whiskey, cigars, and inappropriate conversation about female employees. Most of the men are married, yet never shy to admit just how much money they spend on their mistresses.

The more money they make, the more power they assume they have over women.

So I did everything demanded of me to fulfill the position of CEO for the Beaumont Group. I spent my summer before college in London working at one of my father's offices. As soon as the summer ended, I went straight to Stanford to study business and economics.

Those years feel like a blur. I'd cram all week with classes and studying, then spend weekends trying to escape the pressure by drinking at whatever party was being held around me. In so many ways, life was simpler back then.

Now, as much as humanly possible, I limit interaction with my father. I manage this company, keep my personal life separate, and ensure we deliver the numbers to please him. He may be the patriarch of our family and this company, but it'll be mine one day. All I need to do is persevere and ignore his need for control.

He likes to think he knows what goes on, but the truth is, I'm the master at playing his game. I know the old man too well and have outsmarted his controlling nature many times.

"Chalmers was just wrapping up," I insist. "So, it's agreed we will increase our budget for the project to keep our platform competitive. By doing so, we have confidence from our investors that our launch dates will stick to the agreed-upon timeline. Is there anything else anyone would like to add before we finish?"

"I agree," Will speaks up while staring directly into my father's eyes. "Confidence is key. We deliver this, and moving forward, we will have no issues securing investors for our next project."

Chalmers sits across from me with a sour face. *Fuck him!* That man should retire right now so we don't have to waste time on his irrelevant opinions.

"Perhaps I'm mistaken," my father begins, much to Chalmers's annoyance. He pats him on the back with a laugh that's more unsettling than friendly, a harsh sound that lingers far too long in the room. "Shall we leave the work to the boys? How about we hit the golf course?"

"All right, Beaumont. I could use a day off," Chalmers agrees like it's the worst thing in the world.

Thank fuck! Get the old bastard out of here.

"Everyone is dismissed," my father commands. "Except you, Aston."

Just. Fucking. Great.

Noise elevates as the men chatter while exiting the room. Will informs me he'll call later since he needs to rush to midtown for a meeting with his father-in-law.

As the final person leaves the room and the door closes, my father sits across from me with an arrogant smile. A smile that reminds me I look more like my mother than this bastard.

"I'm guessing you've heard the news?"

Over the years, he has aged, his hair silver but still slicked back in the same style he's had since he was young. He wears a maroon cravat, another piece of clothing that needs to be buried with Chalmers's sport jacket.

I tilt my head. "What news?"

"Your sister is getting married."

My head jerks back at his words. *Damn! This explains why she was trying to call me earlier.* Madelina has been dating Myles for what, a few months? I'm not one to pay attention to other people's relationships, but it doesn't feel long. Still, Myles is a decent guy. I met him years ago at one of my father's functions. Since they've been dating, we've caught up for dinner and drinks, though he's never mentioned marriage. Generally, we talk about business and baseball, since he's also a Yankees fan. His production company is doing well—he's got a good eye when it comes to theater.

"She tried to call me earlier," I inform him. "If it makes her happy, then there's nothing left to say about it."

"The boy is from a good family," he states with a raised brow.

"You mean a rich family?"

"I want the best for my daughter. Is there anything wrong with that?"

Where to begin? I ask myself, as if this old bastard gives two fucks about his daughter's happiness. All he cares about is how our family looks to everyone else.

"Is there anything else we need to discuss?" I quickly check the time on my phone, uninterested in whatever game my father is playing right now. "I have another meeting to attend."

"This wedding will be the perfect opportunity for us to secure a deal with the Whitney Group. Myles Whitney is the son of Roland Whitney. Roland owns the land on the northern border of Cinnamon Springs, where the tree line starts. We've been trying to acquire it for the last twenty years." His voice turns cold as he leans in, eyes fixed on me. "We give the Whitney family a dream wedding for their only son, and then we convince Myles to sell us the land. After all, he will be the new heir of the Whitney fortune. So you give your sister and Myles whatever they want, no matter how costly. You make sure this wedding cements the ties between our two families. Don't screw this up—you understand me, boy?"

I cross my arms, glaring at the man who is supposed to love his children unconditionally.

"You've got to be kidding me," I mumble.

"I don't kid, as you so ineloquently put it, when my business is at stake," he raises his voice.

"You've got more money than you know what to do with," I remind him. "Why do you need some piece of land to make more?"

My father observes me with an unrelenting stare. That same stare would intimidate me when I was a kid, but as I grew older, I learned to meet it with my own.

"Once the Beaumont Group owns the land, it opens up endless opportunities. Cinnamon Springs would benefit from another resort, or perhaps a new golf course with state-of-the-art facilities.

This would give us a steady lead in property investments since the Gellar Corporation acquired the industrial end of town. It's not about needing more money." My father pushes his chair back, standing up. "It's about *power*. Surely, son, you should know that by now."

And with those words, he leaves the room.

My fists clench tight, desperate to punch the wall. Instead, I take a deep breath and decide to find an incompetent asshole I can take it out on in the office.

Then, I will pretend this conversation never happened.

For the sake of my sister.

Across the table, Will is watching me swirl bourbon aimlessly. It's my second glass; the first did absolutely nothing.

After the day I had, Will knew I needed a hard drink and suggested we go out after work. If anyone understands the pressure I'm under, it's Will Romano. He's a billionaire in his own right who owns several tech companies. In the past two years, he branched out into real estate holdings, which is how we met.

"You're letting him get to you," Will is quick to remind me. "Stick with our original plan, and Pops will have no say in the matter."

His sarcastic "Pops" is enough for a slight chuckle. *God, why the fuck is this drink not hitting the spot?* I loosen my tie in an effort to relax.

"You're lucky your dad leaves you the hell alone."

"Maybe, but my father-in-law doesn't," he states. "Before he was my father-in-law, he was my business partner. Try having him look over your shoulder when you're dating his daughter behind his back."

"Dating?" I laugh, shaking my head. "Will Romano wouldn't date. You would have been fucking her sweet . . ."

"Ahem," a voice sounds from over my shoulder.

Amelia, his wife, is standing beside us. I force a grin, pretending I wasn't about to say something vulgar about their sex life. I stand to kiss her hello, having not seen her in a while. They live on the West Coast, but every time they're in the city, we try to meet up for dinner or a drink.

"Your mother ever tell you to wash your mouth out with soap, Mr. Beaumont?" she chides before kissing her husband hello.

My lips curve upward as I attempt to backstep. "The ever-so-beautiful Mrs. Romano, how have you been?"

"Don't try to charm me." Amelia smiles as she rolls her eyes. "What are we drinking tonight, boys?"

The truth is, Amelia is beautiful and sexy, and all the things I dare not say in front of Will. *He struck gold*—enough said. They have three boys, all under ten. And from memory, one could even be a baby, but I'm never one to remember such details.

Her father is Lex Edwards, the mogul of a media enterprise. It doesn't stop there; his real estate holdings are one of the largest in the States. I've met him several times, and unlike my father, the guy is damn intelligent where business is concerned. He's innovative and constantly pushes the boundaries to achieve excellence.

Apparently, my father couldn't care less about money as long as he rules his world.

"Uh-oh. Why the face?" Amelia is quick to scowl. "What did your dad do?"

I glance at her. "How did you know?"

"Because every time you have that face and a bourbon in hand, which I assume is not your first one, it involves the ever-so-powerful Harvey Beaumont."

"Don't you have a kid to take care of?" I tease.

"Actually . . ." Amelia grins, clapping her hands. "We're kid-free tonight. Mom and Dad are here and offered to take the boys. God, I can't remember the last time I slept."

"Last night?" Will reminds her with a huff. "When your sister came over, and the two of you decided to talk about periods so I would leave the room. You were knocked out by the time I was allowed back inside."

"Ah . . ." Her emerald eyes light up. "That old chestnut works every . . . single . . . time."

I scowl. "Women are crafty creatures."

"Speaking of women, I know the perfect person to set you up on a date with." Amelia is quick to focus back on me. "And before you object, hear me out."

Closing my eyes briefly, I shake my head. "Not a chance in hell. You know I don't do blind dates. Besides, I have to meet someone tonight."

Amelia pouts. "I don't believe you."

"Would you like me to show you the texts? I hope you're not a prude." I smirk.

Will laughs while raising his glass of whiskey to his lips. "Is this Bianca, the one with the tight—"

Amelia turns her gaze to her husband with a raised brow. "Tight *what*?"

I sense someone will be sleeping on the couch tonight. *Rookie mistake, Will.* Even I know you don't talk about another woman's tight ass in front of your own wife.

"I'm not sure how to answer this now that your wife looks like she's ready to eat you alive. However, for all intents and purposes . . . yes, Bianca." I raise my hand to stop Amelia as her mouth opens. "Before you lecture me, I don't need to settle down. I'm twenty-six. There's plenty of time for all that later. The topic is closed."

Before Amelia can argue, my phone starts ringing. Seeing it's my sister calling, I excuse myself and weave through the crowd, stepping outside the bar, where it's much quieter.

"It's nice of you to answer your phone," Madelina is quick to scold.

"And happy Valentine's Day to my newly engaged sister."

"Who told you?"

"Father dearest."

"Why am I not surprised? I haven't even told Mom. She's someplace that bans cell phones. *Cell phones interfere with a person's wellness*," Madelina proclaims sarcastically. "Who knew, right? Anyway, let's be honest here . . . are you happy for me?"

"Madelina, if this makes you happy, then I am happy," I tell her honestly.

"I am happy, Aston, but there's something you should know . . ." I purse my lips, waiting for the bombshell—*she's pregnant*. "The wedding is next month, and before you say anything, I'm *not* pregnant. We're having it soon because Myles's grandfather is unwell."

Well, well, it all makes sense now.

Myles's grandfather is unwell, which is why my father insisted I not screw anything up. I assume Roland and Myles will inherit everything, and if Madelina is married to him, then technically, it's all hers, too, given that Myles is an only child. And to top that off, if Madelina has her name on the land my father wants, he will manipulate her into selling it to him.

"Can you plan a wedding in a month?" I question, given that I know nothing about weddings, nor do I care for them. "Isn't that a bit too short?"

"There's a wedding coordinator for the venue. Myles's mother is taking over some of the other plans, not to mention I'll have help from family, which includes you." I hear her voice pick up. "I need you in Cinnamon Springs in exactly one week."

A huff escapes me at the same time a cab honks obnoxiously at a person walking across the street. I live in Manhattan and would prefer to stay here. The thought of going back to a small town upstate is discomforting, even if only for a short time.

"Are you kidding, Madelina? I can't just drop work. I have meetings scheduled in the city."

"Dad said you can. In fact, he insisted," she quickly informs me. "So, are you in? I wouldn't ask if I didn't need your help."

I remind myself I am doing this for my sister, not my father. Despite her being annoying, she is the only family I have.

Letting out a sigh, I drag out the words, "I could work remotely, I guess, if you really need me."

"Perfect!" She raises her voice with enthusiasm. "And yes, I really need you. We'll stay at the house together, it'll be just like when we were kids."

"You owe me big time," I point out.

"I'll add it to the TBPB list."

"The what?"

"To-be-paid-back list. Things I owe you. Like the hundred-dollar bill I stole from you in junior high."

"You said I probably lost it in the locker room," I huff.

"Yeah, remember that bag I had with the ladybugs all over it, which you hated because you have an unnatural fear of the cute little things?"

"I don't have an unnatural fear of ladybugs," I respond stiffly. "They are just very . . . *unpredictable*."

"Anyways, that's what I bought."

"I'm hanging up now."

"One more thing I forgot. Uh, I have wedding brain," Madelina yells over the speaker, much to my annoyance.

"*What?*"

"You won't be alone. What I mean is . . . you'll have help. Remember my best friend, Eva? I've designated her my maid of honor. Now, given that you're my brother, and Myles's best friend is stationed in Alaska and can't make the wedding, Myles asked if you would consider being best man. I said yes, so no declining the very nice gesture your almost brother-in-law has bestowed upon you."

The moment Madelina says her name, an unsettling feeling consumes me, like a shadow creeping over my thoughts. I can't quite put my finger on it, but the bourbon in my stomach suddenly feels like lead. My instincts are screaming at me to back away, a primal urge to retreat from what lies ahead, but I know I can't afford to. Something deeper, more compelling, keeps me rooted.

It was a long time ago. When I was a kid, doing stupid kid things.

As the call ends, a text comes through. It's Bianca. Of course, there's an image attached, and she's leaving nothing to the imagination.

Red lace—how fitting for Valentine's Day.

But my head isn't in it.

And as much as I try to shake off this nagging feeling, the thought of traveling back home to Cinnamon Springs dampens my mood. I left that small town behind for a reason, and the city is now my life.

I text Bianca to let her know I'll meet her in an hour. With my phone tucked back into the pocket of my suit pants, I push the door open and head back inside to finish my drink with Will and Amelia. But it doesn't stop at the second or third, and by the time I reach the sixth, I finally figure out what's gnawing at me and refusing to leave my conscience.

Everleigh Woods.

CHAPTER 4

Eva

My feet dangle over the shallow water as I sit on the edge of the crooked dock.

With a steady heartbeat, I breathe in the crisp air and watch the ripples in the water from the slight breeze.

My hands are tucked into my coat to protect them from the cold, even though I'm wearing gloves. As I sit here and take in the serenity of Peppermint Lake, I try to process my best friend taking the biggest leap of her life.

Marriage. It's not like I'm afraid of commitment, but marriage is huge.

Divorce is even bigger.

Not that Maddy's marriage to Myles will end in divorce, but is forever really forever?

"Shut up, brain," I mutter.

A dark gray frog with mottled skin suddenly appears and sits on a log floating not too far from me. He eyes me dubiously. At least, I think he's eyeing me, but it's hard to tell with his beady eyes.

"I'm calling you Houdini since you magically appeared out of nowhere," I tell him. "When I move in here, I promise to find you a bigger log to chill on if you promise not to poison me."

Houdini ribbits, then hops into the water like he's tired of my BS already.

The natural beauty of this place gives me an escape from my thoughts. My dream is to one day restore the old Edwardian house next to this rusted old dock, which I probably shouldn't be sitting on, and make it my own. People think I'm crazy, and when I say *people*, I mean Maddy and Billie. The house is dilapidated, and nothing at all like the other old properties in town, which are very well maintained. It would need so much work, but that makes me want it even more. Every time I visit, I imagine just how beautiful the property could be with the right vision—and money.

I've tried to explain it to Maddy and Billie several times, the feeling that consumes me when I'm here, but they try to bring me back to reality.

Permits, demolition, construction workers who bend over and expose way too much ass crack. I didn't think that was a thing until we needed some floorboards repaired in the store.

Some things I can never unsee.

I have my deposit saved, ready to strike when the owners who inherited the land are ready to sell. I got my realtor to reach out to them last year, but their lawyer said it was a family property, and no amount of money would make them sell. He wouldn't tell us who owned it.

I call bullshit. How important could it be if they left it to rot all these years?

Still, I long for the day I'll be able to get my hands on this place and officially call it mine. My vision board has a photo of the house, one I took at the end of last year. I promised myself this would be the year to finally follow my dreams. After spending all my time focusing on the café, I'm ready to make the next move as long as business remains steady and the bank loans me the rest of the money.

But until they're willing to sell me the property, my small apartment will have to do.

I sit for a while longer, and as always when I'm here, time is lost on me.

My phone pings with a text.

Maddy

I'm on my way. Do we want tacos? Chinese? Pizza?

I quickly respond.

Me

Why are you even asking? All three please.

Maddy

Roger that

"Goodbye, Houdini. See you soon." I smile as I stand, then make my way to my car to drive to my actual home.

My home is far from a mansion. It's the exact opposite. It's a one-bedroom apartment above the café. Since my whole life revolves around the café, it made sense to rent it. Plus, it allows me to save money. The owner, Mr. Wilburn, charges me low rent in exchange for free coffee and donuts whenever he visits. The man is too generous, always reminding me I'm the grand-daughter he never had.

The complex consists of two apartments. Mrs. Sherman lives on the second floor, and she's lived there forever. She keeps to herself, never complains, and as far as neighbors go, I think I got lucky. My apartment is on the third floor. Besides a living room combined with a kitchen, there's a bathroom, a laundry alcove, and a decently sized bedroom with a walk-in closet.

There's a view of the town church from my bedroom, not that I spend much time gazing out the window. When the bells ring, it's close enough to wake me up from my slumber.

It's nice, and it's convenient, and it will do for now.

As promised, Maddy brought all three cuisines over, and now I'm in a food coma.

There's a bottle of Pinot Grigio teasing me from my kitchen

countertop. Actually, it's two bottles, since there was a sale at the liquor store and I thought *why the hell not*. If I twitch my nose, maybe I'll have some magical power to move objects . . . or, I can get off the couch.

Beneath the beige faux-fur throw, my warm body refuses to move.

I wrinkle my nose, only to get up anyway and take the two steps over to the kitchen to grab a bottle and two glasses. Maddy brought a Merlot, which I'm so not a fan of.

"I forgot to ask you, what did the priest say?" I question Maddy as she sinks into my sofa with a glass of red wine. My eyes watch her cautiously, since red wine and ivory fabric do not mix.

Maddy is quick to correct me: "Minister."

"Potato, potahto," I mumble.

"He brought up my virtue like I thought he would, so I kinda lied."

"Maddy!" I shriek, hugging the cushion in my arms tighter. "You're going to hell for lying to a minister."

Maddy sighs, obviously bothered by something. Earlier today, she was bouncing around like a kid in a candy store, eager to show off her gorgeous ring and tell the world her news. Upon closer inspection, her shoulders are slumped, and her previously styled hair now looks unkempt.

"Look, I have bigger problems to solve."

I sit up, suddenly worried. "Why, what's wrong?"

There's a sadness in her eyes. She shakes her head as if to fight off tears, then blurts out, "It's just my mother—she called me before I saw the minister. She seems less than thrilled at having to fly back here to be mother of the bride. I get it, the whole wellness retreat or whatever the hell she's doing, but this is my wedding."

The first time I met Patricia Beaumont, I was so taken by her poised manner and class. She always wore Chanel and carried herself like the queen of the castle. Not that they live in a castle, but more of an incredibly large mansion overlooking the town.

They have a maid, a gardener, and a cook, if my memory serves correct. At the time, they were the wealthiest family in Cinnamon Springs, and God forbid Mrs. Beaumont ever lifted a finger.

The woman was beautiful, there's no arguing that. Yet, she barely spoke, always shadowing her husband. Their marriage felt forced, the complete opposite of my own parents, who enjoyed each other's company.

I have no idea what to say, given that Mrs. Beaumont isn't exactly maternal.

"You can't be worried about others, Maddy. This is *your* day, and the only people who need to be happy are you and Myles."

"Yes, I guess so . . . I just thought things would be different. I'm her only daughter. I thought she'd want to be more involved."

Leaning forward, I place my hand on her knee and whisper, "I know it's hard. But you can't change her, and you'll go crazy trying. You're creating your new family now, and when you have kids one day, you're going to be an amazing mother."

Maddy nods quietly with glazed eyes. "I'm going to be a soccer mom. Hanging out with the other soccer moms while I cheer on my kids and hand out homemade baked goods to everyone around me."

I chuckle heartily. "Sounds like a plan, though you suck at baking."

"Yes, but you can bake for me. Do you think I need to drive a minivan to be a soccer mom? I'm not a minivan person. I don't think it will go with my aesthetic."

"Your aesthetic of being a mom?"

"No, like I want to be a proper mom but also hot. I don't want to be picking up my kids in sweats with questionable hair that hasn't been washed in God knows how long," Maddy quips.

"Okay, you're spiraling," I inform her, taking a long sip of wine. "Let's focus on getting you married. So, tell me what you have so far."

Maddy pulls out her mood boards for the wedding. She's always been a girly girl, experimenting with colors and different styles but also holding a feminine touch. It comes as no surprise most of the inspiration photos are wedding pictures with lavender and white—the flower arrangements, table settings, and even the bridesmaid gowns.

"Lavender it is," I say with a small laugh. "You mentioned the reception is at the Grand Honey Lodge, and they're catering?"

"Yes, Martha is the wedding coordinator at the Honey Lodge, so all that reception stuff will be taken care of." Maddy inhales a deep breath, then releases it. "We need to sort out the dresses, hair, makeup, cars, photographer . . . What else am I forgetting? Georgina, Myles's mother, is organizing the floral arrangements and—"

"The invitations? And what budget are we working with?"

Maddy rolls her eyes. "Georgina has the invitations sorted. She said they must be handwritten by a calligrapher. As for budget, Daddy Dearest is paying, so no limit, but Myles doesn't want to go overboard. He wants to keep it simple and intimate. Also, no swans or doves. He has a fear of birds."

I motion for her to take another deep breath. "Nothing that can fly and attack you, got it. If Georgina is handling the invitations, I assume she'll keep tabs on any dietary requirements. Also, I can speak to the caterer to make sure we have backup meals in case anyone changes their mind or forgets to inform us."

Across from me, Maddy stares at me with confusion. "Have you done this before?"

"Done what before?"

"Planned a wedding, duh."

"No, but I watch a lot of TLC. And before you start, let's not get into how much free time I have because there's no man in my life."

"Speaking of men . . ." Maddy begins, adding a mischievous

smile. "Myles has a friend, Ken, who is super hot and would totally look great with you."

"You're not setting me up. End of story," I tell her firmly.

Maddy pouts like a spoiled child. "Fine, but when cats start coming to your door . . ."

I roll my eyes.

We spend the next hour making a to-do list for the wedding preparations, so it's clear what Georgina has a handle on and what I can help Maddy with.

The ceremony itself will be held in the gardens at the Honey Lodge. There is a large gazebo next to the lake, which is covered, so even if it rains or snows, the guests will be sheltered. It's absolutely stunning, which is why weddings are booked out in advance. But Maddy's family owns the property the hotel is on, so it's no surprise she was able to secure it.

My eyes dart up and down the list followed by a sudden wave of panic. I try to envision how I'll get this all done and still manage the café. It would be unfair to leave everything up to Billie since she has several medical appointments to attend each week with her mom.

"Uh-oh," Maddy says loudly, eyeing me dubiously. "You're panicked."

I gulp. "I'm fine."

"Nope, you've got on your panicked face, which, by the way, is it also your sex face?"

"I don't have a sex face!"

"Hmm . . . everyone says that, but everyone has a sex face. Mine kind of looks like this . . ." Maddy parts her mouth then rolls her eyes back, looking like she's dead, *not* enjoying herself.

I burst out laughing. "Stop, you're killing me," I cry, wiping the corner of my eye.

Our laughter only escalates until we're both hunched over, unable to make any sounds but an occasional snort from the hilarity of it all.

It takes us forever to calm down, only because we then start laughing about this guy Maddy had sex with back in college who would cry after he came. It was the most bizarre reaction, but every time it happened, Maddy would burst out laughing, only making it worse.

Finally, Maddy stands with a wobble in her step. "It's been a long day and I'm ready to crash. Myles is picking me up in a few minutes." She types something on her phone. My own phone pings beside me, so I pick it up from the coffee table to see a contact card.

Aston Beaumont.

I force a smile as Maddy starts rambling on about calling Aston to plan things out.

Here's the thing . . .

Maddy has no clue what happened all those years ago, and now is not the right time to mention it. Honestly, I don't want to remember any of it, let alone give Maddy a play-by-play of what happened with her brother that night.

Besides, it's all in the past.

"God, I forgot to mention my dad called before I arrived, too. I swear, my brain is all mush right now, and this red wine is not helping. He wants to officially meet Myles's family this Saturday even though he's met them several times, and I doubt Mom will make it back in time. I was like, *you've met them*, and then he lectures me on proper etiquette. I was like, *okay, whatever, add more for me to do.* Just my family—but count ten if my aunts and uncles come—Myles's family, and you, of course. Do you think you can find somewhere nice in town last-minute for just over twenty guests?" she asks with hopeful eyes.

"Sure, leave it to me."

Maddy wraps her arms around me, holding on tighter than usual. I can tell the excitement of what should be the happiest time of her life is slowly overwhelming her. I pull away, holding on to her hands. "We've got this, bestie. Relax and be present, okay?"

With a collected smile, she nods before letting go and opening the door.

As soon as Maddy leaves, I sink into the sofa with a bigger weight on my shoulders.

Planning a wedding was never going to be easy, and unless I change my mindset, this is going to be the wedding from hell.

My best friend doesn't deserve that.

Something draws me to my phone. I lean over, pick it up, and stare at *his* number. However, the longer I stare, the more annoyed I become. The stupid thing is, I don't even know the guy anymore. We were kids.

So, for the sake of my best friend, I begin typing a message.

Me

> Hi Aston. I guess our girl is getting married and we're supposed to make it all happen. We can start planning when you get here this weekend. Hope you've been well. Eva xx

As soon as I hit send, the double-kisses abbreviation throws me into a frenzied panic. I hit the unsend button so fast I don't even realize what I've done until I've done it.

Shit. Shit. Shit!

I blame the cheap Pinot Grigio. This is why vodka is much more my drink of choice. I throw my phone across the living room, resting my head back on the cushion. Then, a ping alerts me to an incoming message. With a mad rush, I reach for my phone, almost falling off the sofa.

Aston

> What did the unsent message say?

This isn't how this was supposed to go. I was supposed to pretend Aston Beaumont has no effect on me whatsoever.

I close my eyes, take a deep breath, then begin to type a message. The only way to redeem myself is with a little white lie.

Me

Sorry, I sent you a message meant for someone else. Anyway, looking forward to planning Maddy's wedding. See you Saturday.

Me

BTW it's Eva.

I wait for his response, but there is nothing.
And, truth be told, I expect nothing less from him.

CHAPTER 5

Aston

Bianca's sultry eyes gaze upward, and she gives a teasing lick of her red lips.

"Have you been a bad boy?" Her fingers trace the zipper of my suit pants before she boldly takes matters into her own hands. "You have something I want to taste."

Inhaling a deep breath, I close my eyes to focus on the woman on her knees, ready to give me a much-needed blow job. My entire body is demanding release—every single goddamn inch of me—from the stress of the past week.

But my head is elsewhere.

I only recognized the number that texted me moments ago because Madelina sent me the contact card earlier tonight. I wasn't expecting an unsent message, so I quickly cut to the chase, impatient as always.

Beside me on the nightstand, my phone pings again, and with an urge to satisfy my curiosity, I focus on the text on the screen.

Did Everleigh just mention another guy?

My chest tightens. Bianca is ready, mouth open wide, but suddenly I'm not in the mood. I place my hand on her shoulder, gently pushing her away.

"Look, I need to make a business call. I forgot all about it . . ."

I try to come up with something else but fall short. "It's to London, and with the time zone, it has to be tonight."

Bianca furrows her brows in confusion, then releases an unflattering laugh. "You're joking, right?"

"I don't joke about business, Bianca," I respond sternly.

She ignores my answer, pulling me back, then shoves her hand in my boxers. Her warm hand wraps around my shaft, yet still doesn't arouse me like it normally would.

"Just relax. I'll take care of you tonight," she murmurs.

How the fuck can she take care of me when my dick went soft moments ago? I stand up, quickly reaching down to zip up my pants. "I'm serious. I need to get back to work."

With an exaggerated sigh, Bianca stands and straightens her short black dress. "You have no idea what you're missing, Aston."

Undoubtedly, she would be a fantastic fuck—she's proven it in the past. Yet, no matter how hard I try, I can't seem to focus on this woman in front of me.

Bianca turns around, her back toward me.

I cross my arms over my chest.

I'm overthinking things.

Whatever the fuck is going on in my head needs to stop right now.

As she gets closer to the door, I take large steps and manage to push the door closed before she has a chance to exit.

Then, I press her against the door and slide her dress up, desperate to shut off the noise inside my head from a ridiculous text message.

"Show me," I demand.

I slide the Rolex onto my wrist and snap the clasps into place. The vibration of my phone prompts me to remove it from my pants pocket. My father's name flashes on the screen, draining my will to live.

"Good morning," I greet him formally.

"Get your ass to Cinnamon Springs this weekend for your sister's lunch." The command, which comes with no greeting, doesn't surprise me at all.

Tilting my head to the left, I crack my neck to release the tension. "Firstly, Madelina hasn't mentioned anything—"

"She hasn't because I suggested the idea last night." His condescending tone does nothing but bore me as I fix my tie. "In the event of marriage, it is important for two families to be introduced to each other properly, despite our past interactions."

I pinch the bridge of my nose with irritation. "Madelina is aware of my business commitments and expects me to be in town on Tuesday."

"And I expect you in town *tomorrow morning*," he demands.

"You know I have work to do, right? Working for *your* company and making *you* money," I argue.

"I'll see you tomorrow, son."

He hangs up before I have a chance to say anything else. It's just after six in the morning and this man has already ruined my day.

My employees are smart enough to pick up on my agitation, avoiding me as I stomp around the office. I cancel meetings where possible to avoid conflict, and when the sun begins to set, I still have a mountain of work needing my attention before driving out tomorrow.

I crawl into bed sometime after two in the morning, but despite my body being desperate for sleep, my mind refuses to shut down.

The frustrating thing is—I have no idea why.

After last night's fuck-fest with Bianca, I should be satisfied. Yet, as I lie here, unable to sleep, my body suddenly betrays me. I reach down and begin to stroke myself, remembering Bianca's full lips wrapped around my cock. A moan escapes me as my hand moves faster, but then the message from Everleigh flashes like lightning, warning me of an impending storm.

My eyes open wide, the darkness greeting me.

"What the fuck?" I mutter.

I slam my fist against the mattress in frustration, then turn to lie on my stomach without finishing what I attempted to start, and somehow fall asleep.

A yawn escapes me as I slowly open my weary eyes. The sound of multiple sirens outside my building is loud enough to be heard from my penthouse suite. My arms stretch above me before I glance at my phone. It's just after six, and, if I calculate correctly, I've had three hours' sleep.

There is no point lying here in misery and fighting the inevitable. I jump out of bed, brush my teeth, and put on sweats to head downstairs to the gym.

After a heavy weight-training session, I head back upstairs to shower and pack my bags. I figure I can drive up to Cinnamon Springs for the weekend, drive back to the city early Monday morning for meetings, and then deal with everything else via video chat. *Honestly, how hard can all this wedding bullshit be?*

It takes me two hours to get out of the city due to roadwork and detours, but once I hit the parkway, it's smooth sailing.

The long, winding road around the bend of the mountain brings back a lot of memories. It's a picturesque scene of maple and oak trees, which, I will admit, calms me to an extent. Perhaps it's reminiscent of my childhood spent climbing trees before the world became a harsh reality.

My Porsche takes each corner with effortless precision, tempting me to put my foot on the gas. The only thing I miss about this place is the open roads, which are the exact opposite of Manhattan's, with their tedious traffic jams.

I rarely have a weekend off, but I often drive to East Hampton just for the hell of it, relishing the open road and the hum of the engine. It's a chance to escape, to let the miles blur as I leave the chaos behind, if only for a little while.

Madelina insisted we stay at our family home. I argued, of course, given that the Honey Lodge's Governor's Suite is more my style. I see the familiar sign to turn off, and the gravel crunches beneath my tires as Beaumont Manor appears before me.

It's smaller than I remember, built by my great-grandfather and his brothers in the 1800s. The natural stone walls and large columns only add to its craftsmanship, along with the manicured gardens and fountain at the front of the property.

The front door opens as Madelina comes running outside. I saw my sister a month ago, back before her vacation, when she stopped by the office, but I notice her face appears rather tanned.

She's already wearing a light blue dress for the lunch. I'm sure the dress is a brand name, but I'm not one to care or pay attention to women's fashion.

I pull the hand brake up, then turn the engine off before exiting the car. My legs are stiff from the long drive.

Madelina is quick to jump up and wrap her arms around me. "You made it."

"Yes," I answer, pulling away. "I was reminded yesterday by the patriarch himself of the importance of my presence."

"I'm sorry. Dad kind of insisted we have a family lunch. Myles had to reschedule some work in the city, too. Anyways, you're here, and that's all that matters."

I remove my bags from the trunk and follow Madelina inside the house. My mother's decor has remained the same, and it's as if the house has been frozen in time. Since my father mainly resides in Manhattan, and my mother spends more time in Europe, this home is taken care of by one housekeeper and a gardener.

"Hilda left some food in the fridge, but aside from that, you'll need to fend for yourself," Madelina informs me.

"I'm sure I know how to feed myself," I deadpan.

"Right, you're a big boy now," she teases. "Dad is arriving soon, and lunch is at noon. It's not overly formal, but make an effort to look nice, okay?"

I drop my bags, crossing my arms over my chest. "Anything else, your highness?"

She shakes her head. "That's it for now."

Given that the lunch is not formal like the wedding, I opt to change into my chinos, a white button-down shirt, and a navy wool coat. The weather is much colder here than in Manhattan, but at least it's not snowing.

I step inside my old room, and everything is exactly how I remember it. All my trophies are still showcased on the shelves, reminding me of a time when lacrosse and football were my life. I lived and breathed the sports, dreaming of playing for the national leagues one day.

But, life had other plans.

Even my bedding looks exactly the same, with the checkered navy-and-white bedspread and pillows perfectly positioned. Much smaller than the king-size bed in my penthouse.

My desk still has all my books stacked on it, with my senior class photograph pinned to the wall. The nostalgia leaves an unsettling feeling, so I don't linger too long. I change and head straight to the lodge.

On this crisp winter day, the sun manages to shine, melting any residual snow.

As I stand inside the restaurant's patio area beside an outdoor heater, Madelina is quick to corner me.

"Be on your best behavior, okay?"

"I'm always on my best behavior," I retort.

"I could list the times when you've lost your temper and argued over politics. I want both our families to enjoy the day. Be nice."

With a glass of champagne in my hand—the server practically forced it upon me as Madelina eyed me from across the room—I introduce myself like the perfect older brother. I despise champagne, but any liquor at this point is needed. My father insists on joining me, which I soon learn is to fabricate a story about Mom. According to Madelina, Mom is on a flight back from Geneva at Father's command. Whatever happened, I'm sure my father was a prick, and Mom had no choice but to follow his orders.

"So, I guess we're going to be family now." Myles appears beside me, dressed in a navy suit with what appears to be whiskey in his glass. I scan the room to hunt down the server and request my beverage be switched immediately. "I'm not sure what I'm supposed to do at this thing."

"You grin and bear it. According to my father, it's proper etiquette to introduce two families upon the event of the marriage. You really had to propose to my sister, huh?" I tease, then rest my hand on his shoulder. "I hope you know what you're getting into."

"Let's see. Your father has made it clear that grandchildren are a must. Not that my mother argued—quite the opposite. And I said, 'How about we get through all the formalities first before kids are discussed?'"

Myles drinks the whiskey in one gulp, then motions for the server. I don't blame him—family events with overbearing parents can be brutal.

"I'm surprised you proposed so quickly," I say, curious.

"Granddad is sick and it's his dying wish to see me get married." The previously upbeat tone of his voice shifts, but I pretend not to notice. "I love Madelina. We have a lot of fun at work."

I nod, unsure how to respond, then his mother pulls him away to discuss some important matter. The room begins to fill with other family members. I thought this was supposed to be a small, intimate event until I see some friends of my father walk through the door.

Myles forces a smile as my father introduces him to a new round of strangers. I can't fault the guy and don't expect him to hurt my sister despite this proposal happening early in their relationship. His intentions appear legitimate.

His cousins, however, have tried to corner me several times. It didn't take me long to figure out Madelina told them I was single. Sure, one is hot, but it would be a quick fuck and nothing else. Blond bob, white pantsuit, and frankly, uninteresting.

Something warns me not to mix wedding events with pleasure.

Ramona—as she introduced herself—is rambling on about her fashion company like I give a shit. I nod politely but scan the room, looking for an exit.

As my eyes wander near the door, a woman walks through alone. I pause to observe her with curiosity. Her long, lean legs in black knee-high boots capture my attention, but soon, my eyes wander up her body to admire the rest of her. I tilt my head with a smirk, and then it dawns on me that she looks familiar.

Everleigh.

Her hair isn't long like back in high school—cut shorter, sitting at her shoulders in loose waves, but still the shade of brown with auburn tints when it caught the sunlight. But it isn't her hair that draws me to her. It's the face of a mature woman. Something about her stirs this unwanted emotion inside of me.

I quickly drop my gaze to the floor to curb these unnatural thoughts but find I'm unable to control myself, lifting my stare back to where she's standing.

The burgundy dress she wears ends mid-thigh. I'm swift to notice her tits sitting nicely in the dress and curves in all the right places.

She is *nothing* like I remember.

Everleigh Woods is a woman now.

And a beautiful one.

Despite my ego fighting me on it.

She catches me staring, and without a doubt in my mind, Everleigh appears annoyed. Her lips press together, jaw clenched. *That's not a welcoming look.*

Madelina steals her attention with what appears to be some dilemma. They both disappear out of the room only to return moments later. It gives me a minute to gain my bearings, finish this god-awful champagne, and excuse myself from Ramona and her boring chatter.

With Madelina by his side, Myles calls everyone's attention, ready to commence what I assume is his speech. I glance to my right, where my father is conveniently standing with Roland Whitney.

"On behalf of my fiancée, Madelina, and me, we thank you for coming today," Myles begins, with a glass of champagne in hand this time. "We know many of you are surprised by how quickly things are happening, but rest assured, we want you to relax and enjoy all the festivities planned in the next few weeks."

Myles continues to talk about his family before Roland takes over, followed by my father. I zone out during my father's speech about family values and find myself distracted by Everleigh. Much like myself, she doesn't seem impressed by my father's lies but politely raises her glass upon his request. As soon as the toast is over, she drinks the entire glass of champagne, almost like she wishes she wasn't here. It doesn't take her long to reach out for another glass as the server walks past.

To be honest, I don't blame her.

This lunch is tiresome at best.

My father is quick to pull me into a conversation with Roland. It starts out rather casually until my father manipulates the topic, and somehow, we end up talking about business.

"Beaumont." Roland pats my father on his shoulder. "Let's celebrate the kids today, shall we? We have plenty of time to talk business after the wedding."

My father displays his poker face, an expression I've seen time and time again when he's annoyed but doesn't want the opponent to see his cards. "Family first," he responds with a counterfeit smile.

There isn't enough liquor inside this room to alleviate the tension.

Eager to escape, I step outside onto the patio for fresh air, quickly deciding that a whiskey or bourbon would be much more satisfying.

There is a bar right next to the lobby serving all types of liquor. I make my way there, praying Madelina doesn't hunt me down to pawn me off on some other damn cousin. As I enter the dimly lit bar, I stop in my tracks.

Everleigh is at the bar, talking to some guy, laughing. They appear to know each other. Then, I see him reach out to touch her arm. She doesn't look fazed, more flattered by his attention.

I've been adulting long enough to know she's fucked, or is about to fuck, this man. I watch with my teeth clenched, subjecting myself to whatever the hell is going on.

I *should* turn around and go back inside the restaurant.

What fool would stand here and watch his sister's best friend with another man?

My feet are itching to move, eager to get away and pretend this doesn't affect me whatsoever.

But something else is forcing me to watch. The same something else that made me look into her eyes that night at the party and kiss her like it was my last day on earth.

I take a breath, dispelling the burning sensation inside my chest, and force myself to leave.

Just like I did when I pulled away and pretended our kiss meant *nothing*.

CHAPTER 6

Eva

Myles is standing beside us looking relieved now that the speeches are over.

With a smile, Maddy places her hand on his arm to reassure him. We spoke earlier, and it was evident he was overwhelmed by the attention.

"You did great," I tell him. "Besides, this was practice for the big day. Not to stress you out, but wedding speeches go down in history as either the greatest speech of all time or an epic fail."

Myles chuckles. "So, what you're saying is I should watch what I drink so I don't make a fool of myself?"

"Exactly."

"Don't worry, my father will make sure the spotlight is on him," Maddy says with an eye roll. "It's always about him."

When Maddy mentioned the small get-together to introduce the two families, I dived headfirst into planning mode. The Grand Honey Lodge has multiple function rooms to host either large events or small, intimate ones, so I secured the Japanese Maple Room, one of my favorite places in town.

It made sense to host it here so everyone can familiarize themselves with the lodge, even though the wedding will be held in a different part of the property. Most of Myles and Maddy's family live within an hour of Cinnamon Springs, but the rest will be traveling in just before the actual wedding.

"Your father has spoken to me in quite some detail about family business and carrying on the legacy," Myles informs Maddy.

She crosses her arms, evidently annoyed. "I told him to leave business out of today. I told Aston as well. Has my brother been trying to talk shop? Because I swear I will annoy the hell out of him when we get home."

"Your brother is fine," Myles says simply.

Aston caught my attention from across the room before the speeches. I was in the middle of eating a salmon puff while in conversation with Maddy's Uncle Frank. He was talking about his house on Martha's Vineyard and the cost of upkeep. When he started mentioning whale watching, boredom crept in and I found myself scanning the room.

That's when I saw him. I had no idea when he'd slipped in, nor why my chest felt like it was up in my throat, causing me to choke on my salmon puff. It was brief, and embarrassing when Frank joked about giving me the Heimlich maneuver.

All of a sudden, I felt like I'd stepped into the Sahara Desert. The shock of seeing him froze me to the spot, making me look stupid and awkward. I rapidly swallowed, but the air was so stifling.

Why was he staring at me like that?

And why does he look so tall and . . .

Don't say it. Don't you dare say it.

I try to focus back on our conversation but find myself scanning the room again.

"Oh my God." Maddy yanks on my arm with sweaty palms the moment Myles is pulled aside by his father. "Myles's mother lectured me on purity. If only she knew how much her son likes reverse cowgirl."

I shake my head, trying to catch up with reality. "Um . . . yeah."

Maddy bites her lip. "What's wrong? You look like you've seen a ghost."

"Um . . . nothing." I wrack my brain trying to come up with an excuse, but everything feels blurry, and *why the hell is it so damn hot in here?* "I, uh, thought I got my period." *Really, Eva?*

"You're not due for, like, what"—she does the mental period math, nodding her head to count the days—"another week? We're period sisters." Maddy gasps, covering her mouth with much exaggeration. "Do you have something to tell me?"

Whoever came up with the term *period sisters* needs a big slap in the face. It's all fun and games when everyone is in sync, but the minute someone isn't, everyone assumes there's a secret pregnancy brewing. Considering I haven't had sex in forever, the chances are, well, zero.

"Absolutely *not!*" I take a deep breath, trying to get a hold of myself. "Ignore me, and ignore Myles's mother."

She raises her hands in defeat. "Okay, calm your farm. I'm going to check to make sure we still have enough food."

"Let me do that. You go mingle."

"Do I have to?" Maddy whines.

A small laugh escapes me. "If I have to play nice, then so do you."

The bar staff are doing a fantastic job, ensuring there is enough for everyone to drink and the food is served at the correct intervals. I make the rounds, chatting to many of the guests before deciding to stick around Myles's cousins' group for a moment.

"So, you're Maddy's best friend," Olivia, his younger cousin, begins with pursed lips. "What's the deal with her brother?"

"Her brother?" I repeat, trying not to look surprised. "What do you mean?"

"Is he single? Because word is he's a billionaire, and boy is he fine."

The girls giggle, waiting for me to respond. The question

itself annoys me. Like, why would I be involved in setting him up with someone? Don't they know I have better things to do than worry about Aston Beaumont's sex life?

"Actually, I have no clue. He lives in Manhattan. That's the limit of my knowledge."

Ramona, another one of Myles's cousins, joins the conversation with a champagne glass in her hand. She brings it to her lips, drinking it in one go before dumping it on a table beside her.

Olivia is quick to interrogate her. "So, what's he like?"

I observed Ramona talking to Aston earlier. To be honest, he looked bored with the conversation, but knowing him, he's too into himself to care about anyone else.

"Smart, sexy, and I'm going to ask him out for a drink," she's quick to inform everyone. "It'll be our little secret, girls."

Again, they all giggle.

Something leaves me unsettled, and the more I stand here pretending to be okay with this potential hookup, the more irritated I become. I try to think of an excuse to leave and end up mumbling something about needing to speak to Maddy. When I glance over, she's busy nodding as her father and Myles's mother are talking. Slowly, she side-eyes me, then quirks the sides of her mouth to smile as if the conversation is enthralling.

I take the opportunity to exit the room and head straight for the bar near the lobby. The champagne is not doing its job. Maybe a shot or two at the bar. Nobody has to know.

As I walk toward the bartender, a man standing next to a barstool looks awfully familiar. As he turns to his side, I instantly recognize the jawline. Sharp, freshly shaven . . .

"Dr. Wilde?"

His attention shifts from the bartender to me, a grin etching his handsome face. I take a deep breath, calming the butterflies inside my stomach. It's been a very long time since a man has made me feel anything, or maybe it's the fact that he's a handsome doctor.

"Please, call me Marco," he insists, then murmurs, "I'm off duty."

My lips curve upward and I move closer, easing myself into the spot beside him. There are a few people in the bar, but it's not overcrowded.

"So, what does an off-duty doctor do for fun besides drinking a . . ." I trail off to pick the glass up, sniffing the liquor. "Gin and tonic."

"Should I be worried you were able to guess that correctly?"

"Since I'm off duty as a patient, I need a strong drink to get through the next two hours," I inform him with a quirk of a smile.

"Oh . . ." He glances back at the room. "It looks like a party to me."

My shoulders fall, and at the same time, a sigh leaves me. "My best friend is getting married."

Marco presses his lips together, observing me with soft eyes. "And you're . . . upset about it?"

I shake my head. "Far from it. There are just some family members who, let's say, are *challenging* to be around. You know how it is."

"When my older sister got married," he begins, still keeping close to me, "every family member interrogated me on when it was my turn. Of course, since I practice medicine, it makes me a target for all my aunties trying to play matchmaker. Some of them pulled out photos of single women from their purses."

My shoulders move up and down, unable to hold back my laughter. "Poor Marco. It's hard being a handsome doctor."

His pout is cute. "So, you're welcome to join my friends and me over there. Mind you, they're all medical professionals, so there are a lot of cringey jokes."

"I'd love to hear them one day." I grin, then pause when I realize it sounded like I wanted to hang out with him, and that's against the rules. "I mean, I'm sorry."

Marco cocks his head, placing his hand on my arm. His touch sends this warm sensation through me, making me want to break all the stupid rules of society. Who says you can't date your doctor? "What are you sorry for?"

"You're my doctor," I state, looking him directly in the eye.

He leans in and whispers, the scent of his cologne lingering. I have no idea what scent he wears but it smells delicious. "I have a lot of doctor friends in case you need a referral."

As he slowly pulls away, I bow my head, trying to hide my grin this time. Slowly, I lift my eyes to meet his, admiring his handsome face.

"I did find your consult rather mediocre," I tease, just as the bartender diverts his attention to me. "Vodka with a twist, please."

Marco rubs his chin, making him all the more irresistible, but then a man calls his name. We both glance over to a group of men waiting for him.

"Listen, I have to go, but expect those referrals soon. I wouldn't want your medical treatment to be compromised," he says with a slight chuckle. "Can I call you?"

"I'd very much like that."

He throws some bills on the counter, then winks.

After Marco leaves, I quickly drink the vodka, my insides vibrating from excitement. It disappears the moment I stupidly open my email. The florist has emailed regarding a meeting about the flower arrangements. She's out of town for the next week, so the meeting has been postponed, which may risk being able to get the right flowers in on time. Given it's winter, there's limited choice, and when I saw the word *artificial* get thrown around, I nearly died for Maddy. She despises artificial flowers.

From there, I begin to spiral, especially when I notice an email from the violinist Maddy desperately wanted. It turns out he and his partner will be away in Italy on the day of the wedding.

Just fucking great.

I release a long sigh, forcing myself to walk back to the main room while trying to come up with an alternative plan. Considering Maddy was banking only on this duo, returning to the drawing board will mean I have to deal with auditions for a new violinist who can play a Beyoncé song for Maddy to walk down the aisle to.

How hard can it be?

I walk into the room, eyes glued to my screen, only to be stopped by an unexpected grip on my arms. The jolt startles me, leaving me breathless and painfully aware of the man holding me. My mind races, stirring up memories I've buried deep—a powerful gaze, and a shadow of the past.

His intensity is suffocating, pulling me back to a version of myself I've outgrown.

Suddenly, I'm sixteen again and facing the boy who broke my heart. The boy who kissed me first then pulled away like I was *nothing*.

No matter how much time has passed, how many boys or men have broken my heart since then, the first one will always sting the most.

And now—he's standing right in front of me.

CHAPTER 7

Aston

As soon as I step inside the room again, Madelina corners me.

"I think it's going well, right?" she asks, nervously glancing around.

A server is a few feet away. I motion for him to come over, and when he does, I take the champagne again and down the glass. It's my only option, since I was a pussy and walked out of the bar instead of ordering a whiskey.

"Sure."

"Okay, what's wrong?" Madelina questions with impatience. "What did Dad say?"

"Nothing out of the ordinary."

"But you look annoyed," she carries on, fidgeting with her hair, which annoys me.

"Well, dear sister, this isn't exactly my idea of fun. I have work to do."

Madelina shifts her attention to Myles's mother, who is calling her over. "Look, I have to deal with Georgina, and that's a whole other level of stress. In case I haven't told you, thank you for being here. Oh, and stop being a sourpuss. Looks like you need to get laid. Ramona is your best bet."

She's quick to abandon me, which causes me even more irritation.

My phone begins to buzz inside my pocket. As I walk through the double glass doors to go answer it, Everleigh is walking toward me, eyes focused on her phone, oblivious to our imminent collision.

Quickly, I reach out, grabbing both her arms to stop us from crashing into one another. She jolts at my touch, eyes wide with fear until her gaze meets mine.

"Fu . . . I mean, you scared me," she heaves, placing her hand on her chest. "It's nice to see you again, Aston."

She's avoided me all afternoon, and if memory prevails, our past has something to do with it. Women are the worst grudge-holders.

"It's been a while," I state simply, holding her gaze.

My stare appears to bother her, as she's quick to pretend to look over my shoulder. The sadistic side of me finds this entertaining. A beautiful woman who once kissed me and almost allowed me to take her virginity can't stand to be in the same space as me.

Cocking my head to the side, I question, "When was the last time we saw each other?"

She scratches the back of her neck, then folds her arms across her chest. "I'm sure you remember. No need for a trip down memory lane," she states matter-of-factly. "Now, if you'll excuse me, I have people to mingle with."

The smell of her perfume, sweet and seductive, floods my memories, reminding me of the taste of her lips. They were soft and sweet and utterly addictive. It drove me fucking crazy. I was just eighteen, but not a stranger to making out with girls. Hell, I'd fucked a few by senior year as well.

Yet nothing, or no one, had ever tasted like her.

I was angry at the world, desperate to escape my father's dictatorship and run away with my own dreams. It fueled the fire burning inside of me as we kissed, and Everleigh's words echoed in my head.

You have everything going for you. You're smart, a straight-A student without even trying. Coach loves you. Your athletic ability is the best the school has seen. I mean, I'm not one to watch lacrosse, but so I've heard. Not to mention, you're pretty. So tell me, why on earth do you think your father should dictate your life?

For the first time, someone saw me for who I truly was. My anger and resentment got in the way of any chance I had of freedom. It changed the way I behaved, the way I saw the future. I had to succeed despite my father forcing this path upon me.

As Everleigh turns to walk past, I grab her arm to stop her, suddenly aware she's fucked with my head.

I'm quick to spout out, "Who was the guy at the bar?"

"Excuse me?"

I narrow my gaze, voice dropping to an icy edge. "The guy at the bar." I repeat each word in a controlled command that leaves no room for questioning.

"He's just . . . wait a minute." She shakes her arm out of my tight grip. "I haven't seen you in eight years, and the first thing you want to ask me is, 'Who was the guy at the bar?' "

A huff slips out as I recall how, even back in high school, she couldn't resist stirring up drama, always needing the last word and acting like she knew everything. My sister was the only one who could tolerate her. "I guess you haven't changed."

"Actually, I have changed," she answers defensively while rapidly blinking. "I'm *not* sixteen anymore, and I'm *not* making stupid decisions. So, I don't know what *your* problem is, but I'm here for one reason only . . . *Maddy.*"

"And I'm here for my sister, too."

"Yeah, right. You don't care about anyone but yourself," she retorts.

"Ouch." I place my hand on my chest with a smirk. "How ironic that you believe you know me, Ms. Woods."

Everleigh refuses to back down. "I know you, Aston Beaumont. You're the billionaire who gets off on controlling the boardroom, then blows off steam, bringing home whatever woman will bend over for you. Your type is exactly who I stay away from. So, if you'll excuse me, I have a wedding to help plan and would appreciate it if you just tell Maddy you're too busy to help me. That way, you're doing us both a favor."

And with her cheeks crimson, she walks away from me and back into the room.

It would be easy to tell my sister something urgent needs my attention back in the city, and it would be just as easy to ignore my father's reprimanding behavior. Yet, something urges me to stay. *Why should I give Everleigh Woods what she wants?*

After all, I enjoy watching her writhe in my presence.

"Not all princesses get their happily ever after, sweetheart," I mumble under my breath.

And I sure as hell am *not* a knight in shining armor.

CHAPTER 8

Eva

The bane of my existence was never supposed to be forced proximity with a man I have loathed for the last eight years.

My cheeks feel like they're on fire as I walk away, detouring to the restroom to calm myself down and splash cold water on my face.

The nerve of him.

I love Maddy, but this isn't going to work. There is no way I can endure spending more than a single minute with her brother for the sake of a wedding. It will be easier if I do it all myself. I mean, honestly, what will Aston contribute anyway? I highly doubt he wants to sit with me and audition violinists playing love songs.

Ramona enters the restroom, trying to maintain her balance. She lets out a hiccup and a small laugh, then covers her mouth. "Oops, maybe I shouldn't have had that last glass of champagne."

"Maybe not." I force a smile, then turn to face her. "Will you be okay getting home? Or wherever you're staying?"

She nods with a wide grin on her face. On closer inspection, Ramona is a beautiful woman. Her skin is flawless, or perhaps it's her makeup. Either way, I'm surprised she's single, since most men would eat her alive.

Okay, that sounded gross, even to me.

Someone get me out of my brain.

"Aston has offered to take me home," she almost sings out loud.

Oh, I mouth, crossing my arms again with my usual annoyance upon hearing his name. "When did he offer to do that?"

"Just then, before I walked in here. I told you he's quite the man. It's hard to find the right guy, you know? The one who checks all the boxes."

"Yeah, I guess," I mutter, then continue, "or maybe he just wants to get you into bed."

Ramona laughs a little too obnoxiously as she leans against the tiled wall. "And? Have you seen how unbelievably sexy he is?"

Suddenly, this restroom feels like a damn jail cell.

Just little old me trapped with Aston's hookup for tonight.

"I have to go make sure everyone is okay. Have fun with him."

I stomp out of there so fast, oblivious to guests walking past me to leave. Maddy is saying goodbye to Myles's parents, so I escape to the kitchen to thank the team. Our conversation takes longer than anticipated, and by the time I get back, everyone is outside in the parking lot or has already left.

Maddy is quick to find me, but Aston is nowhere to be seen. *Thank God.*

Her arms wrap around me in a tight embrace. "Thank you for today. What would I do without you?"

I close my eyes to try to remember Maddy is more to me than a best friend, and all this misery will be worth it for her happily ever after. "I'm glad you enjoyed it."

"Myles's mother insisted we have afternoon drinks at her place. Will you be okay?"

"I will be." I smile, then sigh. "What about you?"

"Afternoon drinks, Eva. That's the only reason I agreed to go. I figure the strong martinis she serves will numb me enough to get through it."

Myles opens the car door for Maddy. He quickly kisses my

cheek to thank me, and then the two of them slide into the car to drive off, leaving me alone with relief that today is finally over.

My car is parked only a few spots away. As I walk toward it, my attention is shifted to a flat tire on the rear driver's side. I lean against the car in self-pity, only for a raindrop to hit my forehead. "Oh no, you better not."

Just as the words leave my mouth, the rain falls hard and fast. I can't believe my luck today. All I need is a pile of dog poop to step in, and I'm officially done.

My hair clings to the back of my neck as the roar of an engine grabs my attention. I glance to my left to find a sleek gray Porsche beside me. The window glides down, revealing Aston in the driver's seat.

"Get in," he demands.

I turn to face him. "I'm not getting in there with you."

"Stop being stubborn and get in the goddamn car before you get sick."

It's a total downpour that even my coat doesn't stop my dress plastering to my skin. My hair and makeup are undoubtedly ruined, so at this point, who cares if I catch a cold?

"I'd rather end up in the hospital than step foot in your quarter-life-crisis mobile," I snap.

His hands tighten around the steering wheel. "If you don't get in, Everleigh, I will step out and put you in this car myself. Is that what you want? A little hands-on kidnapping scenario?" He simpers, voice laced with a daring edge. "If that's what does it for you, I am more than happy to oblige."

My mouth drops. "You are such an ass!"

Before I know it, I'm yanking the door open and sliding into his stupid car. "There. Happy now?"

Aston gives me a sly smirk as he shifts the car into gear. "Buckle up, sweetheart. It's going to be a wild ride."

The last thing I needed today was to be trapped inside a small sports car with Aston Beaumont. My teeth are chattering so I reach out to the heating knob, fingers trembling as I fumble to crank up the warmth.

"Who said you can touch my controls?" Aston questions sternly.

"I'm freezing," I bite back. "Do you want me to die of hypothermia inside your car?"

Beside me, he rolls his eyes. "Ironic, since a moment ago, you were willing to go to the hospital rather than get into my quarter-life-crisis mobile."

"More like penis-extension mobile," I mutter under my breath. "Everyone knows men who drive Porsches have something to prove."

Aston relaxes in his seat, then reaches out to turn up the heat. The car takes only seconds to warm, releasing the tension inside my body.

"If you're still cold, I have a coat in the back you can put on," he offers, but his tone sounds annoyed. "Can't have you dying in my penis-extension mobile."

He takes a sharp turn, causing me to jerk to my right.

"I would get it if you'd stop driving like a maniac," I complain.

I reach over and pull the navy wool coat toward me, feeling the weight of the expensive fabric as I drape it around my shoulders, the soft material cocooning me against the lingering chill. Closing my eyes momentarily, I relish the warmth and allow my body to relax. I'm beyond exhausted, with my social battery completely drained. Hopefully, Aston will leave me in silence for the rest of the drive so I can regroup.

The car's speed slows as Aston takes the next turn smoothly. He briefly glances at me but then focuses back on the road. "Better?"

I don't even acknowledge him, suddenly aware I'm too close to my enemy. With a need to distract myself, I let my eyes wander to his hand resting on the stick shift. Every time he shifts gears, the veins protrude, and I squeeze my legs tight because of the uncontrollable sensation taking over. Why do his hands have to look so . . .

Don't say it, Eva.

He changes gears again, forcing me to turn away as the simple movement makes my urges all the more unbearable. It's been a while since a guy touched me, but it has *not* been *that* long.

"I assume your guy friend will assist you with the tire," Aston alludes in a sharp tone.

I shrug, staring out the window. "Right, my guy friend. Maybe, I could ask."

Aston slams his foot on the gas, obviously bothered by my answer. I turn my head to look at him, and under my intense stare, he shifts his body uncomfortably.

"You seem rather annoyed by my *guy friend*," I begin, keeping my smirk at bay. "One would think you have a problem with me, too."

"I'm not annoyed," he insists. "I just don't want to be planning this wedding on my own while you're busy with some boyfriend doing God knows what."

I raise a brow with a glassy stare. "I'm not a flake. Maddy is my best friend. Besides, weren't you supposed to take Ramona home?"

Aston's eyes widen. *"Fuck."*

"Don't tell me you left her behind without a word." I laugh, the image of a stranded Ramona too amusing to resist. "The poor girl assumed she was getting laid tonight."

"I don't sleep with every woman I speak to, believe it or not," he deadpans, his expression flat as if he's daring me to challenge him.

Big mistake. "Yeah, right. Why else would you take a drunk chick home?"

Aston turns to look at me with a slackened mouth. "Myles asked me to."

I study him closely, noting the way he leans back in his seat, effortlessly relaxed, as if leaving Ramona behind was the most natural thing in the world. "I call bullshit. He did not."

"Would you like to call him to ask?" He moves his hand to his phone, ready to dial. "If you think I'm lying, I'm more than happy to prove you wrong."

"Fine, whatever." My arms fold at the same time as he turns left onto Ginger Grove. I glance around before asking, "How do you know where I live?"

"Madelina," he answers nonchalantly.

"Oh," I murmur as he pulls up to the back of the building. Out front is the café, but back here lies the entrance to my apartment. I unbuckle my seat belt, eyes fixed on the rain pounding against the windshield. My choices are to stay in this confined space, awkwardly silent, or make a dash for it and get drenched before I even reach the door.

A little rain never hurt anyone . . . right?

"Thank you for taking me home," I say, unable to look him in the eye. "I guess we should catch up to talk about the wedding stuff. How about tomorrow morning at my café?"

"Sure."

I nod, then place my hand on the door handle, but something makes me turn back around to face him. "There is no guy."

Aston tilts his head, his gaze sharp and penetrating as he examines me. I shift uncomfortably, suddenly aware of every inch of his attention.

"So the one at the bar looking rather cozy with you was a stranger?" he questions in a rigid tone.

"He is someone I know," I reply honestly. "He's not my boyfriend."

Aston presses his lips flat, then mutters, "Yet . . ."

"What's that supposed to mean?" I ask with a heated glare.

"It means your gentleman friend's body language would indicate he's waiting for the right time to strike."

My body temperature rises as my anger spikes. "And what makes you think I give in so easily?"

He keeps quiet with that stupid smirk on his face. Of course, he just broke the cardinal rule—he called a woman a slut. Okay, maybe not in so many words, but the assumption I sleep around is there.

"You're telling me a man and a woman can't be friends?"

"No! If a man tells you he's happy to be friends, he's waiting for you to get comfortable before getting you into bed."

"Right, so all men are jerks? That's what you're telling me?" I snap, grabbing my purse, barely containing my anger. "You know what? I'm going to pretend this conversation never happened. See you tomorrow morning. And by the way, from now on, it's wedding stuff only. That's all I'll discuss with you."

Despite the rain, I throw open the door and dash toward the stairs, barely feeling the drops pelting my skin. I don't turn around to watch him leave, but the deep, throaty roar of his engine echoes behind me, cutting through the downpour as he speeds off.

As soon as I get inside the apartment, I strip off my soaked clothes and jump into a hot shower. Steam fills the bathroom, easing the tension from my muscles and nearly washing away the weight of the day. But Aston's words linger, refusing to fade.

"What an asshole," I mumble to myself.

When the heat becomes too much, I turn off the water, dry off, and pull on a pair of jeans and a cozy knitted sweater. The café is still open for another hour, so I head downstairs to check on Billie and, hopefully, clear my head.

Billie is wrapping up with customers, and as the door finally closes behind them, I join her in the kitchen, rolling up my sleeves to wash trays and wipe down countertops. The steady rhythm of cleaning brings a welcome calm, if only for a moment.

"How was the lunch?" Billie asks, counting the cash in the register.

I shrug. "As expected."

"You seem tense. Did something happen?"

Denial will only get me so far, but I'll ride its wave for as long as I can. "Just an exhausting day. How about I finish up here, and you leave for the day? You've had a busy one."

Billie wipes her hands on her apron. "You sure?"

"Of course. I'll see you tomorrow."

As soon as the lights turn off, I lean against the wall and close my eyes.

It's going to take all my patience to deal with Aston because he sure as hell likes to make it difficult.

He's a womanizer with only one agenda.

Thank God he appears to despise me just as much.

My phone vibrates on the counter. I don't recognize the number but pick it up anyway.

"Hello, Eva speaking."

"Hello, Eva," the smooth voice sounds over the speaker. "Too early to call?"

My cheeks rise into a grin as my shoulders relax.

"For you, Marco, it's never too early."

CHAPTER 9

Eva

My eyes are glued to the door.

It's just after ten, and I texted Aston last night confirming the time to meet. I kept it formal, reminding myself who I was dealing with. His response was an infuriating thumbs-up.

A group of tourists comes in, and I smile politely before welcoming them. After they take a seat, Chloe, who covers the weekend shifts, takes their order, and a few more customers enter.

Time passes, and so does my ability to accept Aston's poor behavior. I recheck my phone an hour after our meet time, only to see no missed calls or messages. The decent thing to do would be to send me a message to tell me he couldn't make it.

My fingers tap against the screen, typing out exactly what I think of him and his disregard for my time, but then I delete it. I'm too angry to get my words out without calling him *the biggest jerk to ever exist.*

The café becomes busier in the lead-up to lunchtime, forcing me to help Chloe. Billie came in earlier to bake but left before we opened. We have enough fresh donuts to last us the whole day, but given the sudden rain carrying over from yesterday, it's a lot quieter than our usual Sunday crowd.

I head into the kitchen to call Maddy, but I play it cool like I'm not about to rip her brother's head off. The last thing Maddy needs is more stress on her plate.

The call lasts all of two minutes. Maddy left early this morning to head into the city for some important meeting with her cast. Apparently, one of the leads broke her leg skiing, and the understudy is freaking out. She promises to be back tomorrow morning and informs me Aston is at home.

It's all I need to hear.

"Chloe, I need to take care of something." I grab my keys and phone. "I'll be back in an hour."

My tire was fixed late yesterday afternoon, thankfully, since buses barely run in Cinnamon Springs. Burt, the town mechanic, told me he saw it in the parking lot. He replaced the tire, then drove it to my apartment. I tried to pay him, but he refused to accept my money and told me he'll gladly accept a lemon sprinkled donut the next time he grabs coffee.

It's a twenty-minute drive to Maddy's parents' house, and I manage to work myself up even more in that twenty minutes. By the time I arrive at the front of the house, I've already memorized precisely what I'm going to say to him.

The front door is unlocked, so without hesitating, I enter the house and close the door behind me. It's quiet inside the foyer with no signs of anyone home.

Aston's room is two doors down from Maddy's old room. Of course I remember it, along with the bathroom, where I accidentally saw him get out of the shower.

With every step closer, Aston's voice becomes louder. I stand at his door, watching him with my arms crossed. He is pacing the room while running his hands through his hair in frustration, dressed in what appear to be yesterday's clothes. If I'm being honest, he looks like he hasn't slept.

The moment he notices me, he rubs the back of his neck, tension radiating from him. He gives me a terse warning that his call will take a while, but I'm not about to leave. So, I stay by the door, listening as a group of men argue over the speaker, their voices a chaotic mix of frustration and ego.

"Gentlemen, please," he commands while pinching the bridge of his nose. "Let's focus on the next step rather than this back-and-forth. I'll get my team on it today, and we'll see what our rights are before we make the next move."

"Beaumont, there is a lot riding on this," a man warns.

"Yes, John. I'm acutely aware."

The conversation continues for another few minutes before Aston puts his foot down and tells everyone he's hanging up.

As soon as it ends, I raise my arms in frustration. "Have you heard of text messages? You know, like . . . *sorry, I can't make it?*"

"Sorry, I couldn't make it" is all he says.

"I sat there for over an hour waiting for you. You don't think I have better things to do? God, you're such a jerk."

"This is business, Everleigh," he bellows while resting his hands on his desk with his head down. "Not some frivolous party to be planned."

"Oh, so sorry. Yes, of course, the billionaire has business to do. You don't think my time is as important, right? I also run a business, Aston. I may not be a billionaire, but it's my livelihood and the livelihood of my employees."

Aston's back is toward me. He doesn't say a word as I stand in complete silence. My eyes scan the room, noticing it hasn't changed one bit. Once, Maddy made us sneak in here to steal some money from him so we could go to the movies. I remember the moment so vividly, the way I stood frozen with my breath caught in my throat from the fear of being caught.

His phone begins to ring, and the thought of him answering another call while our conversation remains unfinished is enough to make me exhale loudly.

"Madelina," he answers in a tired voice, placing the call on speaker.

"Is everything okay?" she asks, worried. "I had to rush to the city, but I heard you on the phone all night."

"Yes," Aston replies, looking directly at me. "Everleigh is at the house, and we are just about to sit down to discuss some details."

"Thank God. I'll be back tomorrow. See you guys then."

The call ends, but our argument hasn't.

Aston turns his back to me again, this time staring out the window. If I thought he was rude before, I obviously haven't seen just how much of a jerk he can be.

"I'm giving you one more chance," I warn him. "You either want to do this for your sister, or you don't."

"You make it sound so easy," he says in a low voice.

I place my hands on my hips. "I'm sorry spending time with me is such a drag. Do you really hate me *this much*? This is all for Maddy!"

Slowly, he turns around to stare into my eyes. His gaze is penetrating, so much so that I desperately want to spin away, but his pull is much stronger than I care to admit. A fluttery, empty feeling sits in the pit of my stomach.

His eyes look almost as if they've turned dark as he whispers, "Everleigh, you have no idea what I would do for my sister."

Every time he says my name, my chest pounds uncontrollably, leaving me breathless.

And now, I have no idea what to think or how to feel.

"I . . . I think we should—"

"I need to shower," he interrupts, then begins unbuttoning his shirt.

Is he for real right now?

I let out a huff. "We aren't finished talking."

"I'm more than happy to carry the conversation into the shower." He observes my reaction, and his smug expression is annoying as hell. "I mean, this is important, is it not?"

"I don't get you, Aston. One minute I think I can work with you, and the next, you remind me why men are assholes."

"Jerk," he corrects me with a serious expression. "I believe you called me a jerk. And by the way, I'd like to add that your so-called theory is incorrect. I can prove it if you'd like to join me in the shower."

I shake my head in confusion. "Wait, what theory?"

"Guys who drive Porsches have small dicks," he states smugly. "I'm more than happy to prove just how wrong you are."

My eyes widen in disbelief, and at the same time, my cheeks burn with mixed rage and embarrassment. "We're done," I tell him. "I have a wedding to plan, and it's obvious you get off on making my life hell. Goodbye, Aston." I storm out of the room, rushing down the stairs with a desperate need to lock myself in my car.

The moment my driver's-side door closes, I let out the breath I've been holding in.

He will be the death of me.

Despite my animosity toward him, I can't ignore the fact my mind pictured exactly how he would look inside that shower.

My hand grips the steering wheel tight as if it holds some magic power to make this all go away the tighter I squeeze.

But nothing, I mean nothing, will erase my wandering thoughts.

My imagination has betrayed me, along with my body, but the rest of me refuses to let him win. Whatever game he's playing, I'm going to beat him to the finish line. Make his life just as miserable as he enjoys making mine.

I glance out the window to the house's first floor, where his room is located.

"Game on, Beaumont," I whisper with a grin. "Payback is going to be sweet."

CHAPTER 10

Eva

On my drive back from Beaumont Manor, I questioned everything the universe was throwing at me. Aston knows how to crawl under my skin and bury himself in there like a parasite sucking the life out of me. There was a chip on my shoulder the size of Jupiter, so I blasted angry-girl music to release my frustration with the whole situation. I belted out a song at the top of my lungs, trying desperately to erase Aston's infuriating invitation to watch him shower.

The nerve of him.

And the worst part of all of this, a side of me, while minuscule, and I'm talking so minuscule you could barely find it with a magnifying glass, imagined what he would look like naked in the shower.

Yes, that image flashed before my eyes.

And my body reacted almost instantly.

Traitor.

On my way home from the manor, my gas light came on, and while at the gas station, Marco invited me to the Spice House for dinner.

I felt like the universe knew I needed a break.

What's the saying, again? *You can get over someone by getting under someone else?* Or something to that effect.

Not that I'm *trying* to get over Aston.

I'm simply trying to forget he's an asshole.

Besides, Marco is friendly and handsome but doesn't strike me as a man who would take a woman to bed on a first date. He has respect. Unlike the man-whore I know who would bed a woman in the first ten minutes of meeting her.

Nevertheless, my afternoon and mood have improved. I light my favorite strawberries-and-champagne scented candle and nestle into my favorite plush reading chair with a book. Billie suggested this love triangle romance will pull me out of my funk. I enjoyed reading, but not as much as Billie and Maddy. They easily binge read two or three books a week, making it impossible for me to keep up. There are a few book clubs in town, depending on the genre you're into, but I realized I'm a slow reader and can't keep the pace like others.

For me, I want to savor the moment, and the words. When I lose myself, I know the book will linger in my thoughts as I lie in bed falling asleep. Given that I have zero romance in my life, the next best thing is living vicariously through the characters.

Well, maybe not zero since Marco asked me out to dinner.

The plot has started getting angsty, and I am super invested in this billionaire losing his mind over this woman dating another man, until my phone rings and Maddy's name flashes on the screen for FaceTime.

She lets out an exasperated sigh. "Can I please tell you about the day I had?"

I nod, gesturing for her to go on.

"So, I started with work stuff . . . the whole reason I even drove into the city today," she says, rolling her eyes. "And, miracle of miracles, it didn't take as long as I thought. So, I figured, hey, might as well do some shoe shopping for my dress."

I chuckle. "That sounds pretty harmless so far."

"Harmless? Ha!" she scoffs. "I nearly broke my ankle in these ridiculous high heels I thought I could pull off. Who was I kidding?"

"Sounds rough," I say, stifling a laugh. "How high were they?"

"High enough to make me look like I was using stilts. Oh, and then, as if things weren't already on a downhill slide, I get a call from Myles's mother," she continues, her voice dropping as she says it. "I swear, these calls always leave me feeling . . . I don't know, on edge."

"Yikes. Did she go off on one of her rants?"

"Don't even get me started," she groans. "And just when I think I can finally get home, there's this . . . rat."

I blink, holding back a laugh. "A rat?"

"Yes, a rat!" she exclaims. "It darted right in front of me, and I swear, I nearly had a heart attack! I don't know who screamed louder, me or the damn mutant rat . . . Eva, it was so big. I thought it was a cat at one point. I swear to God, it was not a normal rat."

I burst out laughing, unable to hold it in any longer. The rat story continues on, much to my amusement. After she's done with her much-needed vent, I blurt out, "I have a date tonight."

"I've been talking about a mutant rat for ten minutes, and you're only telling me this now?"

"I won't lie to you. The rat story was funny."

"How was it funny?" Maddy raises her voice dramatically. "I nearly died!"

My eyes roll from the drama this woman conjures up in her head. "You didn't nearly die. Do you want to hear about my date or not?"

"Yes, carry on."

"So, it's with Dr. Wilde," I say slowly, then correct myself, "I mean, Marco."

"Hold on one second. Are you dating your doctor?"

"Technically, he *was* my doctor, but not anymore."

"Holy hotness. This is so forbidden!" Maddy squeals, and a horn honks in the background. "Give me all the deets."

"There's not much to tell yet," I admit. "We met not long ago. I ran into him at the bar yesterday when you were spiraling over Myles's family. Then, he called me and asked me out to dinner. Nothing fancy, but still."

Maddy whistles. "The universe is working overtime."

"It's a small town."

"Cinnamon Springs is small but not *that* small," she says, then continues in a rush, "What if he is your prince charming and you marry him? We could double-date with our husbands, and oh my God, what if we have kids at the same time? They could be besties too!"

"Okay, now you're taking it a step too far. I'm not looking for a husband, just someone I enjoy spending time with."

"And someone great in bed," Maddy snickers.

I laugh softly. "That too."

"Okay, but seriously, Eva. What if he is *the one*?"

My laughter dulls to complete silence. We've had numerous conversations about meeting *the one* throughout our friendship. Though, no matter how often we've discussed it, the thought is terrifying. One person for the *rest of your life*? Sure, it sounds fun at times, like when a storm hits and you're in bed by yourself, wondering if it would be different with someone beside you, a man who made you feel safe.

I'm not one to crave children, but sometimes, a mother walks into my shop cradling a newborn, and I wonder what unconditional love for a human being you created feels like . . .

But it ends there.

I still want to experience so much and see more of the world. The only man I dated who was remotely serious was my ex Brady. It was college and we dated for six months. He wanted to graduate, move back to Boston, then settle down and start a family.

The more he mentioned it in the time we dated, the more I retreated and wanted to run. It wasn't the right time, especially since leaving college opened up a world of possibilities.

Even though Brady was a great guy, I wouldn't be here with my own business if I'd stayed with him. God knows, I'd probably have two kids now, since he wanted four in four years.

My uterus shriveled at the thought.

Maybe getting a dog or cat would be the compromise if I never find the so-called *one*. I know plenty of single ladies in town who have cats. They have a club called Crazy For Kitties. There are about ten of them of all ages, and they meet every Thursday at the café for coffee and cronuts. To be honest, they have a ton of fun talking about their fur babies and the books they're reading. It's like a cat and book club all rolled into one.

"How did you know Myles was the one?" I ask, releasing a sigh. "I mean, you're marrying him. So he is the one, right?"

"Of course, silly." Maddy ponders quietly, then continues, "I don't know. I guess there's nothing wrong with him."

"But, surely, there's magic between you two."

"Like orgasms?"

"Yes, but something more . . ." I trail off, lost in my thoughts.

"It's just right," Maddy quickly adds. "Look, all I'm saying is, I hope this guy is decent. He has to be. He's a doctor."

Something tells me Marco is decent.

But is it enough?

Marco is easy to be around. I love listening to him talk, and despite studying medicine for all his adult life, he's managed to travel and see a bit of the world.

"There's this restaurant in Venice, and if it's your anniversary, the old couple who own it take you on a gondola ride and sing the song they danced to at their wedding fifty years ago. Plus, they serve you this delicious almond cake, which they also had at their wedding."

My lips curve upward. "How romantic, but also embarrassing if you're an introvert."

"Very true." He chuckles but holds my gaze, asking, "Have you traveled much?"

"When I was younger, yes, but now that I own a business, it's hard to get away. My schedule suits day trips, so I try to at least go for a drive whenever I get a chance."

Great, that made me sound like I have no life.

Why is this dating thing so hard?

Just relax. Marco won't judge.

Inhaling a deep breath, I slowly release and feel much more relaxed. "My brother, Elliot, lives in France and I miss him. If the rest of the year goes well, I might visit him. It's just that I've been saving to buy a place, so vacations feel less important."

"Hey, you're talking to the person who has student debt that will follow me to the grave," he informs me. "So, I get that completely."

I smile, sighing. "But look at you. You're saving lives."

Marco places his hand on my knee, and his touch excites me. With my gaze fixed on him, I bite my lip teasingly.

"Saving them, yes. One day, I hope to make them, too. When I find someone to spend the rest of my life with."

I can't hold back my grin, but I don't want to encourage talk about the future. Part of me wonders if that is truly what Marco wants or if he is just saying it to get me to sleep with him. Then again, Marco doesn't strike me as someone who needs to lie to get a woman into bed.

Eager to shift the conversation without seeming too obvious, I tell him a story about a customer who came into our store with quadruplets. In the middle of the story, the hairs on my arms stick up as if a cold breeze blew past me—or a ghost. I still my movements, hyperaware of my surroundings while my heart beats erratically.

Then, I see *him*.

The green eyes that insist on haunting me, but this time, they're walking toward us ignited by jealousy.

In just one stare, I have all the warning I need.

Tonight won't end well for any of us.

CHAPTER 11

Aston

A lawsuit was the last thing I expected to deal with on a Saturday night.

I barely slept, maybe an hour at best, and only at my desk when my eyes couldn't stare at my laptop screen a second longer.

It was call after call, and when my father got involved just before ten this morning, he demanded I deal with it. He's at the country club with his buddies, smoking cigars and drinking aged whiskey as if the business world around him isn't burning to the damn ground.

The infuriating thing is—this is *his* fuckup.

He insisted we invest in a brokerage company to get back at some rival, only for us to inherit lawsuits. I warned him to stick to what the Beaumont Group does best—property investment. Of course, he didn't listen because pride was far more important to him.

Our legal team scrambled to resolve the problem before we hit the headlines. All the while this was happening, time was lost on me, and I completely forgot about the breakfast meeting with Everleigh.

Until she stormed into my bedroom, a force of pure determination.

Her cheeks were crimson, her eyes glaring at me, ready to

battle over my lack of consideration of her time. The moment I hung up the business call, Everleigh didn't hold back.

Her incessant nagging was the last thing I need.

Frankly, I am exhausted.

I need a shower and sleep.

But Everleigh disregarded my need for peace.

The woman is relentless.

She did, however, strike a nerve with her sharp, unfiltered words, each one landing like a calculated blow. Everleigh has no idea what I have sacrificed for Madelina, and I've been doing it my whole damn life.

My head swells, tension building as my chest tightens beneath yesterday's clothes. It's been a clusterfuck of a day, and if I survive it without a migraine, I'll be astonished. They have hit me more lately, no doubt induced by the pressure of running this company under my father's watch.

But if only she knew the truth.

How much I sacrifice for my own blood.

My sister. The only person I would take a bullet in the head for.

My mind rushes back to our interaction, replaying how she stormed out of my room, the fire in her eyes unmistakable. I can't help but relish her reaction, savoring the satisfaction of finally setting the record straight and watching as my words landed precisely where they were meant to.

It left me hard as a fucking rock.

In desperate need of release, I step into the shower, turning the water to nearly scalding, letting the heat wash over me and melt away the tension. I battle with myself as to whether I should give in to my urges. Closing my eyes, I convince my hand to move away and turn the faucet off.

Then, I picture *her* for the first time. She's so fucking sexy when she's angry at me.

And it's a record finish.

So much so that I go for round two without a second thought.

The day didn't improve, even after I slept for two hours and my release in the shower. Madelina is in the city for something urgent, leaving me alone with nothing but a questionable box of take-out Chinese in the refrigerator.

All the food Hilda supposedly left behind has been eaten. I can only assume it was my father, and despite him staying in the same house, our paths haven't crossed. Thank fucking God for that.

My mother landed at JFK but chose to stay in the city for the next few days before traveling out here. Honestly, I don't blame her. I know I'm not the only one avoiding my father at all costs.

After his golf game, he calls to lecture me on how I handled *his mess*. His voice carries the husky edge of too much Macallan, laced with his usual condescension. Even though I'm his son, he treats me with zero respect. However, the message is painfully clear—*I'm nothing but a disappointment to him.*

So, I put the phone down and let him rant while I answer emails.

Tomorrow, he'll be sober and won't remember a thing.

It's early evening when darkness fills the house. I stretch my arms and crack my neck to alleviate the stress of staring at my screen for most of the day. The only light in the room comes from my laptop and my phone, which pings continuously with messages.

Little Brat

I'm stuck in the city, there's been an accident on the interstate. Can I crash at your place?

I let out a huff. My sister knows I don't like anyone staying at my penthouse—not even her. It's my sanctuary, the one space I keep solely for myself. No matter how many women I've been with, none have been allowed to stay the night. I am quick to set boundaries, drawing a firm line in the sand. *Fuck me all you want, but you better be gone before the sun rises.*

> **Me**
>
> Fine. Don't touch anything.

> **Little Brat**
>
> I'll sleep on the couch. Wouldn't want to catch cooties from all the women you screw in your bed.

> **Me**
>
> Anything else? You leave me here in this godforsaken town with nothing to do on a Sunday night. I'm starving.

> **Little Brat**
>
> Go to The Spice House. They serve the best tacos and margaritas. Plus it's where all the single women hang in case you're looking for a small-town romance.

> **Me**
>
> Small-town romance? You're delusional. I'm more than happy to continue living my life as your single older brother.

> **Little Brat**
>
> Two words for you. Grumpy/sunshine.

> **Me**
>
> ?

Madelina doesn't respond, but my notifications alert me to someone entering my apartment. I click on the front door camera to watch Madelina removing her coat and knocking over a vase near the coat rack. The sound isn't on, but judging by the way her mouth opens, she's swearing at her clumsy mistake, staring at the glass scattered all over the marble tiles.

"Fuck my life," I mumble.

I grab my keys, wallet, and phone, desperate to leave this place.

The drive into town is dark, and only a few lights can be seen from some ranches nearby. When I hit the main intersection, I turn left to drive down Butterscotch Boulevard. Unsurprisingly, all the shops are closed, the complete opposite of the city. How people don't die from boredom in this town is beyond me.

The Spice House is well lit, which makes sense since it's one of the few places that seem to be open. I park my car in the street, then make my way to the pub. Upon entering, I notice it's bigger than I assumed. The place itself was a jam factory back when I was a kid. In junior high, the owners officially closed it down, and it remained abandoned for years. The brickwork still stands, and whoever owns it now has restored the building with a modern twist.

In the central area, the tables are occupied by families. A few kids are running around, much to my annoyance, but I ignore them and head straight to the bar.

The bartender serves me my bourbon of choice. Beside me, two women are eyeing me up and down. Great! The so-called small-town romance girls my sister informed me about. I press my lips together and take a slow breath to gather my patience.

"You're not from around here," the woman with the jet-black hair is quick to say when I take a seat.

I force a smile, but truthfully, I'm too drained to even think about fucking her or anyone else in this bar.

"I'm not" is all I answer.

"Fresh meat," I hear her whisper to her friend before they giggle. "We have a competitor for the hot doctor."

Hot doctor? Jesus Christ. The women in this town are clutching at whatever they can get their hands on. Despite wanting to take my mind off today, going home with these women seems more tiresome than exciting. I continue to sit, keeping to myself.

"Can you believe the hot doctor is here with Eva?" the other woman complains. "Her donuts aren't even that great."

My eyes widen at the mention of Everleigh's nickname. Unknowingly, my hand has tightened around the glass of bourbon. I slowly raise it to my mouth, drinking the remnants in one go before slamming the glass on the bar, making the leftover ice rattle.

Then, I slowly turn and scan the room. It doesn't take me long to find them huddled in a darker corner of the bar. Everleigh is laughing, and her doctor friend is sitting close, resting his hand on her thigh. It doesn't help that she's wearing a dress that appears too short from where I'm sitting.

My breathing increases like a drum banging inside the walls of my chest. Before I have a chance to calm myself the fuck down, my feet are moving toward where they sit.

Everleigh is telling some story, only to stop talking mid-sentence when her eyes lock onto mine. With her lips flattening, she pokes her tongue into her cheek and inhales a deep breath.

"Well, isn't this a nice surprise." I attempt a forced smile, given the circumstances. "Is this your friend?"

She opens her mouth but quickly closes it. I suspect she was going to say something cutting, but then she contrives a smile, which is obviously as fake as it comes. "Aston, this is Marco. He's a doctor."

The *hot* doctor, according to the woman at the bar. I pause to observe him, then shake his hand politely. "Aston Beaumont."

"Beaumont," he repeats with a curious glance. "Your father is Harvey Beaumont?"

My lips curl, barely opening as I respond, "Yes."

"I believe he golfs with my friend's dad."

I nod, keeping my eyes fixed on Everleigh. It's evident she's irritated by my presence, which I find amusing.

"Aston is Maddy's older brother. We're helping plan her wedding." She's quick to set the record straight.

"Of course, you mentioned the wedding earlier," Marco says.

Earlier?

How long have they been sitting here?

Or is this a post-fuck meal?

Don't even go there.

I attempt to clear my disruptive thoughts, but something is off, and my usual self-control is somewhat compromised.

"We have a wedding to plan, and to get the ball rolling, I suggest we meet up after you're finished with whatever is happening here. Dinner, I presume?"

Everleigh looks completely unimpressed, her mouth slackening while her gaze turns distant. "Wait, are you kidding right now? You, the one who blew me off? You bailed on me without a word."

"Again, I apologize for the emergency that required my attention."

"*Emergency?* It was a business call, Aston. It takes two seconds to send a message to say you can't make it," she reminds me in a huff.

The so-called doctor watches the both of us but keeps quiet. If he's bothered, he doesn't show it. Then, he takes a breath. "I'm going to grab us another drink. Aston, would you like to join us?"

Everleigh's glare is a silent warning, daring me to accept the invitation. The easiest thing would be to stay here and make her life hell. *I mean, why not?* Does she think starting a relationship with the town doctor is a good idea? It would violate some HIPAA code, surely.

"Aston was just leaving," she states. "You said earlier you had so much work to do before we catch up tomorrow, which works much better for my schedule."

I continue to stand there, smug, as Marco waits for my reaction, but it's obvious he isn't stupid and has picked up on the tension between Everleigh and me.

"Yes, I have business to take care of," I respond with a fixed stare. "Tomorrow morning, then. Nine sharp."

Everleigh relaxes her shoulders with a satisfied smile. She is sorely mistaken if she thinks this is how the night will end. I leave them inside the pub, but instead of heading home to work, I park myself at the entrance of her apartment.

There is no chance she is bringing him back here.

I'll wait all night if I have to, even though my conscience tells me to ignore whatever the hell is happening. I have better things to do than act like some goddamn puppy dog wanting attention.

The problem is—*I can't.*

I won't.

Just like when she got the flat tire, and I arranged for it to be repaired and towed back to her place. Given the lawsuit, it was the least of my problems, yet I couldn't stop thinking about it. I paid the invoice and then asked them not to mention it to Everleigh.

Something has a hold over me, and fighting it is proving fruitless.

But I'll be damned if I walk away now and allow another man to touch her.

And that, in itself, is the part I don't understand.

Why the fuck do I care so much?

CHAPTER 12

Eva

There were only two options.

Option one—sit and pretend Aston doesn't exist.

Option two—set the record straight and send him on his merry way.

This was a *date*.

What I didn't expect was for Marco to invite him to dinner, or for Aston to look so . . . I don't know, jealous? I mean, *why would he be jealous*? He loathes me and has made his feelings abundantly clear.

The moment Aston walks away, Marco glances at me, cocking his head with curiosity. This time, I try to smile naturally—not forcefully like I have been since Aston gate-crashed our dinner. Anger and nerves get the better of me, so I take a long sip of my drink and let the margarita work its magic. I breathe a huge sigh of relief, then focus back on Marco.

"I was picking up on some tension between you two," he begins, then continues with a sudden change in demeanor, "I thought you were just planning a wedding."

"We are. Well, I am. Aston is not very cooperative. He drives me insane. All I need him to do is sit down, concentrate, and not act like a jerk. That's too hard for him apparently."

Marco nods quietly. "You are beautiful. I don't blame him."

"For acting like a jerk? What do my looks have to do with it?"

"Well, for starters . . . men have this thing when trying to deny their feelings. They act a certain way."

I shake my head. "Aston has always been like this. He looks at me like his little sister's annoying best friend."

"But, you're not so little anymore—"

"Look, I'd rather not waste my breath talking about him. I'm starving, shall we eat?"

The rest of the dinner is enjoyable. If there's one thing the chef does well, it's the soft tacos with slow-cooked brisket. I polish off three plus another two margaritas, and things start feeling slightly blurry by the night's end.

Marco leans in, placing his hand on mine. "I enjoyed tonight."

"Me too." I grin.

"I would love to invite you back to my place for a drink, but unfortunately, I have an early appointment in the morning." He raises his hands with a mischievous grin. "I promise, I am not making that up."

"Are you sure?" I tease.

He leans in again, this time closer so our lips are almost touching. I press my thighs together, unsure if it's the proximity or the margarita making me dizzy. His hand rests on my knee, the light caresses teasing me beneath the table.

"I promise, Eva, I want to spend the night with you. But work—"

"I get it," I reassure him. "You're saving lives. There will be a next time."

Marco takes care of the bill even though I offer my share, and as we step outside to say goodbye, a few families loiter near us. The kids run around in the cold, making loud noises while Marco stands closer with his hands holding on to my arms.

"I'll call you," he says softly, the warmth of his breath lingering between us. "Tomorrow?"

I punch him playfully. "You better, Dr. Wilde."

And though I know our first kiss would have been perfect, the screaming kids are not. One falls over and sounds like they're dying, so Marco kindly offers to look at the boo-boo.

This is *not* how first kisses should go.

Thankfully, Marco picks up on my vibe and doesn't pressure me into one.

My apartment is two blocks over, so I say goodbye and walk home, enjoying the brisk night air. It's something I do often when I need to clear my head, and after the way tonight ended, plus Aston's gate-crashing, my head needs to be cleared. Cinnamon Springs is one of the safest towns in the county, so I'm not afraid of strolling at night by myself.

That is, until I get to my apartment.

Is that a shadow?

My heart begins to race, panic setting in as I try to get a better look at the man standing near the door. God, I don't even carry mace or anything to protect myself. What good are a tampon and some breath mints when I'm in danger?

As I step a bit closer, the hands running through the curly hair appear to be familiar.

I take larger steps, eyes wide in disbelief.

"Are you stalking me?" I accuse in a high-pitched tone.

Aston raises his brows, pursing his lips. "I would hardly call it stalking."

The guy is relentless. It's bad enough he put me in a sour mood this morning and earlier tonight, but now he just keeps going like he's bored and has nothing better to do than to annoy me.

"Why are you here, Aston?"

"To prove a point to you," he states matter-of-factly but then glances around. "I'm right. Though, your doctor friend is missing. Not enough game, huh?"

I shake my head in confusion. "Right about what?"

"A man and woman can't just be friends," he reminds me smugly.

Not this again.

I drop my gaze to the ground, granting myself patience to deal with whatever Aston is about to throw at me. One minute, I think he's somewhat pleasant and cares about his sister, but the next, he acts like some jealous boyfriend who won't let me play with other boys.

My head begins to spin, thanks to the margaritas. "I'm tired, okay? Just go home."

He places his hand against the brick wall, blocking my way. As he stands this close to me, I smell his aftershave. How can a man as infuriating as him smell so . . . so . . . *delicious*?

I refuse to look him in the eye in case he can read my questionable thoughts, but he inches closer anyway.

"You're telling me you didn't consider inviting him inside?"

"No . . ." I shake my head, still unable to look at him, and manage a lie. "I told you, I'm not into one-night stands."

Aston remains silent, but I know he's watching me. My breathing is ragged, and I'm sweating beneath my coat despite the cold night air.

Slowly, I lift my head to meet Aston's intoxicating gaze. Unwillingly, I swallow the giant lump inside my throat, unable to turn away. I should be angry he's invading my privacy, but I can't seem to gain any clarity, and my heart is beating way too fast for me to focus on anything else.

He tilts his head slightly, leaning into my ear to whisper, "And when he leaned in to tell you how beautiful you look tonight, you didn't envision him removing this sexy dress of yours until you're naked in front of him, begging to be fucked?"

The intensity of his words causes me to bite my lip. My legs press together to stop the desire between my thighs, which, thankfully, is hidden beneath my coat.

"No," I choke.

"Hmm . . . interesting." He touches the pendant hanging from my necklace, then runs his finger down my chest, stopping just shy of my cleavage. My stomach flutters, and beneath my clothes and bra, my nipples harden at the touch of his fingers against my skin. "Your body appears to be betraying you."

"Perhaps you're reading it all wrong," I say, finding my voice and fighting off this overpowering urge to do something I *will* regret later. "See, if I want something, I go for it."

With a satisfied smirk, he murmurs, "A woman who knows what she wants."

"Yes, Aston." I look him straight in the eye and beg myself to remember all the bad things about him, and ignore the part of me that suddenly wants him . . . *naked.* "I'm tired. I'll see you tomorrow morning."

He drops his arm, allowing me to pass, but as I step forward, he stops me again by grabbing me. I glance down, focused on the tight grip around my wrist.

"Sweet dreams, Everleigh. If you need inspiration tonight, I finished twice in the shower after you left. It's a shame you couldn't join me."

My heart almost falls out of my chest. I scramble to respond, but my tongue is tied because my body has now betrayed me entirely.

Then, I shift my gaze and look into his teasing green eyes. He releases his grip on me, the absence of his touch catching me by surprise.

He's just playing. His ego is so big, he thinks he can push my buttons—and for what purpose? All we need to do is get this wedding over and done with, and then he's back in Manhattan where he'll forget all about me—the shiny toy left behind.

"Perhaps you're good for something, Mr. Beaumont. Aside from being the biggest pain in my ass." I pull out my keys to place them in the lock but turn around again. "Tomorrow, and since you're so eager to share your stamina in the shower with me, I expect your attendance at nine will be no problem."

And with those final words, I enter the building and hurry to close the door behind me.

Later, when I'm tossing and turning in bed, I beg myself to fall asleep. *He got to me.*

And I hate him so much for it.

Though *hate* is such a strong word especially for someone who desperately needs to release this tension building down below. I close my eyes, sliding my hand between my legs. The simple touch is enough to make me moan.

Slowly, I move my fingers in a circular motion, this build inside my belly warning me it's only a matter of moments. I bite down, squeezing my eyes shut as the desire climbs and a spread of warmth reaches every part of me.

"*Holy fuck,*" I gasp while arching my back, unable to catch my breath.

My body collapses on the bed, trying to come down from the euphoria. The echo of my heavy breathing is loud inside my room. Surely, this will knock me right out.

An hour later, I find I was wrong.

Another best self-induced orgasm of my life.

And the worst part of it all?

I imagined *him* for the very first time.

Big fucking rookie mistake.

CHAPTER 13

Eva

I wake at stupid o'clock.

I lie in bed beneath the warm comforter, staring at the ceiling in the dark, fidgeting with the bedsheet while trying to find some excuse to get out of seeing Aston today. Every few minutes, I turn my head to look at the clock, only to spiral even further.

Sweet dreams, Everleigh. If you need inspiration tonight, I finished twice in the shower after you left. It's a shame you couldn't join me. His voice replays in my head, causing me to groan loudly in frustration. I throw the comforter over my head, desperate to drown out his voice and the anxiety of having to face him this morning. We never agreed on a place, only a time, but then my phone pings with a text message at the same time as the sun begins to rise.

Aston

See you at nine at the café. I promise to show up this time.

I contemplate a thumbs-up but decide against it. I make myself an extra-strong coffee, double the shot, then continue reading my book. The scene turns spicy when the billionaire takes her on the desk and commands her to look him in the eye while they're screwing. I'm living for the fact that he's in love with her and she's playing hard to get.

The familiar warmth spreads between my thighs, so I put the book down with a huff. The last thing I need is to be physically charged in Aston's presence.

As much as I need a cold shower to bring my body back to reality, outside, the weather is anything but warm. It feels like another cold front hit overnight, and the last thing I want is to get sick before the wedding.

Billie is already downstairs baking, and the smell of vanilla fills the café. Every morning, when I step inside the quiet space before customers arrive, I take a moment to relish it all. The scent of freshly made donuts mixed with coffee brewing is like heaven on earth, and there's nothing in the world I want more than to be here in my happy place.

Sometimes, I think about expanding and opening another store, but nerves get the better of me. What if it fails? What if I throw all my money into my business and end up without any to put a roof over my head? Let alone restore my dream house.

Argh, the spiraling only adds to my mood. I purposely inhale again, desperate for the scent to ignite my happy senses. But this morning, I feel like a truck has run over me.

"Good morning, sunshine," Billie greets me with a lopsided grin. "You look—"

"Tired?" I sigh while scrubbing my hands under the faucet. With my elbow, I knock the paper towel dispenser to dry my hands, and put on disposable gloves so I can help Billie with the toppings. I get to work sprinkling chocolate flakes on the fresh batch Billie retrieved from the fryer, which has already cooled down and been iced. "I had a date last night."

Billie jerks her head back with an incredulous stare. "A date? Well, this explains why you're tired."

It takes me a moment to realize what she means. The coffee is clearly not working its magic just yet. I'm not usually one to drink more than two cups a day, but today might be different.

"Oh no," I say, shaking my head. "It didn't end up that way. I mean, we didn't, *you know.*"

"So, this date was with who exactly?"

"Dr. Wilde . . ." I tell her, then quickly correct myself. "I mean, Marco."

Billie whistles. "That escalated quickly."

I pause my movements with chocolate still in my hands. "Do you think so? There's no rule to say we can't date. Well, there is, but I won't be visiting him as my doctor anymore, so technically, he doesn't doctor me or whatever. You know what I mean."

"Yes, I know what you mean. He won't lose his license if you're not his patient."

Billie slides another tray over to me. This batch is the pineapple donuts—my absolute favorite. The yellow glaze contains a small amount of pineapple juice, which gives it a sweet and tropical flavor. We added it to the menu only recently, after a customer from Australia mentioned them from her childhood. As soon as Billie heard the story, she started creating the amazing treat. There are never any left by the end of the day, making our pineapple donuts one of our bestsellers.

I suggested we use the extra dough to make mini balls as a take-out snack item. These are great for kids and the tourist crowd who use the town as a quick stopover on road trips. I even designed a to-go cup as a souvenir item. My idea was to give them a memento to remember us by, and hopefully, they'll return or tell their friends.

"Anyway, the date kinda went well . . ." I trail off, unsure just how much information to reveal. "I haven't heard from him since."

"What do you mean 'kinda went well'? And I don't think him not texting you in, what"—she looks at her watch—"eight or ten hours is a problem." Billie gasps, pointing her wooden spoon at me. "You're doing it again."

"Doing what?"

"Looking for red flags."

I huff. "I don't look for red flags, okay? They get waved in my face, which is impossible to ignore."

"Okay, so explain why you think it didn't end well?"

"I never said it didn't end well. It's just . . ." I hesitate again, then blurt out, "Maddy's older brother showed up and ruined the evening."

Billie tilts her head in confusion. "How did he ruin it?"

"Long story," I mutter, then exhale loudly. "He's coming here this morning because we need to get some wedding stuff sorted. We have to have some sort of code. If I need an out, I will ask if you ordered the extra cinnamon, okay?"

"Um . . . sure. And then what?" Billie pokes her head near the oven door to check the last remaining batch. "Is there a reason why you would need an out?"

"It's Maddy's brother. I *always* need an out. The guy is a pain in my ass. If the code is used, tell him we need to end our meeting because I need to help with an urgent delivery issue."

"Why don't you just tell Maddy you don't get along?" Billie questions like it's no big deal. "I know she's your best friend, surely she will understand."

"Maddy has enough on her plate," I answer softly, then sigh. "We're adults. I'm sure we can get through this and then never have to see each other again."

The oven dings again, pulling my attention to the clock. *Seven o'clock on the dot.* Right on cue, our regulars are gathered outside, peering in, eager to be let through the door.

I open the doors and greet Mrs. Brimsley first. She has her Yorkshire terrier, Gloria, sitting inside her purse. Gloria is by far the most well-behaved dog I have ever met. Not once have I heard her bark or fuss over the attention she gets for being so cute. With a pink bow and diamanté collar, she is definitely the queen of the Brimsley household.

Mrs. Brimsley is a well-loved socialite in town. I always go out of my way to treat her nicely, so she tells her social clubs, which will bring us more business.

"Hello, my dear." She steps into the store with a smile. "I hope you've got those delicious balls for me this morning."

Thank God Maddy isn't here, or we wouldn't hear the end of it. Billie ushers Mrs. Brimsley to her regular table, then returns to the espresso machine to make her nonfat latte with one decaf shot and sugar-free vanilla. Additionally, Mrs. Brimsley requests room at the top to add cold milk and sugar. It's bizarre, but she tips more than 20 percent, so we don't give a damn how odd it is.

By eight, the morning rush is well underway. It's Monday, so the café is busier than usual as people try to start their week with a bang. Over the next hour, I lose track of time. Billie is serving a customer at the counter who is so indecisive, I can see Billie's patience being tested as she fidgets with her braids. I quickly put together some extra take-out boxes in the back until she calls to me.

"Oh, Eva, sunshine," Billie sings out. "You have a visitor."

"Who?" I yell out, sucking my finger from a paper cut.

Billie pokes her head in the back with a knowing grin. "Um . . . a very sexy man, who you clearly didn't describe in your story."

"His looks have no relevance in my stories."

A snort escapes Billie. "Uh, yes, they do. C'mon, Eva, he looks like he just walked out of *GQ* magazine."

"Keep your voice down. If he hears, I'm sure he'll find a way to use it against me."

I'm taken aback by the fact he showed up, though, in hindsight, I wish I hadn't made such a big deal out of yesterday. Maybe then he wouldn't feel the need to prove a point, and I wouldn't be standing here dreading leaving this kitchen.

"He may be sexy, but his arrogance is not." I breathe deeply, clenching my fists tightly to ward off the nervous energy. Billie watches me with amusement before I shoot a dagger at her with my eyes. "Don't even think about saying it."

She raises her hands. "I said nothing of the sort."

Aston is already sitting at a table, wearing a light blue dress shirt and dark pants. Although he's sans tie, he looks professional for our casual meeting. I glance down at my green apron, ignoring the urge to call him hot to his face. Knowing my luck, I'll accidentally blurt it out and Aston will *never* let me hear the end of it.

Note to self—strangle Billie later.

"Good morning," I say, almost choking on my words.

Aston glances up from his phone, a smirk settling on his lips. "I'm sure it is. Nine on the dot, as promised."

I coerce a smile, desperately trying to forget about the words he whispered last night outside my apartment. With another deep breath, I take a seat across from him. A few customers are still sitting around, but Billie can manage alone.

"So, let's get straight into it, shall we?" I pull out my notebook, filled with yellow Post-its from all the note-taking I did with Maddy. "I've made a list of all the things we need to get done for the wedding day, as well as a few events leading up to it. Now, I've broken it down by—"

"You look good today," Aston interrupts, his gaze locked on me. "Glowing, in fact."

My eyes fall to the open pages of my notebook as I swallow the lump caught in my throat. "I have no idea what you mean, but thank you, I guess."

"You must have had a good sleep," he remarks, his tone dripping with smugness.

This time, I glance up only to see his raised brow and cocky smile. "Actually, it was pretty shitty. Do you want coffee or something to eat? I could probably use another coffee."

Aston leans back into his chair, looking way too relaxed. "Coffee sounds great."

"How do you take it?" I ask, sliding my chair back to leave the table. It's only been two minutes in his presence, and I need a break. "The coffee, I mean."

"I knew you meant coffee. But it appears your mind is elsewhere." Again, with a smug expression.

This is painful.

I wait with annoyance, only for him to say, "Tall Americano, three sugars."

"Three sugars?" I question with my hands on my hips. "Do you want to die young?"

"I didn't get much sleep, much like yourself," he admits.

I would have thought he slept like a baby after working so hard at making my life hell, but something else must be weighing on his mind. My mouth opens out of curiosity, only to close a moment later.

Less is more.

Don't ask questions.

Strictly wedding talk.

Quickly, I excuse myself to make us coffee. Billie is busy taking orders on the other side, which is a good thing since I'm pretty sure she will interrogate me once this is over.

The coffee machine begins grinding the beans, I place the ground coffee into the portafilter, distribute it evenly, and then slide it back into the main machine to begin tamping. My hands reach over for a cup, moving it underneath. When both cups are complete, I return to the table, placing Aston's before him.

"So, this is your place, huh?" He scans the café, including Billie, who is behind the counter pretending not to be stalking us. "Nice."

If there is one thing I'm proud of achieving, it's Donuts Ever After. Everything in here was thought-out, from the woodland-green colored wall filled with artwork showing different types of donuts painted by a local artist to the exposed brick wall with a pink neon sign hanging that reads In My Donut Era.

The booths have a diner-style feel, but my favorites are the small provincial oak round tables I ended up pairing with Hamptons-inspired chairs, a mix of all the things I love. The ceramic vases in the middle of each table mimic a stack of books with artificial purple zinnias sitting inside them.

"Yes, it's mine." My lips press into a fine line. "I'll also take your *nice* as a compliment even though I'm sure you're thinking this place is too cutesy for your liking."

"I never said that."

"You're a guy, a city guy. I bet you drink your coffee from some overpriced coffee shop on Wall Street claiming to have the best blend in the country."

"Actually, you're right." He brings the edge of the cup to his mouth, drawing my attention to his alluring lips. My eyes dart across the room in a panic, only to see Billie with her I-told-you-so face. "Though, this tastes amazing."

"Okay, stop being nice to me. It's weird," I complain. "Can I go through my list now?"

He nods with a scoff. "Go ahead."

I made the list simple so Aston's tasks are easy. After I mention what needs to be done, I wait for his response.

"So, all you need me to do is ensure all the men turn up to the suit fitting, organize the bachelor party, then show up at the wedding?"

"Pretty much. Do you think you can handle that?"

"Not at all," he answers with sarcasm laced in his voice. "I can run a billion-dollar company, but getting a few guys together to try on suits is well above my capability."

"Look, okay, I don't need your bull—"

Maddy appears at the door with cheeks flushed from the cold, distracting us from the near argument. She removes her purple knitted beanie, beaming as she notices us sitting at the table. In a mad rush, she takes a seat and releases a long sigh. "Thank God you two are together."

Billie joins us, asking Maddy if she wants anything to drink. Maddy mentions she left the city at the crack of dawn to beat the traffic, so she is extra wired on caffeine but orders a cinnamon twist since she skipped breakfast. "I was worried this would be too hard for you guys, like there was a beef or something."

"I never said there was a beef." I suck my cheeks in, sputtering those words in a raised voice. "What makes you think we can't work together?"

"Aston is too busy, and you're getting laid by a doctor," Maddy replies casually.

My mouth falls open the moment those words leave hers. Across from me, Aston makes a slight growl. I can't believe she brought up Marco, especially in front of Aston. On top of that, I'm not even sleeping with Marco.

"This is not appropriate to discuss, Madelina," I grit, purposely calling her by her full name. "My personal life should be personal."

"Fine." Maddy rolls her eyes out of boredom. "Can we talk about the dress fittings, please?"

As Maddy talks, Aston remains quiet across from me. I avoid his unrelenting stare and nod when needed as if I'm paying attention to Maddy. All I hear are words like *tulle* and *lace*, but aside from that, my mind is questioning why Aston's mood has shifted.

She glances at her watch mid-sentence, releasing another heavy sigh. "How is it this late already? Myles's mother and Mom are heading out to brunch, and they asked me to join them."

It's just before nine thirty, which is hardly late in the day. Though Maddy appears to be reacting to the caffeine as she annoyingly bounces her leg beneath the table.

"Oh, you didn't tell me your mom is here."

Maddy glances at Aston as something passes between them. I wait to see if either will indulge my curiosity, but both look uncomfortable.

"Yes, I picked her up this morning" is all Maddy says. "It was a long car ride of silence."

I read the signs and decide not to ask any more questions, since whatever is happening appears to be a family issue. If Maddy wants to talk, which I know she will, I'll surely hear about it later.

Maddy says goodbye, reminding me she'll call me later this afternoon, then bolts out the door, leaving us alone again.

Well, not entirely alone, since Billie is still stalking by the counter.

"So, I think we're done here." I push the chair back to stand, notebook in hand, and then smile. "Have a nice day."

As I attempt to turn my back to Aston, he reaches out and wraps his hand around my wrist to stop me. Again with the wrist grabbing, which does something to me I can't explain. I bite my lip, ignoring the blood pumping through my veins. After last night, I thought I got it out of my system, but with just one touch, I'm again proven wrong.

"We're *not* done," he commands.

"I think we are. You have your list of things, and I have mine, which includes visiting a violinist this afternoon, since she's willing to fit me in. So, if you'll excuse me, I have some emails to send out before I leave for the drive."

He lets go of my wrist, but his gaze is unwavering. "I'm coming with you."

"You're not coming with me to listen to wedding music. You'll get bored, then make my life hell."

"I'm supposed to help with these things as well, so I won't take no for an answer." Aston stands, towering over me. His eyes fall to my lips, watching them intently before I see him shake his head like he's been caught up in some sort of trance. "I'll be parked out front at noon."

I fold my arms over my chest. "I'm not getting in your penis mobile again. Look, I can do this myself. I'm sure you have work to do."

Aston doesn't respond, but with his gaze piercing, I know there's no stopping him.

"Twelve p.m., Everleigh. Be ready."

"Fine! But why do you have to be such a jerk all the time?"

A devious smile plays on his lips before he leans in and whispers, "You're an easy target, Miss Woods. But if you want, I'll play nice. Though I'm much more fun when I'm playing dirty." He pulls away, cocking his head with a dismissive glance. As he walks out of the café, I stand still, watching him, not realizing Billie is standing beside me.

"Oh, Eva. You're in big, big trouble . . ." she teases.

I shake my head, blinking rapidly. "What did I do?"

"You've caught the attention of the playboy," she informs me with a bemused smile. "There's nowhere to run now."

"There's always a way to escape," I say, barely above a whisper. "I've escaped him once, and I can do it again . . ."

I *want* to believe my words. I *need* to believe my words.

We just need boundaries. So, they've been crossed a few times already. Big deal. All I need to do is treat him like my best friend's older brother and remember the one I want in my bed is Marco.

And the best way to do that? Make these wedding appointments unbearable for the playboy.

Starting this afternoon . . .

CHAPTER 14

Aston

Madelina knows how to push my buttons without even trying.

Her reckless comment, you're *getting laid by a doctor*, put me in a pissed-off mood for the rest of our meeting. Not only that, but I was also forced to listen to Madelina talk about dresses. Like I fucking care if she wears lace or not.

I insisted on joining Everleigh for this tedious task of auditioning music acts to prove a point—I won't get bored. But now I'm standing here listening to middle-aged women play a Beyoncé song on their violin and cello.

Nobody willingly wants to listen to pathetic love songs.

I can't think of anything worse.

Besides planning this wedding for my sister.

On the car ride over, Everleigh was quiet. It didn't help that I also had a lot on my mind. After leaving the café, I received a call from an investor who pulled out because of the pending lawsuit. My father, of course, ignored my calls and insisted on hitting the golf course again.

Then there was last night . . .

The old man came home on a bender, and my mother was his target. She wasn't there yet, but that didn't stop him from calling Madelina. He so brutally informed her, "Your mother needs to get her ass to Cinnamon Springs because her absence is making me look like a fool."

I knew my sister was upset, and all I could do was hide his bottles of liquor to stop him from drinking more. Eventually, he passed out in bed.

Everleigh sits on the leather armchair next to me, listening to Eunice, the woman who played the violin, explain the notes of the song. It's hard not to succumb to boredom, especially when the conversation shifts to Beyoncé being the greatest artist of all time. It doesn't stop there when other notable female artists are brought up, and then it segues to women's rights.

I'm starting to think these two women are more than a musical duo.

Beside me, Everleigh leans over to whisper, "I know you're bored. I can see it all over your face."

"I'm not bored," I correct her, straightening my posture. "I'm unable to comprehend why music matters so much. My sister is walking down the aisle. Shouldn't the wedding march suffice?"

"A wedding is about emotions," Carol the cello player reveals. "It's about finding the deepest connection with one person and vowing to spend your life with them. Music brings out these emotions."

Everleigh nods, but she's trying to keep a straight face. I observe her side profile, the way her lips deliciously press together while curving upward. She appears confident and poised, making me want to play and have fun with her.

Just admit it . . . you want to see her cheeks turn pink with anger.

I clear my throat. "You'll have to excuse Miss Woods. She's not a believer in romance."

Everleigh snaps her head in my direction as her mouth opens wide in shock. "I'm not the player who brings women to my fancy penthouse and doesn't let them sleep over. What's the longest relationship you've ever had, huh?"

I'm amused by her willingness to bite back so quickly, but truth be told, I've never had a relationship. *I fuck—end of story.*

"So touchy . . ." The corner of my mouth rises teasingly. "Does your doctor friend tell you how he's looking for *the one* to settle down with?"

The color of her cheeks slowly turns the perfect shade, satisfying my sick and twisted need to watch her argue with me over an unimportant matter.

Everleigh opens her mouth to give it back to me, but Carol interjects, "I have an exercise for the two of you. Since the bride and groom usually partake in our auditions, I would like you to stand up as we play the song for the first official wedding dance."

"I'm sorry, Carol. What?" Everleigh shakes her head, panicked. "I will *not* dance with him."

"Hm . . . sounds like you're scared of romance," I mutter under my breath.

"Fine!" Everleigh stands, positioning herself in front of me. "I'll dance with you. After all, this is for your sister, isn't it?"

Carol and Eunice start playing their instruments as Everleigh says, "Just to reiterate, we are waltzing. That's it."

"If you say so."

I watch her take a deep breath, then extend her arm to place her hand on my shoulder. As the music plays, I rest my hand on her hip and then secure her other hand in mine. We move to the tune of the Ed Sheeran song "Photograph." Madelina requested they test this song out, along with two other songs.

With Everleigh's body so close to mine, I fall silent at this unknown feeling of emotion overwhelming me. *What the fuck is this?*

I pull myself out of the thought to ask her with a satisfied grin, "This isn't so bad, now is it?"

"I guess not," she drags out, pretending to be annoyed. "Who would have thought the playboy could dance?"

"Well, if my penis mobile doesn't impress the ladies, I can rely on my dancing skills."

A small laugh leaves her supple lips. "You forgot about your charming personality."

"Right! That's what apparently brings all the women to my penthouse."

"C'mon, there's truth to what I said, so don't lie," she gloats, relaxing in my hold.

I pull away, but only slightly, to look her in the eye. "I never denied it, and I'm the first to admit relationships aren't something I think about. Work has been my life. It's who I am. It defines me. There's no time for this romantic . . . whatever you want to call it."

She presses her lips together with satisfaction, only to respond with, "The billionaire knows what he wants."

I bring her body back into alignment with mine, avoiding her critical stare. "I sense judgment in your tone."

"It's your life, Aston. Who am I to tell you how to live? If it makes you happy, then kudos to you."

It doesn't make me happy.

It doesn't bring me joy.

It satisfies something within me I'm unable to explain. It's a life I am forced into, so there's no choice but to find satisfaction in making billions of dollars. It's not exactly like I can quit and play lacrosse. The dream of following a passion has long died.

"And are *you* happy?" I question her.

Everleigh turns away to stare blankly at Carol and Eunice. Then, she sighs "What is happiness, anyway?"

The song comes to an end before Carol places down her cello. "I think it's the perfect song choice. The two of you looked like a bride and groom on their wedding day."

Everleigh lets go of me in a rush, as if reality has slapped her firmly in the face. "Oh, we had to play the part, right?"

I watch her avoid my gaze and see how her body language tells me something has gotten to her. Unlike moments ago when she was relaxed in my hold, her expression is pensive as she folds her arms, keeping her distance.

Carol and Eunice wait quietly for the green light, but Everleigh doesn't say a word.

"My sister will love it. Can you email me the details, and we'll get the invoice paid?" I reach out and grab Everleigh's hand. "Let's go."

Outside in the driveway, Everleigh struggles to keep up. "Why are you rushing us?"

"You looked uncomfortable," I tell her, honestly.

"I *was* uncomfortable. They thought we were in love or something."

I pause beside the car. "And you're scared of love, romance?"

"Why are you so hung up on that?" She tilts her head with furrowed brows. "You said you're not looking for a relationship."

"I've spent my life around women who are so infatuated with relationships and meeting the right person. I'm finding it hard to grasp you're not like everyone else. Not to mention your best friend is getting married. Doesn't that evoke some sort of biological ticking clock?"

"I'm *not* like everyone else," Everleigh responds sharply. "I would like to settle down one day, but I'm not looking for it. I want to have fun. What's wrong with that? It doesn't make me coldhearted or against romance."

A smirk reaches my lips. "Fun is open for interpretation when you're an adult."

Everleigh crosses her arms, keeping her gaze focused on me. "Okay, so I'll admit it. Sex is fun if it's with the right person. It's not my fault the last two guys were duds."

The thought of other men touching her brings on a state of unrest. I glance away to calm my agitation, then say, "But you're the common denominator."

She slaps my arm, catching my attention. "I am not the dud! I want a man who makes me feel like vanilla isn't the only flavor out there."

I raise my brows, pausing to examine her face. So, the beautiful woman standing before me doesn't like vanilla. How *very* interesting.

I open my mouth to question her, but she quickly interrupts. "We should head back. I have to run a few errands, then close up at three. Billie has an appointment with her mom, so it's just me."

Everleigh doesn't allow me to say anything, impatiently waiting for me to unlock the car. When the car beeps, she opens the door and takes a seat.

She stares quietly out the window on our drive back to town. Not long into our ride, her phone pings with a text message. Everleigh quickly reads it, but almost as if she's been caught doing something she isn't supposed to, she rushes to put her phone back in her coat pocket.

I suspect it's her *friend*.

"Does the doctor enjoy vanilla?" I question with malice, tightening my grip on the steering wheel.

"I, uh . . . wouldn't know," she simply states.

It's all I need to hear.

And with a satisfied smirk, I keep quiet for the rest of the drive.

When we reach the front of the café, I put the car in neutral but keep the engine running. Despite my reluctance to come back to Cinnamon Springs, there is something nostalgic about being in a place you grew up in. Sure, it's nothing like Manhattan—the exact opposite, to be frank.

But sometimes change isn't a bad thing.

"So, the music is checked off," Everleigh says quietly, unable to look at me. "I've got the photographer covered at the end of this week. Actually, could you organize the cars for Maddy? I'm not into cars, but clearly you are."

I nod silently.

"And that's it." She sighs, still avoiding my gaze. "See you around."

She opens the door to get out of the car, leaving me no chance to say anything. Upon stepping out, her phone slides out of her coat pocket and onto my leather seat, and before I even have a chance to let her know, she slams the door shut.

I pick up her phone and read the message on the home screen.

Marco

I'm looking forward to seeing you tonight.

A burning sensation rips through my chest, causing me to slam my foot on the gas and take off without returning her phone. I almost run a red light, but then am forced to stop as a mother duck and her ducklings waddle across Main Street without a fucking care in the world. My hands grip the steering wheel until my knuckles are stark white, suddenly not caring for this small-town bullshit.

As soon as they're safely across, I accelerate the fuck out of there. My anger spikes as I drive around the town in a circle to end up where I started—in front of Everleigh's donut shop. The lights are turned off, and a sign on the door reads Closed. I turn off the engine and wait.

But the jealousy consuming me doesn't resolve.

The longer I sit here, the more consumed I become.

I need to calm the fuck down.

Minutes pass as I stare out the window and watch some families play in the park near the town gazebo. A little boy is kicking a ball around, laughing as his father softly tackles him. I can't recall a time my own father ever played with me. It was always business in our household.

I pull my gaze away from the park and back to the front of the café. It's empty, so I assume Everleigh is in the back. Finally, I exit the car.

The door to the café is not locked, surprisingly, so I turn the knob and enter at the same time as it chimes.

"Sorry, we're closed," Everleigh yells from the back.

I take steps toward the counter until Everleigh appears.

The moment she lays eyes on me, her lips press together in a slight grimace. "What are you doing here? I have to close up, and then I have an errand tonight," she informs me.

"Another date?" I grit out.

She lets out an annoyed huff and twists away from me to return to the kitchen. I follow her until she's cornered and has nowhere to run. The kitchen is small but ridiculously organized. Everywhere I turn, something is labeled so there's no confusing what belongs where.

"You didn't answer me," she repeats, her tone unsure. "What are you doing here?"

I reach into my pocket and pull out her phone. "It seems the doctor is looking forward to getting you alone tonight."

She snatches the phone from my hands, stepping back, her eyes smoldering with resentment.

I move closer, trapping her against the stainless-steel countertop. My calm demeanor is short-lived as once again, Everleigh's presence evokes this uncontrollable jealousy within me.

I won't allow him to touch her.

My breaths come coarser and faster until I can't take it anymore. Fueled by the adrenaline running through my veins, I bring my hands to her thighs and lift Everleigh, so she's sitting on the counter.

Her honey-brown eyes take me in as her chest rises and falls, with soft, shallow breaths escaping her gorgeous, pink, kissable lips. I'm drawn to the way they part, and I remember how they tasted like fucking heaven the night I gave in all those years ago.

That night, I ignored how she made me feel because I was stupid and immature.

But now we're adults.

And I bet she will taste just as fucking sweet.

Beside me, a tub of vanilla icing sits opened. Without even thinking, I dip my fingers into the icing, then bring it to my mouth, running my tongue along my fingers before sucking it off.

She watches me take it in, eyes wide, unaware a small moan has left her lips. I'm rock fucking hard beneath my pants, desperate to taste her. This teasing is doing nothing to help the situation and is very unlike me.

I don't tease. Women beg me to take them without any effort on my behalf.

But Everleigh is not like other women.

She's the poisonous apple dangling from the forbidden tree. With just one taste, I'm crossing into uncharted territory. I have to—*I must*—be strong enough to kiss her and walk away like it's nothing more than a game.

"Vanilla isn't always so bad, now is it, Miss Woods?"

CHAPTER 15

Eva

"Vanilla isn't always so bad, now is it, Miss Woods?"

My body movements still, frozen at his forced proximity.

The kitchen becomes increasingly hot, making my breathing uneven. The scent of Aston's cologne is so intoxicating, like a mixture of soap and masculine energy all rolled into one.

Thinking straight is . . . is . . . *challenging*.

It's just a scent. Remember the man who drives you crazy. It's all a plot to lure you into some sort of trance so you forget about his unforgivable behavior.

Then, I accidentally feast my eyes upon his lips.

It all comes back.

The night he kissed me.

The night I wanted *all* of him.

I suck in a breath, fixated on his tongue, gliding against his fingers before his lips wrap around them and finish the sweet treat. A moan leaves my parted lips, but this time, I have *no* control. Underneath my skirt, moisture builds between my legs, and a dull ache torments every inch of me.

"I, um . . ." I'm unable to find the right words, overcome with brain fog. "Your tongue is . . ."

The corner of his mouth twitches as he presses into me. I feel him hard against my body, only adding fuel to the burning fire.

"You were saying?" he teases, leaning into my neck near my earlobe. "About my tongue?"

My body is ignoring any rational thoughts trying to fight their way through. With his body so damn close, the urge to taste him is *too* dangerous.

This is Aston Beaumont.

Get yourself together.

But Aston likes to win, and maybe just once, two can play his twisted game.

"I have work to do," I whisper back, my voice firm, a spark of defiance flickering in my eyes. "And a date tonight."

He pushes himself into me, lifting my hair in his fist while placing a kiss on my neck. My skin feels like it's on fire, forcing me to close my eyes before my body betrays me entirely and combusts right before him.

"What makes you think I'll let another man touch you?" he murmurs, running his tongue along my skin.

"I'm not yours," I remind him while holding back my moan. "Anyone can touch me."

Aston retracts his lips at a slow and agonizing pace. With his gaze piercing into mine, he raises his thumb and drags it against my bottom lip.

The desire to bring his mouth to mine and taste him is overwhelming, but then he runs his hand below my chin, against my chest, and continues as I take in a breath when he rests his hand on my thigh.

In a rush, I wrap my hand around his wrist, stopping him from doing anything else, but his wicked smirk becomes my damn weakness. I let go, freeing him to do whatever the hell he pleases, swallowing the lump forming inside my throat.

He slides his hand beneath my skirt and against my panties.

His eyes widen with a tortured stare, and at the same time, I throw my head back and bite my lip, desperate to control the urge to give myself to him entirely.

"Don't do that, *Everleigh*." He growls my name. "Don't make me demand we fuck right here and now."

My head falls forward as our eyes connect, and I become trapped in his commanding stare. I reach for his wrist again, and I pull him away this time. The loss of contact is unbearable, but watching him tortured in my presence spikes my adrenaline.

"I'm going to be late," I inform him as his jealous stare torments me. "Can't have the doctor sitting around waiting for me."

He pulls back only slightly, pressing his lips together firmly. "Maybe I should send you to the doctor with your pussy dripping wet with my cum. Would that be a better solution?"

I roll my eyes to get a reaction from him. "And what makes you think I'll let you come inside me, huh?"

Aston observes me with a mischievous grin. "Sweetheart, you'll be begging me to come inside you. Mark my words."

A vibration sounds in the quiet room. With his stare still dominating me, he reaches into his pocket and retrieves his phone to answer it. "Beaumont," he greets coldly.

I sit in awkward silence while the person on the other end of the line is clearly having a good old rant. Bowing my head, I focus on the floor, thinking of ways to get myself out of here before my clothes come off. This phone call is the splash of cold water we both needed.

"The meeting isn't for another twenty minutes," Aston informs the person sternly. "I'll fix it, trust me."

I twist my body to release myself from his entrapment, then hop off the counter. As I press my hands on my skirt to flatten it, Aston ends his call.

He takes a step closer. "This isn't over, Everleigh."

Just as I'm about to tell him nothing started, a knock on the door distracts me. I glance at the clock, noting the time.

"It's our delivery guy," I tell him, thankful for the interruption. "You should probably go. Your meeting sounds important."

Aston tucks his hand in his pocket, cocking his head.

Quickly, I leave the kitchen to let Jeremiah into the store. He waits patiently outside with boxes of soda and other supplies I ordered late last week.

"Hey there, Jeremiah. You're early."

He tips his head with a grin. "For you, I like to come on time."

"I bet you say that to all the girls," I tease.

With my hand holding the door open so Jeremiah can wheel his cart full of boxes inside, Aston exits the kitchen with a less-than-pleased expression.

Jeremiah is cute. We flirt, but that's where it ends. If I'm being honest, most girls in town think he's cute and friendly. There is nothing I can fault him on. Perhaps he is vanilla—universally liked.

"Mr. Beaumont was just leaving," I announce, shooting Aston a glare sharp enough to cut through steel. "Your meeting?"

"Yes," he responds, keeping his tone arctic. "I have business to take care of."

Aston walks to the door but stops just shy of where I am standing. Jeremiah continues to unload the boxes as Aston inches closer. "Another one wanting to get you into bed. My, my . . . aren't we popular in town?"

I have half a mind to slap him in the face. "That's an asshole thing to say. Go, Aston."

And with his shoulders back, radiating superiority, he turns and walks toward his car.

Maddy has spoken for a solid thirty minutes about veils. She's still undecided if she wants one.

However, being her best friend, I listen and give advice occasionally when I can get a word in, even though my head is elsewhere.

"The veil is supposed to symbolize purity, innocence, and

modesty," Maddy sputters in a panicked tone. "Am I any of those things?"

My phone vibrates, alerting me to a text message. My lips press together firmly as I read the message with anticipation.

Marco

> The Mountain Lounge just called me. Apparently, there is some electrical problem and they're closed for the night. Any suggestions of where we should meet? I'm more than happy to cook dinner for you if you're up for staying in. I promise to behave 😊

The truth is, I haven't responded to his earlier text because I completely forgot. After Jeremiah left, I locked the shop, came home to lie on the couch, and stared into nothing. I needed time to process what happened earlier with Aston and cool myself down because finishing what he started was too tempting.

Then Maddy called, leaving me no time to think about anything else.

I quickly respond.

Me

> Raincheck? I'm sorry, Marco. It's been a long day and I have an early start tomorrow. Are you free later in the week?

I don't want him to think I'm not interested.

"Eva, are you still there?" Maddy questions.

"Yes," I answer quickly. "The veil. Just wear it if you want, and if you don't, so be it."

"That's all you have to say?" Maddy complains before continuing, "What's gotten into you? Is it the doctor? Does he have a small ding-dong?"

I scrunch my nose. "Please don't call it that. It's disturbing. And for the record, I haven't slept with him."

"Oh, right. So what's the problem?"

"One of many . . ." I trail off, careful not to mention Aston. "Veil aside, the string duo is booked. I've got some things to check off tomorrow, and then I'm free for dress fitting on Friday."

Maddy squeals. "Fabulous. What would I do without you?"

"Get married at city hall?"

"Funny! I won't lie to you, I don't blame people for doing exactly that."

We end the call with a promise to catch up tomorrow. As for me, I yearn for complete silence to decide my next move.

I stare at Marco's text again.

He is a great guy with so much potential. I mean, how many men like Marco will I cross paths with in my lifetime? The dating pool is slim pickings. Well, at least, in Cinnamon Springs it is.

Aston got to me.

My fingers quickly type another message to Marco, but then I erase it. None of my words are coming out the way I intend them to. Frustrated, I throw my phone onto the other side of the sofa and head to the kitchen to grab something to eat. As I pull open the cupboard door on the hunt for something to satisfy my craving, I hear the ping across the room.

"Don't read it," I say out loud to no one but myself. "Food. You need food because you're hangry and not making any good decisions right now."

I find some chocolate and devour it to cure the cravings for sex, which have consumed me since the moment I saw Aston lick his fingers. With a mouth full of fancy chocolate my brother sent me from France, I drag my feet back to the sofa and grab my phone.

Aston

Are you behaving, Miss Woods?

A smile graces my lips, much to my annoyance. Obviously, the chocolate has cured my mood.

Me

Not really. I just shoved expensive French chocolate in my mouth. I don't know how long it's been sitting in my cupboard.

Aston

You do know you own a donut store. If you were craving something sweet, you could probably find it in your store kitchen. Maybe something vanilla?

I sink into my cushions, relaxing for the first time today.

Me

Are you only texting me to see where I am or who I'm with? Stalker, much? Remember, I'm single, and the doctor checks all the boxes.

Minutes pass with no response. I put my phone down to turn on the television. With a bored flick of the channels, I recheck my phone to see if he has read the message, but no response.

Two hours later, it's obvious he was playing a game.

Annoyed with myself, I reread the text I sent Marco. He responded letting me know his schedule is booked but he may be free later in the week. I feel terrible but know if I went on tonight's date, I'd be using him for revenge sex, which is not fair to Marco.

Instead, I lie in bed by myself.

And I refuse to satisfy my sexual urges by thinking about Aston again.

I can't stay ahead of whatever game we're playing if I break my own rules.

"That photographer was cute, wasn't he?"

Maddy half pays attention to the road, almost driving us into a ditch. I grab the dashboard and say, "Be careful and pay attention. You're getting married. Stop looking at other guys," I reprimand her.

"He was cute for you."

A huff escapes me. "I'm done with men."

"How can you be done with men?" Maddy raises her voice while pressing harder on the gas. "What happened to Dr. Hottie?"

"I have a lot on my mind with the wedding coming up. Now wouldn't be the time to start something serious," I lie, but then change my mind. "It's on pause. I still plan on continuing when I can get my head together. It's not like I'm interested in anyone else. Marco is a great guy, and I would be stupid to let him go."

Yes, I have a lot on my mind.

A lot from some jerk who never messaged back—it's been over twenty-four hours.

The worst part is that he's read the message, and it only reinforces my image of him playing his game and using me as a pawn.

"Shit, I didn't realize the time," Maddy says in a panic. "I have a dinner with my parents and Myles's parents at my place."

"Is that why you're driving like a maniac?" I hold my breath as she takes another sharp turn. "Look, we're five minutes from your place and it's fifteen to mine. How about I drop you off, and we'll work out the car situation tomorrow?"

Maddy sighs. "You're a lifesaver."

I glance at my phone. There's nothing but email notifications. We pull into Beaumont Manor, where Myles's parents' Mercedes is parked out front.

"Great, they're already here and probably conspiring to get me to wear the veil I don't want to wear," Maddy complains.

She puts the car into park as I unbuckle my seat belt. "So, is it just you guys for dinner? As in, Myles's parents and yours?"

"Yeah, Myles is back in Manhattan. A potential female lead for a new play flew in to audition from London, and Aston is AWOL as usual."

Oh, I mouth, but I'm uncertain how to respond. I'm sure whatever is occupying him, he has a spare moment to respond to a text.

What an *ass*.

I exit the car at the same time as Maddy, only to notice Mrs. Beaumont walking toward us dressed in what I assume is a designer knitted baby-blue dress. She crosses her arms to shield her body from the cold.

It's been a long time since I have seen her, but even though time has passed, she still looks as beautiful as I remember. Perhaps this wellness retreat or whatever the hell it is actually works. Her face is flawless, with minimal makeup on her porcelain skin. Upon closer inspection, Maddy has similar traits, but it's evident Aston inherited his mother's genes.

"Eva, it's lovely to see you again." She leans over to peck my cheek, the scent of her Chanel No. 5 lingering. "You are just as beautiful as I remember."

"Thank you." I smile politely, then say, "It's been a while, Mrs. Beaumont."

The corners of her lips curve forcefully. "Yes, it has. Will you be joining us for dinner?"

"Actually, I was just going—"

Maddy pinches my arm. "Eva is staying."

I glance at Maddy with wide eyes.

The last thing I want to do is spend the night eating dinner with Maddy's father, who will no doubt find a way to make me feel small. Not to mention, I woke up early to open the store and spent the rest of the day with Maddy to meet with the photographer. After yesterday's encounter with Aston, the last thing I need is this forced dinner, given that I'm exhausted.

Maddy pleads with her eyes, and it's not lost on me.

I press my lips together, then contrive a smile. "Sure, thank you for the invitation."

Mrs. Beaumont claps her hands. "Excellent. I will have Hilda set the table for another guest." She walks back to the house while I stop Maddy from leaving.

"Thanks for the peer pressure. This is *your* family," I remind her in a huff. "I was going to order takeout tonight and watch *Love Island*."

Maddy wraps her arms around me. "Have I told you lately that I love you?"

"You owe me."

"I know, I know," she sings playfully.

The lights are on inside the manor, showcasing all the fancy chandeliers. The place looks much more alive than when I visited the other day. The dining room is set up to seat eight people, but I count the plates again, wondering who the extra guests are.

"I thought it was just your parents and Myles's parents," I say out loud.

Mrs. Beaumont appears from the kitchen. "Viviana will be joining us. I ran into her earlier, so the timing was perfect."

"Viviana?" Maddy repeats, only to roll her eyes moments later. "Did you invite her to the wedding?"

"Madelina, she is an old family friend. Of course I invited her."

Maddy places her hands on her hips. "This was supposed to be a small, intimate wedding. How many guests are we up to now, huh? And, let me guess, Aston is coming to dinner then?"

His name catches my attention.

"Yes, your brother will be here."

"Does he know you invited Viviana? I mean, she's his ex, Mom. I would be livid if you invited my ex."

Mrs. Beaumont releases a sigh. "Your father insisted."

My thoughts start to cloud, and I'm unable to think of ways to get out of this dinner. Sitting at the same table as Aston and his ex will not be pleasant. I mean, he doesn't do relationships, so basically, she was a fuck buddy. Maybe not even a buddy, but a quick fuck, and that's it.

Mrs. Beaumont turns away to head toward the kitchen, with

Maddy at her heels arguing over the guest list. My hands twist as I fumble with my excuse, only to yell out, "I'm not feeling the best. Maybe I should head home—"

The hairs on my arms stand while my breaths become uneven. I close my eyes momentarily, addicted to this rush that's consuming every inch of my body.

Then, a voice whispers behind me, "You're not going anywhere."

CHAPTER 16

Eva

Mr. Beaumont takes a seat at the head of the table.

He arrived not long ago, making his presence known like it was such a big deal. Maddy appeared to be the only one who greeted him with a smile, embracing him while he doted on his only daughter.

Mrs. Beaumont retreated to the kitchen to check on dinner, barely saying a word even when he leaned in to kiss her on the cheek. It was apparent it was purely for show—possibly one of the coldest interactions I've ever witnessed.

As for Aston, his demeanor changed the second his father gave him a stern look. Something passed between them, the tension mounting in the room. I have no idea why he insisted I stay, given that he hasn't spoken two words to me.

I knew the next hour would be torturous.

Damn me for having no backbone and agreeing to support my best friend.

Then, Viviana arrives.

I hate to admit it, but she's attractive—if you're into blondes. She's wearing a gray knitted turtleneck dress that hugs every curve, accentuating her full, perky boobs. Her hair is pulled back into a sleek bun, giving her a polished, refined look.

My wraparound denim dress and knee-high boots look out

of place. My hair also took a hit with the wind earlier—Maddy calls it my sex hair.

Which would be great if I were actually having sex, which I am not.

Of course, Aston sits beside Viviana, across from me, with a mischievous smirk. He dressed appropriately for dinner in dress pants and a black button-down shirt. His sleeves are rolled up, making him look incredibly sexy, and his smug expression is warning me to pay attention to his next move.

This man knows how to push my buttons.

"I'm pleased we are having dinner tonight," Mr. Beaumont begins, raising his glass to toast. "I apologize my wife couldn't make the luncheon on Saturday."

Mrs. Beaumont keeps her poise, staring blankly at her husband like a puppet waiting for the next move.

"What matters is we're all here now." Roland Whitney raises his glass. "Aside from my son. It's always a challenge to pull Myles away from the city, especially when he's on the verge of supposedly casting the next Patti LuPone. With the wedding not far away, he's trying his best to get all his work done."

Everyone raises their glasses in a toast, then sips the rich red wine—a bold, velvety blend with hints of dark berries and a subtle oak finish that lingers warmly on the palate.

Maddy smiles, but I can see in her eyes that she is over it already.

Myles's mother glances at Maddy and asks, "And I assume both you and Myles will be living in Manhattan?"

"We're looking around Brooklyn, actually," Maddy replies.

"Brooklyn?" her father questions with an arrogant laugh. "My daughter will *not* be living there."

Maddy shoots dagger eyes at Aston but shifts her focus back onto her dad, evidently annoyed by the comment. Maddy is low-maintenance when it comes to the finer things in life, which surprises most people since she comes from a wealthy family.

To this day, she still uses my Netflix login because she can't be bothered paying for it. "I like Brooklyn. Besides, not everyone can afford a penthouse on the Upper East Side."

"The company pays for that penthouse," her father quickly informs everyone. "The perks of being employed by the Beaumont Group."

Across from me, Aston takes the glass and drinks the red wine in one go. His muscles have tensed. Every now and then, he looks my way, but I quickly distract myself. My attention is drawn back to him when Viviana leans over to whisper something in his ear.

"Georgina," Mrs. Beaumont calls softly, "Viviana's family owns a lovely property on Martha's Vineyard. Madelina mentioned you were looking for a place?"

Myles's mother wipes her mouth with her napkin. "It would be nice to find a place for our future grandchildren to spend time with us on vacation."

Underneath the table, Maddy's knee begins to bounce. It happens when she's anxious. I move my hand to her thigh and squeeze it tight. Maddy wants kids, but I know she plans not to start trying for at least three more years. She wants to do so much before she settles into family life.

Mr. Beaumont rests his fork on his plate. "Quite an investment, Roland."

"Yes, but like Georgina said, we are thinking about our future grandchildren." Myles's father lovingly places his hand on his wife's. "It's time for me to retire, Harvey. Pass the reins over to my son. With my own father quite frail, we're learning to enjoy the simple things."

I want to laugh, given that a house on Martha's Vineyard is far from simple, but keep my expression still.

"Once the kids are done with Broadway," Mr. Beaumont responds condescendingly. "It's important to keep the family name alive. Is it not?"

"Harvey, please. The kids are enjoying themselves," Myles's father informs him.

The answer doesn't please Mr. Beaumont. He raises his glass to his lips before following with, "A big portfolio to manage, Roland. I can't see how Myles can continue to focus on Broadway and manage all your investments. Perhaps we can sit down and look at some alternatives. I mean, if Madelina is to focus on bearing and raising children, it's important Myles also has the time to be around for his family."

Aston narrows his gaze while his hands sit on the table curled into fists. I'm drawn to the way his knuckles turn so white. He relaxes them, only to reach for more wine. Not that I've been counting, but I swear it's like his third glass in the space of ten minutes.

Then, his eyes reach mine, and something in his tortured stare pulls me in. I knew he wasn't the biggest fan of his father, but assumed because they worked together, things got better since high school. The more I hear Mr. Beaumont talk, the more I realize their relationship is still strained.

"Enough business talk, and how about we cool it down with the baby plans," Maddy interjects, a welcome relief. "So, Viviana, are you and my brother getting back together or what?"

I hold back my urge to gasp, instead reaching for the wine to ease my irritation. I'm glad Mrs. Beaumont served multiple bottles on the table. It's almost like she knew everyone needed a bottle just to get through this damn uncomfortable dinner. Since I'm driving, my one glass is my limit, so I try to savor it even though I desperately want to drink it down in one go, much like Aston.

"Madelina," Aston mutters, his jaw clenched. "Are you really asking that question?"

Viviana places her hand on Aston's to calm him down. My stomach hardens. Aston doesn't move, welcoming the gesture as I bitterly turn away for the sake of my sanity.

"Aston is my date for the annual Cures For Cancer Charity Ball. It's kind of our thing."

Our thing?

I force myself to keep my gaze fixated on the plate of roast beef and vegetables in front of me, but the burning sensation in my chest is hard to ignore. *Why the hell am I so bothered by this?* It's not like he's my boyfriend or anything. God, we haven't even kissed.

Well, recently, anyway.

"Nice," Maddy says simply, before blurting out, "So, what else is happening with everyone? The weather has been pretty drab, and the roadwork at the corner of Ginger Grove and Butterscotch Boulevard is a real hindrance. Oh, and Eva is dating Dr. Wilde."

An unflattering gasp leaves my lips. "Maddy!"

"What? It's not a secret."

Wow, Maddy will throw anyone under the bus to take the attention off her. Given that this dinner is for her family, I'm taken aback by the overshare of my personal life.

"Dr. Wilde is a respectable physician. Everleigh's personal life is perhaps not the ideal conversation to have when we're hosting guests, Madelina," Mr. Beaumont scolds.

"Better than all the plans for my future," Maddy mumbles under her breath.

At first I dare not look across the table, but the sadistic side of me slowly lifts my gaze, only to be met with the scornful eyes of the man who warned me last night that no other man could touch me.

But that was before Viviana came into the picture.

"My relationship with Dr. Wilde is private. Besides, his name is Marco," I correct her while everyone watches me curiously. "He's not *my* doctor. Just for clarification."

Maddy rolls her eyes, then sighs. "Is he your plus-one at the wedding? You never told me. I mean, of course you can bring him, it's just we keep adding people and it was supposed to be only one hundred people."

"A wedding is a time to celebrate, Madelina," Georgina interjects. "You only get married once."

"Exactly," Mr. Beaumont agrees. "Considering you're not paying for the wedding, I don't understand why additional guests should be a problem."

Beside me, Maddy lowers her gaze to avoid an argument. Despite her earlier outburst regarding my personal life, I can't help but feel sorry for her. Maddy only wanted something intimate, and judging by the conversations had tonight, this wedding is becoming a bigger event than she anticipated.

My hands twitch nervously beneath the table. "I'll get back to you about Marco. It depends on a few things, I guess."

This night is going progressively downhill. I desperately eye the bottle of wine, wishing I could drink all this tension away. The temperature inside the room increases to an uncomfortable level. My breathing becomes much faster, forcing me to reach for the glass of water to calm myself down. As I bring the glass to my dry mouth, I catch a glimpse of Aston staring at me with his lips pressed flat and eyes burning with jealousy.

My head falls, desperate to control the desire consuming me. I'm all shades of fucked-up. How can this man across from me turn me on with his toxic behavior? Everyone knows jealousy is a red flag.

"Excuse me, I need to use the restroom," I inform everyone.

I wander down the hall to the restroom toward the back of the house. Inside, I wash my hands before resting them on the countertop to gather my thoughts.

The creak of the door catches my attention.

I don't look up, consumed by my racing heart and the adrenaline running through my veins. Whoever has just opened the door has made their presence known.

My eyes close to control my breathing until Aston's body presses up against my back, and his lips find their way to my neck.

"Perhaps I didn't make myself clear yesterday," he murmurs, placing small kisses on my skin, which drives me insane. "I won't allow another man to touch you."

I open my eyes, staring at our reflection in the mirror. "Then I won't allow another woman to touch you."

He pauses mid-kiss, meeting my gaze with a brutish smirk. "Jealousy looks beautiful on you."

"I never said I was jealous."

Aston moves his hand toward the base of my neck, keeping me locked in this position. With his eyes still focused on the mirror, he brings his lips to my earlobe.

"So, Viviana getting down on her knees and begging to take me in doesn't make you jealous at all?"

My chest rises and falls rapidly, making it difficult to respond. Inside my stomach, a swirl of desire threatens to take my entire body into meltdown mode, warning me my next move is dangerous.

"Does me getting down on my knees begging to take the doctor in make you jealous?"

Aston presses against my ass, his hard cock only making me more turned on.

I'm no longer in denial; his shaft is *big*.

"Sweetheart, the only cock you'll be taking in is mine. You understand me?"

I purse my lips together, then tease, "And who says my body belongs to you?"

His lips angle into a wicked grin as his hand moves toward the hem of my dress. I suck in a breath, forcing myself not to combust as he nears the edge of my panties. *He wouldn't dare, not here inside his parents' home with his entire family sitting inside the dining room waiting for us.*

"The biggest mistake you can make, Miss Woods, is questioning my authority," he rumbles.

His hand moves in the opposite direction from my thighs to the belt holding my dress together. In a swift move, he tugs on the knot and exposes my bra and panties. A slight growl escapes his lips as his eyes burn with desire, admiring my body.

I follow his every move. The way his hand shifts to my neck to hold me in place, his other hand gliding back down into my white lace panties. The moment his fingers rub against my clit, I let out a moan.

"Be a good girl and keep very quiet," he warns, glancing briefly at the door. "We wouldn't want to be caught, now would we?"

I can't even think straight, let alone string together a sentence.

Ashton's fingers dive inside me, sending me into a delicious trance. I close my eyes, momentarily lost in his scent, allowing it to intoxicate my senses.

My body shivers in anticipation, and upon opening my eyes, I see the turmoil in his reflection as he slowly slides another finger inside of me.

Another moan accidentally passes my lips, forcing Aston to cover my mouth with his hand. "I warned you to be quiet." He pushes in more as I scream into his hand. My thoughts are incoherent, desperate to push the boundaries. "Good girl. Now look at me."

His tortured gaze is enough to push me over the edge.

I'm falling into a beautiful abyss, struggling to control my body. I buckle in his embrace, tightening my grip on his wrist while I ride out the most intense orgasm I have ever had.

It takes me several moments to gather my composure and control my ragged breaths, only for him to remove his fingers from inside me and turn me around so we're face-to-face.

He brings his fingers to his lips and sucks on them with ease. "You taste just how I imagined."

In a bold move, I take his fingers and bring them to my mouth, sucking on them as well. The scent of my arousal lingers between us, only making me want more.

With a roguish smirk, he rubs his thumb against my lip. "Next time, you'll be taking me into this beautiful mouth of yours."

What is he doing to me?

And the frightening thing is, I know there will be a next time.

CHAPTER 17

Aston

I *can smell her all over my hand.*

The temptation to slide my cock in and take her inside the bathroom is impossible to ignore, but I know it won't be long until someone comes looking for us. With every moan escaping her beautiful lips, I fight the urge to fuck her to oblivion.

Miss Woods is my target.

I want to own her here and now.

My hands instinctively cover her mouth to hide her delicious moaning, but all it does is send me into a frenzy. I thrust my fingers into her, groaning as they slide in so effortlessly. Her soaked pussy smothers my fingers, and inside my pants, I'm ready to fucking blow.

The unbearable pain of holding back is a whole other torture.

I control the moment, but the truth is—I am tormenting myself just as much.

Avoiding our reflection in the mirror is futile. I watch her body melt into me, and her tits bounce inside her white lace bra. All the while she rides my fingers until she loses control and comes all over them.

Then, I taste her.

And she tastes like *perfection*.

She brings my fingers to her lips and I watch her taste her own juices.

Fuck, I am on the verge of exploding right here and now!

Yet, the fear of being caught weighs heavily on my mind.

For now, I have to stop.

But I need this power trip. I need to be the only man she thinks of when her body is falling into an abyss and her pussy is throbbing with cum, dripping from the intensity.

The only voice in her head.

The only scent she can smell.

And I need this doctor douche gone for fucking good.

Everleigh exits the bathroom first, leaving me to gather myself and try to calm my cock, which feels beyond unbearable inside my pants. I pace up and down, but it doesn't seem to work.

Next, I try to splash cold water on my face, but not even that helps.

My phone pings, and in an effort to distract myself, I read the email. It doesn't take long for my anger to shift toward my father. The prick is trying to avoid the press by palming everything off on me. The media giants are hot on my heels, and avoidance will get me nowhere. I've spent the last year working my ass off to close essential deals, only for them to be jeopardized over *his* actions.

I exit the bathroom and head back to the dining room. Thankfully, the conversation has carried on to the wedding plans—anything to avoid talking business or Everleigh's so-called love life.

That was the straw that broke the camel's back.

And by that, I mean my patience.

Across the table, Everleigh avoids my gaze. Her cheeks are still flushed, making me hard beneath the table again.

Fuck my life—I need to get out of here and take her somewhere.

Damn, anywhere but here.

I bet her pussy will clench nicely against my cock. She's tight, and I got off on just how tight she was.

Viviana turns to face me, raising her brows. "You were gone a while."

I clear my throat. "A phone call."

"Still the same man I remember," Viviana scoffs with her glass of wine in hand. "All work, no play."

Inadvertently, my eyes wander across the table to meet Everleigh's. "I wouldn't say there's no play."

The little rise in the corner of Everleigh's mouth before she turns away purposely is enough for me to know she wants more.

And sweetheart, this is far from over.

"Madelina suggested we be each other's plus-one for the wedding." Viviana places her hand on mine. "What do you think?"

It takes seconds for Everleigh to snap her attention back onto me. Jealousy looks like perfection on her, but to keep things civil, I simply respond with, "We'll see."

After dessert is served, Myles's parents announce they're leaving. I shake Roland's hand politely, grateful the night is over. All I can think about is getting Everleigh out of here so I can own her body entirely. When Viviana lures me aside to suggest we return to her parents' ranch tonight, I tell her I'm busy.

Look, she was a decent fuck years ago. But from memory, I was drunk the times we had sex. We barely spent time together between her schedule and mine, even though our families labeled us as dating.

My response to her invitation doesn't sit well, especially since she glances at Everleigh and then back to me as if piecing the puzzle together. Before she can say another word, my father requests I join him inside his office.

For the first time in my life, I welcome my father's demand for my presence. However, knowing he will test my patience,

I grab a whiskey bottle from the drinks cart and pour myself a glass, downing it in one gulp.

I let out a rasp, then walk down the hall toward his office.

Once inside the dimly lit room, I close the door. As a child, I avoided coming in here at all costs. My father repeatedly warned my sister and me that this was *his* space. Nothing at all has changed. There's still the large wood-grain table with his old-school feather pen that was passed down from my great-grandfather. The smell of cigars lingers in the air and has seeped into the books lining the tall, dark brown shelves.

There are no photographs of us, just a picture of his prized possession—his Rolls-Royce.

I take a seat across the table, only for him to belittle me the moment our eyes meet. "Your lack of cooperation has jeopardized our plan."

"*Our* plan? You mean *your* plan."

"Now you listen to me . . ." He points his finger at me as his nostrils flare. "You play your damn cards right or else."

"Or else what?" I stand up, yelling back. "You need me. Without me, you couldn't pull off half your ridiculous stunts."

My father expels an arrogant laugh. "You think I need you?"

"Well, I'm the one having to speak to the media about this damn lawsuit. Who else is going to defend *your* actions and maintain the integrity of *your* company? As for Roland, you think he's going to allow Myles to sell you all this land after newspapers are calling you greedy? It's important to the Whitney family to keep things close, and yet here you are trying to buy this land to sell it off to wealthy people willing to pay stupid money just to have a town that is exclusive to billionaires. Since you're very out of touch with what is actually going on, you need *me* to bring you back to reality."

Across from me, my father juts his chin with a stiff smile. "Everyone is replaceable."

Fury twists inside of me. "Are you giving me an ultimatum?"

"I'm demanding you pay attention to my instructions, Aston," he answers in an arctic tone. "Once your sister is married, the land will be ours. If anyone can convince Myles and Madelina to sell, it will be you."

"What makes you think it will be that easy? I just told you, Roland made it clear everything would be passed on to his son and kept in the family."

My father's dismissive glance grates on my last nerve. "And his son is marrying my daughter. You think it's a coincidence they are getting married?"

I take a step back, fixating on his blank stare. "What did you do?"

He leans back comfortably in his leather chair. "Son, you still have much to learn about the game."

"It's not a game when Madelina is involved," I bellow, clenching my hands into fists. "What did you do?"

He continues to observe me with an arrogant smirk. "Roland invited us to join them at their ranch this weekend. I expect you to be there."

And with his phone in hand, he dials a number and requests I leave the room.

I storm out, fuming at the thought of him involving Madelina in his fucked-up game. As I walk past the dining room, I enter without thinking and grab the bottle of whiskey. This time, I don't pour a glass, I simply bring the bottle to my lips to down the hard liquor. An unflattering rumble escapes me as my mother watches on.

"Aston . . ." she calls softly.

"Don't start, Mother. I'm leaving."

With the bottle in my hand, I rush out the door only to hear footsteps follow me to the car. *Fuck, why won't everyone leave me alone?!*

"You're not driving," Everleigh calls out behind me.

I bow my head, refusing to answer. My hands grip the glass bottle like my entire life depends on it. "I need to get out of here," I hiss.

She snatches the keys from my hand, much to my annoyance. "Fine, I'll take you wherever you need to go."

My gaze flickers to hers. "You're not driving my car. Nobody drives my car."

"Then I guess you won't be going anywhere."

I lower my chin to my chest, letting out a huff. Everleigh moves to the driver's side while I climb into the passenger seat. God, everything about this feels wrong. It's almost like I have no power, sitting here like a fucking moron unable to drive my own car.

The loss of control prompts me to take another swig of the bottle as Everleigh attempts to insert the keys into the ignition but sees no ignition.

"Um . . ."

"Foot on the brake, stick out of gear, press this button." I exhale, then turn to her and question, "Do you know how to drive a stick?"

"Yes," she declares, rolling her eyes. "Can you trust me, please?"

"Fine."

The engine starts with a loud roar, a sound that always manages to calm me.

Everleigh does, in fact, know how to drive a stick.

And as the dark road greets us, I sink into my seat and continue to drink straight out of the bottle.

"What happened back there?" she asks, breaking the welcome silence.

"It's not worth talking about."

I hear her sigh. "Why do you let him get to you, Aston?"

My head shakes unwillingly as I stare out the window. "You have no idea who my father is."

"Maybe. But I know what I feel. And for as long as I've known your father, he has made me feel . . ." Everleigh pauses, then continues, "Uncomfortable."

"Among many things he makes a person feel," I mutter.

"We don't have to talk about it," she falters, quickly glancing at me, only to focus back on the road. "Unless, of course, you want to. No pressure."

I take another long drink, allowing the liquor to burn. "Then let's not."

"Okay, fine," she answers. "Where do you want me to take you?"

"Your place," I tell her.

"My place?"

"Yes. Is that a problem?"

"I'll make a deal with you. Stop drinking, and you can come back to my place. Otherwise, I will dump you on the side of the road right here in the pitch black and let a bear feast on your drunk ass."

I hand the bottle to her, and she places it in the middle console. "Good boy. Now, don't throw up on me, because I'm a secondary vomiter."

The Bluetooth sounds with an incoming call. My sister's name flashes on the screen as I reach over to decline the call, but Everleigh pushes my hand away to hit answer.

"Maddy, it's me," she says, twisting her mouth. "I'm driving Aston's car."

Madelina sighs over the speaker. "Is everything okay? I came back into the room, and you guys were gone. What did Dad say, Aston?"

"It's not your problem," I tell her.

"Well, Dad is drinking again, and Mom is packing a bag to stay in a hotel." Madelina sounds worried. "I'll stay here to make sure he's okay."

"I'm coming back home, Madelina." I twist to look at Everleigh but press end to terminate the call. "Turn around, we're going back."

"You want to go back?"

A heavy weight sits in the pit of my stomach. "My mother and sister need me."

Reality has pulled me out of my selfish existence once again.

The silence in the car allows me to overthink, so by the time we get back to the house, the darkness reminds me of what my life has become.

The *knight in shining armor* for all the wrong fucking reasons.

Everleigh turns the engine off and then places her hand on mine. "Do you want me to go in with you?"

"No, I will take it from here."

"Okay," she whispers. "I'll call someone to pick me up—"

"Take my car," I interrupt, quick to unfasten my seat belt. "I don't want you getting into some car with a stranger."

"There's no Ubers or cabs out here. I would have called a friend who I trust."

I tilt my head, annoyed. "A doctor friend?"

Everleigh's penetrating gaze does something I can't explain. As I stare into the pools of her honey-brown eyes, even in the dark, they ignite something inside me.

"No more games, Aston. Just go inside and deal with what you need to." She sighs, then reaches out to caress my cheek. "You know where to find me if you need me."

Her touch terrifies me.

I pull her hand away, then say, "I'll call you."

After exiting the car and taking a few steps, I hear her drive off.

There are more significant crosses to bear right now.

And when my father has taken to the bottle, his only target is my mother. I've heard it repeatedly, the callous words he throws in her face like she owes him her life.

I enter the house and hear him yelling.

A weight sits inside my chest when I see Madelina seated on the sofa, holding back her tears.

As for my mother—she's left once again.

So, for the sake of my sister's emotional state, I go on the hunt for my father and remind myself the only person I will allow him to hurt is *me*.

CHAPTER 18

Eva

Rain is pouring outside on this cold winter morning, forcing patrons to stay inside the café longer than usual.

I'm so ready for spring.

The dark clouds and sound of raindrops tapping against the glass windows do nothing to improve my already somber mood. It feels like this season has dragged on longer than usual, and I ache for the days when the sun kisses my pale skin.

Billie is busy waiting tables as I work the espresso machine behind the counter. We often swap, depending on how busy we are. Billie has the patience for customers, and I have the patience for what can often be a temperamental machine.

Our regulars sit at their usual tables, savoring their morning coffee and donuts. Then, there are the remote workers—laptops open, brows furrowed in concentration as they stretch a single coffee over three hours, monopolizing a full table. I can't stand them.

Some are college students. They spend more on treats than the remote workers, even though most are cash poor. We often catch them taking pictures of their food and posting them to their socials while busying themselves on their phones over what I assume is meant to be a study period.

"That guy over there didn't even want coffee," Billie huffs, placing the tablet down on the counter beside me. "He wants fricking tap water."

I shake my head, lips pressed together. "How do we bring in customers who actually want to eat? Maybe Maddy is right. I should look into hiring a marketing team or something." I know signs about table occupancy are necessary, but the last thing I want is to drive people away. It feels like a no-win situation.

It's not like the café isn't doing well—we're in the black. But we need something to boost profits. The locals love us, sure, but that only goes so far when the tourist season slows down. If I did want to open another café one day, we would need to bring in more business, not to mention more staff.

Billie shrugs. "Maybe some marketing might work . . . it's just the winter lull. When spring is here, people start traveling through town again."

My shoulders slump as I clean out the filter in the machine. Billie is an optimist, the exact opposite of me. I'm not sure when I became so cynical, or perhaps the appropriate word would be *moody.*

"You have a point." I slip my hand into my pocket, fingers brushing against Aston's keys. I pull them out, and immediately, Billie's eyes catch the emblem on the key.

He hasn't picked them up, called, or texted to ask for them back. I considered reaching out, but after last night, I don't know what to think.

Things took a turn.

I wasn't expecting to be pulled into their family drama; not only that, I wasn't expecting to see this other side of Aston. Something got into him, and it wasn't pleasant. He was angry and hurting over what can only be described as an argument with his father. I wish he would have opened up to me, maybe he would have calmed down. But the moment I offered to stay with him, he shut me out and that was that.

"Whoa, you have some explaining to do." Billie's eyes widen.

"Did the hot older brother stay over? It's his keys, right? Wait, what about the doctor? Are you playing the field?"

I try to hush her, since her voice travels and all the questions give me a headache. *So does the lack of sex.* "No. Nothing of the sort. It was a long night, and something happened, but it's not what you think."

"Okay, sure. So, I should ignore what I think?"

"Yes! We did *not* have sex."

"With who, though?"

"With Aston!" I yell out unexpectedly.

A few people turn, forcing me to smile and pretend I didn't yell out my best friend's older brother's name. "Look, there's a lot at stake. So it wouldn't be a good idea even if I wanted to, which I don't. You don't mix best friends and their older brothers with pleasure."

Billie removes a plate from the stack of clean ones to serve three jelly-filled sugarcoated donuts to table five. "He certainly seems to rile a reaction from you."

"He does," I admit, remembering our encounter in the bathroom. "But, we're all adults. Once this wedding ends, he'll be long gone back to the city, and I'll be here."

"With the hot doctor . . ." Billie trails off with a knowing grin.

Right on cue, Maddy walks in, looking a bit frazzled. "Aston sent me to pick up his keys for him," she says, barely meeting my gaze.

I hand her the keys, noticing her tension. "You all right?"

She lets out a sigh, fiddling with the key ring. "I'm fine. Just . . . meeting Georgina for tea. *Again.*"

I raise an eyebrow, unable to hide a smirk. "A tea party? Who are you, Alice in Wonderland? Isn't that her second one this week?"

"Third, and the Mad Hatter at this point," Maddy mutters, rolling her eyes. "She's gone full mother-of-the-groom mode. Myles is her only kid, and she's milking it for all it's worth."

I chuckle. "And you're the perfect future daughter-in-law, smiling through it all."

Maddy laughs, but there's a weariness in it. "I try, but she's pushing every button. I mean, who needs three tea parties to plan a wedding?"

"Maybe she's just excited." I try to keep a straight face, but Maddy sees right through me.

"Excited? *Excited?* Eva, she has this massive binder for table placements alone."

"Sounds like you're in for quite the ride," I say, shaking my head. "If you need a break, you know where to find me."

"Trust me, I'll take you up on that." She sighs, clutching Aston's keys like they're the lifeline she really came for.

For the rest of the week, I busy myself with wedding preparations.

The flowers take forever, but I manage to order everything from the bouquets to the arrangements for the ceremony and reception.

Billie offered to bake the cake, and given that she's great with desserts, I took her up on the offer with Maddy's approval. Then, the pastry chef at the Grand Honey Lodge insisted he bake the cake and threw a tantrum when Maddy mentioned Billie making the cake. What we both didn't know was that Georgina had already discussed it with him. Honestly, it wasn't worth the stress, so I encouraged Maddy to just let him do it to avoid any further conflict.

Now, with those details sorted, the next major item on the list is dress shopping—a task I dread more than anything. It's not that I dislike wearing a dress—it's just that once I find one, I prefer to stick to it. The thought of trying on endless gowns and parading in front of others under the unforgiving lights of a dress shop makes me want to crawl into a hole and hibernate until it's all over.

But Maddy is my best friend, and as her maid of honor, I need to be present with a smile on my face.

The wedding dress shop is about forty-five minutes away, two towns over. It's owned by a friend of Georgina's—apparently, they're bridge partners. Of course, that connection only adds another layer of pressure to this whole dress-shopping ordeal.

We take a seat on the white bouclé sofas as an assistant serves us champagne. Aside from Georgina and Patricia, two of Myles's cousins join us. One of them being Ramona.

The owner, Helena, takes dresses to the back changing room for Maddy to try on. I know exactly what she wants and doesn't want, so hopefully, she will find the dress here because I have checked, and Helena can make alterations, even given the short notice.

We chat among ourselves, mainly about dresses and fabrics. It's all civil until Georgina, out of nowhere, says, "So, Patricia, I hear your son is single. Quite the handsome boy."

"I'm not quite sure, Georgina. My son likes to keep his private life private."

I pretend to be busy on my phone but listen attentively to this conversation. Considering I haven't heard from Aston for almost a week, I'd also like to know what's going on.

"Ramona, dear," Georgina calls out softly. "Perhaps the two of you should have dinner. You're not getting any younger, my love."

Ramona flattens her lips, then sighs. "I could reach out, I guess."

"Why not do it now?" I say loudly, the sarcasm lingering in the air. "I'm sure he will agree to dinner. He is single and ready to mingle."

I don't know where that came from, but I want her to text him to see if he responds.

"You think I should do it now?" Ramona asks, reluctance clear in her voice. Her fingers fidget with the edge of her sleeve, twisting the fabric nervously. "At the lunch, he seemed preoccupied."

"Seize the day," I tell her before releasing a breath. "If you're nervous, I'll do it for you. Pass me your phone."

Surprisingly, Ramona hands me her phone. Quickly, I type a message but realize that if I want him to respond, it can't be too needy, or he'll get spooked. It's not like I want him to go on a date with Ramona. Actually, that thought makes my stomach turn.

But I commit to the damn challenge like a child.

"How about this . . ." I announce while typing. "Hey, would you like to catch up for dinner or drinks? Myles's mother suggested I text you. Kisses, Ramona."

"*Kisses?* Don't you think that's a bit . . . *forward*?"

I shake my head. "Forward is you wanting to go home with him at lunch last week. This is fine."

Ramona's eyes widen, but no one else appears to hear as the curtain to the dressing room opens. Maddy carefully walks out in a sweetheart pleated-satin corset dress with a chapel train.

"Oh, Maddy," I gush, choking on my words. "You look stunning."

Patricia nods with approval, but Georgina looks less than pleased.

"Maddy, darling. Wouldn't a covered neckline be more appropriate?"

Maddy glances at me, pleading with her eyes for me to say something.

I stand, fixing the skirt, and say, "I think this dress is beautiful. After all, Maddy is the bride, so the decision is *all* hers."

Patricia tilts her head but remains quiet, observing her daughter. "You look gorgeous. However, I guess it wouldn't hurt to try on something with a covered neckline. A bit of lace can look elegant."

I shrug at Maddy, and with a heavy sigh, she agrees to head back to the changing room to try on another dress. Patricia follows her with a few of her own choices for Maddy to try on.

This happens another five times.

I've already drunk three glasses of champagne, so I can ignore the forced conversations with both mothers.

As for Aston, he hasn't responded. I feel bad for Ramona, who has also drunk several glasses. Between the two of us, this *won't* end well. Thankfully, Maddy drove, so technically, I could get blind drunk if needed.

Maddy walks out again, but this time—she is glowing.

I take a deep breath, covering my mouth, holding back the tears I so desperately want to cry from seeing her in the most *perfect* dress. The sheer bodice creates a semi-off-the-shoulder illusion with nude tulle and floating tattoo lace. It's not as covered up as Georgina would like, but it's a great compromise, in my opinion.

The floating lace continues over the long sleeves, with the back of the dress open. Unlike some of the other designs, this dress hugs Maddy's curves. The most stunning piece of the dress is the extra-long scalloped train made with corded lace.

"This is the one," Maddy whispers, gazing at me with dancing eyes. "It feels perfect."

I jump up, wrapping my arms around her in a tight embrace. "It's so you."

"It is me." Maddy pulls back with a grin.

As if the universe knew, the dress fits Maddy like a glove, needing minimal alterations. This is music to our ears given that the wedding isn't far away. I reach for the tag on the dress, almost fainting from the hefty price. With $100,000 I could open another *two* cafés.

With the gown now chosen, next up are the bridesmaid dresses.

Maddy chooses two different styles so as not to overwhelm us. The three of us have agreed to try on both of them to see which one suits us better. The first is beautiful, suiting each one of our body types. The dress has a draped cowl neckline and a rich satin back.

"The color is berry hue," the sales assistant informs us.

The second dress is lovely, too, with its intricate lace and flattering fit, but there's no denying the first one steals the show. It has that perfect mix of elegance and charm.

Helena and her assistant crouch beside me, carefully pinning the fabric in place, murmuring about adjustments and tailoring as they work.

Maddy leans over, scrolling through photos on her phone to show us potential hairstyles, her excitement bubbling over. She tilts the screen toward me, displaying an elegant updo wrapped in tiny pearls. It's no surprise Maddy is enjoying this fitting, since costumes and fancy dresses are her thing. I'm just glad she's finally able to be in the moment. All week she's been stressed with changes to the wedding plans.

Just then, Ramona's phone pings from the chair. The sound cuts through our conversation, making us all glance over.

"What's going on?" Maddy questions.

My lips press into a grimace before I blurt out, "Ramona asked your brother out to dinner."

Ramona's eyes widen in surprise. "Thanks a lot. And for the record, his message says he's seeing someone."

My body freezes, my focus shifted to my flipping stomach.

"Really? And besides, Mom told me in the changing room *you* texted him." Maddy's mouth slackens, and then she continues, "He's been in a horrible mood this week. I swear, he has man periods. If he's seeing someone, wouldn't he be getting laid and, therefore, be in a better mood?"

"Madelina," her mother snaps. "We do *not* discuss such matters in public."

"C'mon, Mom." Maddy rolls her eyes. "Your son is the biggest player there is. Not only does he not do relationships, he has this rule where no woman is allowed to stay over. He does the deed and sends them on their merry way."

Her mother closes her eyes as if trying to unhear Maddy's

words. A deep sigh escapes her, and she pinches the bridge of her nose, looking torn between disbelief and disappointment.

Meanwhile, I feel like the biggest fool for letting Aston get to me, or more so, for allowing him to give me the best orgasm of my life inside their guest bathroom.

I reach out, grabbing another glass of champagne.

Helena warns me not to get any on the dress, but at this point, I need to forget about Aston. But Maddy doesn't shut up.

"Aston will never settle down. He's never even been in love," Maddy continues with her rambling. "In high school, he slept with two best friends, and they both lost their virginity to him that night."

I gasp. "I thought that was a fake rumor!"

A satisfied smile graces Maddy's lips. "Nope, just my big brother."

"Madelina, *enough*. Your brother is a hard worker and does more than you'll ever know for this family. If he chooses to live his life like this, then so be it." Patricia stands to grab her purse. "Ladies, I have a dinner later and must prepare."

Georgina also leaves but doesn't give her opinion on Aston's personal life. As for us girls, we sit on the chairs, exhausted from the day.

"Maybe I dodged a bullet not dating your brother." Ramona sighs dejectedly. "He's really handsome. I mean, drop-dead-gorgeous handsome. Did you know he doesn't even have social media? I tried to stalk him, but instead, I found all these images of him on this social page. College girls run these accounts that have vision boards with him all over them. He's been seen on red carpets for different galas and once his photo leaked, girls from NYU went nuts."

"Wow!" I gasp, surprised by this revelation. "That's some next-level stalking."

"Oh yeah." Ramona nods, continuing with, "They see him around Manhattan, and they call it suit porn."

I raise my brow. "Suit porn?"

"Okay, enough." Maddy rises from the chair. "We are talking about my brother. If you bring up his penis size, you're dead to me."

❧

On the car ride home, I fall quiet. I lost count of how many glasses of champagne I consumed, but things started to blur, given I hadn't eaten.

Maddy receives a call from Myles, so I use the time to close my eyes and fall asleep.

We're outside my apartment when I wake, and the sky has turned dark.

Maddy puts the car in park and turns off the engine. "Do you think there is more to love than just that feeling?"

I shake my head to wake myself up. My head is throbbing, but I try my best to come up with a response. "What do you mean?"

"I mean . . . I look at couples who have been married for like fifty years. There has to be more to it, right? Like, is love enough?"

"I think love has different elements and layers," I begin. Then release a shallow sigh before saying, "It's companionship, equality, respect, and connection. When you're old, sex isn't going to be what keeps you together. Does that make sense?"

"Yeah, marry your best friend," she murmurs, dropping her gaze to her lap. "My parents are not an example of a good marriage."

I don't want to agree with her, but it is the truth. Mr. and Mrs. Beaumont are anything but loving toward each other. Again, I have no idea why they don't just call it quits. Their kids are grown, so it's not like divorce would be a big deal.

"Break the cycle, Maddy. Just because they choose to be miserable doesn't mean you have to."

Maddy nods. "It's been a long day."

"It certainly has. But your dress is amazing, and that's another thing checked off your list."

She laughs. "You mean *our* list?"

"Right, *our* list." I laugh a little too obnoxiously. "Thanks for reminding me." I let out a hiccup.

"And you're buzzed." Maddy falls into a fit of laughter again. "Will you be okay? I need to meet Myles for dinner. I kind of want to bail, but we haven't spent much time together with everything going on, so I feel bad."

"And hot pre-wedding sex?"

"I told you, we're holding off."

"Bummer," I complain, then open the door of the car. "I'll be fine. Have fun at dinner."

Maddy drives off by the time I reach my door. I take a quick shower inside my apartment and throw on some sweats with a tank top. Considering it's cold outside, my body is overheating like I've run a marathon.

The headache refuses to dissipate, and after searching my cupboards for medication, I come up empty-handed. I let out a groan, grabbing my beanie and a thick coat to wear over my tank.

My sneakers sit at the door, so I stop to put them on, catching a glimpse of myself in the mirror before pulling on my coat. "Son of a bitch," I bark upon noticing my nipples stand out beneath my white tank. Walking back to my bedroom to find a bra is too much effort, so I button up my coat to cover the ladies.

No one has to know.

The grocery store is a block from my place, and at this hour, it's blissfully quiet—most people are home by now, settling in for dinner. The fluorescent lights hum softly overhead, casting a cool glow over the empty aisles as I grab the essentials and toss them into the basket. The faint smell of freshly baked bread lingers in the air as I make my way through the store. When I reach the self-checkout, the silence is comforting, broken only by the gentle beeps as I scan each item—the sound oddly soothing.

I exit the grocery store and step outside into the cold, only to bump into another body.

"Oh my God. I'm so sorry!"

"Eva?" the voice says, forcing me to glance up. Marco's sheepish grin catches my attention. "Well, this is a pleasant surprise."

I hug my grocery bag close to my body. "You look well. And before you think it, I look like crap. It's been one hell of a week."

Marco chuckles, his handsome smile lightening my mood. "Is everything okay?"

"I guess. I've been busy planning this wedding, which has been harder than I thought. Today, I spent six whole hours watching Maddy try on dresses. By the end of it, I was so wasted on champagne that I'm now expecting the worst hangover."

"Ah, hence the Tylenol and"—he reaches for my grocery bag—"burritos?"

"The cure to any hangover," I reply with a small laugh, then sigh. "I'm sorry I haven't called."

"I'm sorry I haven't called either. There's a new strain of flu going around, so the clinic has been going nonstop."

"So I've heard. Chloe wasn't feeling well yesterday, so I sent her home. The last thing Billie and I need is to catch a virus. I'm so ready for winter to be over."

"If I had a dollar for every time I've heard that this week."

I hesitate, then ask, "Apart from that, you've been well?"

Marco drops his head, only to raise it moments later. "I would be better if we actually went on a proper date, uninterrupted."

A soft sigh escapes me, the guilt weighing heavily on my shoulders. There's no doubt in my mind Marco is a good man who would treat me the way I deserve to be treated.

But this is not fair to him.

Not when my body is craving someone else.

"I'm sorry, Marco. Things have just been—"

"It's okay." Marco offers a warm smile. "I should probably go, but just for the record, you look beautiful tonight, Eva. You always do."

Marco leans in, kissing me on the cheek, lingering as his lips touch my cold skin.

As he pulls away, I allow myself to gaze into his eyes, only to be distracted by the roar of an engine as a familiar gray Porsche pulls up to the curb.

It takes only a few seconds for the door to slam and Aston to appear. He's dressed in a navy suit with a tie, looking deliciously sexy. *God, now I get the whole suit porn thing.*

I shake my head, snapping myself out of this daze. "What are you doing here?" I ask, annoyed.

"What am *I* doing here?" he repeats, moving closer to me.

Marco takes a step back, his face clouding with hurt. "I didn't realize you were together."

"We're not together, Marco. Far from it."

"I think I'll just leave," he says, eyeing Aston.

Aston doesn't breathe a word, but I know his smug ass is relishing in the fact that he has gotten his way. With a half-smile, Marco turns his back and walks into the grocery store.

The moment the automatic doors close, I snap my attention back to Aston.

"God, Aston. You haven't spoken to me for a week. Not even a text. According to Maddy, you bailed and went back to the city. So, as far as I'm concerned, you're bored playing your game with me, which means I am free to do whatever the hell I want."

"Get in the car," he demands.

"No."

"I said . . . get in the car, Everleigh. Stop being a pain in my ass."

"And I said . . . *no!*" I raise my voice. "Oh, and by the way, aren't you involved with someone? It's bad enough you hurt Ramona's feelings."

His eyes fire back with frustration. "Get. In. The. Car."

"I live a block away, asshole. I am *not* getting in your car."
I turn my back and begin walking, refusing to turn around. I
expect to hear the sound of his engine revving, but instead all I
hear is silence.

My door is only a few feet away as I turn the corner. I retrieve
my keys from my pocket and open the door, only to smell his
scent before he says a word.

There's no turning back now.

Aston followed me here.

And the scary part is—part of me wanted him to follow me.

It's no longer about the cat chasing the mouse.

It's the mouse running with the thrill of being *caught*.

CHAPTER 19

Aston

The night of the dinner ended just as I anticipated. My father drank himself into a stupor while calling me the biggest disappointment of his life. It's nothing new, and frankly, I can take his drunken slurs. It's better me than Mom or Madelina.

He knew better than to show his face the following day. Mom stayed at the hotel, and he drove to Boston for a few days. God knows what business he had there, and I did not care to ask. It made sense to drive back to the city, given that remote work is much more complex than I thought, and Madelina was kind enough to fetch my keys from Everleigh so I could drive back.

And that in itself is a whole other mind-fuck.

Everleigh evoked something inside of me, something I can't explain.

No one, and I mean no one, drives my car.

But it isn't the car that made me question everything, far from it. It's how she made me feel that night. I lost control inside that bathroom, and afterward, she saw a side of me I wish she hadn't. The moment her hand caressed my cheek, I pulled away. Scared of how a simple touch made me feel like I deserved better.

Hence my need to escape to Manhattan and back to where I thrive on my own.

Will sits across from me inside the boardroom after everyone leaves the room.

"What the hell was that?" he blurts out.

It was five hours of torture listening to plans of how we *could* come out on top after my father single-handedly destroyed my hard work from the past year. The Beaumont Group is known for its property investments, and my father's ego is causing our stakeholders to lose confidence in us. This *panic plan* is not how I intended to spend the last five hours.

"That is the result of my father giving zero fucks," I answer coldly.

I push the chair back and stand, facing the window. With my arms crossed, I give myself a much-needed moment to think.

"We need to come up with a game plan. Strategize against these old fuckers because this will *not* happen. You worked your ass off the last year, and those acquisitions will go ahead, mark my words," Will responds sternly. "Your father has officially gone mad."

"He certainly has," I mumble, gazing at the tall buildings surrounding us. "I need some time to think about how to handle this."

"But time is of the essence," Will reminds me. "Look, I know you have your sister's wedding, but do you really need to go back to Cinnamon Springs?"

"Yes, eventually. There's other business I need to take care of."

Will remains silent behind me, but then he can't resist when I don't offer. "What other business?"

I turn around. "Just someone."

"Someone?" Will grins annoyingly, only to shake his head. "Are you getting laid in your small town?"

My lips press together into a grimace, refusing to answer his question. Technically, I am *not* getting laid, despite thinking about how sweet Everleigh would be to fuck. I've laid in bed every single night since I felt her explode all over my fingers, thinking about ways to forget it happened so I can move on with my life.

"I am not," I state simply. "Things have gotten a little complicated with someone from the past."

Will nods with an arrogant smirk. "I know that look, buddy. Been there, and hey, look at me now."

My lips curve. "You're married to the ball and chain?"

"Hush. You let Amelia hear you say that, and you'll wish you'd never said a word." Will grabs his phone and slides it into his pocket. "Let's sort out this shit here so you can go back to your small town and get laid by whoever it is you can't stop obsessing over."

"I don't obsess over a woman." I'm quick to set him straight, clearing my throat and fixing my cuff links. "That's not my style."

Will rests his hand on my shoulder. "It may not be your style, but with the right woman, you'll have no control. Mark my words, Beaumont."

The week doesn't get any better. I fly to DC to meet with an investor to ensure we still have them on board despite the legal proceedings surrounding my father. Our attorneys are working around the clock, but assure me this will be settled in the next few weeks, and business will resume as usual. I crave normalcy, wishing I could sleep at night without all this grief weighing on me. I'm surviving on caffeine and adrenaline to get me through the back-to-back meetings. It's taking its toll on me, but I know I can't slow down. The moment I slow down will be the moment the wheels come off the tracks, and my father will have another thing to hold over my head.

I sit in another meeting, wired on my third espresso of the day. A text message from Ramona, oddly, finds its way to me. The random question surprises me, since I forgot all about Ramona. I ignore the message, not wanting to meet for dinner. Aside from the fact that I couldn't think of anything worse, I'm in the city with far too much work on my plate.

Then, my phone pings again.

Little Brat

> BTW, Everleigh made Ramona text you.
> Please don't sleep with her then ghost. This
> wedding is already stressful enough.

The text catches my attention. It makes no sense that she would encourage me to date another woman unless, of course, Everleigh wants to date someone else.

That thought pushes me into action.

I need to be back in Cinnamon Springs.

"Gentlemen, I need to be somewhere important."

Will observes me with a smug expression. As for Lex Edwards, his father-in-law, I expect him to question my decision to leave, but he glances at Will and something passes between them.

"We'll resume this via video chat tomorrow, shall we?" Lex says, keeping his expression neutral.

I nod, then leave the boardroom without another word. Instead of going to my penthouse to pack a bag, I drive straight out of the city and onto the parkway.

The open road gives me too much time to think, so I put my foot on the gas, speeding through the mountains until the town's lights appear before me. Night has fallen, and despite my reluctance to return, I'll admit there's something about being here that gives me a sense of peace.

I head straight to Everleigh's apartment without stopping at home first. If she's not there, I'll wait for as long as needed.

I drive down Main Street without thinking, focusing only on two people standing outside the grocery store—Everleigh, laughing with the doctor.

My hands grip the steering wheel, slamming my foot on the brake to park the car in front of them. Everleigh turns and presses her lips together in a grimace.

What the hell is she thinking?

Anger spikes through me as I exit the car to confront her. Instead of looking surprised, she pinches her mouth with a stiff stance, and questions, "What are you doing here?"

It's evident my absence has made her look elsewhere, which is why she so easily pushed Ramona to text me. I shift my gaze from Everleigh to her doctor friend, still unable to control the fury springing to life as my mind conjures up all these scenarios.

The thought of him touching her . . .

The thought of him being *inside* her . . .

Everleigh doesn't hold back her feelings, once again losing her shit like I'm the one doing something wrong. She's angry, insisting I leave her alone.

But that only makes me want her more, so I follow her all the way to her door despite her warning me to back the hell off.

Hastily, she turns to face me with a frown. "Why do you insist on making my life so miserable?"

Before I can respond, she swiftly turns around to enter her apartment.

I follow her inside without an invitation as she throws her keys onto the nightstand and then removes her wool coat in a mad rush. Upon placing her coat on the rack, she mutters, "Your new girlfriend won't be happy you're stalking me."

Beneath the ivory coat, she wears a ribbed white tank. My body instantly reacts to the lack of undergarments.

Fuck, she's wearing no bra!

And her nipples are . . . are . . . taunting me.

I bite down on my lip, but then the doctor circles back in my mind. *Did she intend to hook up with him, which is why she's basically going commando?*

I'm unable to turn away, staring at her breasts with a stir inside my pants. They're perfect. Nice, perky, and demanding to be sucked between my lips.

"Okay, great, now you're not even paying attention to me . . ." She trails off, only to glance down to see what I'm looking at.

Panicked, she quickly covers her chest by folding her arms, and at the same time, her cheeks turn bright red. "I was getting Tylenol for a headache and couldn't be bothered getting changed, okay? A headache you don't seem to be helping."

"And the doctor?"

"I ran into him." She throws her arms in the air again, only to remember her bare chest, covering it up immediately. "Anyways, what does it matter? You're seeing someone, right? It's why you rejected Ramona, which is so not cool."

I take a step forward, closing the distance between us. It's too easy to hold her gaze and watch her panic. "Tell me, Everleigh. Why did you make her text me?"

Like a frightened little mouse, she inches her way back to the wall. "Who said I made her text you?"

"A birdie."

"I have no idea who would have said that. Myles's mother said you were a very handsome man and that Ramona should date you. That's all that happened."

"Interesting," I murmur, placing my hand against the wall to stop her from running. "It's nice for an old lady to admire my handsome looks."

"Yeah, well . . . that's what happened," she barely manages to say.

I run my thumb against her bottom lip, observing her breathing as it falters. "Is that all that happened? You didn't take Ramona's phone and text me, asking me out to dinner?"

Her eyes are firm on mine. The flush of her cheeks makes me desperate to remove all her clothes and taste every inch of her delectable body.

But I hold back.

Teasing her is much more fun.

"So what if I did?" she admits, but her eyes soften. "You're seeing someone."

I can't look away. This hold she has over me drives me to the brink of insanity. I tell myself to control my actions, but the longer I stare into her honey-brown eyes, the more control I begin to lose.

"Am I, Everleigh?"

She reaches out and grabs my shirt, pulling me close, and our mouths crash into a deep kiss. The warm sensation spreads throughout my body and straight to my goddamn dick at the taste of her soft, supple lips.

Just like I remember from all those years ago.

Inside the hallway, we kiss feverishly as I push her against the wall, lifting her up so her thighs wrap around my waist. I press into her to ease the throb in my pants, losing myself to the taste of her lips and barely coming up for air until she pulls back, slightly out of breath.

"Aston," she murmurs as I bury myself in her neck, spreading kisses on her heated skin. "We can't do this. Maddy—"

I pull back, gazing intensely. "Even more reason why we will. You think my sister is going to stop me?"

Everleigh catches her breath, staring deep into my eyes. "But . . . you're off-limits. I can't betray Maddy. If she knew we kissed years ago and I kept it from her all this time, let alone finds out we've, you know, fooled around, it won't end well. You know how sensitive she is about feeling betrayed."

"Madelina doesn't need to find out," I state firmly. "It'll be our little secret. Besides, we're adults. What I do is none of her business."

"It is her business if you're doing her best friend." Everleigh gasps. "I don't want to lie to her."

"You're not lying if you don't say anything," I murmur.

The apartment is small enough for me to figure out the living room is a few steps away. With my hands lifting her body, I carry Everleigh to somewhere more comfortable, refusing to pull my mouth away from hers.

Our kisses deepen, soft moans escaping her beautiful lips as we come up for air, breathless, with our attention anchored on each other. I want nothing more than to own her entirely, but I savor the moment until I'm sitting on the sofa. Without a second thought, I pull her down so she's straddling me.

The light coming from the hallway filters through to the living room, enough so I can see her clearly. Even in the dark, her beauty radiates, and all I want is to slide myself inside her and watch her come on top of me.

My hands rest on her hips, but the urge is too strong to fight. Slowly, I lift the bottom of her tank and pull it over her head, exposing her tits.

Fuck, they're perfect.

I grab her hips again, pressing down to alleviate the pressure in my pants. Everleigh's weighted gaze falls upon my lips, hungry and impatient, while her chest rises and falls. I beg myself not to hurt her, but the animalistic side of me wants to ravage her.

My mouth moistens as I cup her tits in my hands, caressing them with a groan passing through my lips. At a teasingly slow pace, I wrap my tongue around them and watch her crumble.

"Tell me to stop again," I murmur.

I need to hear her beg for it.

Her lips crash to mine with urgency, almost as if she won't allow me to stop. My tongue aches to explore all of her and taste her sweet wet pussy, but I pull back slightly.

"Answer me, Everleigh."

Her soft moans escape, but she doesn't answer. Instead, she climbs off and stands before me, eyeing me with a lick of her lips.

I wait with bated breath.

Slowly, she gets down on her knees, positioning herself in front of me.

Fuck.

Zero chance of stopping.

She reaches out and toys with my belt, her hair sliding across her shoulder and exposing her neck. Her skin, so delicate and pure, taunts me, making it hard for me to control my urges.

My muscles tense as my heart beats strongly, causing me to hold my breath while waiting in anticipation. With the pull of my belt, Everleigh unzips my pants until my boxers are visible.

I unbutton my shirt, exposing my chest, only for her to pull my boxers down, allowing my cock to spring free.

Her eyes widen. She gulps, then whispers, "You're so . . . so . . . hard."

There isn't a second to respond as she takes me deep into her mouth.

A groan escapes me as I watch her wrap her tongue around my shaft to take me all in. Saliva builds around her mouth, and the delicious sounds make me clench because I'm ready to fucking explode.

Just as I'm about to remove her sweats and make her sit on top of me like a good cowgirl, a knock on the door startles us.

"Fuck!" Everleigh pants, pulling back in panic. "Um . . . who is it?"

"It's Maddy. Hurry up, I really need to pee."

Her mouth falls open as she stands in a mad rush. Beside us on the sofa, there's a dark sweater that she reaches out for to put on before she says, "Oh my God. You need to get out of here."

"I can't get out of here," I inform her while sliding my cock back into my boxers, zipping my pants carefully. "Who do you think I am, Spider-Man?"

When I'm done with my pants, she reaches for my arm, pushing me to the bathroom, eyes wide with fear. "Hide in there."

"I'm not hiding in there. Relax, Madelina won't suspect anything. We'll just say we were discussing the wedding."

"Aston," she begs.

"Answer the door, Everleigh," I demand again, annoyed my sister has cockblocked the night.

Everleigh turns on the light and runs to the door. "Sorry, I just got home from the grocery store. Well, ran home because I was so cold."

Madelina's voice gets closer. "Is that why your cheeks are red?"

"Yes, have you ever run up my steps?" Everleigh questions.

"Uh, yes, I just did because I need to pee . . ." Madelina pauses, then glances behind Everleigh, frowning at the sight of me. "What are *you* doing here?"

"I was waiting for Everleigh," I lie, then smile forcefully. "We agreed to meet tomorrow to sort out the cars for the wedding, but I have a meeting, so I thought I'd drop by now to see if she could squeeze me in."

Madelina observes both of us, but given that she is my sister and I've known her my whole life, she doesn't suspect anything. The twinkle in her eye would suggest she thinks we're planning something special for her wedding. A surprise, as such.

Everleigh casually sits beside me, tucking her feet under her legs. "Yeah, I was at the grocery store with Marco."

Great! This is the one lie I don't want to get on board with.

Madelina claps her hands with excitement. "Wait, so hot doctor is back on?"

"Yes, it's back on." Everleigh forces a smile, then continues, "I was just telling Aston about my upcoming date."

I do everything to remain calm, sporting a blank face rather than exposing my jealousy. While I want to show Everleigh how I *really* feel about this, her pleas to keep this from my sister are in the back of my mind.

"Oh my goodness, I'm so excited," Madelina squeals annoyingly. "You're going to have the hottest sex ever. You think he will wear his white coat, and you'll do it on his desk?"

The muscles in my neck tighten as I mutter, "Don't you need to use the bathroom?"

"Oh, damn. Hold that thought."

Madelina rushes to the bathroom, leaving me alone with Everleigh. The apartment is small, with the bathroom only a few steps away.

"I had to lie," Everleigh whispers. "Don't give me that look."

I lean in close, holding her gaze with an intensity that makes her flinch. My voice drops to a low, commanding tone, each word measured and firm. "This isn't over." There's no room for argument, no softness in my expression. I am making it clear that whatever she thinks, I'll have the final say.

Everleigh holds my stare. "I never said it was."

I consider waiting this out until Madelina says, "Hey, can I crash here tonight? I could really use some girl time."

"Of course." Everleigh smiles, then turns her attention back to me. "I guess we'll meet tomorrow, then? Just let me know when you're free after work. I have a spare hour before my date with Marco."

The burning sensation inside my chest refuses to dissipate, even though her so-called date is fictitious. With a fixated stare, I nod. It's all I can do so my sister doesn't unravel the truth.

I step out of the apartment with a heavy weight on my shoulders. On my walk back to my car, which is still parked in front of the grocery store where I left it, the cold winter air awakens my senses.

One thing has become abundantly clear.

This is far from over.

CHAPTER 20

Eva

Maddy hugs the spare pillow as we lie in my bed watching *Gilmore Girls*.

It's our comfort show, where no thinking is required, and the fast-paced banter calms our chaotic minds. I've lost count of how many times we've binge-watched it.

"I just don't understand why you want the rich playboy. Everyone knows Logan will never settle down with one girl," Maddy says, eagerly starting our usual argument.

Team Jess or Team Logan.

Dean is not an option in either of our eyes.

"And you think Jess can settle down? His trauma is next level."

Maddy huffs. "He was willing to run away with Rory."

"And why should she give up all her dreams?" I argue, keeping my stance firm on the subject. "Just to run away with some bad boy wearing a leather jacket."

It's the same old argument, no matter how many times we've seen it. We both turn silent, focusing on the screen. Unlike Maddy, my head isn't completely here.

Not since Aston left.

I try hard not to think about our kiss, or should I say, kisses. And I'm definitely trying not to think about the way he lifted my tank top and devoured my breasts like a hungry beast deprived of food.

But most of all, I am especially trying not to think about his cock looking so delicious. He wasn't wrong when he said his car wasn't compensating for his goods. If anything, I am the loser who assumed he was not well-endowed.

Boy, was I so very *wrong*.

And it is perfect. How can a male organ be so perfect? I've slept with only a handful of guys, but let's just say there have been some questionable ones. One was crooked and another was skinny but super long. *Oh God, stop thinking about cocks.*

I glance over at my phone sitting on the nightstand. Even if I want to text Aston, I won't risk it with Maddy by my side. Lying here beside her, my guilt is already at an all-time high. So, it's a small lie I'm keeping from her. This won't go anywhere, so why should I mention it and add more to her already full plate?

Maddy lets out a yawn. "Are you waiting on a call from your hot doctor?"

"Or a text," I lie, then end up yawning, too. "Maybe he's super busy at the hospital."

My phone pings with a message from Aston.

Aston

We're far from over.

I press my lips together, holding back a smile as the words spread to every part of my body in a mad delight. With a deep breath, I control my need to text him back and place the phone on the nightstand, face down, on silent.

"What did he say?" Maddy questions in a tired voice.

"Um, nothing. Just that he'll call me tomorrow."

A thickness forms in my throat, prompting me to change the subject. I forgot to ask Maddy how her dinner with Myles was, so I ask now in an effort to distract her from my love life.

"It was fine. I guess Myles is overwhelmed with work, and his dad really wants him to take over the business."

I raise my brows. "Would that mean leaving Broadway?"

"I don't know what it means, to be honest. It's a bit of a sore topic, so I'm trying to stay out of it."

"Maddy," I begin softly. "You can't stay out of it if he's going to be your husband. Things will change. Myles's family will soon be your family, too."

"Oh, trust me, I know." She sighs, then turns to face me. "It just feels . . . complicated."

I move a loose strand of hair away from her face. "Complicated for now."

"What if it's complicated forever?"

"It's only complicated if you keep resisting the change. One thing at a time, okay? We need to get you to the altar first. Don't get caught up in all this business talk."

"It just feels like I'm losing myself to everyone else's wants. I was on a video chat with my team about a production later this year. We were discussing the costumes because it's a period drama, and you know how much I love that. In the middle of this, my phone is blowing up with Dad insisting I have a discussion with Myles about the future. How do I tell my father to kindly leave me alone when he's paying for the whole wedding? It makes me sound ungrateful."

"You pick your battles. Tell him your focus is on the wedding, which is just around the corner."

"You're right." She nods, then turns to lie on her back with her eyes on the television screen. "Is my brother being a dick or actually helping? You can tell me the truth."

My fingers twist the blanket as I clear my throat. "Um . . . a bit of both. You know him, controlling and busy with work."

"You'll tell me if he treats you like dirt, right?"

"Of course," I mumble, trying to keep a blank face. "I can

stand on my own. I'm a big girl now. Don't worry about your brother. I can handle him."

"Okay, the last thing I need is more stress on top of my ever-growing list of things stressing me out. I honestly don't think I've been this stressed in my entire life."

"It'll be over soon, and you know I'll help you with whatever you need."

Maddy turns over on her side, gazing at me. "What did I do to deserve a best friend like you?"

My lips curve upward, but my indiscretion brings me back to reality. If it were Marco I fooled around with and not Aston, I'd be sharing all the sordid details. Instead, I'm hiding this secret just to protect my best friend. "Go to sleep, Maddy. You need to rest."

Maddy expels another yawn, which then prompts me. We fall into a vicious yawn cycle until I glance over and notice she's sleeping. With soft snores passing through her lips, I tug on the blanket to cover her body.

I watch her sleep, ignoring the guilt seeping into my conscience. Maddy is my ride-or-die, and Aston is someone who has piqued my sexual interest. That's where this needs to end.

Despite the yawns, I struggle to fall into a deep sleep, tossing and turning for most of the night. All the while, Maddy is fast asleep, so I try not to wake her with my constant movement.

I give up when the clock hits five, deciding to take a shower and head downstairs early. It takes me forever to decide what to wear, but I opt for jeans and a black knitted sweater with cherries all over it. Before I leave, I write a note on a piece of paper and stick it to Maddy's head, letting her know I'm downstairs in the café.

It's still dark outside when I turn on the lights in the kitchen. The café doesn't open until seven, leaving us time to let the dough rise before frying and icing. I throw all the ingredients into the mixer to prepare, but then my phone rings with Billie's name flashing on the screen.

I press answer, putting the call on speaker. "Hey. Everything okay?"

"Not really," Billie replies with a worried tone. "Mom's had a reaction to her new medication, and I need to take her to the ER."

My hand immediately reaches out for my phone to bring it closer. "Do whatever you need to do. I've got this covered. Will you be okay?"

"I have to be, don't I?"

I can hear the trepidation in her voice. With a heavy weight sitting on my chest, I take a seat on the stool and try to think of other ways to help Billie.

"I'll call Chloe to help out. Take as long as you need," I offer, feeling helpless.

Billie rushes to say goodbye so she can take her mom to the ER. I'm praying Marco is at the hospital and can maybe help her out. Given that we are a small town, the hospital isn't that big and sits on the border of where two other towns meet. I've visited only a few times, but each time, it was busy, as they are always short-staffed.

I take a breath, mentally preparing myself to work independently for the day. It's only after I mention Chloe on the call that I remember she drove into the city to take her sister to look at student housing near the NYU campus, since she's transferring there next semester.

Maddy enters the café just before seven, helping me out with the morning rush before leaving for a meeting with the caterer at nine. Before she leaves, I assure her I will be fine on my own, since our regulars have left, so there won't be too many customers in the store.

I've wiped down all the tables and restocked the glass cabinets with fresh donuts when a small bus stops at the front entrance. The doors of the bus open, and a bunch of elderly people slowly take each step off the bus and gather on the sidewalk. There are at least twenty of them, and they don't look like locals.

One lady doesn't take long to turn around and point to the café. They all nod in agreement, and before I have a chance to prepare anything, they enter one by one and occupy all the tables.

Great.

I lose track of time, taking orders and mustering up my patience when three customers list their dietary requirements. They felt it was important to inform me. Then they proceeded to tell me the whole story about their hip surgeries, which led to all these problems to begin with.

At the counter, I work the espresso machine, making sure I prepare each order correctly. God knows what will happen if the lady at table five accidentally drinks cow's milk instead of soy.

God does know, and so do you, after she gave you a descriptive breakdown of her bowel movements.

The machine expels a grinding sound while crushing the coffee beans. As I momentarily glance up, I see Aston standing at the counter wearing a charcoal-gray coat with a light blue dress shirt. The shirt is slightly unbuttoned, exposing a small amount of his chest.

He cocks his head, rubbing his chin while looking deliciously sexy. "So, you are alive, then?"

Those green eyes dive into my soul, stopping my ability to breathe for just one moment. I shake my head to pull myself out of the trance, then respond, "Billie's mom is sick, so it's only me today. It was fine until this busload of customers arrived."

I wait for him to say something to rile me up, but instead, he removes his coat and moves behind the counter. "Where do you need me?"

"Um . . . what are you doing?"

Aston throws his coat under the counter and begins to roll up his sleeves. "I'm helping you."

The corners of my mouth curve as I fold my arms. "You can't help me. I bet you've never even made your own coffee. You've probably got some hot maid who brings it to your bed each morning along with a happy ending."

He continues to fix his sleeves as my eyes are drawn to the veins on his muscly forearms. Sitting on his wrist appears to be an expensive watch, but he leaves it on, unbothered by it.

"The maid was hot, but my coffee was not. So I fired her," he deadpans.

"Wait! Are you joking or serious?"

Aston shakes his head with a smug expression. "If I can run a billion-dollar company, I can make coffee."

I opt to give him the benefit of the doubt and spend the next few minutes teaching him. To my surprise, he quickly picks up the instructions and starts to work.

"You're a lefty," I tease, watching him closely. "So cute."

"I'm surprised you didn't pick up on that when you were in the bathroom with me," he responds with an irritatingly smug expression, then leans in to whisper, "I guess you were too busy coming on my fingers."

Heat rises to my cheeks, but I flatten my lips to hide my embarrassment. "Okay, we're violating some sort of work code here."

"Oh yeah, which one, Miss Woods?"

"Sexual harassment," I tell him. "For now, I'm your boss. So behave or else."

He keeps his grin to himself. "I never pictured myself as a submissive, but here I am, I guess."

A small laugh escapes my lips. As Aston takes to the machine like a pro, it allows me time to take the remaining orders and finish icing the rest of the pineapple donuts. As usual, they're a hit.

"Pineapple donuts, eh? That's new," Aston mentions casually, then motions for me to glance at the old lady sitting at table three with two of her friends. "See that lady wearing the blouse with the upside-down pineapples?"

I glance over to see the bright pink shirt with pineapples scattered all over. "Yeah?"

"She's into swinging."

My eyes widen in disbelief. "Why would you say that?"

"Pineapples on clothing, specifically upside-down ones, means you swing," he informs with a gleam in his eye. "So, Grandma likes to take it on both ends."

My mouth opens, then I slap his arm. "What's wrong with you? Why would you tell me that? Now it all makes sense. She told me she had a hip injury. The injury must be from the swinging."

Aston keeps his laugh at bay. In that split moment, gazing at him, I realize it's been a long time since I've seen him genuinely smile. Most of the time, he's acting like an asshole to get a reaction from me.

And the truth is—he looks so devastatingly handsome when he's happy.

I demand that we work in silence since the swinger talk has left me somewhat disturbed. I find myself glancing at her to see if there's any truth to what Aston said. The ladies all seem to be giggling at something as swinging grandma shows them a picture on her cell phone.

The two ladies cover their mouths, almost as if they're embarrassed.

I wrinkle my nose and imagine the picture to be some old dude's penis.

God, why did you even say that in your head?

An hour later, the group leaves. They finalize their bills and head back to their bus.

And that's when I breathe a sigh of relief, turning to face Aston. If it wasn't for him, I would have gone insane trying to wrangle this crowd. Not to mention, they tipped generously because we were so accommodating.

"Thank you for helping me."

"My pleasure," he states simply.

"If only business were thriving like this every day, then I might be able to open a second café one day."

"Well, if you ever need an investor," he mentions with a grin, "Manhattan has a big swinging community and those pineapple donuts would be a drawcard."

"Eww." I cringe, shaking my head before laughing. "Manhattan would be a dream. Though, should I be worried you know so much about the swinging community?"

"I know *of* the swinging community, but that does not mean I partake in such activities. I'm selfish. If I want someone, I want them all to myself." Aston gazes over at me. "But I'm serious, if you are looking for an investor."

I drop my head, staring at the floor. "I want to do it myself. Save my money and open when the time is right, plus there's a house I'm working toward purchasing. I'm trying to adult the right way."

"I understand. If you change your mind, the offer is on the table."

I could never imagine being in business with Aston. When I initially borrowed from the bank, it was a small amount that I managed to pay off in the first year. The timing right now isn't ideal. I don't feel confident expanding when sales are not as great as I would have hoped. For now, I've parked the idea, but never say never.

"Listen, I spoke to Maddy last night . . ." I begin. He cocks his head, waiting for me to finish. "She asked if we are getting along. Look, I know things have, um . . . escalated. But I think we should stop and just be friends. For Maddy's sake. I don't like lying to her, and that's exactly what I'm doing. What *we're* doing. We fooled around, so be it. Time to move on."

Slowly, he places his hand in his pocket and retrieves his phone. He taps on the screen to read a message, then places it back in his pocket.

"If that's what you want, Everleigh," he responds in a notably cold tone.

I nod, then avoid his eyes. "That's what I want, Aston."

Reaching beneath the counter, he fetches his coat and pulls

it on. I lower my gaze, ignoring the sick feeling in the pit of my stomach.

I know I'm doing the right thing.

I need to end it before it starts.

But why does it feel so damn wrong?

Aston presses his lips together in a slight grimace. "I hope Billie's mother recovers."

With his back toward me, I watch him walk out of the café, never turning around.

My shoulders slump as I bury my head in my hands.

This didn't need to be so difficult.

It should have been easy.

But as I stand here and think about all the reasons why being friends is the right thing to do, my body argues *every single point*.

It's only a matter of time before I lose all control and break the rules.

My phone sits beneath the counter where Aston stored his jacket. I reach down to view a message on the screen. It was sent earlier this morning, during the rush, when Maddy was helping out.

Aston

You're driving me crazy.

It's four simple words.

I want to smile, laugh, kiss his lips, and tell him the exact same thing.

He is driving *me* just as crazy.

But we're just friends.

I made sure of it.

And friends don't go saying things like this.

As much as I want to text him back, I tuck my phone away and remember the fun is over.

Besides, I have a wedding to plan and a best friend to honor.

The reason why I'm not in bed with Aston and standing here miserable instead.

CHAPTER 21

Eva

Billie needed time off while her mother stayed in the hospital under observation.

I manage to open every morning, with Chloe starting later and taking over the afternoon shift.

At least this way, it gives me time to check things off my ever-growing list. Somehow, that list has multiplied, and little things need attention before the wedding, which is only around the corner.

As for Aston, I haven't heard from him, though I'm not surprised. We ended our fun somewhat amicably, but considering I threw around the friend card, he's ghosted me and has been anything but a friend.

I briefly asked Maddy if he was still in town, and she replied yes. Apparently, her father insisted Aston spend time with Myles's father. I assume it was business related, and I didn't ask any more questions.

All I can do is keep myself busy and ignore the pestering hollow in my chest.

Billie received positive news that her mom was going home this morning. I quickly prepared a care package and some food, sending it to her house so Billie wouldn't have to stress for the rest of the day. There is an amazing pie shop two blocks over, and Billie's mom loves the chicken potpie.

The morning is relatively quiet, only adding to my somber mood. I have managed to clean the kitchen, do inventory, and order more supplies. After my conversation with Aston about expanding, I found myself scrolling through leasing options in the city out of boredom. The prices were over-the-top, so I backed away before I spiraled for no reason. I'd have to sell a hell of a lot of donuts to even come out in the black.

At just after ten, Maddy bursts through the door with tears streaking her flushed cheeks.

"Maddy, what's wrong?" I rush to her side, motioning for her to sit.

She stares at her hands, trying to control her tears. I bring her in for a tight embrace in an effort to comfort her. Slowly, she pulls away, reaching inside her purse for a tissue.

"This wedding is stressing me out," she frets in a shaky voice, then continues, "Georgina just informed me some family friends of theirs will be in the country and would like to come to the wedding. Not only that, my father invited some business associates, too. This was supposed to be a small, intimate wedding. When did this become a circus? And no one is listening to me. Just because money is not an issue doesn't mean I want a big wedding."

I rest my hand on hers. "Just breathe, okay? I can contact the caterer to increase the head count and make a note of it on the seating chart. It can still be what you want despite the additional head count. We can make it work. Is that the only thing bothering you, though?"

Maddy shakes her head. "I have all this work to finish before I officially go on leave next week. There's a ton of stuff to do, not to mention Georgina is driving me up the wall. She's already picking out nursery patterns for the kids I'll supposedly be having soon. Owls . . . apparently owls are cute."

With a heavy nod, I listen to her repeat the conversation Georgina threw upon her this morning. It's obvious that with all the stress of the wedding, Maddy isn't thinking straight and is trying to please everyone.

"Give me the list. I'll take care of it. As for the whole baby thing, I can't help you there, but I'm sure Myles can have a word with his mother."

"But you're busy here. With Billie gone, I don't want to burden you," Maddy whispers before biting her nails to curb the stress.

I pull her hand away from her mouth as I always do to break the bad habit, then tell her, "Don't worry about me. Billie is back tomorrow. Chloe can cover for me this afternoon. She'll be here in fifteen minutes. Tell me what you need."

"It's too much, don't worry about it," Maddy sulks.

"Maddy, it's fine. Trust me."

She sighs heavily. "There is a store in Manhattan that has the jewelry I need to pick up for the wedding and another store for the shoes. Mom suggested I try my entire outfit on, but I just don't have time to go to the city. The stylist wants to do a test run for my hair and makeup. How hard is it to get my hair in a bun?"

I can't argue this one. It's not hard to get Maddy's hair in a bun. I've done it several times for her.

"It's fine, I can do it."

"Are you sure?" Her eyes plead with an inner soft glow. "You have so much going on here."

"I'll drive there now and back tonight. Billie works the morning, so I can sleep in if I'm tired." I reach out to squeeze her hand. "Can you chill now, please?"

Maddy sinks into the chair with a slack expression. "I don't know what I'd do without you. It feels like you're the only one who actually cares about me."

"Okay, now you're being a bit dramatic." I stop myself from rolling my eyes. "So many people care about you and love you."

"Oh yeah? It doesn't feel like it."

"C'mon, Myles, for starters. I mean, he has agreed to do the whole sickness-and-health-till-death-do-us-part thing," I joke, smiling softly, only to falter momentarily. "And, um . . . your brother."

She shrugs. "Hasn't felt like it lately. He's been in a mood."

It piques my interest. I pretend to be fixing the condiment box in the middle of the table when I say, "Oh yeah? That sucks. I haven't spoken to him. I guess he's busy with work."

"Well, he should be helping you."

"Honestly, Maddy. It's fine."

"Do you want me to talk to him?" she questions, tilting her head to wait for my answer. "I don't know what Dad is dragging him to these days, but he promised me he would help you."

The last thing I want is for Aston to feel obligated to spend time with me.

"Look, I better get ready to drive to the city." I push my chair out, standing up. "Send me all the details. I'll drop the jewelry and shoes off tomorrow. Now go home and sort out your work stuff. Deal?"

"Deal." She smiles.

~

I have this love-hate relationship with Manhattan.

Every time I drive in to visit, it feels entirely brand-new, like a place I've yet to discover and explore. There are so many emotions when you stand on the sidewalk and glance at the tall buildings surrounding you. It makes you feel alive, like you could conquer the world.

Then, some moron honks his horn, almost giving me a heart attack, while a homeless guy takes a piss right in front of me. *Yep! It's a love-hate relationship, all right.*

I park my car in the garage close to the stores where I need to pick up the items for Maddy. Usually, I'd take the train into the city to avoid the chaos, but given that I have to leave when it gets dark, I thought it would be best to drive back home.

The first stop is some fancy shoe store. Maddy's mom suggested the place because they do custom pieces. Finding the place and picking up the shoes wouldn't have taken me so long if the sales assistant hadn't rudely questioned me about the order, which involved a call to Maddy. I had to place her on speaker, and by the end of the encounter, I was annoyed.

I'm trying to take some stress off Maddy, not add to it because of some rude salesperson. It was all very *Pretty Woman* minus me being dressed like a hooker.

Next, I walk a block over to the jewelry store. The store is all white with gold chandeliers hanging from the ceiling. Very extravagant but expected of a jewelry store of this caliber in Manhattan.

There are rows of display cabinets housing expensive pieces, and a few customers are trying on some necklaces. According to what I overhear, one man appears to be picking out an engagement ring with his soon-to-be sister-in-law. I try not to stare too long, but the flirtatious behavior between them is such a red flag.

The sales assistant quickly serves me and brings the order from the back. Since the bill is already finalized, I thank her and decide to have a quick bite to eat before driving back. Given the value of the shoes and jewelry, I'm way too nervous to wander the streets.

As I walk toward the exit, the security guard politely opens the door for me. I step out onto the street, only for my attention to immediately fall onto Aston leaning against a sleek black Mercedes with his arms crossed.

He's dressed in a tuxedo, looking so damn handsome with a devilish grin on his face. His usually curly hair is slicked back into a more formal style. The corners of my mouth curve upward as I take steps toward him with a fluttering stomach.

"Wow! So now you're stalking me James Bond style?" I tease with my gaze fixed on his. "I'm assuming Maddy told you I was here."

"I've come to ask you for a favor . . ." he begins, taking a step closer. I inhale his aftershave, the scent as intoxicating as ever. "I have a charity event tonight, and my companion is unwell. Since you're my *friend*, as you so kindly put it, I'd like for you to please be my plus-one."

"Your companion?" I question, poking my tongue into my cheek. "You mean date?"

A smirk lingers on his lips. "*Friends* don't get jealous."

The burning sensation in my chest makes it difficult to breathe, let alone say anything. I hate that I *miss* him. How can I miss someone I barely spend time with?

"I haven't spoken to you for a week, but you're already dating?"

Aston reaches out to grab my bags and places them inside the car without even asking me. "No, Everleigh. Viviana was supposed to attend this charity event as my companion, but she caught some stomach virus and is unable to make it."

"Viviana . . ." I trail off, lowering my gaze to avoid his eyes.

In the middle of Fifth Avenue, the beat of my heart is the only thing I can hear. Not the traffic, not the sounds of people chattering as they walk past me. It's just my stupid heart and the feelings it's begun to catch.

Aston's finger connects with the base of my chin. Then, slowly, he lifts my head so our eyes meet. "It's not what you think."

"What do I think, Aston?"

"You think that because I'm a man, I ran straight between someone else's legs."

"And did you?"

He shakes his head, keeping his stare fixed on me. A simple stare in the middle of this busy street leaves me questioning everything in my life.

How his stare evokes this unwanted emotion inside of me.

How his smirk makes me want to slide beneath him and demand he take all of me.

How his smile, the most beautiful of smiles, fills my heart with this fullness, I can't even begin to explain.

"Now, will you be my plus-one for tonight?"

"I don't have anything to wear," I remind him.

Aston reaches into his pocket and pulls out a plastic card. "This is for the Plaza. You have a room waiting with a stylist, hairstylist, and makeup artist. I'll pick you up in one hour."

I stare at the key in shock. Then, I realize one hour is a short amount of time.

"One hour?" I complain, crossing my arms. "You do know it takes a girl longer than that to get ready."

"Hurry up, then," he urges with a grin. "The clock is ticking."

Aston opens the back door of the Mercedes and motions for me to slide in. The car has a driver who so kindly takes me to the Plaza. It's only three blocks away, but the sea of red lights brings the car to a standstill two blocks from the hotel.

We pass time by talking about the city, the weather, and when I'm all out of small talk, Aston gets a work call. Unlike the ones I've heard him on previously, he isn't arguing and ends the call rather quickly. The driver pulls up at the Plaza.

"I'll be waiting right here," Aston informs me.

"You mean you don't want to come up and watch me shower, then get changed?" I tease.

Aston cocks his head. "Always playing with fire, Miss Woods."

With the clock ticking, I rush to my suite to be greeted by a team of professionals. I have only five minutes to shower before they work on my hair and makeup. Since I had no idea this is how I would spend the night, I run on adrenaline trying to get everything done in time.

We opt for simple makeup, nothing overdone, with my hair pinned half up. The satin dress is off-the-shoulder with a sultry split thigh. The color is a beautiful sage green, matching the jewelry the stylist arranged for me to wear.

I feel like a million dollars.

And according to the stylist, the necklace around my neck is worth a million dollars, so I need to be careful tonight and watch the people around me. The pendant hanging from the necklace reminds me of the color of something, but I can't quite put my finger on it.

With five minutes to spare, I make my way down to the lobby, where Aston is waiting for me. My heart starts beating incredibly fast when his eyes land on me.

And then I make the connection.

The necklace reminds me of his eyes.

His lips part as I move closer to him, careful not to trip in these sky-high heels.

"You look breathtaking, Everleigh," he murmurs with soft eyes. His longing stare makes me hold my breath in anticipation, until I'm forced to let it go. Then, he extends his arm. "Shall we?"

I link my arm to his before we walk out of the hotel and toward the car parked at the entrance. Once again, he opens the door politely as I slide in and take a seat.

Unsure of what to say, I sit quietly on the drive to the ball. Aston is just as quiet until he pulls out his phone and sends a quick text. I don't ask any questions, praying the entire evening won't be this awkward.

When we reach the venue, paparazzi are scurrying around, snapping pictures of everyone. Aston kindly exits the car first, then reaches out for me to join him.

With all the attention on the car, I begin to worry about any photos leaking and Maddy finding out. The sudden thought makes my stomach churn, so I drop my head, hoping my face isn't caught and splashed all over the internet.

Somehow, I need to think of a reason I agreed to go tonight without Maddy thinking it was anything more than a favor.

But that's a later problem, as the event demands all my attention.

The ballroom takes my breath away, unlike anything I've

ever seen. Instead of the usual stiff, formal setup, wisteria cascades from the ceiling and strands of fairy lights weave through the branches, casting a soft, enchanting glow over the space. It feels like stepping into a magical forest, each table nestled amid the greenery, giving the room an intimate, almost otherworldly atmosphere. The lighting is dim but warm, enough to see the sparkle in people's eyes and the soft shimmer of the decor, enhancing the fairy-tale-like allure surrounding us.

Aston takes my hand and guides me to our table—the most prestigious one in the room. All eyes turn our way, tracking our every move. I'm not used to the attention, given that the last event I went to was a wedding for a college friend, and of course it was all about the bride and groom.

As we take a seat and get comfortable, Aston introduces me to all the guests seated at the table. It's easy to see why everyone has their eyes on our table—the men are *hot*. When I say *hot*, I mean *drop-dead gorgeous*. With Aston beside them, I feel like I've stepped into some fairy tale where all the men are so sexy, there is bound to be a happily ever after.

Will Romano is Aston's business associate and friend. He is also the first to glance at Aston with a knowing smirk. A knowing look passes between them, but Aston keeps quiet.

His wife, Amelia, also looks at Aston with a grin. She's gorgeous, with emerald-green eyes that are almost identical to the man near her, who apparently is her father.

And I'm not one to find older men sexy, but damn—this man is fine.

"Aston has told us nothing about you," Amelia says, scolding Aston with her dagger eyes. "I'm glad he brought a date."

Aston is busy talking to Will, so I lean in to correct her. "It's not a date. We're just friends. I'm a plus-one. Actually, a last-minute plan since his actual date is sick."

Amelia shakes her head with a grin. "That's how it always starts."

Sitting on Amelia's other side is her mother, Charlotte. I try not to stare in awe since her mother looks more like a sister. The family genes are strong and she looks a lot like her mother, too.

"Millie," Charlotte chides. "You're reading too many romance books."

I laugh, enjoying their company. "You sound like my best friend, Maddy. She's Aston's sister."

Amelia places her hand on top of mine, her eyes wide as she holds her smile. "Wait a minute. Best friend's older brother? This will *definitely* end well."

"Everleigh, please excuse my daughter." Charlotte eyes Amelia dubiously. "She doesn't get out much since the kids were born."

"Mom!" Amelia shakes her head with pressed lips. "For complete transparency, Dad is Mom's best friend's older brother. They've now been married for, like, what . . . a million years?"

"Thirty," her father intervenes. "And yes, Everleigh, please excuse our daughter. I'm glad you could attend tonight. This charity is important to our family, so the more, the merrier."

Amelia is chill and nothing at all like a billionaire's overprivileged daughter. In saying that, Maddy is nothing like that, either. I enjoy chatting to Amelia for most of the night as the men leave the table to talk business. Normally, I would be pissed if my date—but also *not date*—left me to fend for myself, but it's fun hanging out with just women sometimes.

Charlotte is just as chill as Amelia. They have a great mother-daughter bond, making me miss my own family. I decide to visit my parents once the wedding is over and maybe take a trip to France to see my brother. It's been way too long.

"May I have this dance, Miss Woods?" Aston is standing beside me with his hand extended, waiting for me to join him. Since I danced with him at the violin and cello audition, this doesn't seem like a big deal.

Yeah, but you didn't have feelings then.

Amelia presses her lips together to hide her smile, but she's doing an awful job at it. Will leans in and whispers something in her ear, only for her to shake her head as if he said something dirty to her.

The dance floor is full, and since we haven't been served any food yet, I'm surprised so many people are already dancing. According to Charlotte and Amelia, the charity auction takes place after dinner.

Aston places his hands on my hips as I wrap mine around his neck. We dance to the band playing "Can't Take My Eyes Off You." The singer has a soft, velvety tone, with his spin on the song giving it a slower vibe than how it's usually performed.

"I really like Amelia," I tell him.

He chuckles softly. "If I tell her that, she'll want to double-date every time she's in the city."

Unsure what to say, I continue with the same topic but avoid the whole double-date thing. "And Charlotte and Lex. They seem really chill."

"Charlotte, yes," he agrees with a twinkle in his eye. "But Lex, he's a shark in the boardroom. My father loathes him."

I try not to roll my eyes. "Your father loathes everyone."

"That is true. Lex has taught me a lot. If I ever need anything, he's always been there for me. If only my father could take a page out of his book."

"I've only spoken to him for a few minutes, but I can see that."

"It's hard to trust people in our industry . . ." He trails off, then sighs. "Not everyone plays fair."

"Well, as long as you do. You can't control everyone, Aston. Just your own actions," I remind him softly.

"You make it sound so easy."

I still my movements, raising my eyes to meet his. "Being a good person is easy."

Seconds pass as I wait for him to continue dancing. With his hands still around my waist and our bodies almost touching, his gaze pierces into me while I try to read him.

"My life isn't easy," he says with reluctance. "There's a lot of responsibility and pressure on me to perform a certain way. Everything is calculated, nothing is done because it is my choice."

"That's not true." I manage to smile. "It was your choice to bring me here as your plus-one. I'm sure there are plenty of other women you could have asked."

"Yes . . . but with you, it feels like I have no choice in the matter. My head tells me all types of things, but my body doesn't listen." I wait with bated breath until he murmurs, "The night doesn't have to end here, Everleigh."

"We agreed to be friends," I blurt out.

"*You* wanted to be friends." His soft gaze has turned fiery. "I wasn't lying when I said you are driving me crazy."

As I fall prey to his penetrating stare, my lips begin to tremble and the air surrounding us becomes thick and unbreathable.

It's impossible.

I can no longer resist him.

Aston Beaumont is all I think about.

I move forward, pressing my body against his to whisper in his ear, "How far away is your place?"

CHAPTER 22

Aston

Everleigh's hand is firm in mine as I hurry to get us out of here.

The dance floor is crowded, forcing me to zigzag through the couples dancing. People try to stop me to say hello, but I smile politely and ignore being pulled into some trivial conversation.

I have only one thing on my mind.

Everleigh.

Will, the bastard, shakes his head with an *I told you so* smirk. Earlier in the night, he and Amelia both cornered me with their opinions. Frankly, they were both like nagging parents. When Amelia stepped away, Will quickly laid it out for me—if I touch Everleigh, it's game over.

He called it.

I'm done trying to fight it.

The car is waiting outside in the valet parking. I open the door and motion for Everleigh to get in, following quickly behind her. When we're both inside, I tell Henry, the driver, to take us back to my apartment.

I keep my hands to myself despite my need to touch her. This stupid car doesn't have a privacy screen, and I don't want Henry to have a free show.

Not when Everleigh is involved.

Thankfully, my penthouse is only four blocks away, and because it's late, the traffic is flowing, so we make it there in record time.

As soon as we are in the elevator, I press her up against the mirror and smash my mouth to hers. I fucking missed the taste of her, spending the week away in this torturous mind-fuck after she insisted we just be goddamn *friends*.

It didn't help that my father was on my back, forcing me to spend time with Roland Whitney. The old fellow wasn't too bad, but my father has plans, and my getting into Roland's good graces is one of them. The distraction helped somewhat, but every moment I allowed myself to think about Everleigh, my willpower became weaker.

She carelessly moans into my mouth when the door pings open on my floor. With our breaths uneven and my dick hard beneath my tuxedo pants, I manage to enter my pin code into the keypad to open the door.

My hand reaches out for hers again to lead her into my apartment before I close the door behind us with a kick of my foot. Everleigh scans the main foyer with a curious gaze as I step behind her, wrapping my arms around her waist while kissing her neck.

"Your place is huge," she barely manages to say, only to moan softly when I suck on her neck like a bloodthirsty vampire.

I turn her around, retaking her lips. This time, there is no stopping me.

I need all of her.

Now.

As I pull away, she watches me with lustful eyes as I lead us into my bedroom. I push the door open to the dimly lit room. Outside, darkness has fallen, and frost has blanketed the floor-to-ceiling windows on this cold night. There are drapes that I could pull shut, but the windows are tinted so no one can see inside.

Just like before, she looks around the room with a smile playing on her lips. "This is such a bachelor pad," she teases.

I want to tell her I'm done being a bachelor, and all I need is her naked in my bed, but I refrain, knowing the sheer lust of this moment is fucking with my thoughts.

We stand at the foot of the bed as my finger runs across her collarbone. Her gaze falls on my lips, hungry and impatient, while her chest rises and falls. I see the slight fear in her eyes, but fuck it, I'm getting off on her being scared of me.

I open my mouth to speak but shut it again, conflicted by all the emotions fighting for attention at this moment. Instead, I sit on the edge of the bed as she leans down and crashes her lips back onto mine with urgency. My hands come around to grip her ass, squeezing her cheeks in my hands with a need to smack her and make her yelp.

Then, I slowly pull away because I can't take it anymore.

I need all of her.

"I want you to undress for me." My eyes are commanding.

Taking a step away, she moves her hand to the back of her dress and begins unzipping. At an agonizingly slow pace, I watch her reach for the straps of her dress until they glide down her arms and fall to her waist. She's wearing only her white lace bra, so I lick my lips in anticipation, waiting for her to push the dress past her waist and to the floor.

The moment she does, I ache to be inside her. My eyes wander all over her perfect body standing before me in her lace underwear. She steps forward, running her hands through my hair while I teasingly kiss her stomach.

I can't take it anymore, needing to see her mouth take in my cock. My hand wraps around her wrist as I seat her on the edge of the bed. I'm standing before her with this need to control her mouth. It's all I can think about.

Everleigh's amber eyes watch me so innocently. No matter how hard I try to ignore them, they pull me in like a force I have zero power over.

This won't end well.

The moment you touch her, you'll never want to stop.

I'm distracted as she toys with the button of my pants, eagerly trying to remove them. I reach to wrap my hand around the back of her neck, desperate to push down and have her take me all in.

But I stand and watch, reining in my patience to observe just how beautiful she looks in my bed. She manages to pull down my pants as I unbutton and remove my shirt, leaving me only in my silk boxers.

Unknowingly, she's biting on her bottom lip while tugging on my boxers until I spring free. Her eyes, wide with curiosity, find me, and as our gazes lock, she opens her mouth to take me in.

I buckle when her mouth wraps around me, the uncontrollable groan escaping my lips while the rush of pleasure floods my entire body. My eyes close when all of my body tenses from the sheer gratification of knowing she's the one making me feel this way.

My hands grab her hair, pushing her deep until I hear the sucking noises echo in the room.

Fuck, I don't know how long I can last.

I ache for more, so I remove myself from Everleigh's mouth and push her to lie down, then climb on top, pinning her beneath me.

Our kisses deepen, the rush only adding to the intensity, but then I insist she straddle me. There is nothing sexier than seeing a beautiful woman riding my cock.

But given that it's Everleigh, it's all of my fantasies come true.

As Everleigh sits on top of me, still in her bra and panties, I trail my finger down her chest as she unclasps her bra. The moment her tits are exposed, I bite down on my lip, using every muscle I have to stop myself from blowing right this very second. They're fucking flawless—round, supple, perfectly positioned light pink nipples, fully erect and expressing how turned on she is right now.

She's unaware of just how sexy she is.

And I need to show her.

As our gazes lock, the silence speaks loudly between our shallow breaths. Every forbidden fantasy of her—all of them that became a mind-fuck—is happening right in front of me.

And all those years ago, when I kissed her at the lake, I regret not taking the one thing that could have belonged to me all this time.

I could have been the only man to have ever touched her.

To *own* her.

But I was young and foolish, caught up in my own insecurities, only to land right here.

My throat begins to thicken as I pinch my brows together, losing all hope of resisting the one person I'm not supposed to touch.

The one person who has this hold over me.

This one person who terrifies me.

I can't hold back, running my fingers along her curves, taking her tits in my mouth as she moans so carelessly, arching her back. My tongue rolls around her nipple, sucking gently with a small tug of my teeth. I knead them between my fingers, unable to control my urge to ravage her, begging her silently to let me have her completely and hoping she doesn't get scared, pulling away at a moment's notice.

This *friend* thing? It was *never* going to work.

And this time, I won't hold back.

Everleigh's moans deepen, pleasure and pain all rolled into one. Every beautiful sound warns me she's close when we haven't even begun. We have all night, and I refuse to have her leave my bed.

I pull back, sadistically waiting for her to beg.

"Don't stop," she pleads, pushing my head back into her breasts.

Like a hungry beast, I ravage them with a sick and twisted need to ensure she wakes up sore. I need her to feel me all over her, to be the only man she will ever think about again.

But then, she shuffles off me and removes her panties.

Fuck.

I stare between her legs. *How can a pussy be this fucking perfect?*

And why in the hell does this all feel brand-new? Like I'm some teenage boy experiencing his first sexual encounter.

Everleigh hovers back over me, but not before eyeing me with a knowing look. I wait for her to climb on, but she then opens her mouth to say, "We need protection."

Fuck! I completely forgot for the first time *ever.*

Reaching for my nightstand, I open the drawer and remove the foil packet.

Tearing at it between my teeth in desperation, I quickly place the condom on the tip of my shaft and slide it down.

What I would do to feel her bareback.

Clutching the back of her neck, I draw her close to me, my mouth eager to kiss her deeply and have her moan in my mouth when I slide inside her.

"Do you want me to stop . . ." I ask, out of nowhere. "Once I'm inside you, Everleigh, there is no turning back."

"Aston," she breathes, sliding herself on as her mouth parts slightly.

I close my eyes, biting down as the sensation grapples my shaft and pleasures me without even the slightest movement.

"I've been waiting for this. Fuck me, *please.*"

Her begging spurs on the beast within me. I grip her hips, watching her body ride me. Everleigh doesn't know just how sexy she is. Goose bumps cover every inch of her body, and her nipples are hard as I pinch them softly. Her cries are mixed with moans, the sound fighting for attention with the grunts my body expels.

As I shuffle my body so I'm sitting up against the headboard, it allows me to bury myself deeper within her. I push myself with urgency, but at the same time, she tells me to go deeper.

Everleigh's face is in line with mine, so close that we lose ourselves in the heat of the moment, and kissing her becomes an addiction. Our tongues feverishly battle, only adding to the heat of our intense fuck.

Pulling away while arching her back, she calls my name until I slide my hand behind her neck again and beg her to look at me.

And at this moment, our eyes connect so profoundly that my emotions run wild in fear.

This isn't just a moment.

For argument's sake, if this is a onetime fuck, how do I even begin to forget how easily I'm willing to give up everything to be inside her?

How nothing matters because the desire drives me to make careless decisions.

How everything I know is a blur because I *need* this woman in my life.

But then she scrapes her thumb on my bottom lip, causing the feverish spell within me to intensify.

"Come with me," I demand with a rasp. "I want you to come with me, Everleigh."

Her lips smash onto mine, and the taste is so delicious. I beg my body not to release now, willing the restraint to last a little bit longer so we both feel the rush in sync.

My hands lace around her neck, our foreheads touching as I thrust inside her with a grunt. She rides my cock, a rhythm building momentum until all I feel is her muscles tighten around my shaft. My body jerks forward, a shiver following as a deep groan escapes me, and my body basks in euphoria, unable to stop this mind-blowing release that has left me at a loss for words.

My eyes blink rapidly, sweat dripping off my forehead while I try to gather my bearings. *Fuck!* I've never experienced anything so intense. Not even when I've had threesomes where two girls both fucked me at the same time. Those weren't my finest moments, simply a power trip that has nothing on Everleigh.

Our breaths, uneven, echo inside the room.

Slowly, she slides herself off, collapsing beside me and pulling the satin sheet over her.

I discard the condom, tossing it on the floor, and turn to face her.

"I should head home," she says, breathless, as I spread tiny kisses on her arm.

Without even thinking, I climb back on top of her. I'm held hostage by her deep stare, shades of brown locking me in some sort of trance. Every rational thought is buried deep inside, and I can only think about being inside her again.

I will *not* let her leave this bed.

I kiss her shoulder, trailing her skin until I'm on her lips. "Stay."

She pulls away with a vacant expression. "But you don't let anyone stay over. It's your rule."

"Rules are made to be broken, sweetheart."

I'm hard again, eager to go a second round. As I reach for the nightstand to remove another condom, Everleigh stops me, her stare boring into me.

"I'm on birth control," she whispers.

I close my eyes momentarily, trying to calm my racing thoughts. I've never gone bareback on a woman, no matter how many have told me they're on birth control.

But this isn't just any woman.

I take a deep breath and slide myself in, her arousal utterly wet as she moans even louder than before. Her pussy wraps around my bare cock, and all I can think about is just how perfect she feels.

Like everything missing from my life.

To burn with desire and lust, to taste the forbidden fruit of the woman I've fantasized about for the longest time, is the greatest punishment if our hearts choose to get involved.

When all the pieces complete the puzzle, there will be no turning back.

And for someone who doesn't believe in falling in love, the only one set to get her heart broken is the woman I'm inside.

My sister's best friend.

CHAPTER 23

Eva

*S*tay.

It's the one word that changed everything.

One simple word that carries so much weight.

Aston Beaumont broke his own rule.

But instead of making me feel like the luckiest girl in the world, that one word terrified me.

A man like Aston doesn't just break the rules for anyone. His personality thrives on structure and control, and everything he's done tonight is against his normal behavior.

From the moment he told me on the dance floor that I was driving him insane and he never wanted to be just friends, my body took over. It was like some spell had been cast, and nothing could break it.

I needed to taste him, feel him all over me.

When he slid inside me for the first time, it was different from anything I'd ever experienced. No man has ever made me feel the way he did—this feeling of being empowered yet worshipped at the same time.

Being inside his penthouse and lying on his bed awakened something within me.

I'd be a liar if I said I hadn't thought about this moment. It's one of those things I'd fantasized about, and acting it out was another mind-blowing experience. I exploded into this beautiful abyss, barely able to think straight when the moment was over.

As I lay beside him, naked and vulnerable, he asked me to stay before sliding back inside and pulling me back into a moment where all I want is *him*.

Aston is *insatiable*.

It didn't stop the second time.

He devoured me all night long until we both collapsed from exhaustion. I've lost count of how many times I blissfully buried the nagging feeling of not using protection even though I'm the one who stopped him. He did pull out, coming all over my stomach the first time he went bare. I take birth control, so at least I can relax and not worry about getting pregnant.

"I think you broke me," I whisper, trying to hold back my smile but finding it impossible.

Aston brings my hand to his mouth, kissing my fingers gently. "I think you broke *me*."

"You can't break a stallion."

He chuckles. "I'm a stallion?"

"Yes. I'm sure this isn't the first time you've broken a woman in bed."

Aston turns to lie on his side, watching me with his brows furrowed. "What makes you think I bring women here and spend all night fucking their brains out?"

I stare at the ceiling, unable to look at him. "You're the billionaire every woman wants."

He climbs on top of me so our eyes are forced to meet. "And you're the untouchable woman every man fantasizes about. You don't see how men react to you. Trust me, Everleigh, when I say my jealousy has been tested many times."

"Please, I haven't had sex in forever."

"And why do you hold back?" he questions, staring at my lips. "Do you know how unbelievably sexy you are?"

"Because . . . I don't know," I mumble. "Sex can be great, but it's better when you have a connection."

"But the doctor . . ." He trails off with a jealous tone etching his words.

I roll my eyes, pursing my lips. "I haven't had sex with Marco, okay? We haven't even kissed. Does that answer all your questions? I'm sure you've had sex with a ton of women in the last month."

"No." His stare bores into me. "I've been fixated on trying to have sex with just the one."

"Well," I say, unable to think straight. "I have nothing to say."

"Good," he affirms before sliding down and settling in between my legs. I moan with delight as he runs his tongue around my sensitive clit.

He can't possibly make me come again.

Aston slides a finger inside of me, slow and easy, since I'm raw after the multiple times he's ravaged me. At a steady pace, the heaviness in my belly builds while his tongue circles my swollen clit to the point of no return. I clutch his hair in my hands, riding out the orgasm until I can barely breathe.

Damn, he did it again despite me thinking I was done.

A yawn escapes me, and then another. I nestle into his chest, barely able to stay awake.

Beside me, I hear him whisper, "Good night, Everleigh."

I wake to the sound of sirens blaring. It's still dark outside, and Aston is fast asleep beside me. The clock on the bedside table says five past five in the morning.

The reality of last night is scattered around the room—the messy bed, our clothes strewn all over the floor, the one discarded condom we used. Neither one of us left the bed.

Slowly, I rise from the bed to use the bathroom, then put my dress back on while carrying my heels. Careful not to wake him, I keep my footsteps to a bare minimum.

At the foot of the bed, I stop to watch him sleep, admiring his sculpted chest exposed as he lies on his back.

This man is like some Greek god, perfect in every way.

My eyes are drawn to the tattoo on his chest, the one he got the night of his graduation. I still remember his cold stare as his friend inked him.

It feels like a lifetime ago, but in the same breath, like it happened yesterday.

But tonight, things changed.

In his touch, my body belonged to him. Our words in those heated moments, while careless, made us believe it was just us and would be just us forever.

This is Aston, not some man with a connection to my existing world. I've yet to think of an excuse to make Maddy believe it was a platonic night. Yet the longer I stand here and think about how I need to lie to my best friend, the more the guilt eats away at me.

It begins to suffocate me, questioning all my actions last night and every move I made that led me to right here.

With a deep breath, I take the initiative to leave, but not before removing the million-dollar necklace I am still wearing. I'm surprised it didn't break when he had me in a chokehold, fucking me from behind.

Gently, I place it on the table beside him.

If I stay, my heart will only become more invested, and who knows what will happen next?

It has to be a goodbye.

At least—for now.

I leave the city and end up in my thinking spot by Peppermint Lake.

A sudden drop in temperature sends small snowflakes floating down from the sky. I glance up, allowing the snow to rest on my tired face. The cold ice, combined with the cool air, brings me back to reality and away from the noise of the city.

I close my eyes, caught in the memories of last night. Every touch, every sound, replays like a movie on repeat. When I open my eyes, I see Houdini has appeared beside me, making me gasp as I bring my hand to my chest. I'm pretty sure it's him, if he is a *him*. The same dark gray color and mottled skin.

"Okay, listen, if you're gonna keep surprising me, could you at least make a sound? You know, *ribbit*?"

A croaking sound emerges from his tiny body.

"Thanks, just a bit too late," I mumble, then glance at him again. "Do you want to know something interesting? I slept with my best friend's brother last night, and things are so weird, I don't even know what I'm supposed to do. Do I call him? Was it a onetime thing? I rode him bareback for Christ's sake!"

Houdini stills all movements. I knew it, he's just as shocked as I am.

"I know, what was I thinking? I wasn't! I'm never thinking around him. Why does he make me feel like nothing else matters?"

With a short and stout body, Houdini continues to sit in close proximity to me. I try not to make any sudden movements so as not to scare him.

"What do you think, Houdini? Have I caught feelings for him? If it's a yes, jump back into the lake. If you think this is a fling I'll get over, stay perfectly still."

I wait with bated breath, but then Houdini spots a bug of some sort and hops in the opposite direction of the lake.

"Great, you're of no help to me."

As much as I want to stay here, ignoring all my problems, I know I need to head to the café and help Billie.

"I'm sorry I'm late!"

I rush through the door and straight behind the counter,

where Billie is preparing two hot chocolates. There was no time for a shower, just a quick outfit change into a pair of jeans and a wool blouse.

His scent lingers all over me.

My entire body aches, and when I reach up to grab a clean plate from the shelf, I let out a groan, unknowingly.

"You look . . ." Billie falls short of words, observing me with her lips curved. "How can I put this politely?"

"Like death?"

"Freshly screwed," she blurts out.

"Billie!" I gasp, surprised by her choice of words since she isn't vulgar like Maddy. "That's very unlike you."

She shrugs, her smile fading. "Yeah, well . . . I could use the distraction."

"Is everything okay with your mom?" I ask, worried.

"For now." Billie sighs heavily, then smiles. "Anyway, can we go back to your exciting love life?"

"Okay, listen . . . there is no love, so technically, no love life."

"Sure. So, was this bestie's older brother?" Billie waits with hopeful eyes. "It was, wasn't it?"

I glance around, then pull Billie into the kitchen. "Yes, but please promise me you'll say nothing to Maddy. I don't want her getting involved, and I already feel guilty for having to lie to her."

Billie holds up her pinkie finger. "I swear I won't. Only if you promise not to tell anyone a hot surgeon gave me his number, and he's possibly double my age."

"Age gap?" I grin with a nod. "You go, girl."

"It was a very McDreamy moment. I mean, age ain't nothing but a number, right?" Billie shakes her head, then places her hands on my shoulders. "Tell me everything that happened last night with Aston."

I start with Aston appearing at the jewelry store and then continue with the rest of the night. As the story progresses, her eyes widen with enthusiasm.

"This is the most exciting thing to happen to you in the time I've known you," Billie is quick to tell me.

"Really, am I that boring?"

"I wouldn't throw around the word *boring*, more like *picky*. You red-flag all men before they even have a chance to prove their worth in the bedroom. Now you've had, like, what, multiple orgasms with the hottest guy ever?"

"A lady never tells. But let's say six for all intents and purposes."

Billie purses her lips with a silent nod. "You're falling for him."

"No, I'm not." I choke the words out quickly.

"I'm sorry. I will correct myself. You've *fallen* for him."

"It's not like that, okay? It's just been a buildup from high school. More of a what-if scenario," I rush, spluttering my words. "Once this wedding is over, this will be over."

"You really believe that?"

"I have to, Billie. Aston is not the guy for me." As the words leave my mouth, I check my phone to see if Aston has texted. There's nothing from him, and even though I should send him a text, something makes me hold back.

Last night changed everything.

I don't know where we stand.

But given Aston's history with women, it wouldn't surprise me if I'm just a notch on his belt.

Except he asked me to stay.

The day turned out to be quiet, which should have been a welcome relief, but only added to my stress of low numbers this season.

When I finally arrive home, I take a long-needed shower. The hot water feels like heaven, but upon spreading the soap all over my body, I notice small bruises near my thighs.

A smile graces my lips as I remember when he positioned himself between my legs and gave me the best head of my life. He used his hands to keep my legs spread wide open, which I assume led to the bruises.

The water cascading down my body stings my sensitive nipples. *God, he really did a number on me.* I use the soft loofah beneath, but the moment it accidentally glides against my clit, I moan with desire. *How is it possible for me to want more?*

I decide to get out and put on my silk black pajamas to relax for the rest of the night. With my hair damp and brushed away from my face, I set up camp on the sofa with my laptop. In the background, I put on *Love Island* again. I've missed a few episodes, so I'm not up-to-date with who is sleeping with whom.

This week's focus is finishing plans for the bachelorette party and the seating chart for the reception. Maddy's mom offered Beaumont Manor to host the girls-only party. I wasn't sure if Maddy would approve, but since we didn't have much time, she happily accepted and gave me a list of things she requires.

Ramona, however, texted me to say she could get male strippers if we need them. I'm still on the fence, not wanting to make the party that kind of cheesy.

My phone pings with a text beside me.

Maddy

I'm coming over after dinner. Did Ramona text you about strippers? Like, how hot are we talking?

Me

I saw a pic and let me sum it up in two words: WILD STALLION. See you soon.

The guilt rears its ugly head again. If I were to say something, maybe she might understand given that we're all adults now and can make our own decisions.

With every minute that passes, I twitch nervously in anticipation. It all becomes a bit too much, so I rumble through the kitchen cupboards and pull out a bottle of gin someone gave me for the opening of the café. Luckily, I also find a bottle of tonic.

My stare is blank, and I am unable to concentrate on the screen. The gin has gone down nicely, so I make another and decide to call my parents instead. It's been a while since I last checked in, and of course, nothing much has changed. They got some new animals, including an exotic bird, which Dad treats like a third child. When we hang up, I call my brother, needing to hear his voice.

"If it isn't the queen of Cinnamon Springs," he teases upon answering. "You're alive, lil sis."

"Barely," I tell him. "This wedding planning is killing me."

"Wedding planning? Whose wedding?"

"Didn't I tell you Maddy's getting married?"

"No, but then again, maybe you did and I forgot. It's been busy, and I haven't had a moment to stop. Everyone wants a taste of *Cannes*," he says in an overdone French accent.

"Right, because you're a Michelin star god." I smile proudly, even though he can't see me. "Do you mention that when trying to hook up with the ladies?"

He chuckles. "No, I rely on my good looks."

"Gross." I laugh loudly. My brother is a good-looking guy. He's always been one to capture the girls' eyes, but much like Aston, he never settles down. "So, what's new with you?"

"I'm dating someone," he says, with a weight to his admission.

"Get out of here," I shout, then calm down. "Really?"

"Yes, her name is Nicole, and she is American. We've been seeing each other for four months."

"Four months? Wow! Is this the longest relationship you've ever had? Do I smell wedding bells?"

"No," he quickly informs me. "Since you're so nosy, remember Briella? I dated her for longer."

"Oh God, how could I forget?" Briella is someone my brother dated while still living here in Cinnamon Springs. She ended up following him to college, but things took a nasty turn. Apparently, once she got a taste of freedom, she no longer wanted her high school boyfriend and was caught hooking up with other guys at frat parties several times. Poor Elliot had his heart broken over and over again. "More like Cruella. What a waste of time. Do you even know what she's doing these days?"

"Some husband in finance and three kids."

I chuckle. "Consider yourself lucky."

"So, what about you? Are you actually trying to let men date you, or are you still red-flagging everyone?"

"I don't red-flag everyone." I sink into my sofa, annoyed. "God, you're just like Billie."

"Wait, is Billie the hot one?"

"Don't go there," I warn him. "To answer your question, my dating life is complicated."

"Complicated because you make it that way."

I sit up, pulling my legs to my chest. "I don't make things complicated. I'm the *least* complicated person to go out with. If it's not working I—"

"Pull the plug," Elliot finishes. "And there's your problem."

My guard is up while annoyed by my brother's comment. He makes it seem like I don't care and just end things if the guy isn't working out. It's not at all like that. What's the point in pursuing a relationship if I think my heart will get broken? I know what it feels like, and I would never wish it upon anyone, let alone myself, again.

"Eva, just admit it. It's not complicated, you're spooked."

"You're spooked," I retort.

There's a knock on the door, so I jump up to answer it. I expect it to be Maddy after her dinner, but I open the door to Aston, who is standing on the other side in his gray sweats and his usual navy coat.

"Um . . . Elliot, I have to go."

I hang up the call as Aston tilts his head in curiosity. "Elliot?"

"My brother," I blurt out, quick to remind him.

"Right, yes, forgot about him." Aston's expression softens. "Can I come in, or am I banished to the hall for being a naughty boy and breaking the *friend* code?"

The corners of my mouth lift. "You can come in, but just letting you know, Maddy is coming over."

"Of course she is," he deadpans before closing the door behind him and following me to the sofa. I sit on the other end, keeping my distance. I'm not immune to how his presence affects me. How can someone look so sexy in gray sweatpants but equally as sexy in a suit? It's usually one or the other.

But it's not what he is wearing, it's Elliot's words lingering in my head. *Do I spook easily?* I don't consider it being spooked, more vigilant with my heart.

There's a difference.

"The wedding is right around the corner," I start by trying to ignore the voices in my head, but stop upon his unrelenting stare. "What?"

He rubs his stubbly chin. "You don't want to talk about leaving this morning?"

I shrug, focusing back on my screen. "What's there to talk about, Aston? We both lost control last night."

"And you still believe I'm playing you, am I right?"

"I don't know what to b-believe." My words falter, and I'm unsure how honest to be with him. "We just need to get this wedding over and done with. Can we at least pause things until then? I know you're not bothered by hiding from Maddy, but I am, and if you care for me in the slightest way, you'll understand why I'm feeling so torn over this."

The powerful sound of silence lingers in the room. Of all the words we could say to each other right now, perhaps this is the loudest. Besides, with Maddy coming over, the last thing we need is an argument between us.

Aston finally sighs, asking, "Okay, what do we have left to do?"

I go through my list and read from my screen. "So, this is my spreadsheet. Red means outstanding, orange means pending, green means complete."

"Show me." He yanks the laptop from me, only to place his fingers on the keyboard to start typing, but then he stops, reaching into his pocket to remove black-framed reading glasses.

"Are you touching my spreadsheet? I'll let you know I spent hours on that and have a system."

"Your system needs tweaking," he brags, passing the laptop back. "Here you go." His eyebrows raise with a smirk teasing his lips.

I press my legs shut, trying my best to ignore the heat rising between them while I glance at him. "Since when do you wear glasses?"

"Since staring at screens all day became blurry," he admits.

"Huh." I rub the back of my neck, then swallow with a struggle. "They look good on you."

"Is that why your nipples are hard?"

I glance down, rushing to cover my chest. "No funny business. You are here strictly as a friend helping me plan this wedding."

"Right, so I have to forget about how you came five times last night?"

"Six," I mumble, taking a slow drink from my glass. "But who's counting?"

"Apparently, you," he teases.

I smack him with the pillow as he scowls. *Why does he have to look so irresistible in those glasses?*

"Can you be normal, please? Pretend nothing at all happened last night," I beg of him.

"Impossible." His grin is driving me crazy. "However, since my sister is about to knock on that door, I will pretend . . . *for now.*"

The knock on the door comes as no surprise not long after that. Maddy quickly enters my apartment and plonks herself on the sofa between us. It almost feels like a parent chaperoning two teenagers. I laugh inside my head but make sure not to show my feelings in front of her.

We chat mainly about the wedding, but Maddy admits she's done talking about it and needs to unwind. Her mood has been off since she walked in, but sometimes it's better to let her cool down than give her a platform to air her grievances and make them ten times worse.

Hogging the remote, she switches to a movie, which is apparently some thriller. It doesn't help that she talks through most of the movie, annoying both Aston and me.

"You know where this is going to go, right?" Maddy questions as I start to become uncomfortable when the man presses the female lead up against the wall and pulls down her panties. "Yep, he's going to go in bareback. If a guy goes in bareback, it means he's in love with the woman."

I choke on my own saliva.

Maddy and Aston wait for me to pull myself back together, but I dare not look at Aston.

Maddy pats my back. "You okay?"

"Yeah, sorry."

She then turns to face Aston. "You're a guy. What do you think?"

"I think, as your brother, you asking me this question is disturbing."

"I've never done it, to be honest," Maddy admits, ignoring her brother. "Always used protection. Those high school sex-ed classes are really ingrained into me."

"Did you need to share that?" Aston complains, raising his voice. "In my eyes, you're still a virgin."

I burst out laughing. "That boat has long sailed. It sailed in senior year, and since then, a lot of sailors have ridden the ship."

"You make me sound loose. I've slept with six guys in total, including Myles," Maddy informs us both.

"Madelina," Aston groans, rubbing his face with his hands. "Shut the fuck up. You're getting on my nerves."

"This is girl talk, and if you want to hang out with us, then you need to partake. Now, Eva, on the other hand, is picky as fuck. Her count is small because she red-flags everyone."

"Okay, listen," I begin defensively. "When did I become this red-flagging person? Earlier, Elliot was saying the same thing and—"

I cut myself off as the both of them stare at me. I've revealed too much, so I close my mouth and beg myself to stop talking.

"Since you red-flag every guy!" Maddy raises her voice. "If we dissect your red flags, you're possibly afraid of commitment or picky as hell. The doctor is the only one you haven't red-flagged."

Maddy watches me with curiosity. I keep quiet, unsure of what to say.

"Oh, you've red-flagged him! Eva, what now? Is it his penis? Too small?"

My head shakes before I say, "God, no."

"Too much foreskin?"

With a frown, I quickly tell her, "I agree with Aston. This is disturbing. I haven't red-flagged the doctor, okay?"

"So, you're still dating him?" Maddy pushes, refusing to drop the subject. "Is he your plus-one for the wedding? You never told me. We can squeeze him in, but you're really leaving it last-minute, and I'll be honest, Eva, I'm not coping well with last-minute changes."

"I, uh . . . not sure."

"We need to give numbers to the caterer next week," she reminds me with a raised voice.

"Stop spiraling! This is all under control. How about we go back to watching the movie?"

For the rest of the movie, both Aston and I remain quiet and allow Maddy to ramble on. I barely listen, my mind exploding with so many questions.

There's another knock on the door, and I gladly jump off the sofa to answer it.

As I open the door, Myles is standing in the foyer.

"Hey, Eva, is Maddy here?"

"Yes . . ." I answer slowly, wondering how he knew I lived here. "Come in."

"I'd rather talk to her in private."

I'm thrown off by his rigid tone as Maddy appears beside me, gently placing her hand on my arm. "It's okay, I'll be back in a moment."

Closing the door behind them, I head back into the living room.

"Do you know what that's about?" I ask, only for Aston to purse his lips, keeping quiet. "What's going on, Aston?"

"It's just family stuff. Best you don't get involved."

His words hurt slightly, not because I want gossip or anything of the sort, but because I am genuinely worried about Maddy. Myles's tone was off, which is probably why this is bothering me so much.

When Maddy returns, her usually jovial face appears tired and worn down.

"Is everything okay?" I question, worried.

"We'll talk tomorrow. I just want to go home."

Aston grabs his keys without arguing, then glances at me one more time. His eyes bore into me, and all the flags waving at me to be careful with my heart, slowly come down.

I hate that even after last night, I want him.

And that whole bareback conversation began to eat away at me. Aston Beaumont is not in love with me, far from it. Just because he had a moment of weakness, it doesn't mean anything. The guy isn't capable of love, and to be honest, maybe I'm not either.

Yet my heart is anything but in agreement.

The weight inside my chest reminds me of what is missing in my life.

Who is missing from my life.

No matter how hard I try to fall asleep, all I hear is his voice, see his face, and feel his touch all over my body.

It's too late . . .

I have fallen for the one man I promised myself I would never fall for *again*.

CHAPTER 24

Eva

What do you mean there are no chickens?"

Maddy is yelling into the phone so loud that customers inside my café pause their conversations to gawk at her. My hand reaches out to pull the phone away so I can take over this conversation before it gets out of control.

"What's happening with the chickens?" I ask, pressing my hand to my forehead.

"We don't have any," Sal, the lodge's head chef, informs me. "A bird flu has knocked the poor buggers out, so we can't get them in time for the wedding."

"Right . . ." I breathe, then follow with, "What other animal can we sacrifice for this wedding?"

Sal lists a few options, none of them satisfying Maddy when I say them out loud. It isn't that all the chickens have magically fallen off the face of the earth, but Sal and his team can't secure supply for the event.

Since Maddy left my apartment last week, she's been on edge. The shoes I'd picked up from Manhattan were too tight, but given that they were custom-made, she has to grin and bear it on her wedding day because it's too late to do anything else. I joked about wearing flip-flops, but it didn't go down well.

On top of this, the minister performing the ceremony has come down with shingles, so there was a last-minute call around to have someone replace him.

All those problems are somewhat resolved, yet something is still bothering her. The night Myles came to my apartment, Maddy simply said they had an argument about his mother. I assumed it was over table settings or something but decided not to push Maddy to open up about it.

Instead of talking about it, she snaps at everyone, which is getting tiresome. I also assumed she got her period, but I don't want to rile the bridezilla and mention we are definitely no longer in sync. Therefore, the period sisters' ship has sailed.

"Sal, let me get back to you in fifteen minutes." I end the call, glancing at Billie, who looks just as worried about Maddy. Between the two of us, we've been trying to talk Maddy off the ledge all week.

Maddy has taken an Oreo cheesecake donut from the glass display, munching on it with a frantic look in her eyes. It's her third donut in a row, but neither of us dares tell her to take it easy.

"Why don't we do the beef and fish? There's also the vegetarian option for those who want neither," I suggest softly.

"Georgina insisted on chicken. She doesn't eat anything but chicken." Maddy raises her voice again.

"Maddy, there is no other choice here. I'm sorry, but as your maid of honor, I need to put my foot down. Georgina will need to eat something else." Taking a deep breath, I follow with, "We can get her a bucket of Kentucky Fried Chicken. Then she can't complain she ain't got no chicken."

Billie laughs, but Maddy narrows her eyes with an exaggerated sigh. I keep my smile at bay, though the image of Georgina eating a bucket of chicken at the wedding is hilarious. This is going to be an exhausting day, and it hasn't even reached lunchtime yet.

"I'm the one who has to deal with her, Eva. For the rest of my life," she enunciates, refusing to lighten up. "This wedding needs to be perfect. It's almost like you don't care because it's not that important to you."

"The wedding *will* be perfect and I'm doing my best here," I emphasize, trying to ignore her jab. "It'll be perfect, just with beef."

Bowing her head, she grabs her purse from the counter. "I'll go deal with this."

Maddy doesn't say goodbye, only sulks while leaving the shop. I glance at Billie, tilting my head in confusion, then rush to follow Maddy until we're outside on the sidewalk.

Thankfully, the weather is warming up and the sun is shining for once. My skin so desperately needs it after the long, cold winter we've had. The warm weather means more people are out strolling the streets, which is great for business.

"Hey, what's gotten into you?" I question, stopping her at the front of the store. "I understand you're stressed, but from day one, you said this would be easy. Why are you letting something as trivial as chicken get to you?"

"This is the biggest day of my life, and so many things are going wrong," she complains, bringing her shaking hand to her forehead.

"That's why I'm here," I remind her, then smile softly. "You know . . . to take the stress off you."

Maddy crosses her arms. "Yeah, well, you've been busy."

My hands slip into the pockets of my jeans as I smile at the elderly lady walking past with her two toy poodles. Maddy's tone comes across as cold and resentful, and I try to ignore the nagging feeling she suspects something has happened between Aston and me. She's not one to keep a secret, so if she was onto something, I'm sure she'd tell me.

"I'm trying my best here, Maddy. Let me worry about all of this, okay? We have the bachelorette tomorrow night, then the rehearsal on Saturday." As she drops her gaze to the sidewalk, I place my hand on her shoulder. "By Sunday, you'll be Mrs. Whitney. You need to relax and be in the moment."

Maddy nods in silence. Then slowly says, "Okay, beef it is."

She presses the button on the new silver BMW Myles's parents bought her as a wedding gift. Maddy has never cared for cars and was happy to drive her red Jeep around town. With a noticeable weight still resting on her shoulders, she gets into her car and shuts the door.

I wait for her to open her passenger window to say something, but she drives down the street instead, leaving me standing alone.

My shoulders curl, prompting me to take a deep breath and pull my phone out of my back pocket to text Aston. For the past week, Aston's father insisted he attend meetings. Why they were so important before the wedding is beyond me. It's easy to see Harvey Beaumont barely lifts a finger, instructing all his workers to do his work, including Aston.

Aston is the CEO, though he never gave a straight answer when I asked what it entails. He has a lot of power, that much I know, but ultimately, his father owns the company, and Aston's shares are no match.

In the space of five days, Aston's driven back to the city twice and flown to Boston for the day, so I didn't get to see him at all. We texted with our usual flirtatious banter, but not once did I want to admit I missed him. He mentioned last night he would be driving back to Cinnamon Springs after dinner with some clients from Manhattan. So, I assume he is here.

I type quickly, hoping he'll respond.

Me

Is it just me, or has Maddy turned into bridezilla this week?

The three dots appear, and then his text flashes on my screen.

Aston

It's not just you. This morning, we got into a fight about cereal.

Me

Okay, now I don't feel as bad. What are you doing today? Are you getting ready for the strippers tomorrow night?

Aston

What answer will make you so jealous that you'll want me to come over and fuck your pretty little brains out?

Me

Nice try, buddy.

Aston

I'm with Roland at the country club in Cherry Tree Creek. He's just introduced me to his friend's daughter, who has joined us. Have I told you I despise golf?

Me

Wait! Is this a setup?

Aston

I've red-flagged her. She has a Hello Kitty golf club.

Me

Um, how old is she?

Aston

Ten

Laughter escapes me as I reread his texts. Aston is super competitive and always has been. In high school, he used to get into fights with other teams all the time. I'm surprised he never got expelled.

Aston

She's kicking my ass, it's rather embarrassing.

> **Me**
> Watch out, she'll post it all over socials and your reputation will be ruined.

> Poor baby. I'll try to be nice to you then.

> **Aston**
> Luckily, I don't believe in socials so my reputation may be salvaged. If you want to be nice to me, I can think of many ways, starting with you naked on all fours.

> **Me**
> We made a deal, remember?

A few seconds after I hit send, my phone rings with Aston's number flashing on the screen.

"No," I answer with a grin. "Be a good boy and stick to the agreement."

"Firstly, this kid really is kicking my ass, so I think you should feel extra sorry for me," Aston responds in his velvety voice, which does nothing to curb my desire. "And secondly, you know the wedding is three days away—that's a whole seventy-two hours."

"I think you can survive," I tease, leaning against the green lamppost. "Besides, not to gross you out, but since you've grown up with Maddy, I think you're accustomed to the girl talk. I'm possibly out of action for the next few days."

"You think that will stop me?"

"Um, yes!" I scowl, but my body reacts immediately with a flurry in my stomach. "You do know what I'm referring to?"

"Yes, Everleigh. I'm well aware of how the female reproductive system works. However, there are other places I've yet to explore." His voice stiffens, and like me, I assume he is struggling with this stupid rule I put into place—*let's pause until the wedding is done.* It's Maddy's special day, and we must focus on her.

"Okay, maybe it's best we end this conversation. Golf pants are tight and leave nothing to the imagination."

Unable to hold back my laughter, I follow with, "Bye, Tiger Woods."

I'm grateful Georgina is not part of the bachelorette, nor is Maddy's mother. Patricia checked herself into a hotel with a day spa to de-stress before the wedding. From my observations, I think Patricia has had enough of Georgina. Honestly, I don't blame her.

Beaumont Manor has a beautifully landscaped garden, so setting up the long wooden table in the middle of the large open patio makes sense. Draped from the wooden pillars are festoon lanterns to enhance the lighting, and because it's still cold at night, I rented some outdoor heaters and positioned them near the tables to keep everything nice and toasty.

This has always been my favorite area of the property. It's next to a medium-size pond with lily pads floating on the surface during the warmer months. In the distance, you can see the mountains with leftover snow blanketing the peaks.

But most of all, I love how if you stand quietly, you can hear the sounds of nature coming to life.

In high school, Maddy's parents would host fancy parties out here. Tonight, we are letting loose and celebrating the end of Maddy's singlehood.

There are twenty of us here. Some of Maddy's friends from work and college, Myles's cousins, and family friends, too. Billie canceled at the last minute as her mom isn't feeling the best. I really wish she could be here but didn't want to make her feel guilty.

The dress code is all white, making it easy for everyone. Most women have turned up in dresses, except for Maddy, the star of the show, wearing a white pantsuit. Beneath the low-cut blazer, she has nothing on, exposing the middle of her chest and the curves of her boobs. The gold necklace she has hanging between her cleavage, with a diamond cross lying flat against her olive skin.

I opted for a two-piece—a cropped lace corset with a matching skirt. The skirt's slit runs up to the top of my thigh, showing my leg in my sparkly knee-high boots. I brought my coat but thoughtfully organized plush blankets for everyone to place on their laps to keep them warm if the outdoor heating isn't enough.

"You've done an amazing job," Carolina, one of Maddy's college friends, says out loud. "And to pull this off in less than a month. Are you sure you don't want to plan my wedding?"

I smile proudly. "Think I'll stick to running Donuts Ever After."

The server pulls out a chair for me to sit beside Maddy, who is sitting at the head of the table. With my shoulders back and a knowing grin, I take in all my hard work.

It looks spectacular.

The table is decorated with gold-plated china and cutlery, and white linen napkins are embroidered with Madelina's Bachelorette in pink. Centered on the table are hot-pink roses in these gorgeous mosaic vases next to candles burning inside lanterns. Everything has come together just how I envisioned, including the male servers who are supposed to be shirtless. At the last minute, I felt sorry for them and suggested they wear a bow tie with a jacket so at least you can still see their abs, but so they won't suffer in the cold.

We have a professional chef from Brooklyn cooking dinner for us and a bartender who concocted signature cocktails. They are pink, of course, and taste very feminine. That's if it is possible for a drink to taste feminine. I guess *fruity* would be the more appropriate term.

After everyone has arrived and is seated, I stand and raise my glass. "To Maddy, the bride-to-be. May this night be as wild as you were back in high school."

All the women laugh, including Maddy, who quickly disagrees playfully. "I'm still wild, thank you very much. Who else would get married a month after being proposed to?"

While this is Maddy's night, I'm quick to observe she's had a number of drinks already.

The servers march out of the house carrying gold platters with plates of food. Since Mediterranean is Maddy's favorite, serving all the dishes she loves to eat made sense. Aston knows the chef at a restaurant Maddy visits often in the city and paid him to cook tonight.

We start with *Zeytinyağlı yaprak sarma*, as pronounced by Maddy. It's made from vine leaves with a rice filling and slightly sweet cooked onions, then seasoned with fresh parsley and dill. They are so yummy, but I make sure not to overindulge and leave room for the other courses.

Next, we are served lamb shish kebabs with bell peppers, tomatoes, and onions. On the side, there is a simple Greek salad. The food tastes amazing, and even though I promised myself not to overeat, I devour everything and leave no room for dessert.

With my stomach full, I turn to Maddy and say, "Are you having fun?"

She hesitates, then drinks her cocktail before requesting the waiter serve her another. "It's what I wanted, right?"

"Yes," I answer with raised brows, questioning her tone. "You did want this."

Maddy becomes distracted by the girls seated across from us telling a story about another friend's wedding. Apparently, the bride's ex showed up right before the vows and made this long speech about how he never stopped loving her. All hell broke loose, and then the groom and ex got into a fistfight. It sounds like a reality television show.

When the story ends, Ramona stands up with a grin on her red-stained lips. "Did somebody say dessert is next?"

This is the code for *Watch out, some dick is gonna flop out.*

The girls all look at each other in confusion until "Pony" by Ginuwine plays loudly, and three men wearing togas walk around the table.

I want to crawl into a hole and die. For them, not me.

Maddy surprises me by raising her napkin and swinging it around. I'm not sure how much she's had to drink at this point, but I can tell by the way she's dancing that it's more than I've had.

The men circle Maddy, practically shoving their crotches in her face. Since I'm sitting next to her, one of their butt cheeks rubs against my arm. I shudder at the contact, removing myself from the table to give them more space.

The cocktails keep coming, and by my fourth one, I start to loosen up and have more fun. The togas eventually come off, much to my surprise since I wasn't expecting to see so much *manhood*. At least they are wearing thongs, but the teeny piece of gold fabric isn't enough to hide everything. One guy's balls accidentally slip out, but I think he's more embarrassed than we are.

Ramona is a loose cannon, rubbing her body up against one of the strippers, who keeps eyeing me. It wouldn't surprise me if she goes home with him at this stage, if that's even legal. I have no idea what the stripper code of conduct is these days.

We play games, dance to music, and laugh so hard I nearly pee my pants.

Maddy is blind drunk, slurring her words and talking crap about the wedding. As soon as I hear her mention how she wasn't sure about walking down the aisle, I know she'll pass out soon.

Thankfully, Myles's cousins don't hear, as they are too busy trying to flirt with the servers, who seem to have let loose, too.

Maddy is the type of drunk to get sad and cry about first-world problems. I'm the exact opposite. I want to party harder and dance my life away like I'm eighteen without a care in the world.

"I think I should get some water into you soon," I tell her, observing her glazed eyes. "You look ready to crash."

"You ever loved someone so much you can't think about anything else? And it hurts so much when you're not with them?" Maddy's questions come out as a giant slur.

"Maddy, you're just drunk. I'm sure that's how you feel about Myles."

She points her finger into my chest, pushing a little too hard and hurting me. "But what if I don't?"

"Well, you're lying because why would you agree to marry someone you're not in love with?"

She bursts out laughing. "You're right!"

"See, everything is going to be okay."

"But what about you?"

I raise my brow. "What about me?"

Maddy motions for me to come closer, then giggles in my ear. "I gave the stripper your number. He thought you were hot."

"Why would you do that?" I raise my voice, only for two girls across from us to look over. "I'm not interested in dating someone. I already—" I cut myself off, almost carelessly mentioning Aston.

"Relax, why not have a little fun? You sure need to. It's not like anything is happening with the doctor or anyone else. You wouldn't lie to me, now would you?"

I shake my head without even thinking.

Maddy hiccups this time, her face looks pale. She reaches for another drink, quick to distract herself.

"Speaking of dating," Hailey, Myles's other cousin, pipes up. "What is the story with your brother, Maddy?"

My body stiffens at the change of topic, but I quickly add, "We tried to set him up with Ramona, but apparently, he's seeing someone."

The moment it leaves my mouth, I hide my satisfaction. There's no chance in hell any of these girls will touch what's mine.

Did I just say what's mine?

"I tried stalking him on Instagram. Turns out he doesn't have one." Hailey pouts. "Everyone has Instagram. He's probably sneaking around with someone he wants no one else to know about."

For some odd reason, it never occurred to me to stalk Aston online. Talk about a red flag on my end. How could I have been so distracted with everything going on to not cyberstalk the man I've slept with?

"My brother refuses"—another one of Maddy's loud, obnoxious hiccups breaks her train of thought, but she continues, slurring—"to go online. He likes things to remain private. I don't even know who he is supposedly dating, but whoever it is, he's not breathing a word. God, she could be my sister-in-law."

I clear my throat. "I highly doubt he will get married. That's not his style."

"How do you know?" Maddy accuses, her brows furrowing. "What if he meets the one woman with whom he wants to spend the rest of his life, huh? He's not a robot, Eva. Just because you hate him doesn't mean other women do."

"I never said he was a robot. Plus I don't hate him." I drag the words out and then take a drink to ease the tension building inside me. "Aston doesn't strike me as someone who wants to *settle down*. That's all."

"Yeah, well, you weren't there this morning when he was rambling on about one day wanting to get married and have kids. Trust me, I know my brother. He has changed."

The lump inside my throat thickens, forcing me to stand up and say, "I'm going inside to get you a bottle of water. You need to sober up."

But truthfully, *I* need to sober up.

Aston wants to get married and have kids.

That is absurd.

One of the servers offers to go instead, but I kindly tell him I need the walk.

With the fresh night air caressing my heated skin, I try my

best to drown out the conversation between Maddy and me. Something is crawling beneath the surface, pestering me to pay attention, but I have no idea what the voices inside my head are even trying to say.

As I step inside the kitchen, the staff have cleaned up and only two people remain. I open the refrigerator door to pull out a bottle of water, only to close it to see Aston on the other side.

His presence makes me jump in shock, and my hand presses against my chest to still my racing heart. He's supposed to be at the bachelor party, which is being held on some fancy houseboat on Peppermint Lake, owned by his business acquaintance.

I immediately notice the black suit jacket and pants he wears with a white shirt beneath. The shirt is partially unbuttoned, exposing his tanned chest. I'm quick to inhale his scent, only to remember he shouldn't be here.

"Aston, why are you here?"

He takes my hand, not saying a word, a look of desperation in his eyes. In a mad rush, he pulls me up the back staircase leading to the end of the south wing. I beg him to slow down since the heels of my boots are higher than I typically wear.

Aston ushers me inside the bedroom, closing the door behind him. Then, he unexpectedly smashes his lips onto mine, causing me to gasp. I can taste the liquor on him and suspect he's had more than a few drinks.

My hands press on his chest, pushing him away. "Aston, we can't. Maddy and everyone are downstairs."

"I need you." His voice breaks in the dark.

"But . . ." I breathe, dropping my chin. "We agreed."

I glance into his eyes, and despite the room being dark with only the light of the moon illuminating the space around us, his pain is evident. I reach for his cheek, caressing it gently. "What's wrong?"

"I don't want to talk about it."

"Okay, but how can I fix it if you don't tell me?"

"You can't fix everything, Everleigh," he mumbles.

I place a soft kiss on his lips, hoping to calm him down. "No, I can't, but I can at least try."

He doesn't say another word, taking my hand and leading me to the bed. As I lie down, he climbs on top of me. Unlike the night in his apartment, this feels different. There's something behind the urgency of his kiss, and the touch of his lips makes me forget how to do the simplest of things, such as breathe.

"Aston . . ." I moan into his mouth mid-kiss. "We shouldn't be here."

"Everleigh, please, I need you."

I hold on to him, wrapping my hands around his neck until he pulls away to undress me. When I'm completely naked beneath him, he takes a moment to drink me in before sliding inside of me. I gasp at the fullness swarming my belly, and this time, he takes me at a slow pace. In and out, kissing every inch of my skin and making sure nothing is missed.

Then, he stops and holds my gaze as if this moment will save him. Whoever he needs saving from, I want to be the one who wears the cape and promises him nobody can hurt him. And in this vulnerable moment, the reality of this cat-and-mouse game we've been playing becomes crystal clear.

It's no longer a game.

Not when my heart is suddenly the one caught in the trap.

CHAPTER 25

Aston

Chalmers slides the thick pile of papers in front of me.

Night falls outside as the two of us sit in my office. It's been an incredibly long day, and the last thing I want is to spend my night here in the city, but my father left me no choice.

He's been on my back all week about wrapping up outstanding deals and insisting I spend time with Roland Whitney. One moment, he wants me to do one thing, and the next, another. He's giving me whiplash.

My eyes reluctantly scan the first page to see the Whitney Group name in bold on the front. As I continue to read silently, the contract's content becomes apparent.

My father will get his hands on the land he has so desperately wanted over the last two decades.

And Madelina is his bargaining tool.

The children she will be forced to bear in exchange for land to be transferred to the Beaumont name. All Roland and Georgina want is to be grandparents, which will grant them their wish as well as please my father.

I push the contract back to Chalmers, then stand up to pace the room with a fresh swell of anger rising within me. "I don't understand why my sister must be involved," I bellow.

Chalmers sits back in his chair, keeping the smug expression on his aging face.

"C'mon, kid. You know your father by now," he chides.

He's right.

I should know my father by now.

My arms cross over my chest as I stare out the window, trying to think of ways to end my father's irrational thinking. This week alone, I closed one deal and secured our investors for two more in the works. The stock market rose in our favor, and we are tracking solid growth in this fiscal year alone.

"I will deal with this after the wedding," I mutter while pinching the bridge of my nose. "My sister's happiness is more important to me."

Chalmers tips his head with an arrogant smirk, then says, "Don't think the old fella will let this one go. Be careful. If you don't play nice, you'll pay the price one way or another."

He leaves my office, only for me to slam my fist on my desk the second he is gone.

I sit in my chair, staring at my screen until a headache spreads across my temples, forcing me to close my eyes. My mind drifts to a time when life was simple and the weight on my shoulders was less because I was naive enough to think my life belonged to me.

My phone dings with a text message alert. I retrieve the phone from my pocket and see Everleigh's name on the screen.

Everleigh

There's a loud banging sound coming from my neighbor's apartment, and I'm not sure if I should tell her to keep it down.

Me

It depends. What do you think she's doing?

Everleigh

What do you think she's doing?

A smile spreads across my lips as I type quickly. The headache slowly dissipates, the tension easing.

> **Me**
>
> Oh, I see. You're in a bit of a pickle. I guess you could go over and politely ask her to keep it down, but you do run the risk of seeing her in sexy lingerie. How old are we talking?

Everleigh

> Old enough to be your grandmother. She has a new boyfriend who is half her age. Kudos to her, but seriously, he's a machine, and she's the cowgirl having a good time.

> **Me**
>
> So, what you're really trying to ask me is to come over so you can give her a run for her money?

Everleigh

> I'm serious! I have an early start tomorrow and am exhausted from today. We got boxes of supplies in, and I've been moving stuff around. All I can say is we better start picking up more business, or I'm out of this town and this building.

> **Me**
>
> Don't stress. Cinnamon Springs always peaks during spring break when people are traveling. As for your neighbor problem, you know where to find me.

Everleigh

> You're all the way in the city.

> **Me**
>
> Yes, I am. It takes me exactly two hours and five minutes to get to you.

Everleigh

I'll remember that . . . after the wedding.

I reread her text, releasing a drawn-out sigh. Every part of me is desperate to touch Everleigh and lose myself in her again. The thought of not being inside her until this wedding is over will drive me to the brink of insanity.

My fingers type before my brain can think clearly.

Me

For you, I'll wait.

The three dots appear forever. *What the hell is she typing?* As I wait, I shut down my computer to head back to my apartment for a quick rest so I can drive back to Cinnamon Springs early in the morning to meet Roland. The bachelor party is tomorrow night, but thankfully, I'll be done with all my urgent business before it starts.

My computer makes the shutdown noise, and at the same time, my phone pings.

Everleigh

Thank you.

Two words that make me stop my movements.

I'm not sure what the hell is going on, wondering why my chest is rising and falling at a rapid rate and why my stomach flips, leaving me queasy.

I contemplate texting back but decide some things are better left unsaid.

When you have money, planning a bachelor party is a walk in the park. The sky is the damn limit.

A business buddy of mine, Eli, owns a houseboat bordering Cinnamon Springs and Cherry Tree Creek. When I pitched the idea to Myles, I explained it wasn't an ordinary houseboat. This one is a crossover between a private yacht and an apartment, moored next to a private sandbar with its own pier. The space is around 4,350 square feet and comprises four en suite bedrooms, a terrace, and a swimming platform. Not that I expect anyone to jump in the freezing-cold water, but then again, bachelor parties always have a way of getting out of control.

It's decked out like a luxury apartment and offers unparalleled waterfront views of Peppermint Lake and the mountains surrounding it.

I have a yacht moored at Safe Harbor, but it's nothing compared to this vessel—there's no way it could fit everyone on board. Eli made a fortune from cryptocurrency, and this is just one of his many toys scattered across the globe.

Myles's guest list comprises thirty guys. Most are college buddies, a bunch from work, and some family acquaintances. Unfortunately, my father insisted on joining when he found out Roland would be there.

Unlike Everleigh and her bachelorette planning, I delegated most of this task to my assistant. She planned the catering and liquor, and organized a poker table. As for the other entertainment, I called for reinforcement. Will's father has connections in the industry. I didn't ask why or how but simply paid the invoice to ensure the girls would be there on time and entertain the men.

Madelina had already warned me to keep it somewhat clean.

I've been to several bachelor parties, all ending in pandemonium. The worst ones are those in Vegas. Sin City never ends well, not when rules are made to be broken.

The night starts relatively relaxed. The boys throw back a few shots, urging Myles to drink away his second-to-last night of freedom. Most of the guys are already married, leaving only five still single.

It's always the married ones who party the loudest.

Gino, Myles's buddy from college, cranks up the sound system and dances out on the terrace without a care in the world. I take a few shots myself, trying to ease the tension in my shoulders and arms from the golf session with Roland. I don't mind the guy, but golf isn't a sport I'm fond of. It's a sport used to talk business, something my father taught me earlier in my career.

Give me a football any day over a club and golf ball.

"Hey, Beaumont, come out here and smoke with us," Gino yells over the music.

It doesn't surprise me someone brought weed to the party. The last time I smoked it would have been at college at some frat party while I fucked whoever would spread their legs for me. *How times have changed.*

The only woman I want to spread her legs for me is at my sister's bachelorette party, hopefully behaving herself and not allowing any male stripper to touch her. Everleigh saw my jealous streak when Dr. What's-His-Face attempted to touch her and should have learned her lesson.

"I'm going to check on a few things," I tell Gino as Myles begs me with his eyes to take me with him.

"Be nice to the groom," I warn Gino playfully. "He better come out of this alive, or my balls are on the line."

A few of the guys stay outside to smoke, while others sit around the large poker table inside. My father is leading the game, counting his chips with a cigar resting between his lips. The bastard is impossible to read, his facial expression blank until the last minute when he reveals his cards.

Steven, Myles's groomsman, pushes half his tall stack into the middle of the table. Carefully, he watches my father, waiting for a reaction. It's down to the two of them, and the stakes are high.

My father stares blankly at his stack, counting his chips quietly as everyone waits in anticipation. After what feels like the longest minute ever, he pushes his entire stack farther to the middle and calls, "All in."

Almost everyone gasps except for me.

This won't end well for Steven, and the poor guy has no clue just how cunning my father is.

Steven begins to sweat, beads dripping from his curly black hair onto his forehead, and after much deliberation, he finally concedes and sputters, "I fold."

My father grins while bringing Steven's stack toward his own and doesn't show his cards, much to Steven's annoyance.

"C'mon, Harvey. Take me out of my misery," Steven begs.

"Rule number one in poker," my father preaches with a satisfied smile. "Always make your opponent believe you hold the better hand."

"Dammit," Steven mutters, only to reach out and drink his whiskey in one go. "I'm broke as fuck now."

Another game starts, but I opt to walk away. Glancing down, I check my watch. A waitress comes over to advise me the entertainment has arrived. I thank her and meet the three girls at the door.

Will's father delivered on his promise. The women are all beautiful, and despite them wearing coats, I can tell the men upstairs will be pleased. One is slightly older, maybe in her mid-thirties, with fiery red hair and bright green eyes, albeit contact lenses. Her stage name is apparently Poison Ivy. It's very fitting since she looks just like the DC character.

The second lady is blond, looking like a young Marilyn Monroe with a mole perched above her lip, just like the icon herself. I peg her as being in her late twenties.

As for the third woman, she appears much younger. Her long brown hair reminds me of someone I can't put my finger on. Unlike the two other women who come across as boisterous and outgoing, the younger one keeps to herself.

I give them directions to the bedroom at the back of the houseboat to change and leave their belongings. As I return to the main living area, my father stops me.

"Chalmers told me you refuse to cooperate." His stern voice is far from the earlier laughter at the poker table. "Don't disappoint me, you understand? You do the wrong thing, and our entire family will suffer."

"This is not the time to discuss such matters," I tell him, keeping my tone as calm as possible.

"We *will* discuss matters when *I* say so," he voices coldly.

"Why don't you go back to stealing whatever money you can at the poker table," I deadpan. "Surely, you didn't need Steven's money."

"It's never about money. It's about power. You need to get that through this arrogant head of yours, or else you will pay the price."

Of course, another threat comes from the man who is supposed to be my father.

"Please, enlighten me as to why power is so important to you. Why, instead of being my father, you treat me like one of your goddamn puppets."

His gaze flickers, warning me I've pushed the wrong button.

"The measure of a man is what he does with his power. My father treated me no different, and because of that, look at how powerful the Beaumont name has become. One day, I'll be gone, and it will be your responsibility to carry this name, which is why I promoted you to CEO. You'll have your own son who will then carry the legacy." His words are a warning. "A son you will bring into this world with the right woman who will fulfill the role as the next Mrs. Beaumont."

I cock my head, surprised to be hearing this for the first time. It sounds to me like he'll be choosing my wife. Nothing should surprise me anymore, the man has no care in the world for what I want.

"I don't want to know what you expect me to do next. As for right now, I'm going to make sure this party doesn't end up a mess."

For my sanity, I step away from him and back to the main terrace where everyone has gathered. A roar erupts as the music changes, and the three women strut out of the room. Myles is already sitting in the middle, appearing awkward and less enthused than I thought he would be. Gino catches on, passing a blunt to Myles to help him chill the fuck out.

The girls do their work, teasing Myles as their clothes slowly come off. I watch from the railing of the boat beside Roland. Earlier, he was playing poker and enjoying himself. Surprisingly, he doesn't seem bothered by his son getting lap dances.

I drink the bourbon from my glass, quietly watching Myles. The rest of the group cheers him on while trying to touch the girls. They don't seem bothered by it, especially when the men slide bills inside their panties. Steven and his broke ass borrowed money from Gino just so he could have some fun.

Unlike other parties where I've been blind drunk and partaken in activities involving women, tonight feels entirely different.

All I can think about is Everleigh.

What she's doing.

The sound of her voice.

The smell of her skin.

If only I could escape this godforsaken party and see her.

I turn to face the dark water, desperate for a moment's peace as my father's words haunt me.

A son you will bring into this world with the right woman who will fulfill the role as the next Mrs. Beaumont.

It explains why on several occasions, he's pushed Viviana onto me. To please him, I did date her, but it quickly ended, much to his disappointment.

"You see all that land across those mountains?" Roland points across the water. "My grandfather migrated from Ireland and bought this land so his future family would never have to worry about money."

"Quite the gentleman," I state simply, my eyes suddenly drawn to a spot on the shore across from us. "Family is important to you."

"Your father is pulling out all the stops to get me to sell it to him. However, it's more than just selling him land. Behind those mountains, we have farms. All of which produce agricultural export products. I know Myles is reluctant to take over, but I hope I can find someone to help him and that we can keep it in the family. I owe my grandfather and father this. One day, I hope Myles and Madelina will also produce a son to carry the Whitney name for generations."

"I understand, Roland. My father can be very persistent . . ." My words trail off as I remember why the spot across from me seems so familiar. The abandoned house by the lake was where we partied on graduation night.

The night I boldly kissed Everleigh and, in the same breath, pushed her away because I was young and foolish.

The walls of my chest tighten at the memory of that night.

You have everything going for you. You're smart, a straight-A student without even trying. Coach loves you. Your athletic ability is the best the school has seen. Not to mention, you're pretty. So tell me, why on earth do you think your father should dictate your life?

I had gazed at Everleigh coldly that night, so afraid of how she made me feel by believing I could defy my father. For a moment, I thought about giving it all up to follow my dreams.

But fear crippled me.

It destroyed any fight I had left.

"I'm sure you understand." Roland interrupts my wandering thoughts. "I'm surprised you're even considering moving to Dubai. It's a long way from Manhattan."

I tilt my head in confusion. "Excuse me?"

"Harvey secured the partnership last week by investing in a hotel chain. He negotiated the terms and offered you as the bargaining tool. Are you telling me you had no idea?"

"What do you mean he offered me as the bargaining tool?" I splutter, momentarily beyond words.

Roland places his hand on my shoulder. "Aston, go speak to

him. If you're not happy, I'm sure there's a compromise you can agree on."

Slowly, I turn around to face the guys all having fun and laughing. Two of the women are joining in, smoking a joint and dancing with Gino and another guy. I angle my head, cracking my neck with anger thrumming through my veins. I scan the area, hunting for the man whose death I wish to plot.

He's nowhere to be found.

My feet move in large steps, searching the entire vessel until I hear noises inside the room at the back. I place my hand on the doorknob, turning it until the small crack is enough for me to see what's happening.

The young brunette woman dances in front of my father, swaying her hips with a vacant stare in her eyes. He sits on the edge of the bed, the corner of his mouth quirking as the smoke lingers from his cigar.

Then, he wraps his hand around her thigh and squeezes it tight, forcing her to move closer to him. My hands curl into fists, the rage pouring through me like hot lava. I see the fear in her eyes and suddenly push the door open with a bang.

She covers her bare chest in a panic, but my father grins like a complete and utter asshole. I warn her with my eyes to leave, and thankfully, she hurries out and avoids what could have been with a man who gets off on control. I knew my parents' marriage was far from a loving relationship, but he's taken it too far this time.

Does he really think he can get away with fucking some young girl the same age as his daughter?

"Jealous, son?" he boasts, standing up to meet my stance. I'm much taller than him, despite his ignorance. "I don't think your little girlfriend would be too pleased to see you touching another woman. So, I thought I'd do you a favor."

Resentment festers within me, mixed with cold fury.

"You think I don't know you've been wasting time on your

sister's best friend? How devastating if your sister finds out you've both been lying to her."

My nostrils flare as I demand, "You leave Everleigh out of this."

I don't wait to argue with him, leaving his smug face behind as I bail on this party to see Everleigh. The bastard somehow knows I've been with her, and the only rational answer is someone told him I brought her to the charity event, and he assumes we're dating.

My Porsche is parked outside. I don't even think twice about getting in and driving home despite the bachelorette party still going on.

When I reach the manor, I roll my car in quietly and park it out front. I know they will be in the back, so I head to the kitchen and decide to text Everleigh, only to see her walk in.

Her face becomes concerned the moment she sees me, but I don't waste any time taking her hand and leading her to my bedroom.

It's all become too much.

The conversation with Roland about my father's secret deal and me moving to Dubai, to seeing my father willingly cheat on my mother with a young stripper, to him bringing up Everleigh like she's worth nothing.

All I want to do is forget.

So, I kiss Everleigh and make it clear I need her.

She wants to save me, but it's too late.

I'm beyond being saved.

Even from myself.

Everleigh provides me with an escape. I lose myself in her body, fucking her quietly as everyone parties outside. Her body becomes my new addiction, and no matter how many times I kiss her, or how many times I push myself in deeply, I still want more.

I fucking blow, seeing goddamn stars.

Collapsing on top of her, we lay quietly, trying to catch our breath.

"I should go back downstairs," she whispers. "They could be looking for me."

My lips press against hers but without the urgency this time.

"Come back here, please," I beg of her. "Stay with me tonight."

"Aston . . ."

"I need you," I murmur.

With a silent nod, she kisses my lips and promises to return when Maddy is asleep.

I lie in bed, staring at the ceiling. My mind is conjuring up a thousand ways to quit my role as CEO and free myself from the reins of my father. The more I try to develop scenarios that will work, the more roadblocks I face. Many of them legal.

Sometime later, my door opens, and Everleigh steps through. She quietly tiptoes to my bed and hovers without saying a word. I pull back the sheets, which prompts her to strip her clothes off and climb into bed with me.

Her warm skin envelops me, and I know the most significant thing weighing on my mind isn't my father.

It's my heart falling for the girl I almost had all those years ago.

CHAPTER 26

Eva

Aston woke me up by sliding himself inside me.

Something changed between us last night.

His usual aggressive sexual appetite was slower and sensual, and all it did was make me want him more. I realized there was so much emotion behind a slow burn, and thoughts ran rampant while my body reached new heights.

And when the sun peeked through his dark drapes, a new day promised so much more.

Unlike the last time we slept together, in his apartment, I stay snuggled into his embrace after we both climax.

I want to stay like this forever. And with a lopsided grin, I keep the thought to myself.

"I'm going to have to get out of this bed soon and check on Maddy," I say softly.

"Hmm . . . not yet."

"But soon, okay?"

His embrace tightens as he makes it obvious he doesn't want to let me go. I turn to face his perfectly sculpted torso, spreading tiny kisses on his chest.

"We broke the rules," I remind him.

"I'm done playing by the rules, Everleigh." His voice wavers. "It's only a matter of time before Madelina finds out."

I lace my fingers into his. "I know. Just give me time, please. I want to tell her myself."

Aston raises my chin so our eyes meet. "And what exactly will you tell her?"

"That we, um, are together." I pause, waiting for his reaction. "We *are* together, right? Unless, of course, this is an open relationship type of thing?"

He kisses my knuckles softly. "I want you all to myself."

My face rests on his chest as I run my fingers against his tattoo. The small cross is barely noticeable beneath his sparse chest hair. "What happened last night?"

Aston's muscles tighten beneath me. He's always had difficulty opening up, so I'm not counting on him telling me anything.

"He got to me."

"Your father?"

A sigh escapes him. "Yes. I was standing with Roland and looking at that old house where we kissed before I left for college. I still remember how you told me no one else should plan my life for me."

I place a kiss on his chest. "I still believe that."

"I just needed to see you."

With a shuffle, I glance up to look at him. "One day, I'm buying that house."

Aston chuckles. "I don't think it's habitable."

"Houdini thinks it is."

"Houdini?"

"A frog. He comes and goes, hence the name."

"Right . . ." Aston trails off. "Are you smoking a joint while you're talking to your imaginary friend?"

I smack his chest with a grin. "He's not imaginary! Though, I do admit talking to a frog does make me sound cuckoo. Do you know how many times I've thought about lying in this bed with you? I hated how much I thought about you in high school."

Aston kisses my forehead. "I've also thought about you in this bed. I was just the fool who couldn't see past his ego."

We lie together for another hour, but then reality becomes unavoidable. I reach for my phone to ensure Billie opened the store, and Chloe came in to assist. With Billie's mom still recovering, I tell Billie to leave early. Chloe can run the store today, and anyway, I plan to stop by later.

As for tomorrow, our store is officially closed for the first time ever. Chloe offered to open up and work, but I wanted one day to relax and be focused on my best friend.

Aston is dead tired, falling asleep again, so I muster my way out of his arms to put my clothes back on. Sneaking out of his room feels so juvenile as I tiptoe down the hall to Maddy's bedroom.

Just like Aston, she is fast asleep. So I grab my bag from the room and head straight to the shower. By the time I'm completely dressed and downstairs, no one has joined me.

I sit at the kitchen counter and enjoy a strong coffee prepared by Hilda. With my focus on my phone, ensuring emails are up-to-date and everything is ready for the rehearsal dinner tonight, I don't hear footsteps behind me.

"Good morning, Everleigh," a voice calls.

My body twists on the tall stool to see Mr. Beaumont behind me. I force a smile and offer him some coffee, which he accepts. *So much for a stress-free morning.*

"I know I haven't had a chance to speak to you privately," he starts, slow and steady. "However, now would be the perfect opportunity to thank you for all your time and effort in making my daughter happy."

I drop my gaze, focusing on the cup between my hands. "Maddy's happiness means everything to me. She's my best friend."

"Yes, I'm aware the two of you have a close relationship. I'm sure once my daughter starts her own family, it will be difficult for you, given that she'll no longer have time to focus on anything else."

This time, I raise my eyes to meet his. Thank God he looks nothing like Aston because it would be much harder to loathe him. "If Maddy chooses to have a family, I will be there to support her. I understand the true meaning of family, unlike some others."

"My daughter knows what is expected. What she doesn't need is a best friend encouraging her to go against what is best for our family."

I cross my arms, annoyed by his sheer disrespect for Maddy's wants. "Maddy deserves to make her own decisions, as does Aston. They're no longer kids."

"See, Everleigh, your lack of understanding is the reason why you'll never work out with my son."

"Excuse me?"

"I'm no fool. Who do you think owns the building you slept in? And did you expect to attend the event without me finding out? When a woman is standing beside my son, everyone is watching, including me. After all, the next Mrs. Beaumont will be more than a small-town café owner."

Mr. Beaumont cocks his head with an arrogant smirk while I stand here in shock. Just as he is about to open his mouth again, Maddy walks into the room groaning.

"I will never drink again," she mutters.

With a shaky hand, I slide a tall cup of Americano toward her. Maddy despises coffee with no milk, but today, she needs the extra jolt of energy.

Mr. Beaumont leaves the room when his phone rings. The piercing sound is enough to make Maddy block her ears. Even after he's gone, the tightness in my chest lingers from his callous words. Not only does he know about me and Aston, but I'm considered not good enough.

Me, a woman who started her own business without billions of dollars to fall back on.

Everything I've worked hard for isn't good enough for a man who has proven impossible to please.

Maddy cringes when she sips the steaming coffee. "This tastes like ass."

"I'm glad you know what ass tastes like," I mumble, turning away while trying to hold back my emotions.

An email comes through from the restaurant confirming numbers for tonight—so far, no one has pulled out—prompting me to respond quickly. There are a few other things I need to do today, and time is of the essence, so I finish the remaining coffee inside my cup, desperate to get out of here. "I have to run some errands."

Just as I hop off the stool, Aston walks in wearing his checked red-and-black bottoms with no shirt. I swallow with great difficulty, avoiding looking at his hot body, but Mr. Beaumont's words continue to haunt me.

"Why do you look so happy?" Maddy questions grumpily. "And why aren't you hungover? What about Myles? God, tell me everything that happened."

"I'm going to head to the café," I say with a smile. "I'll see you both tonight."

Aston leans against the counter, crossing his toned arms. The corner of his mouth lifts, he's teasing me with his piercing green eyes.

Mr. Beaumont is *wrong*.

Aston will do whatever the hell he wants, and after last night, it's clear he wants me.

My head falls to hide my grin as I take a step toward the door.

"Oh, Everleigh?" Aston calls, forcing me to turn around. I take in a deep breath, preparing myself to face him again. When our eyes meet, he cocks his head with a smirk. "I'll be at your place twelve sharp to finalize the things we discussed last night."

"What things?" Maddy asks, eyeing both of us.

"Wedding things you made us do," Aston snaps, shaking his head. "You know, once this wedding is over, everyone has to return to their own lives."

Maddy folds her arms. "Oh yeah, and who do you have to go back to, huh?"

"My personal life is no one's damn business."

Back in high school, it wasn't uncommon for me to get stuck in the middle of their sibling arguments. Evidently, nothing has changed.

"Okay, listen. Can I just say one thing before this gets out of hand?" They both glance at me, waiting for me to say something. "You both need to chill out. This is a time for celebrating love."

Maddy's lips press together. "That sounded corny."

"You're right, it did," I concur, only to turn my back on them again and yell over my shoulder, "Now, both of you grow up and stop arguing!"

"Are you moving people around for your own sick and twisted pleasure?"

The finalized seating chart is on the screen as we sit on the sofa. Aston insisted I stay naked, which, might I add, is incredibly uncomfortable when you're trying to do serious things, and your boobs are just hanging there saying hello. I negotiated and was able to wear his T-shirt instead.

From the moment he arrived, he made sure to fuck me in every which way possible. Against the front door, in the kitchen on the counter, where he apparently had the best "meal" of his life, on this very sofa.

"Yes." He grins, pulling my laptop from me. "You see, Josephine was married to Larry until he was caught doing the housekeeper. It was one hell of a nasty divorce because he also knocked her up."

My hand slaps against my mouth to hide my shock. "Don't you dare! That's so mean!"

"But is it?" He raises his brows with a slow smile building. "What's life without a little fun?"

"You're a bully," I tease before he places the laptop down and pins me to the sofa.

Aston kisses me deeply, then fixes his gaze on mine. "Would a bully fuck you for the fourth time today and make you come again, huh?"

I shake my head, unable to hold back my simper.

Aston grazes his hand against my thigh and brushes it against my clit, causing me to gasp. With a devilish smirk playing on his lips, I expect him to slide himself in me until his phone vibrates on the coffee table beside us.

It's like the tenth call he's had since he got here two hours ago, and like all those other calls, he chooses to ignore it.

"Fuck my life," he complains, resting his forehead against mine. "I can't even fuck my girl in peace."

A warmth radiates throughout my body from him calling me his girl. I'm not that type—you know, the one who gets all fuzzy over cutesy nicknames and stuff—so why has the simplest of endearments left a drumming sensation in my chest?

Almost like I belong to him.

"You know, all those years ago when you kissed me, I hated you for being a dick afterward," I admit, running my fingers down his cheek. "And do you want to know what's really funny?"

"What?" he murmurs, watching me intently.

"I spent years trying to buy that piece of land. Something always drew me to it, even before we kissed. Being there always brought me so much joy. Then you went ahead and ruined it." I laugh softly.

"I'm sorry," he says faintly.

"It's all in the past," I remind him. "It'll be mine one day, when business picks up and whoever owns it agrees to sell it to me."

Aston cocks his head with a grin. "You love it that much?"

"Maddy and Billie think I'm crazy, but I don't need them if Houdini will hang out with me. I'd love to restore the home, rebuild the porch, sit outside with a good book, and take it all in."

"A good book . . . like smut?" he teases. "I could get on board with this project, but your frog friend sounds a bit possessive."

I smack his arm. "How do you know about smut?"

Aston shrugs with a smirk, only for his phone to ring again.

"I should probably go." He sighs dejectedly, then continues, "We have to be at dinner in two hours."

As he stands up, I grab his arm to pull him back to me. "But why do you have to go now?"

His mouth curves in amusement. "Because I can't turn up in sweats with your pussy smell all over me."

My nose scrunches at his crass remark. "That sounds gross."

"Trust me, sweetheart, it's the exact opposite of gross. The last thing I want is some other man smelling you on me."

"Well, if you put it like that," I deadpan.

"I am putting it like that." His eyes search mine with desperation. "No one, and I mean no one, gets to touch you but me."

This is the biggest red flag to exist.

Aston Beaumont thinks he owns me.

And while a part of me is terrified of what that might entail for us, I bury the feeling and ignore it for now. After all, he did call me his girl.

The sentiment brings a grin to my face.

After Aston leaves my apartment, I also have to prepare for tonight. I choose to wear a long, high-neck dress that reaches the floor. There is a split down the side, which comes mid-thigh. I style my hair in a bun and away from my face.

Once I am dressed and have done my makeup, I drive to Pecan Peaks, a town over, for the dinner.

The only people attending tonight are Maddy and Myles's family and the wedding party. Since there are only twelve of us, I've reserved one round table in a quieter part of the restaurant. The dinner is nothing fancy, with large platters of Italian food served instead of multiple courses, keeping the night intimate for the almost-married couple.

Aston arrives with Maddy, but since they are preoccupied talking to Roland Whitney, I don't get a chance to say hello to either of them. When Maddy finally steps away from the conversation, she barely acknowledges me. Her body language is off. She appears weighed down, as if carrying some burden.

As for Aston, he looks my way a few times but also appears to be in some sort of mood. I don't know what's happened in the last two hours, but I wouldn't be surprised if they got into another fight before coming here.

I sit beside Ramona and across from Aston. Next to Aston is Patricia, who doesn't seem like herself either. *What the hell is wrong with this family tonight?*

On her other side, Mr. Beaumont makes sure everyone can hear him.

His voice triggers me, but I pretend to be nice for the sake of my best friend.

With Myles two seats away from me, I lean over to ask, "How are you feeling after last night? Ready to walk down the aisle?"

He reaches out to kiss Maddy's hand, but something is amiss. She glances down at her plate of creamy pasta alla boscaiola with a blank expression.

"I'm ready." He smiles, then chuckles lightheartedly. "Last night was interesting. I know a few of my boys went home broke after Harvey cleaned them up in poker."

"Of course he did," I mutter under my breath. My head tilts to observe Mr. Beaumont. His need to win doesn't surprise me one bit. Everything is a power trip to that bastard.

More bottles of wine are brought to the table to prepare for a few speeches. While most of the speeches are reserved for the wedding day itself, it's common for family members to say a few words at a rehearsal dinner.

I glance across to Aston again, but he ignores me as if I've done something wrong. There's no way to get him outside to talk without raising suspicion, so I text him quickly, with frustration building inside of me.

Me

Why are you acting like a dick?

He drops his attention to the screen but then places his phone back into his pocket.

Did he just completely dismiss my text message?

A tightness inside my chest makes it difficult to focus on whatever Ramona is talking to me about. Her voice is drowned out as my veins begin to pulse with this anger swelling inside of me.

Mr. Beaumont rises from his chair, capturing everyone's attention. My throat feels like it's closing up as I attempt to listen to this asshole's impending speech.

"It is my greatest pleasure to welcome you tonight to our final dinner before my daughter, Madelina, officially becomes the new Mrs. Whitney," Mr. Beaumont begins, raising his glass as everyone gushes over the sentiment. "I believe love is a sacred thing, and the moment you find it, you hold on to it and spend a lifetime creating memories, hopefully with my soon-to-be grandchildren."

The guests seem to laugh at his dig, and Maddy contrives a smile to please everyone.

As for me, I struggle to listen to a man who makes everyone believe family is always first, when he single-handedly puts *business* first. Not to mention I'm worthless, according to him.

"I will save the speech for tomorrow when my darling daughter makes me the proudest father and marries her future husband."

Myles cheers, then raises his glass to say, "Okay, we get it. You want grandkids, too. You do know you have a son as well, right? No pressure, Aston."

Mr. Beaumont brings his glass to his lips to have a drink,

thrusting his chest out with an expression radiating superiority. "My son will be busy in Dubai starting two weeks from today. The Beaumont Group has acquired a rather lucrative chain of hotels, and Aston will be the new CEO of the Emirates portfolio. Perhaps he can find a wife there if he must. After all, he will be living there indefinitely."

A brutal coldness hits my very core, making my entire body freeze. I stare blankly at Mr. Beaumont, trying to register what he's just said. He glances at me while adopting a pondering pose, only to then focus back on everyone else at the table.

My chest suddenly demands my attention. My once-beating heart feels like it has stopped, forcing me to gulp for air.

An uncontrollable shudder takes over until I direct my gaze to Aston. His normally vibrant green stare would usually fill me with warmth, but as I look at him for comfort or a reason for all this madness, all I see are dull eyes staring back at me.

He lied to me.

All this time, he lied to me.

I push my chair out mid-speech, ignoring the weakness in my legs. Maddy diverts her attention to me but doesn't say a word as I turn my back to leave the table. My feet move as quickly as they can given the tight dress around my legs. I push the main door open, smacked in the face by the cold air against my heated skin.

The sound of the door opening again forces me to turn around.

Aston has followed me but is smart enough to keep his distance.

"I hope you followed me because you have a damn good reason why I had to sit there and hear from your father that you're moving to another country *forever!*" I thunder, unable to hide my emotions.

He takes a step closer, clenching his jaw. "Everleigh, it's not what you think."

"It's not what I *think*?" I take a step back, refusing to get close to him. "Don't do this again!"

"Do what again?"

"Make me feel like I'm nothing, that my feelings mean nothing." My voice trembles from the nausea hardening my stomach. "God, Aston. Here I was, falling in love with you, thinking you have changed. You had all the time in the world to tell me you're moving, but no, you lied."

"I have changed!" He runs his hands through his curly hair, trying to control his anger. "You have no idea how much I sacrifice to protect others. This isn't about you, okay? This is about my father dictating everyone's life."

I stare at the man who made me believe I'd fallen in love with him.

A man who broke my heart all those years ago, only to break it again.

"For as long as you allow this man to control your life, then as far as I'm concerned, you haven't changed, Aston." My eyes widen as I swallow hard. "I'm not going to stand around, allowing my heart to break even more. After all, I'm just a small-town café owner unworthy of your family."

"Everleigh, don't do this . . ."

I bow my head, unable to look at him. "Tomorrow, we make sure Maddy has the best day of her life. After that, whatever the hell we were doing is done."

My feet move toward my car, parked a few feet away. I beg myself not to cry, not even a single tear. However, the moment I sit inside alone and realize Aston never followed me, a lonesome tear falls down my cheek and rests on my lips.

I press my head against the steering wheel, fighting the urge to sob. My chest hitches, but I know I have to get myself together to drive out of here.

Not one person has come outside to check on me.

Not fucking one!

I quickly send Maddy a text saying I am not feeling well, but as I hit send, my phone begins to ring, and Billie's name flashes on the screen.

"Billie, I can't really talk right now," I rush in a shaky voice. "My . . ."

"Billie, you're cutting out," I almost yell. "What are you saying?"

"My mom's gone . . ."

CHAPTER 27

Eva

Seraphina lies peacefully in her bed as the doctor examines her lifeless body.

I hold Billie tight, proud of her bravery while she pulls herself together as much as possible under the circumstances. For a long while, Seraphina had been unwell, and Billie's life was put on hold to take care of her. Seraphina's passing comes with mixed emotions. There's the grief of losing a mother, a woman Billie has looked up to her whole life, but in that same breath, Seraphina is no longer in pain.

The doctor on call also happens to be *Marco.*

He explains to us that Seraphina passed in her sleep. Her heart was just too exhausted to function anymore. Marco continues explaining what will happen next and who will come to collect her body.

My arms wrap tight around Billie, doing my best to shield her from the grief even though I know it's impossible. At times, she spoke about the possibility of losing her mother, but reality never compares.

"I'm just going to call my Auntie June and my Uncle Daniel," Billie mentions softly.

"I'll be here," I remind her with a faint smile, wishing I could do more, but I know just being here is probably all she needs right now. "I'll stay with Marco."

Billie takes her phone into her bedroom, leaving me alone with Marco. I watch him take out a notebook. I assume he's recording important details for the coroner when he starts writing notes.

"She's not in pain anymore," I mention quietly.

He shakes his head with his mouth pressed firmly. "The truth is, her heart was weak, and it was just a matter of time."

I nod silently. My eyes wander back to Seraphina, admiring her beauty even in her eternal sleep. Then, I think about the funeral and all the moments when Billie will need someone to lean on. She'll also need some time off, so I mentally try to plan how I'll juggle it all, only to remember what happened tonight with Aston.

It all becomes too much, and just like in the car, another tear finally falls.

"Hey," Marco calls softly, placing his hands on my arms. "It's going to be okay."

My lips begin to quiver, wondering how the most genuine man is here comforting me, yet the one my heart has so desperately fallen for is with his family planning his future without me in it.

A future he chose to hide from me.

"It's just too much," I sob, trying to control my raging emotions. "Maddy is getting married tomorrow, and I'm supposed to be there for her, but Billie needs me. I can't be everywhere."

Marco embraces me, and no matter how hard I try, it's not the same.

It only shows how strong my feelings are for Aston.

How I've fallen so head over heels in love with him without even really knowing.

"There's no way you can prepare yourself for something like this. It's what I tell my patients, and it is that thing we call life. It comes, and it goes. And sometimes, it's out of our control. All we can do is take it one day at a time." Marco gazes at me softly. "Do you think you can do that for me?"

Quietly, I nod.

My fingers fumble nervously before I say, "I'm sorry, Marco, about everything that happened between us."

He remains silent, leaning down and placing his notebook back into his doctor's bag. "As I said earlier, Eva. Some things are out of our control."

"You're too nice to me. I don't deserve it."

"Take care of yourself. I'm a big boy, Eva. It's not the first time things haven't gone the way I wanted them to," he says in a low voice, only to tilt his head. "I heard a car outside. It's most likely Morton, the funeral director."

I leave the room to open the front door. Morton arrives with his colleague to take Seraphina away at the same time as Billie's family arrives.

It all becomes a blur.

The loud sobs Billie expels when Seraphina's body is covered and carried out on a stretcher . . . I hold on to her for dear life, wishing to God someone could take her grief away. I'm unable to stop my own emotions, as a soreness builds in my throat and lungs from the heavy tears I shed with my friend.

In the late-night hours, people come by to pay their respects.

Instead of sleeping, we make cups of coffee and stay awake as Billie's family tells fond stories of Seraphina. It's so lovely that everyone remembers the good times. Just like Marco said, we can only take it one day at a time, and today has been the hardest.

Outside, the sun rises, and the promise of a new day greets us. I sit in the living room with Billie all night as she shows me albums of her childhood. Seraphina was truly Billie's best friend.

Billie gently touches the photograph of herself dressed in a flower girl dress for her auntie's wedding. She sighs heavily before she asks, "You think Maddy will understand if I don't come today?"

"Of course she will understand, Billie," I assure her. "Please don't worry about the wedding."

"Can you maybe not say anything unless she notices?" Billie pleads with hopeful eyes. "I don't want to ruin her day."

"I promise I won't mention anything, okay?"

Billie's Auntie June enters the living room with a fresh pot of coffee. Like us, she looks exhausted and trying to hold it together. I gently take the coffee cup from her but then glance at the clock on the wall.

"Go on, I'll be fine," Billie insists, giving me a little push. "You need to get home and get ready. The wedding's only a few hours away."

I sigh, leaning down to kiss her. "All right, but I'll check in before the ceremony, okay?"

She smiles. "I know you will. Now go."

As I get into the car and drive back home, my eyes are beyond tired from staying up all night and all the tears I so easily shed. Even with copious amounts of coffee, nothing can take away my level of sheer exhaustion right now.

There's no time for a nap, so I take a quick shower and then go straight to the Grand Honey Lodge to help Maddy get ready. Once Maddy is done, my hair and makeup shouldn't take too long.

All I need to do is get through today.

"One more day," I breathe to myself.

As I pull into the parking lot, I see Aston pacing by the door. The moment he notices my car, he storms toward me with flushed, mottled skin and wide eyes, ready to go to battle.

I get out of the car, only for him to yank my bag from me, pulling out my phone.

"It didn't occur to you to pick up your phone any of the times I called you?" he hisses, nostrils flaring as he stares at me in a blind rage.

I glance at the screen to see twenty-seven missed calls.

My eyes close, wishing all of this would just go away. My patience has worn fragile, and nothing I say or do will come out rational. I am tired. I am so tired of life and spinning in this vicious cycle with Aston.

"Don't start," I warn him. "Not now."

"I was worried sick about you! God, Everleigh. You could have driven into a ditch last night."

"I'm not sure why you care. You've never worried about me before." I place my hands on my hips, suddenly angry at him for everything that happened last night. "I mean, you're going to live on the other side of the damn world. That didn't seem to bother you in the slightest."

"Jesus Christ, Everleigh. I wanted to tell you, but—"

"But what? You spent all day with me yesterday. It's clear I am nothing more than an easy fuck to pass the time while in Cinnamon Springs. Or did Harvey get to you?"

"It's not like that," he mumbles, unable to look at me. "We need to talk properly."

I point my finger at him. "*No*, we *don't*, Aston. All the talking has been done. You know just how to break my heart, don't you? So, if you'd kindly get out of my way, I need to make sure my best friend gets married today."

There are no words left to be said.

I enter the building, making sure to slam the door behind me as hard as possible.

We are done.

I am done.

Nothing, and no one, can change my mind.

All the bridesmaids are dressed with their hair and makeup finished.

During my dress change, I get my period. Why not add something else to the already fucked-up twenty-four hours I've had! Luckily, I carry tampons, but given that the dress is made from silk, I pray it doesn't seep through during the ceremony. It could explain my mood, but it's no match for walking around with a broken heart. Everything I do hurts, and no matter how much I try to distract myself, it all comes back to one thing.

It's over before it even began.

And although it's the last thing I want to think about, I remember how Aston has been entering me bareback. Even though I'm taking birth control, that's only 99.9 percent effective.

Thankfully, I am *not* that 0.1 percent this month.

Ramona and Hailey have drunk a bottle of champagne between them. They offered me some, but I was not in the mood. It's bad enough that the makeup artist had to use more concealer to hide the dark circles under my eyes. The girls giggled, thinking it was funny.

But they don't know the hell I've been through.

I check the time with Georgina to ensure we aren't running late. With Patricia in the room, we wait for Maddy to exit the main suite. It takes a few minutes, but she eventually walks out quietly, and we all gasp at how beautiful she looks.

"Maddy, you look perfect," I gush, helping her with the long veil that follows her from the suite. It's made from this expensive lace and passed down from Georgina's great-aunt.

Everyone fusses over Maddy until it's time to head outside to where the ceremony is being held. When everyone leaves the room, I stay back to have a moment with my best friend.

After last night, Maddy has barely spoken two words to me nor responded to my text about leaving. I narrowed it down to nerves, but after spending the night with Billie, I'm too exhausted to focus on anything else.

I fix her train, then open the door so we can head to the main area, where Mr. Beaumont will meet Maddy to walk her down the aisle.

As I hold on to the door handle, Maddy stands perfectly still, staring at me like she's seen a ghost. With her mouth downturned, I pause momentarily, ignoring the sudden quiver in my stomach.

"Maddy, what's wrong?"

"I . . . uh . . ." She stutters on her words, playing with the expensive necklace around her neck and tugging on it, almost like it's choking her. The skin surrounding it turns red, making it obvious she's rubbing it too hard. "I-I can't do this."

I do my best to remain calm, knowing it's common for the bride to panic before walking down the aisle.

"These nerves are normal." I smile, trying to ease her thoughts. "How many movies have we watched where this happens? Cold feet are part of the process."

She bends down to fall to her knees on the floor. Maddy covers her face, rocking back and forth.

My moment of calm is suddenly taken over by worry. I bend with great difficulty, rubbing her back, trying to calm her down.

"I think I'm going to be sick."

I rush to grab the trash can near the end table, pushing it beneath Maddy as she hurls violently. With deep breaths, I try not to puke myself, quickly grabbing some tissues for her to hold on to and removing the trash but still keeping it near.

"Do you feel better now?" I ask softly.

She shakes her head with bloodshot eyes. I notice her skin has developed a rash, and I see her chest rise and fall with her erratic breathing.

"Maddy, what's going on?"

"I . . . I can't do this," she fumbles, anxiously twisting her hands. "I don't love Myles the way he deserves to be loved."

"Okay," I respond, unsure what else to say.

"This doesn't feel right," she cries. "Please, Eva, call my brother."

My lips press together in a slight grimace. "You want me to call Aston?"

"I need him."

"But . . ."

"I need him!" she shouts this time.

The last thing I want to do is speak to Aston, but this is a crisis, and I'm out of my depth here. I search for him and tell everyone that Maddy needs a few moments alone to fix her dress. *What other lie should I have come up with?* It seems much easier than stating the truth right now.

Aston is standing at the altar beside Myles. His head is bowed, his fingers intertwined while he waits like everyone else. *Thank God Mr. Beaumont is nowhere to be seen.* I try to gain Aston's attention. His eyes lock onto mine, but I fight my heart right now and urge him with my eyes to follow me.

He leans in to whisper to Myles, then carefully exits down the side of the manicured garden to where I'm standing. Patricia is sitting at the front and watches me cautiously. Nobody else has noticed yet.

Aston reaches out to touch my arm with a concerned expression, and it's evident he didn't sleep either. "Everleigh, what's wrong?"

"Maddy needs you," I rush.

We both head back inside, running down the long hallway until we reach the bridal quarters. My hand shakily reaches for the door handle, flinging it open, and that's when Aston sees Maddy crouched on the floor.

"Madelina?"

She runs to him, clutching his tuxedo jacket while he wraps his arms around her. His skin bunches around his eyes, and he has a pained stare as he's looking back at me.

It breaks my heart to see my best friend like this, and equally breaks my heart to see the man I love hold on to her and not be able to take her pain away.

"Don't make me do this." She sobs uncontrollably. "Please don't make me marry him."

Aston holds on to her tighter. "I won't make you do anything you don't want to do. Just tell me what's wrong."

"It's . . . it's not right," Maddy stammers, her head shaking. "This doesn't feel right."

"It's just cold feet, Madelina." Aston tries to soothe her.

"No, Aston. This is *not* just cold feet. I'm not some actress being all dramatic in an audition for *Wicked*. This is my life!" She takes a breath, then releases it. "I'm sick of all these lies!"

"What lies?" Aston questions.

"All the lies. The lies I tell myself, and the lies the two of you insist on telling me. I've watched you and Eva hate each other, then like each other, then hate each other again. I saw you change before my own eyes. You, out of all people, mentioned settling down."

I swallow the lump inside my throat, unsure how to react. The truth has come out at the worst possible time.

Maddy turns to face me with a tearstained face. "You think I didn't realize you were falling for my brother? Why did you lie to me, huh?"

"I . . . I, um . . ." I trail off, lost for words. "I wanted to tell you but—"

"Both of you fell so damn hard right in front of me! Only for me to realize I don't feel the same way about Myles. From the moment he proposed marriage, something felt forced. Almost like someone was pushing him, but I didn't listen. I wanted what I thought was a fairy tale, but it's not. I should have DNF'ed this relationship months ago."

Aston cocks his head in confusion.

"DNF stands for *did not finish*," I say faintly.

"I lied to myself all along," she sobs. "I can't walk down that aisle and marry him. I can't have children with a man I'm not head over heels in love with."

The door opens for Patricia, who walks in with concern for her daughter.

"Madelina, sweetheart. We're running behind." She notices Maddy's tears, then frowns. "What's wrong, honey?"

Maddy shakes her head and chews on her bottom lip as tears continue to fall down her perfectly made-up face. Patricia reaches out to embrace Maddy. She holds on with a vacant stare, then glances at Aston with a pained expression. They stand together for minutes on end with Maddy crying openly. I keep my distance from Aston, unsure what to do after Maddy revealed the truth about us.

But right now, this isn't about him or me.

The door opens again, this time much louder, with a thud. I don't have to turn around to know who is breathing heavily behind me.

"What the hell is going on here? People outside are whispering," her father barks.

"I'm sorry, Dad. I won't marry Myles."

Mr. Beaumont clenches his hands into fists, rage seizing him as he shouts, "You *will* marry him. Do you understand me, Madelina? There is too much riding on this!"

Maddy cowers, scared by his vicious words. I straighten my shoulders. I may be nothing to him, but it doesn't make me any less of a person. For once in his life, someone needs to tell him to shut the hell up and stop acting like the biggest asshole to ever exist.

When I'm about to open my mouth, Patricia beats me to it.

"No, Harvey. I will *not* force our daughter to marry some man she is *not* in love with," she states adamantly.

An evil laugh escapes him. "And what is love, Patricia? Is love sneaking behind my back with some poor man who works in the stables? Birthing *his* son, not *mine*?"

Patricia curls her lips, showing her teeth. "A man who has more integrity and compassion than you will ever have in your lifetime."

He moves closer, pointing his finger in her face. "You and your son are nothing without me!"

My eyes blink repeatedly, trying to understand what is happening here. I glance back and forth, only realizing now what Mr. Beaumont has revealed. Maddy has stopped crying, and as for Aston, he stands in complete and utter shock.

But then, something clicks.

His muscles and veins strain against his skin, and a guttural roar passes his lips. I've never witnessed him this angry, and I'm scared to see this side of him. This isn't a momentary reaction— this is a lifetime of being made to feel like he would never be good enough to carry the Beaumont name.

And now, it all makes sense.

"Step away," Aston warns with a snarl.

I yank on Maddy's arm, motioning for us to leave. Mr. Beaumont steps toward Maddy, but Aston presses his hand on Mr. Beaumont's chest to stop him. Aston's tall stature overshadows him as he continues to stare at him ferociously.

"You want to ruin this family just like your brother?" he accuses Maddy wildly.

Maddy looks into my eyes, begging me to help her. I hold on to her hand tight, then stare directly into the devil's eyes.

"Maddy and Aston didn't ruin your family," I inform him with a hard stare. "You did, Harvey Beaumont."

And with the truth said, I leave the room with my best friend so she's not forced to make the biggest mistake of her life.

A mistake her father had planned all along.

CHAPTER 28

Aston

Anger thrums through my veins, unapologetic in its ferocity.

His eyes *burn* with resentment.

The resentment was so poisonous it destroyed his ego and made him a monster.

My entire life now makes perfect sense.

From the moment I was born, my existence reminded Harvey Beaumont of what it feels like to lose. What it feels like to lose *control.*

His wife, my mother, chose someone else.

Yet, we all paid the price for her infidelity.

My sister is standing beside Everleigh with her head bowed, clutching onto her, as my father continues to spit hateful words. On many occasions, I have witnessed him lose his temper, consumed by raw anger and frustration.

But nothing, and I mean nothing, will ever compare to what I am seeing now.

For once, my mother is standing straight, holding her head high, and no longer imprisoned by the man who held her affair over their marriage.

A marriage built on lies and deceit.

It was hardly a moment to feel proud of her sudden strength because in the end, all the lies they spun destroyed one person's life.

Mine.

I motion for my sister to leave before she changes her mind. If there's anything *her* father does well, it's manipulate those he claims to love. I also have my guard up, unsure of just how far he will take it. If he dares lay a finger on any of the women inside this room, his life is over.

I will make sure of it.

And then, Everleigh stands up to the man who despises strong and confident women. He is never shy in expressing his opinions on what he believes a woman's role should be.

But like all of us, she is done with his mind games.

"Maddy and Aston didn't ruin your family," she informs him with a hard gaze. "You did, Harvey Beaumont."

Everleigh holds Madelina's hand to usher her out of the room quietly. As they step outside, I quickly follow to grab her wrist, stopping her momentarily. My hand dips into my pocket to retrieve my car keys, handing them to her. "Take my car, get her out of here," I command.

Everleigh's honey-brown eyes glisten, a depth of sorrow pooling beneath her lashes. Her lip quivers, the faintest movement that betrays the tears she's fighting to keep at bay. My hand aches to reach out, to trace that trembling lip and smooth the lines of worry etched into her face. But reality tugs me back, reminding me of the battles I have yet to fight, the promises I still need to keep.

And I'll be damned if Harvey drags Everleigh into this mess I once called family.

The door closes behind me as Harvey splutters, "Do you realize what you have done? You have single-handedly allowed your daughter to destroy *our family*! How do you expect us to recover from this?"

My mother drops her gaze to the floor, and with my chest tightening, I pray she doesn't give in to him. I've spent my entire life watching her fall victim to his emotional tirades and abuse. She deserves to get out now and stop living this lie.

She lifts her gaze and straightens her shoulders, drawing strength from some reservoir hidden beneath the surface of a woman who has been downtrodden. "There is no *us* anymore, Harvey. I'm filing for divorce." Her voice is a fractured whisper, but each word is laced with the weight of every moment leading to this one.

"Divorce? I won't allow it!"

He inches closer to her, his face twisting with rage, a crimson flush darkening his cheeks, his jaw clenched so tight it trembles. My eyes catch the rigid set of fists, knuckles white against his skin, and I know all too well how his barely contained fury can erupt.

Before he can take another step, I lunge forward, my voice dropping to a low, lethal hiss, "Touch her, and you die." The words slice through the air, each one an unmistakable promise.

A flicker of uncertainty flashes in his gaze as he steps back, but the fury seething within does not ebb. It radiates like the sun, simmering and waiting for an excuse to burn.

I feel my own pulse pounding in my ears, my fingers twitching, my body taut with readiness—I will gladly make good on my threat.

But then a gentle touch grounds me. My mother's silent presence steadying the storm inside me. Her fingers, soft yet firm against my arm, convey the restraint she is urging on me. "Aston, honey, perhaps you could leave us alone for a moment?"

"No chance in hell," I voice coldly. "Whatever is said will be said in front of me."

Harvey's expression deepens, his eyes narrow to slits as he plants his feet wide. His mouth curls back into a snarl and he bellows, "Beaumonts do not get divorced."

The threat hangs thick in the air, every syllable a dangerous promise.

I stand my ground, meeting his fury with an unwavering stare, my stance a silent shield between this bastard and my mother.

"And I will tell the world just who you are if you make me

stay," she counters, keeping her tone calm. Her composure seems to slice right through him but only stokes the fire in his glare. "We can either end this amicably," she continues, her tone smooth. "Or you can see what I'm capable of."

My mother's sudden backbone catches me off guard, a spark of resilience I hadn't seen in her before. For a moment, I wonder if she needs me here, standing guard and defending her. Maybe she is stronger than I ever realized.

But as much as I want to believe in that strength, I also know I'll never forgive myself if he lays even one finger on her. So I stay, a silent sentinel, prepared for whatever comes next.

"You're both completely worthless to me!" His blinding rage has stripped away any pretense, baring the ugliness underneath. "I spent months securing this marriage. Do you think I enjoy wasting my time? If it weren't for you playing these childish high school games with your girlfriend, your sister would have happily walked down that aisle by now, proudly and without hesitation. I warned your girlfriend not to get involved!"

The pounding in my ears is incredibly difficult to ignore. The adrenaline spins inside me, a tornado gaining momentum, building and building until I'm on the verge of tearing everything apart to cause maximum destruction.

Then he laughs—a vile, twisted sound that slices through my haze. "Did you honestly think I would allow you to marry and have children with a woman who brings no value to our family?" His voice drips with mockery. "I could destroy her just as easily. Oh, wait! I think I did, when I said you were leaving for good."

A sensation I can't even name floods through me, igniting my strength and amplifying my rage to a new level. I don't think, I just move—charging for Harvey, shoving him against the wall with my hand pressing into his neck, pinning him there. His smug expression falters as he meets my gaze, and I feel my grip tighten. Every ounce of fury I've held back is surging through my fingertips, waiting to be released.

"Aston," my mother calls urgently, cutting through the haze of my anger. "Let him go."

I press my lips close to his ear, my voice a low, dangerous murmur. "Don't you ever, and I mean *ever*, talk about the woman I love that way again. Do you understand me, *Harvey?*"

My mother pulls me toward her, motioning for us to leave. Just as I turn my back, Roland, Georgina, and Myles enter the room in a flurry. I've lost count of how long it's been, but I assume everyone has now caught on that Madelina is either running behind or running away.

Roland narrows his gaze on me, reading the room. There's a gleam in his eye, albeit slight. I've spent enough time with him to know it's a sense of pride.

I have finally stood up to the man who has controlled my entire life.

"I'm sorry, Myles," I say, my voice steady. "Madelina can't marry you."

Myles bows his head, hiding his reaction, as he absorbs the blow. Beside him, Georgina's reaction is far less subdued as she presses her hand to her chest.

Obviously, she doesn't know how to read the room.

"What do you mean she *can't?*" she questions with a high-pitched cry. Her tone cuts through the tension in the room. She can't see it—doesn't understand what's unraveling before her.

I glance back to Harvey again, then to the Whitneys, letting my gaze settle on each one of them, letting the truth of the moment sink in. "I'm sure Harvey can fill you in," I say, my words weighted with finality. "After all, his plan has backfired and ruined everyone's lives. All he wanted was your land, not the happiness of your son or his only child."

And with those words said, I take my mother's hand, feeling the tremor in her grip as we turn away from this monster.

And with each step, a new vow forms—I will never allow him to hurt her again.

CHAPTER 29

Eva

We both sit in complete and utter silence.

Aston insisted we take his Porsche and get the hell out of the Grand Honey Lodge. He never said it, but I assume he was worried Maddy's father would try to manipulate her decision and pressure her to walk down the aisle.

I don't blame him because the thought had crossed my mind.

The car is parked beside the abandoned house overlooking Peppermint Lake. The usually crystal clear water is looking slightly murky from the turnover in seasons. As I look a little closer, I see the organic matter from the bottom of the lake floating on top, but it's all a part of nature and what I love the most about living here in Cinnamon Springs.

There is so much beauty to be found in each season.

Only today, a darkness cast its shadow over this normally happy town.

Earlier this morning, the sun graced us with its presence, only to be overshadowed by fast-drifting clouds warning us of an impending storm. When we checked the weather forecast a few days ago, there was supposed to be a chance of light showers in the early evening. But as they say, when it rains, it pours.

Even Houdini is nowhere to be found. I don't blame him, to be honest. Sometimes, I wish I could disappear, too.

Maddy has been quiet since the moment we left the Grand Honey Lodge. We avoided running into anyone on our way to the car and drove to somewhere no one can find us, which makes sense, at least for now.

While this is usually my happy place, it's also my place for peace and reflection. It's my place to sit and think when I'm feeling overwhelmed or lost, and at times, it's been the place to breathe in the fresh air with the need to just survive.

I hope, by bringing Maddy here, it will be her place to realize just how strong she is for being able to walk away.

Buried in my purse is my phone, but I refuse to check it, assuming there are a million missed calls, all of them asking where the bride is. There's a high chance Myles will know the truth by now, and while I respect my best friend's decision, a part of me feels sorry for him.

It won't be easy telling his family and friends that the wedding is not going to proceed.

That the bride changed her mind.

"We don't have to talk, or we can talk," I voice hesitantly, then continue with, "I'm here for you, Maddy. I'm always here for you, first and foremost."

Her vacant stare is worrying. Beneath her eyes, her face has turned puffy from all the tears she's cried today. I ache from seeing her in such emotional pain, but I am unsure how to help her get through this. All I can do is be a friend who listens, holds her when she cries, and then reminds her this, too, shall pass.

Just like Marco said, *one day at a time.*

After a longer period of silence, an exaggerated sigh escapes her parched lips. "I've humiliated Myles."

"This is one moment in time, Maddy. Your emotions were running high, and you were upset."

"I'm still upset." She lowers her gaze, fumbling with her hands. "I always defended my father, even though I knew he treated Aston differently than me. I just never knew there was a reason behind it. I honestly thought it was a normal father and son relationship."

"He showed his true colors . . ." I trail off. It's not the right time to voice my opinion on Harvey Beaumont. At the end of the day, he is still her father.

But to me—he is scum.

I also worry about Aston, knowing he must be in so much pain at learning the man he knew as his father is not. As much as I want to reach out to him right now, Maddy needs me. I know deep down inside, Aston will put his sister first. He always has, and that's one of the reasons why I fell in love with him.

Why I still love him.

"Do you hate me?" I ask, barely above a whisper.

Maddy shakes her head slowly. "I could never hate you, but I do need time to process everything. You lied to me, Eva. All that time you lied to me. It hurts to be lied to by the one person you always trusted to tell you the truth."

"I didn't want to, but I was scared of losing you and adding stress onto your already full plate. It was stupid, I know. I was just so in my head." I sigh, dropping my gaze to the dead grassy patch on the ground. "There have been a lot of revelations today. You take all the time you need."

Suddenly, her breathing becomes irregular, like a wave of panic has hit her. "I need to get out of Cinnamon Springs, but I need to get out of this dress first. If you take me back to your place, people will look for me there. How about Billie's? Can you call her? She'll understand and no one will find me at her place, and I'll be able to get out of this dress and take a train somewhere."

With a heavy chest, I tell her the truth. "Um . . . there's something I need to tell you. Billie's mom passed last night."

Maddy's eyes widen in shock. "Why didn't you tell me?"

"She asked me not to. Plus, I knew you had a lot on your mind. I got the call when I was about to leave dinner last night. I drove over and spent the night with her."

"I don't know what to say." Maddy expels a long breath. "She was so young."

"She was—"

"I want to see Billie. I need to make sure she's okay," Maddy rushes.

"Why don't we go back to my place? You can get changed, and then I can drive you over."

Maddy nods quietly.

Before we leave, Maddy pauses mid-step. "This place . . . I understand now why you want it so much."

My shoulders relax as I take in the lake one more time before leaving. "It was my first love—maybe that's why it's always had a special place in my heart."

As Maddy settles into the car, I start the engine, and the loud roar takes a moment to settle down. It's not hard to remember this is Aston's car, his pride and joy, so I take extra care in driving back into town and ignore the pain inside my chest from the smell of his scent lingering in the car. A scent that reminds me of how *broken* my heart is right now.

Back at my apartment, I help Maddy remove her dress as we both stay silent.

It's bittersweet, and I can see her hesitation as I hang it on the coat hanger. The two of us just gaze at the dress, numbed by the reality staring back at us.

"They'll call me the runaway bride," she murmurs.

"So, let them." I reach into my closet to pull out a pair of jeans and a sweater. Luckily, Maddy is my size. "Everyone in this town will talk, then they'll get over it and find something new. It's the cycle of Cinnamon Springs."

"I wish I'd stopped this wedding sooner."

"But you didn't. So stop beating yourself up over something you can't change. It's done, Maddy. You need to focus on healing, not wishing you'd done things differently."

"You're right."

With much reluctance, Maddy pulls her phone out of my purse to call Aston. She doesn't even look at the screen, which must be swimming in missed calls.

"Aston," she says softly. "It's me."

She drops her gaze to her feet, listening to him speak. I step out of my bedroom to give them privacy but struggle to ignore the constant wave of nausea in the pit of my stomach. I haven't slept or eaten, and all the adrenaline is slowly wearing off.

As I stand inside my living room, staring blankly out my window at the bare trees slowly coming to life, my head begins to spin.

Maddy exits my room, wiping her nose. Her splotchy skin has returned from the obvious tears she's just cried over the phone. "I'm going to drive to Billie's, then meet Aston later."

My chin lowers to my chest, avoiding eye contact with her. I've done everything I can, but in the end, they need each other right now.

And who's going to take care of you? The voice whispers inside my head.

Maddy takes the keys to the Porsche and then walks toward the door. She opens it to step outside but stops momentarily. "Eva?"

"Yes?" I barely manage to answer.

"Are you and my brother still together?"

Holding back the tears I've fought hard this entire time to keep at bay, I shake my head. As the door closes behind Maddy, a sob escapes my throat.

I'd held it together for Billie as she grieved her mother, and we watched her be taken away.

I held on to Maddy as she broke down in my arms and needed her best friend to comfort her.

And I also told the man I love, a man who has consumed all of me, to let me go.

We have nothing.

We are *nothing*.

As I stand here inside my apartment, my weakened knees finally giving up as I fall to the floor with the world spinning around me, I realize I'm not all alone.

It's just me and my broken heart.

The worst company any girl could have.

CHAPTER 30

Aston

My fingers trace the rim of the glass, slowly gliding against the smooth edge, and I eye the amber liquid with a desperate thirst.

Madelina is still in Cinnamon Springs but apparently drove to see Billie, whose mother passed the night before. The moment Madelina informed me of this news, I desperately wanted to reach out to Everleigh.

But my own pain is too much.

And I'm drowning in this dark abyss, unable to pull myself out.

We ended up on my yacht, away from the small town that is wreaking havoc on everyone's lives right now, and from my penthouse, which is technically owned by the Beaumont Group.

My mother sits beside me on the deck. Her silence speaks a thousand words as we both stare out into the bay, trying to come to terms with what happened.

All we see is darkness.

And hope that the sun will eventually rise.

I fall asleep on the deck, alone and surrounded by bottles of bourbon.

The sun eventually rises, but it retreats behind dark clouds and threatens an unpredictable storm.

It is a new day, but to my mother, it's her first day of freedom.

She continues to remain silent, almost as if the shock of walking away from my father has frightened her. At first I worried she would find an excuse to go back, but then I realized my strength was what she used to stand on her own two feet.

As another day passes, and the dark night falls upon us again, she finally releases a sigh as we both sit on the deck with our legs dangling off the side. Our silence over the last few days has spoken volumes, but now we need to talk.

"When I first met Harvey, he was charismatic and incredibly loving," she says out of nowhere, forcing me to pay attention. "I thought to myself, *I've found the perfect gentleman.* So very handsome and romantic." A small smile graces her lips as if it happened only yesterday. She takes a breath and then follows with, "Then, the FBI reopened the death of his brother."

As kids, me and my sister begged my father for a pool, only for him to demand we drop the subject. Then, we found out through the town librarian, Mrs. Glimore, that my father's twin brother drowned at five years old, leaving my father the only child of my now-deceased grandparents.

I still remember Madelina asking our father what happened and him refusing to answer. Instead, he went on an all-night bender only to come home drunk and fight with our mother. Something smashed in the middle of the night during their argument, and we knew never to bring that subject up again.

I bring the glass to my lips, tasting the bourbon and allowing it to slide down my throat with ease. It no longer burns.

"People spread nasty rumors," she admits with sadness. "But an old neighbor came forward and said he saw it all with his own eyes—they were playing, and it was all innocent. By then, it was too late. The memories of losing his brother changed him forever."

She presses her lips together, lost in thought. Slowly, she continues, "I tried my best to help him, but he turned into this cold man, and that's when I met your father."

A pain smacks the back of my throat as I croak, "Who is he?"

Mom exhales, drinking the bourbon in one go, something I've never seen her do. Usually, she's all about wine or champagne. As I observe her briefly, even her appearance has changed. Normally, she is poised and well put together. I've never seen her with her hair in a messy bun, and wearing sweats, of all things. Granted, they're massive and belong to me, but still.

"Sawyer King," she states simply, with a yearning gaze. "He owned the ranch where I would ride horses to get away from it all."

A heaviness rests on my shoulders, forcing my body to slump. "Where is he now?"

She shrugs. "We lost contact a long time ago. Your father— sorry, I mean Harvey—made sure of that."

There are so many questions, but my mind is still reeling from the fact Harvey is *not* my father. All along, he treated me as if he had something to prove, and I was nothing but a pawn in his game. As I look back, there were signs. Every so often, he'd make a dig, but I brushed it off as his sick and twisted humor.

"I don't understand why Harvey pretended to be my father," I say out loud, my tone raspy from the strong liquor.

"He didn't want his reputation ruined. It was easier for him to pretend than for everyone to learn his wife had an affair."

It's all so fucked-up.

I rub my face in my hands, unsure what to do from here. Everything has changed, and my entire existence is one giant blur.

"But all these years, you paid the price, Mom."

"For you, Aston." She reaches to touch my cheek. "Always for you."

I place my hand on hers, then squeeze it tight. "So, now what?"

"There's a lot I need to sort out, Aston," she mentions softly. "But I'm here for you. I'm sorry it felt like I took his side all those years. I thought I was protecting you by saying nothing and following his instructions. I was facing my own demons, trying to escape, only to find myself addicted to pills. These wellness retreats weren't retreats, they're rehab centers."

My chest caves, knowing that all along, my mother was in so much pain she jeopardized her own life.

"You've sacrificed enough," I tell her, then state firmly, "You need to be happy."

Her arms wrap around me, pulling me into a much-needed embrace. I've heard there is no greater love for a son than from a mother, and at this moment, I know she gave up everything for me. That is unconditional love.

"And what about Everleigh? You love her?"

I ache at the mention of her name. For the last day, I've buried my emotions and hated myself for the cowardly act of not fighting for what we had.

The wound is wide open and exposed to severe pain. Instead of screaming, telling the whole world just how miserable I am, the pain cripples me. Forcing me into a cone of silence where my tortured thoughts imprison me.

And for now, I can't fix us, not when I am drowning without a life jacket.

But then, a raw emotion consumes me when I realize . . .

"I think I always have."

∞

My eyes divert toward the glass table beside me, where a large pile of papers sits with a note on top. Contracts. Everything that still ties me to the Beaumont Group. I reach for the yellow note, bringing it closer to read as my eyes are blurry and unfocused from the bottle of whiskey I drank earlier this evening.

Three nights in a row of drowning myself in my sorrows.

Avoiding everything to figure out who the hell I am.

Madelina checked in briefly. She opted to stay in a secluded Airbnb farther upstate until Billie's mom's funeral later in the week.

It feels like a world away, but my sister deserves this break. I'm aware her failed wedding made news headlines in Cinnamon Springs, only adding fuel to an already burning fire. A bunch of bored reporters looking to bank on people's misfortunes.

As for me, I've barely managed to pick up the broken pieces of my existence, staring outside the shell of my body like a stranger. This vicious cycle I find myself in spiraled out of control. It's been days since I slept, days since I showered, and the beard is a reminder of how unbothered I've become.

The only ray of hope is when Everleigh sends me a text.

Everleigh

> I'm here as a friend if you need me.
> You're not alone, Aston.

But I am alone.

She isn't in my arms, all because I fucked up and allowed Harvey to ruin what I deserved. The pain of it all only forces me to drink myself into a more profound stupor, miserable as I struggle to climb out.

So I don't respond.

The Aston Beaumont she supposedly fell in love with doesn't exist anymore.

And until I find myself, I am worthless to everyone.

My eyes strain to see the sun peeking through the drapes. As I glance around the room, it takes me a few minutes to realize I'm in my penthouse.

I don't even know how I got here.

Beside me on the bed, there are multiple empty bottles of liquor. I twist my body in an attempt to sit up, but my muscles ache, and a shooting pain stabs my hand. Slowly, I raise it, only to see a bandage wrapped around it and blood seeping through.

There's glass smashed on the floor and a liquid stain running down the wall. And with no recollection of last night, the truth becomes increasingly clear.

This is not the man I am.

Harvey Beaumont may have raised me, but if there's only one thing of value he has taught me, it's to always make your opponent believe you hold the better hand.

I take my first shower in days but trim the beard instead of removing it entirely. With the glass cleaned up and the empty bottles tossed in the trash, I choose to wear my best outfit—my Zegna suit, which was custom made for me in Italy.

I am on a mission.

And that mission begins inside the boardroom.

My moment of confidence is shadowed by the lawsuits Harvey has insisted on throwing at me. I know it's a punishment for Mom leaving him, which is why I hired the best attorneys to fight him. The games have only just begun.

Inside the boardroom, there is a team of six attorneys, all belonging to Lexed Enterprises, which is Lex Edwards's corporation. He called me after hearing of the lawsuits, then offered me his team without even asking what the hell happened.

Lex and Will sit with me in the meeting, since they are both stakeholders and part of existing deals. Lex makes my father look even more pathetic, and for that, I'm grateful.

Across from us, the monster has graced us with his presence.

And his lawyer begins firing away with just how ruined I supposedly am.

Lies, all of them to protect *his* reputation.

My nostrils flare, angered by the deceit this man has conjured up to salvage his ego.

The temperature inside this room suddenly becomes unbearable as the four walls begin to close in, trapping me in this fucking nightmare.

But then, he mentions all the land Harvey lost because I didn't sign the contracts, and I remember the abandoned house that sat on that very land. It was the night of the bachelor party when Roland urged me to stand up for what I believed in.

The night I allowed myself to fall in love with Everleigh.

To my father, it was a house on a piece of land he planned to destroy to make him more money.

To me, it was the house the woman I love dreamed of making hers.

A piece of land, which became a piece of *us*.

I hear her voice urging me to fight. Encouraging me to stand up and own my life because it belongs to me and only me.

Lex leans over to whisper, "I have your back, son. You know what you need to do."

People will call me a fool for going up against the man who deals *all* the cards.

But the only fool is the one who doesn't fight for everyone he loves.

And doesn't know his own worth.

"There is only one thing I will tell you . . ." I say, straightening my shoulders and staring into Harvey's cold eyes. "Game over, Beaumont. I win, you lose."

CHAPTER 31

Eva

The days blur together.

I fell asleep on the couch again, only to wake up in the dark. My sleep cycle is beyond screwed. I've lost count of what day it is, blinded by the persistent headache that refuses to leave me. My mouth is dry, unable to swallow normally. I reluctantly pull out my phone and purposely ignore all the missed calls and messages from the last few days.

Not a single one is from Aston, even though I texted him to let him know I was here if he needed me.

The loneliness is palpable.

So I call the one person in the world who never lets me down: my brother. It's daytime in France, I think, but I am too tired to even check. Family is exactly what I need right now.

"Elliot," I cry softly over the phone as he answers. "Are you awake?"

"It's nine in the morning, Eva. Of course I'm awake," he answers in a rush, with noise surrounding him. "What's wrong?"

"Everything! Everything's gone wrong. Billie lost her mom, Maddy pulled out of her wedding, and I . . ." I trail off, holding back what happened with Aston.

"Eva . . ." He raises his voice. "Hold on, let me go into my office."

There's the sound of shuffling and people yelling in the background. I assume he's at work in the kitchen. It suddenly becomes quiet, and then Elliot breathes, "I'm back."

"Elliot," I whisper as another fat tear falls down my cheek. "I don't know what to do. It hurts. Life hurts right now."

"It's fine to be upset, Eva."

"Is it?"

"You're always the strong one. The first one there if anyone needs help or if anyone needs saving," he says with conviction. "But sometimes, you need help. You need saving."

"I'm just . . . I'm so tired."

"And that's your red flag."

"My red flag?"

"Yes, *your* red flag. Eva, you have to put yourself first so you can help others. Your battery is depleted, and until you can recharge, you can't be everything to everyone."

Elliot is right. I'm forever trying to help everyone, and sometimes, I don't take a moment for what I want.

Like Aston.

I was too far in my head, so worried about Maddy's wedding that I lost my patience and pushed him away. He tried to explain, but I was too upset to even listen to him. My guard was up, and I didn't know how to pull it down for the man I love.

And my other red flag . . . pushing people away because I'm scared to get hurt.

"How do I start to take care of myself?" My shoulders curl as I touch my temple, only to close my eyes, overwhelmed. "Billie will need time off, but I'm not sure how long that will be. Everyone in town is badgering me on what happened, like I'm some sort of news outlet."

"I'm coming back home," he states adamantly.

"Elliot, you can't come back home."

"You need help with the café."

"Yes," I barely admit in a whisper.

"Then consider this a nonnegotiable."

"But you have your Michelin-star restaurant," I remind him. "And what about Nicole?"

"Eva, you're my little sister. Family first, okay?"

My hand instinctively covers my mouth. I'm relieved to know I'm not alone and my brother is here for me. "Thank you, Elliot. I miss you."

"Miss you too, sis." He chuckles softly. "Listen, I have to go, but can we talk more later tonight?"

"Deal," I say before hanging up.

My arms hug the cushion as I continue to sit in the dark. Outside, the rain gently taps on the window, but the sound is somewhat comforting.

I think about what Elliot said.

The words finally ingrained into me.

I need to take a moment and think about myself. Otherwise, I'm no good to anyone else.

Later in the day, Elliot calls to check in on me. He told the restaurant he was coming back to the States for at least the summer. I will be glad to have him back, even if it sounds selfish. More than ever, I miss my family.

Although I promised him I would take care of myself, I find little to no time for self-care. Billie needs help with the funeral preparations. I never realized how much was involved, but nevertheless, it had to be done.

I closed the store for a week, which got everyone in town talking. Not that I cared since I didn't have the mental bandwidth to deal with them anyway.

Maddy texted to check in, letting me know she is not too far away and is staying at an Airbnb until the funeral. I know it's important for her to attend and be there for Billie, even if it means traveling back to Cinnamon Springs.

I'd heard Myles and his family had taken off to Ireland, but like all the rumors in town, I took it with a grain of salt.

Today is the day of the funeral, and I stand behind Billie in case she needs me. Her family grieves at the front, comforting each other as Seraphina is laid to rest.

When "Amazing Grace" plays, and the coffin is lowered into the ground, I stand next to Maddy and bow my head, allowing myself to mourn a woman who deserved a better life.

Her legacy, a young woman named Billie Mae Reynolds, will live on, and I silently pray for Seraphina to protect her daughter from heaven above.

At the wake, family and friends stop by to pay their respects. Billie insisted all the guests wear bright colors to honor her mom, so this is nothing like a regular funeral gathering where everyone is dressed in black.

Billie joins us after a few guests have said goodbye and conveniently taken some food home. Everyone brought a dish so there are plenty of leftovers.

I rub her lower back, knowing it's been a long day. "How are you holding up?"

She sits beside me on the chestnut leather sofa, resting her head on my shoulder. "I'm okay. Mom would have been so happy to see everyone."

I smile back at her. "You're strong, and I'm proud of you."

On my other side is Maddy. She drove in early this morning and is flying out tonight to some retreat her mother recommended in Switzerland.

Billie leans over, catching Maddy's attention. "So, how long do I wait to set you up?"

"Me?" Maddy points her finger at herself. "I'm done."

"For now." I roll my eyes, then knock into her shoulder playfully. "You're not done forever."

"Why not? Men are too complicated."

"Right . . ." Billie grins, then says, "I'm glad you said that. Because it's not a man asking."

My head tilts with curiosity. "Have you thought about playing in the same field?"

"You mean, have I thought about chewing the cooch?"

I scowl, then bury my head in my hands. "Maddy, it's a wake, for God's sake."

Billie laughs, snorting unexpectedly. "Oh, sorry, but Mom would have laughed, too."

"You know what? Life is too short. Give her my number."

Billie motions for Maddy to glance out the window where the young woman is standing. She's pretty, with long ginger hair tied into a bun. A man is conversing with her, and he looks remarkably similar, so I assume it's her brother.

"Oh, you didn't tell me she had bangs," Maddy says in a disapproving tone.

I throw my hands up in the air, then smack them on my thighs. "Okay, now that's taking it too far."

"What about you?" Billie questions with a smirk.

"What about me?"

"The reverend's son asked about you."

I scratch the back of my neck. "Um . . . isn't that frowned upon? You know, dating someone holy. Besides, I'm really not interested."

Maddy crosses her arms. "She's not interested because she and my brother can't seem to get their shit together."

"Maddy, I have my shit together . . . kind of," I answer defensively.

"Then why are you so miserable?" Maddy questions with annoyance. "Why is he so miserable?"

"It's complicated."

"Well, by the time I get back from this wellness retreat, you better be married and giving me nieces and nephews."

I turn and gaze into my best friend's eyes. Maddy's expression softens as she reaches out to squeeze my hand. "My forever might have fallen apart, but yours doesn't have to."

We may have been walking in the opposite direction in life, but I know Maddy will always remain by my side.

Because that's what best friends do.

And I count myself the luckiest girl in the world to have a best friend in Madelina Eleanor Beaumont.

CHAPTER 32

Eva

Wat in the ever-loving world is going on here?"

Elliot stands beside me on the corner of the street as we stare at the long line waiting to visit the store. He arrived yesterday morning, so I picked him up from the airport and told him to crash at my place.

We both tilt our heads at the same time, counting the people, but lose track when we notice many are in groups. They're sitting on the ground, all on their phones, but appear to be in good spirits.

I scratch my head in confusion. It's been slow the past month, and because I closed up the week of the funeral, revenue has taken a nosedive. Billie was taking some time off, and briefly mentioned a change in scenery. I completely understand her need to get away but hoped she would return so we could put our heads together to drum up more business.

But perhaps the tides have turned and the universe is finally listening.

"Eva, when you said it was a simple donut shop, you failed to mention the lines would be bigger than at my restaurant in Paris."

"I, uh . . . I have no idea what's going on," I answer, dumb-founded.

We move closer to the girls who are sitting at the front of the line.

"What's happening?" Elliot asks.

The girls eye him up and down, then bat their lashes with overbearing grins. "We're waiting for the best donut store to open."

"Um . . . thanks," I say, then scratch my head again. "But I don't understand."

"Some stores we've been to are so mid, but yours looks delish," another girl says. "It's totally the talk of the town!"

I narrow my eyes, still confused. "As in, Cinnamon Springs?"

"Duh . . . Manhattan."

It still doesn't make sense.

Then I overhear one of the girls say, "He's like, so hot. As soon as Cassie told me he opened an account, I was like, *baby, I'm following you.*"

Elliot extends his hand. "Pass me the keys. I'll get started."

We did a bit of a rundown yesterday when he arrived, but given that I've been closed for a week, I expected there to be a small crowd, just the usuals, nothing at all like this.

"So you guys all traveled from Manhattan?" I ask, flinching my head back slightly.

"We're from Bridgeport," two girls respond in unison. "And the group behind us are from Jersey."

"Wow, so you guys left at what time?"

"We left at midnight. I mean, when the hottest CEO tells you to run, you run. It's about time he opened a social account. When my girl Keira told me, I swear I screamed and reposted it everywhere."

I nod, then ask with my eyebrows squished, "Where did you see this post?"

The girl in front hands me her phone, and on the screen is a profile page of the one and only Aston Beaumont. And what appear to be two hundred thousand followers. My mouth opens in shock, since I have one thousand followers, and most of them are people in this town.

How did he manage to open an account and gain so many followers so quickly?

The profile picture is a photograph of skyscrapers, but then I glance closely at his one and only post. It's an image of the front of my store, and the caption reads:

Donuts Ever After deserves a Happily Ever After #roadtrip

I read the post again, waiting for it to sink in. Aston knows how important my store is to me. And for someone who loathes social media, I know just how big of a gesture this is from him.

My cheekbones rise, unable to hold back my smile as heat radiates through my chest.

"We won't be too long, okay? As soon as our batches are done, we'll open the door."

⁓

The morning can only be described as complete and utter chaos. I ended up calling Chloe for reinforcement, and thankfully, she was free.

At first, Elliot was preparing donuts, but then the girls kept asking about the hot guy in the kitchen. So, I swapped and put him on coffee duty. It makes sense since the last thing I want to hear about is how hot my brother is. Besides, to flirt with him, they have to continuously order, so it's a win-win. The sales are the highest I have ever seen, making this our most successful day ever. Maybe Maddy is right, I do need to invest more time in marketing.

"Miss Woods?"

"Mr. Fenech," I say politely while trying to complete an order for a dozen mixed donuts. "What would you like to order?"

He removes his flat cap and places it on the countertop. "Oh, Miss Woods, I'm here on official business."

"I see." I glance at the line, trying not to be rude. "Um . . .

I'm kind of busy right now—would it be possible to talk once I close?"

"Of course, Miss Woods."

"May I ask what it's in regard to?"

"It's best we talk about it when you have time. How about you drop by my office when you're done?"

"Sure," I tell him.

At the end of the day, Chloe closes the door as the three of us collapse on the chairs. I don't think, in the entire time I've been open, this has ever happened. My entire body is throbbing in pain, and my feet are swollen even in my sneakers.

"I'm exhausted." I almost cry from tiredness. "How do you do this every day?"

"Well, I have a team of about ten kitchen staff, so that's the secret," Elliot answers with a cocky grin.

"Right," I barely manage to reply. "I can't even talk. I'm so tired."

"I heard them say they'll be back tomorrow." Chloe drags out her words. "Plus, this famous influencer is driving here, too."

"I don't even have enough supplies to deal with this," I say loudly, jumping to my feet in a sudden panic, only for my phone to ring with Mr. Fenech's number flashing on my screen. "Shit, I promised to meet Mr. Fenech at his office."

"I've got this," Elliot informs me. "Go do what you need to do."

"But how do you know what—"

"Two words for you—"

"If you say *Michelin star* . . ." I interrupt with a grin. "I swear to God I will—"

"Do what?" Elliot teases. "Just go, you're being a pain in my ass."

"Do you see how my brother treats me, Chloe?"

She laughs, sliding farther into the chair from exhaustion. The store is still a mess, so Chloe offers to clean up the dining area before leaving. I thank her, then reach over to hug Elliot. "Did I say thank you for coming back to Cinnamon Springs?"

"Yes, but for my ego, please say it again."

This time, I pinch his cheeks like I used to when we were kids. He scowls, annoyed by my show of affection. I love having him back and hope he'll change his mind and want to stay longer than the summer.

I decide to walk to Mr. Fenech's office, since it's only one block away. However, halfway there, I realize it's a stupid idea because my body feels like jelly.

The moment I enter his small office, the receptionist greets me and offers me a beverage.

"I'm fine, thank you. Is Mr. Fenech available?"

"Yes, please enter his office."

The office is small, with papers scattered all over his desk. Organized chaos, I assume. It smells like cigars, a scent I'm not overly fond of, and his furniture is vintage.

"Miss Woods, please take a seat."

"So, what is so important you needed to see me today?"

"The owner of the land you've wanted has decided to sell. Naturally, I knew you were interested, so before it is placed on the market, I thought I would ask you if this is still something you want."

I shake my head in shock, pressing my hand to my chest. "Um . . . yes. I think. I've been so preoccupied and haven't had a moment to think about it."

"The owner is asking below market, but I will let you know there are conditions for the property."

"Right, conditions . . ." I trail off, then release a breath. "So this is a big surprise. I mean, I have to speak to the bank again, but surely it won't be a problem. At least, I hope it's not. Business has been slow, but after today, I think we're on a winning streak."

Mr. Fenech waits for my incessant rambling to finish. "I thought it would be. I know you have a lot of questions, and the owner wants to move fast. Perhaps we can arrange to see the property, and you can ask as many questions as you need?"

"That would be great. Is there a time?"

"How about now?" he answers promptly. "I will call to make arrangements if you give me a moment."

"Okay," I say, with a new thirst for life.

He dials a number on the office phone but speaks quietly into the speaker. I try to make a mental calculation in my head of how much money I have saved. I'm praying it's enough, and hopefully, after today, the store will bring in more customers, relieving any financial stress.

"Right, the owner will meet us there in ten minutes. Shall we?"

Mr. Fenech's old Mercedes-Benz smells like mothballs and cinnamon. It's an odd combination, but nevertheless, it's the least important thing on my mind. I pray for this to all come true because it is something I've been dreaming of for the longest time.

He parks the car behind the house, and as we both exit, loose twigs and leaves crunch beneath my feet. We step into the clearing, and the moment we do, the dilapidated house comes into full view. Many would say it looks like a horror movie house, but I see the bones of a home I plan to make *perfect*.

"Did they say what time?" I ask loudly.

"Now," a voice behind me says.

I don't turn around, my stomach flipping at the sound of *his* voice. My heart starts to hammer inside my chest, and when I slowly turn, Aston is standing across from me.

Just like me, he looks tired. Dark circles have formed around his normally sparkling green eyes, and he has a beard. Though he looks damn sexy with one. My fingers ache to touch him, to show him I was wrong and need him more than I ever cared to admit.

"What are you doing here?"

"I'm here on business," he states, but there's a gleam in his eye.

He removes a bunch of papers from inside his suit jacket. I turn to look at Mr. Fenech, but he simply grins and walks back to his car, leaving us alone. I scan the area, but see no Porsche. All I notice is a small dinghy docked next to the modest wharf.

"The conditions of the property . . ." Aston begins, clearing his throat before continuing, "Number one, any house changes must be in accordance with its heritage listing."

I place my hands on my hips, unable to hide my smile. "Well, duh."

He glances at me, attempting not to smirk. "Number two, all plants and fauna must add to the nature reserve."

"Right. Don't plant something that will make this entire forest extinct. Got it! Is that all?"

"And third . . ." He bows his head, and when he raises his eyes to meet mine again, a glaze shimmers around his pupils. "You please forgive a man who is irrevocably in love with you and has been miserable since the moment he acted like a coward and never fought hard enough for what he wanted. I thought about all the ways to beg for your forgiveness, but the only way you would truly understand just how sorry I am, was to do something that made me extremely uncomfortable. If opening a social media account meant crazy girls would go nuts and chase the latest trend, then it's one step closer to you fulfilling your dreams. For my entire life, I wasn't allowed to have my own dreams. But you have yours, and I want to be a part of them."

"Aston," I call softly as my lips quiver. "You're *in love* with me?"

He reaches out to caress my cheek. The touch is like a jolt of much-needed electricity, lighting up my heart and soul.

"It's always been you. All those years ago, you were the only one to believe in me," he admits, fixating on my lips. "And because of you, I've finally learned my worth. I love you, and no amount of money in the world matters if I don't have you, Everleigh."

A tear falls down my cheek, only for his thumb to slowly wipe it off as I smile back at him. "That's one hell of a speech. How will you ever top that?"

"The day you marry me," he whispers with his lips curving, only to then gently rest his hand on my stomach. "The day we find out you're carrying our baby. The day you bring our baby into this world. I plan to never stop telling you how much I love you, Everleigh Woods."

I jump into the arms of this unbelievably sexy man who has just made my world complete. His lips brush against mine, and softly, he kisses me, a kiss that melts away any doubt I have left.

My hands hold on to his jacket as I pull away, only slightly. "So, do you really own this land, and are you selling it to me, or was this a ploy to get me here?"

"I own this land, but I don't plan on selling it to you. I want *us* to make it *our* home."

A squeal escapes me. "You're moving back to Cinnamon Springs?"

"Kind of." He chuckles. "I was thinking we could live half here and half in Manhattan. The new job I was offered is pretty flexible, so—"

"Wait, you got a new job?"

He nods proudly. "Yes, I no longer work for Harvey Beaumont."

"Wait a goddamn minute. You actually quit?"

Aston takes my hand, sitting me down on the same log where we sat all those years ago. The nostalgia brings butterflies to my stomach, the same time a hummingbird lands in the tree beside us and makes a buzzing sound.

"I quit. Of course Harvey tried to sue me, but I preempted the move and hired the best lawyers to countersue. Remember Charlotte Edwards, Amelia's mom?"

"Yes, how could I forget?"

"She connected me with attorneys who are sharks in the industry. Lex is no stranger to lawsuits, so he has the best team working for his corporation, Which is where I'm working now."

My eyes widen, still in disbelief. "And what will you be doing?"

"The same as before, but managing a portfolio of hotel chains on the East Coast."

There are so many changes, all of which are happening in such a short amount of time. I have so many questions, and I am unable to calm down my racing thoughts.

"But you said you left the Beaumont Group, so does that mean you lost everything?"

"My father thinks I lost everything because he paid for my apartment, car, and bills. But since the moment I was paid a salary, I invested in property and the stock market. So, I still own two apartments, a motorcycle, and a yacht."

"Hold on . . ." I raise my hand, leaning my head back. "You own a yacht?"

Aston unconsciously parts his lips, a lingering smile reflecting his own happiness. "There's so much you don't know about me, Miss Woods."

I run my fingers through his hair like I've done many times before, but this time it feels so different. My hands wrap around his neck while he rests his hands on my hips as I murmur, "I can't believe my store went viral. Did I say thank you?"

"You can thank me later, in bed, on all fours." He teases my bottom lip. "Actually, cowgirl. Think that's my favorite."

I laugh, falling in love with him even more. "I guess this is where we start, right?"

He moves away from my hips to cup my face with his hands, but then stops abruptly.

"Um, so your boyfriend is watching me," Aston says while trying to keep a straight face.

"Huh?" I turn around, only to see Houdini sitting on the railing of the porch. How the hell did he get up there? "I guess I should formally introduce you. Aston, meet Houdini."

Houdini croaks on cue, prompting me to laugh.

"I'm just letting you know, Houdini gives great life advice."

Aston's lips lift into a wide grin. "And what life advice has he given you?"

"Watch this," I tell him. "Houdini, if you think Aston is just trying to get me into bed again and will dump me to go back to being a playboy, croak once. If you think I'm supposed to stay with him forever and ever, jump in the lake."

Houdini sits perfectly still as we wait in silence.

"I don't think Houdini is as intuitive as you thin—"

With a large leap, Houdini lands on the icy ground and hops straight into the lake. My lips lift upward into the biggest smile as I dance with excitement, at the same as time the sun appears from behind the clouds. If you look around, the beginnings of a new season are upon us.

I wrap my arms around Aston to bring him even closer. "So?" I ask, teasingly.

Aston tilts his head, leaning down to kiss me deeply before pulling away. I moan at the lingering spell of his kiss.

A smile brightens his entire face as he says softly, "Forever sounds nice, don't you think?"

I found my home in the man who broke my heart at the tender age of sixteen.

My best friend's older brother.

The biggest red flag of all.

Aston

Two Weeks Later

One more time."

Everleigh laughs beneath me, attempting to squirm out of my hold as I kiss the base of her neck.

"You've broken me!" Her pitched voice is cute, but not as cute as the beautiful smile on her face. "Seriously, I think my vagina is broken."

"I'd like to bet all the money in the world it is not broken."

She bites her bottom lip, a move that drives me crazy. Just as I'm about to prove to her how wrong she is, a knock on the door interrupts us.

"It's room service. I'll get it," she says.

"You think I'm going to allow another man to see my girl naked?"

Everleigh rolls her eyes with a hidden smile teasing her mouth. "Firstly, you don't know it's a man. And secondly, I was going to wear a robe."

I hop off her, then grab the robe from the chair and place it on, tying the belt around my middle. She brings the sheets to her chin, hiding her mischievous grin.

My hand reaches out to open the door, only to see a young

man carrying a silver tray. He eyes me, then notices Everleigh in the bed. I clear my throat, prompting him to pay attention to me and only me.

"I'll take it from here," I warn him, then sign the bill and add a tip.

I could be an asshole and not tip him for looking at my girl, but I circle the 20 percent before closing the door behind me.

"I'm starving," Everleigh calls, then lets out a yawn.

"Lucky for you, food is meant to improve stamina."

"Or, it can put you to sleep," she teases.

"You're lucky you're so damn hot," I tell her, then bring the plates to the bed.

Everleigh insists we turn on the television and watch some trashy show involving people marrying strangers. Before now, I barely had the time to watch any TV, but this show becomes interesting when one of the women reveals she's attracted to another woman's husband.

We're starving, finishing the food off, and leaving the plates completely clean. With our stomachs full, we watch the show with light commentary every so often.

It's been a whirlwind of events and both of us are trying to catch our breath.

When I approached Roland and asked to buy the land from him, he signed over the title so I could start my new future. I expected him to reject my offer based on his previous mention of wanting to keep it in the family, but his change of heart worked in my favor.

Everleigh hasn't been able to contain her excitement, constantly showing me her Pinterest boards for inspiration. I love watching her gush over wainscoting, even though I don't really care for wainscoting.

All I want is to make her happy.

And since that moment two weeks ago when I professed my love, I haven't let her go.

So much so that we ended up in a hotel, because her brother cockblocked my plans.

I wrap my arms around her waist, kissing her shoulder. "Sleep . . . we have a big day tomorrow."

"I know." She yawns but tightens her hold on me. "But I miss you."

"I'm not going anywhere," I whisper.

She turns around so our eyes meet. Her lips find mine, and my urge to be inside her roars back.

"I won't hurt you, baby," I tell her softly.

Her fingers reach out to caress my face. "I know."

My hands slowly glide down to her beautiful, perfect tits. Slowly and agonizingly, I tease them between my fingers, then tug on them softly. I spent the day ravaging her, so I know her body needs a break.

Beneath me, her soft moans become more intense. My hand reaches down to enter her, but she stops me with her lips curved into a delicious and wicked smile.

Everleigh climbs on top. Reaching down, she grasps at my shaft, causing me to tense at her touch. Slowly, she eases me in until I'm completely seated inside her.

I rest my arms behind my head, watching her ride me at her own pace. Every single inch of her is perfect, and the more my eyes admire her body, the harder it becomes to resist blowing inside her.

A maddening rush suddenly grips me, so I reach out and grab her hips, rocking her harder. Our bodies move in sync, and even though we spent most of today exploring one another like it was our first time, I still crave more.

It will never be enough.

"Come with me," I demand.

My blood is pumping hard, and every single part of me tingles in mad delight as her pussy clenches around me. My body combusts, and all I can see are bright stars.

We catch our breath, both of us parched from the physical activity.

"Okay, now I'm officially broken," she says.

I bring her to me and kiss her softly. "I think you broke me, too."

Everleigh chuckles. "I broke the stallion?"

"The stallion may be broken." I wince.

"Oh no." She laughs again. "Well, you have come how many times? I think it may call for a world record. Unless, of course, the stallion rode too many mares during his single days, and his record is yet to be beaten."

I turn to face her as my eyes fall upon her lips. "No one, and I mean no one, has ever made me feel the way you do."

"You'll do anything to get me into bed," she whispers with a smile. "But if that's your way of telling me you love me . . ."

My cheeks rise. "I love you."

"Okay." She laughs, rolling her eyes. "Round six, here we go, I guess."

We arrived at the store just as Elliot opened the door.

Back in high school, I saw him around, but since he's a few years older than me, we didn't run in the same circles. He's a decent guy who doesn't seem bothered by much, especially when Everleigh is repeating her list to him for the tenth time.

"Okay, so that I remember," Elliot says, touching his lip. "I use this switch to turn on the espresso machine?"

He hides his smirk, and I hold back mine.

Everleigh is too easy of a target.

Everleigh's eyes widen. "Are you really asking me that?"

"*No*," he shouts. "Oh my God. For the millionth time. I know how to run this place."

"He did get a Michelin star," I remind her.

"Yes, but does the Michelin star make coffee for Mrs. McGregor the way she likes it?"

Elliot tilts his head, rubbing his stubble. "Who's Mrs. Mc-Gregor?"

"You met her *this morning*!"

"I'm kidding. Relax," Elliot drags. "Grande flat white with a triple shot of espresso and nonfat milk, extra foam but only on the bottom half of the cup. Shot of caramel and no sweetener."

Everleigh crosses her arms. "Fine, you win."

"And we will both win if we leave now," I urge, tugging on her sleeve.

Our bags are packed and waiting in the car. I organized for a driver to take us straight to the airport so we don't miss the flight.

Elliot hugs Everleigh, giving her more suggestions of where to visit around Paris. We have two whole weeks to ourselves before I am due back in Manhattan. Elliot and Chloe are managing the store, with Billie returning early next week.

Since my so-called viral post, the store has been incredibly busy, but Elliot insisted he could manage. Frankly, many of the customers are young women, and apparently, Elliot has also gone viral. The small-town chef has a major following. It wasn't my place to inform Everleigh her brother is more than busy after-hours, since she was worried he may get bored.

With the success of the store, Everleigh mentioned the possibility of opening another store in Manhattan with Billie taking over. After the death of her mother, Billie decided she wanted a different pace. It made sense, and so did calling the broker to organize some appointments when we return.

Everleigh insisted we wait until later in the year, but the rule of thumb in business is to strike when the iron is hot. We argued and had make-up sex, and now Everleigh is open to inspecting some storefronts.

The traffic is smooth with no major delays on the interstate.

My phone rings in my pocket, so I remove it to see Madelina's nickname flashing on the screen.

"Hey brat," I tease upon answering. "You're on speaker."

"Yeah, you're on speaker so I can hear just how amazing Europe is!" Everleigh's eyes light up. "Is it just as fun as when we went?"

"Sure." Madelina laughs over the speaker. "Though instead of chugging tequila shots in a rowdy bar in Dublin, I'm lying on a lounge chair in Saint-Tropez and being served by extremely good-looking men."

I breathe a sigh of relief, not because my sister is enjoying gawking at French men, but because she finally sounds like the weight of the world has been lifted off her shoulders.

Harvey has decided to disown her, much to her disappointment. Unlike me, Madelina did have a relationship with him, but since our family name was dragged through the tabloids the last few weeks, Harvey has gone into hiding.

Frankly, I don't care where he is as long as it's far away from me.

"You need this break, Maddy. Just soak up the sun and enjoy your freedom," Everleigh reminds her. "We'll see you in a few days when you're back in Paris."

"See you guys then."

We hang up the call, only for Everleigh to rest her head on my shoulder.

"Do you think Maddy will be okay?"

"My sister will bounce back. She always does."

"But she sounds lonely," Everleigh murmurs. "I know Myles wasn't the love of her life, but where do you think she's going to find him?"

I shrug. "Maybe he's right under her nose. Give it time, Everleigh. Madelina needs to heal."

"It's going to be hard coming back to Cinnamon Springs. Maybe she'll meet a French guy and fall in love . . ."

"Perhaps" is all I say.

Everleigh changes subjects and begins to complain about these two girls who ordered a pineapple donut to share, then stalked Elliot when he locked up yesterday.

"You know, he's probably going to bring them back to your apartment," I tell her.

Everleigh's eyes bulge. "Like a threesome?"

"Sure, why not."

"He should settle down," she states adamantly.

"Leave the guy alone. Much like Madelina, his time will come."

I'm waiting for her temper to flare. She looks sexy when trying to argue with me over something I couldn't care less about. Suddenly, her eyes dart to the window.

"Um . . . the driver is going the wrong way. Excuse me, sir, you're—"

"Everleigh, he's going the right way," I inform her.

We drive into the private area of JFK, where all the private jets are stationed. The one we're flying in has been prepared and is ready for takeoff. All they're waiting for is us and our bags.

"This is our plane? I don't understand," she mumbles, looking at the tarmac.

"Which part?" I ask, then continue, "Because we need to get on board so I can finally join the mile-high club."

She slaps my arm as I kiss her hand. "You own this plane?"

"I own shares in the plane. Another perk of working for Lex Edwards."

The driver stops the car at the base of the stairwell. I exit the car, then open the door for Everleigh. Her eyes are wide with surprise at the thought of flying in such luxury.

"So," she says, eyes dancing happily, "any other surprises up your sleeve?"

I might have broken her heart twice, but I'm going to spend a lifetime making sure it only beats for me.

This trip to Paris will be something to remember.

My sister has made sure of it, planning the whole thing behind her best friend's back because Madelina insisted Everleigh needed to get her *forever*.

Starting with the diamond ring, which sits inside my black leather suitcase.

I reach out, take her hand in mine, then tease, "I guess you'll just have to wait and see . . ."

ACKNOWLEDGMENTS

The small town of Cinnamon Springs wouldn't have come to life without a serendipitous moment in my bookstore. Who would have thought my small special edition romance bookstore in a country town just outside Sydney would be where it all began.

To Anthea from Simon & Schuster Australia—You walked into my store, and the moment I felt your energy, I knew you were someone meant to be riding shotgun with me. Actually, I'm shotgun, and you're the driver because without you and your pom-poms cheering me on to absolutely everyone, none of this would be possible.

To Emilia from Atria Books US—Thank you for taking a chance on an Aussie gal who is low-key envious of your Manhattan office. You've given me the opportunity of a lifetime, so for that I'm forever grateful.

To Kinza and the team at Pan Macmillan UK—A big thank-you for giving me this opportunity from across the pond.

To my cheerleaders—Claudia, Chantelle, Willow, Kay, and Kim. I love you all more than words can say. Thank you for being my unpaid therapists.

And last but never least—my best friend.

We'll celebrate with a pineapple donut while we argue over who our four boys look like.

P.S. They're all me 😊

ABOUT THE AUTHOR

Kat T. Masen is a *USA Today* bestselling author from Sydney, Australia. She is the founder of Books Ever After Romance Store, and spends way too much time on BookTok. She lives with her husband, four boys, and a needy pug. Find out more at KatTMasen.com.

Atria Books, an imprint of Simon & Schuster, fosters an open environment where ideas flourish, bestselling authors soar to new heights, and tomorrow's finest voices are discovered and nurtured. Since its launch in 2002, Atria has published hundreds of bestsellers and extraordinary books, which would not have been possible without the invaluable support and expertise of its team and publishing partners. Thank you to the Atria Books colleagues who collaborated on *How to Break My Heart*, as well as to the hundreds of professionals in the Simon & Schuster advertising, audio, communications, design, ebook, finance, human resources, legal, marketing, operations, production, sales, supply chain, subsidiary rights, and warehouse departments who help Atria bring great books to light.

Editorial
Anthea Bariamis
Emilia Rhodes
Rosie Outred
Elizabeth Hitti

Jacket Design
Josie O'Malley

Marketing
Kelly Jenkins
Zakiya Jamal

Managing Editorial
Michelle Swainson
Paige Lytle
Shelby Pumphrey
Lacee Burr
Sofia Echeverry

Production
Brigid Black
Kyoko Watanabe
Kiara Codemo
Briana Skerpan

Publicity
Jasmine Aird
Sierra Swanson

Publishing Office
Neysha Santos
Suzanne Donahue
Abby Velasco

Subsidiary Rights
Amy Fletcher
Ben Phillips
Nicole Bond
Sara Bowne
Rebecca Justiniano